THE ADVOCATE

Special Victims Unit

ဆာ ❧ ಆ

Dawn Mattox

Morningtide Publishing
PO Box 4262
Yankee Hill CA 95965

MORNINGTIDE PUBLISHING
PO Box 4262
Yankee Hill CA 95965

E-mail: info@theadvocatebooks.com
Website: www.theadvocatebooks.com

Print & eBook Cover Design, Print Interior Layout and Design, by Melissa
Alvarez at BookCovers.Us/BookCoversGalore.com
Cover Art: Shutterstock ©Chepko Danil Vitalevich
Inside Art: Shutterstock ©Andrey Armyagov
Editors: Alice Duncan@aliceduncan.net
        Catherine Wolcott @ catherine.wolcott@outlook.com
eBook Formatting: eBookadaptations.com

REVIEWS

Disturbingly realistic. One hell of a gripping story! If you read only one book this year, make it this one! **I gave it to a friend, who gave it to a friend.**

Paper View Book Club

SVU was a **mind bending, life changing** story for me. I couldn't put down! Sunny McLane gripped my heart and soul. I will never go back! **Never be the same!** Thank you, Dawn Mattox!!!

Fearless and Free (reviewer)

This book completely blew me away. SVU is a **wildly compelling** story about the destructive ways that we hide our private sorrows and the **consequences of such dreadful secrets**.

Word Wise Book Reviews

OMG!!! Better than good! A psychological thriller that had me tearing through the pages!!! SVU is a totally addictive book that I will read again while waiting for the next one. **More please!** I need to know what happens next.

Living in Suspense Book Club

Just plain brilliant! I was glued to the pages. The story was gripping and the men hot and sexy. Excellent writing. A true suspense thriller that I could not put down. **Five stars!**

Woman2Woman Book Club

Days later and I am still stunned! Possibly the most compelling book I have ever read. **This book does not disappoint**. I was captivated to the very last page.

Thrills for Life (reviewer)

Mainstream Christian and unafraid! My, Oh My . . . how refreshing!! And the couple of cuss words didn't kill me. The descriptions are graphic, but more than acceptable considering the vital nature of the story. **This is a book that women of every faith should read!**

Christian Suspense Book Reviews

DISCLAIMER

This book includes fictionalized accounts of violence against women. They are composed of variations and compilations of the many stories Advocates will hear over the course of their careers and is not intended to reflect poorly on any field of advocacy.

Names, characters, places brands, media and incidents either are the product of the author's imagination or used fictitiously. Any resemblance to actual persons, living or dead is entirely coincidental. Any references to events or locals are strictly fictionalized accounts of those events for the purpose of fictionalized entertainment.

The author acknowledges the trademarked status and trademark owners of various products referenced in this work of fiction, which have been used without permission. The publication/use of these trademarks is not authorized, associated with, or sponsored by the trademark owners.

The Motorcycle Clubs exist, but the characters herein are fictional characters and portrayed as individuals acting outside of their Club's purview and are nowise intended to discredit or disrespect these organizations.

All actions taken by law enforcement agencies are fictionalized accounts and individuals and are nowise intended to discredit or dishonor the dedicated men and women who work in the field of Criminal Justice.

Only the dynamics of Domestic Violence, the tireless work of advocacy and law enforcement, the setting in northern California, and identity of the dogs are true.

DEDICATION

To
The Holy Spirit

ಖ 🕊 ಐ

The *Lord* answered me saying, "Write the Vision that he may run who reads it, for it is for an appointed time. In the end, it will speak. Though it tarries, wait for it, because it will surely come."

ACKNOWLEDGEMENTS

Special thanks and appreciation to:

Harriet, who wrote, "Your writing is just beautiful.
You have changed my life forever.
How can I repay that?"

Shirley, who always had words of encouragement:
"I am praying for you.
Now, get back to work!"

Catherine, my friend and content editor,
whose knowledge and help was priceless.

My dear Sue, who wrote,
"I am in awe of you, Dawn."

To my husband Ken, who ate sandwiches
and spent many evenings alone while I wrote.
He never complained. Not once.

To my sons, who always inspire me:
each in his own unique way.

Thanks to each reviewer and friend
who read this book.

Each of you gave of your time.
This is the most precious gift.

GOD BLESS

ADVOCATE

Noun: *believer, operative, intermediary*

Verb: *minister, caution, guide, prepare*

PART ONE

"LEAD ME NOT INTO TEMPTATION..."

CHAPTER 1

ಋ 🕊 ಞ

"Please God, don't let me die! I don't want to die. I'm not ready. Okay—I'm ready—but I still don't want to die."

How many bones have I broken? I tried not to think about internal injuries, but the nightmare stories of motorcycle crashes roared through my brain anyhow. Horror stories that centered on death and dismemberment. Everybody knows somebody who has died on a motorcycle. Warm blood trickled down my face—or was it tears? — It was too dark to tell.

My gloved hands kept a finger hold on the canyon wall, booted toes bit into the narrow ledge, heels jutted into outer darkness. The Harley was somewhere far below in the surging Feather River, and while it hadn't been much to look at, it got me where I needed to go. Until today. Good thing I wore a helmet—California law. I was pretty sure my head was still attached to my neck. Life had been a maze of twists and turns, but I wasn't prepared for the deer with the alien eyes standing in the road.

To hell with Walt Disney. Whoever thinks deer are Bambi-cute has never seen one straight ahead while doing fifty-five around a blind corner on a moonless night.

"I'll never criticize deer hunters again. God... just let me live, and I'll join the NRA. Promise!"

I was losing my grip in every sense of the word. My hands had a tenuous hold on the rocks while my heart reached frantically for the spiritual one. Neither one seemed too promising.

One boot slipped sending bits of granite splintering and tumbling into the night. "Jesus! Help me!" I plan on going to heaven when I die—it's just that I had other plans for tonight... like TV and a hot shower. And what about my dog? Who will take care of her? "Oh God!" I pleaded, weeping bitterly, "Please... don't let me fall."

"Let go."

The words rode the night breeze. Maybe I had a head injury after all.

"Let go!" Louder, stronger this time.

No headlights or people anywhere. Above me, a narrow, twisting highway gouged the slopes of the Sierra Nevada's. Below was the distant rumble of the Feather River.

Beacon bright words sliced through the night illuminating the muddle of my thoughts. I recalled an object lesson about a mountain climber who died in the dark while dangling at the end of his rope. He kept hearing God tell him to "Let go"—but he was afraid. His frozen body was found the next day—hanging in the air just a few feet from safety. He didn't trust God. He couldn't "Let go!"

The fateful words returned. This time, a whisper that drowned the thundering rapids below. "I may not have a choice here, Lord," I whimpered. Blood mixed with tears and coursed down my face. I was only twenty-nine. I hadn't hit the dreaded thirty yet, although thirty was sounding pretty good at the moment.

Motorcycles are my heritage, and I relish the wind washing over my face and the rush of unbridled freedom. But the iron horse is also a means of escape. When today's crisis work triggered hellish memories that unleashed a storm of fear and anger, memories had sent me racing up the canyon, just heartbeats ahead of a pack of ghost riders on my heels; their captain, swathed in black, closing the gap until I swore—I could hear his familiar laugh.

ℰ 🕊 ℭℛ

The sixties were a bizarre time in American history and culture. It was also the time when the "King of Violence" wed the "Queen of Love." Mom was looking for "peace and love;" Dad was just looking for a piece.

True love—cosmic fate—found them on the rolling green of Golden Gate Park. Miss Natural swaying on an LSD high to Jefferson Airplane's *"One pill makes you larger... one pill makes you small... and the ones that mother gives you don't do anything at all,"* looking hot and easy to Mr. Born to Be Wild. A match made in heaven—Angels batting zero—Satan scoring a home run.

I was born in a rustic cabin about three miles from the tiny rural-remote community of Feather Falls in Northern California during the great hippie "back-to-the-land" movement of the seventies, daughter of passionate non-Christian political believers that "the end was near." I was the only child born to Lefty and a free-spirited young woman named Starla before she left me to "find herself" as a tree-hugger in the California Redwoods. Later, she would go on to produce a rainbow assortment of colorful offspring fathered by one-night stands with multi-cultural lovers.

Life had always been turbulent in spite of the solitude and tranquil environment. I recall the day the tsunami hit that forever changed the landscape of my life.

I walked home from the little country school much as I had for the past six years.

Frito, my one-eyed Chihuahua-mix (half Chihuahua, half gopher), laid in front of the door like the last forgotten chip at the bottom of an empty bag. He had one good eye, two good ears, and a heart the size of the giant cedars and ancient ponderosa pines that crowned our tired little cabin—more of a shack really—at the bottom of a long dirt driveway.

"Frito" I called, as I had each day after the mile-long trek home from school. Three grades in three rooms, it was the closest structure to our home in one direction, and neighbors Joyce and Kenny lived about the same distance in the other.

Ever vigilant, waiting for the sound of his tired mistress this time each day, Frito had exploded into life with happy yapping, exuberantly wriggling with uninhibited love. He alternately sampled nature's pantry by licking my fingers, stained purple from wild blackberries I had devoured en route, and sniffing apples I had picked on the trail home.

I dropped the schoolbooks in a heap and we swapped kisses before I put him back on the floor, fearful that Starla would catch us and fulfill her threats to get rid of "that nasty little dog."

"Frito, where's Mama?" I asked my ratty little friend whose breeding, much like my own, remains one of nature's mysteries.

Starla's absence was typical and Dad was rarely home before Friday night. Something felt different, and yet familiar. Something felt wrong. Frito whined anxiously, dogging my steps as we rambled from room to room. I searched past my tiny bedroom and through the living room and dining room that were divided by an old Franklin wood stove. I peeked into the large kitchen; it's inside walls covered with black felt paper and furnished with a small propane refrigerator, a large white Wedgewood gas-and-wood combination cook stove, a deep double sink, and a wall of cabinets.

Checking upstairs in my parents' sanctuary-bedroom, I called softly for my mother in case she was napping or weaving on her loom or doing yoga. I didn't want to disturb her meditations. No Starla. The walk-in closet (*walk-in* because it had no doors) revealed that her clothes and the large leather suitcase she had found at the local dump were missing. She packed that bag several times a year, whenever life became unbearable. Like a wild bird trapped in a cage, beautiful, colorful Starla had regularly beat her paisley wings against the bars of tradition, longing for freedom.

A familiar dread crept over me as I stepped through the sliding glass doors, searching for final confirmation. I noted Starla's van was gone and sighed with relief that she had left Frito behind. Maybe it was out of the kindness of her heart, or maybe it was because she couldn't afford his dog food. Most likely she had left him because he was a bed-wetter.

Sitting on the step, scooping my dog into a child's embrace, I mothered him, bravely mumbling words of encouragement.

"Don't be scared. I'll take care of you," I hastened to assure both Frito and myself with a puppy-love hug. "We'll always have each other," I promised. "And we have food," I continued, considering the orchard, the chicken coop, and the bomb shelter Lefty had constructed just behind Starla's all-natural Japanese bathhouse. We had a lot of survival stuff: toilet paper, MRE's (Military Meals Ready to Eat), survival food that tasted like leftovers from World War I, guns that were probably smuggled back from Vietnam, and plenty of gasoline to feed the generator and Dad's Harley.

ဆ ✢ ca

Lefty, my dad, was a Hells Angel out of Oakland. His biker name was "Lefty" because he had lost his left hand along with parts of his mind and soul in Vietnam. He preferred a hook to an anatomically correct prosthetics. Yeah, he rode his Harley and he rode it with a hook. Lefty never made any modifications to the bike—except the night he got drunk and attached a hose clamp on the left grip to keep his hook from sliding off. Lefty did a lot of things with his hook—including beat my mom, the flower child.

Dad was the guy who came home mostly on weekends. He usually rode in with friends; "business" associates with party-hearty supplies loaded in their saddlebags. He also brought Logan home for my sixteenth birthday. It was a party to remember, a night impossible to forget. The night I met pure evil.

ဆ ✢ ca

Jasmine was my first major case as Butte County's new Victim Advocate and ultimately, it was the stress of this case that would lead me to the bend in the road, the deer, and a new direction for my life.

I instantly liked Jazz, as she called herself, and her two adorable little girls. She was twenty-three years young when we first met at my office. Bright and beautiful with golden dancing ringlets, she seemed to possess an air of childlike innocence that matched her appearance. Tucked behind her skirts were two of the sweetest little girls this side of heaven. Jazz will always have a special place in my heart. The first client always does.

After two years of internship with Butte County District Attorney's Office, I wrote the grant that established the first Special Victims Unit. My position, unique to the DA office, was "Advocate," and my job was to integrate services between victims of rape and domestic violence and the justice system.

My work is all about setting boundaries, yet I readily swept them aside in a surge of generosity toward Jazz and her children. I broke the rules by becoming emotionally attached and using my personal money to buy them groceries. Both actions were "unprofessional," but like most sin, it felt good at the time. I never paused to consider the consequences.

Jazz's husband, Bryan, had moved the family to Butte County when he inherited a plumbing business and trailer in a park. Bryan had forced sex upon Jazz in front of their children. Unlike victims of domestic violence, victims of sex crimes have the power to choose whether or not to press charges. And she did press charges—sort of. When it came time for the preliminary hearing Jasmine minimized the seriousness of the assault and degree of her injuries when giving her testimony. Charges were reduced and Bryan snapped up the offer to plead guilty to sexual battery instead of spousal rape. Jasmine grabbed the girls and fled the 150 miles to the sleepy town of Mt. Shasta. Bryan served a little jail time but refused to pay his fine. He promptly filed for child custody and hired a process server as a means to locate his wife and family.

Mornings always begin with coffee. Coffee triggered the need for a bagel and cream cheese, which would go well with granola and yogurt, plus a healthy side of fresh fruit. I turned on the local news, sat down to indulge my cravings and promptly lost my appetite—throwing it all in the trash.

The lead story featured Bryan, who had caught up with Jazz and the girls in Mt. Shasta and severely beaten her. My stomach may have been empty, but my anger bubbled like a can of soda, dropped and rolling across a hot parking lot, fit to blow. *I warned her.* She was a fool to return to a place she and Bryan had shared in Mt. Shasta. Now Bryan was back behind bars, this time charged with Section §273.5 of the penal code for felony domestic violence.

Without intervention, it was likely that Jazz would minimize her injuries again. Women leave and return to their abusers an average of seven to nine times before making a complete break, whether it happens over thirty days or thirty years. It left me wondering if she would recant again.

No word from the news anchor on the whereabouts of the girls.

I struggled to calm myself. I knew that I couldn't blame Jasmine. Most people seek the familiar when stressed.

Wasn't I also a fool? Wasn't I hiding in plain sight from my abuser? What will happen when Logan finds me? My blood ran cold at the thought.

Bryan's vindictive assault on Jasmine had sent shockwaves of flashbacks through my system and fueled a burning need to get away. I needed to run, and my Harley was my drug of choice.

I flew up the canyon prepared for some emotional backlash. What I hadn't prepared for, was the deer.

෨ ⚥ ෬

The Feather River Canyon is not a forgiving place, even for an experienced rider. Slashing its way nearly seventy miles through the heart of the Sierra Nevada Mountains, it finally comes to rest near Lake Oroville, not far below my home in Yankee Hill. The canyon walls shear off both up and down in places. Looking up is a neck-breaker and down is the Feather River in spring flood.

How long have I been hanging here? It felt like a lifetime. It would take a miracle for anyone to find me. Fatigue and dizziness washed over me. Gripped by cold and saturated with fear, shaking with violence that caused more rocks crumble, the fragile ledge finally gave way. Fingertips clinging to failing hope—*"Agggh"*—my body thrashed in space before final surrender. Pausing, hanging in midair for a moment, heartbeats away from wherever destiny would take me, I took a deep breath and replied to God's prompting. "Whatever you say, Lord." I let go.

ഇ ॐ ൙

The steady thunk-thunk-thunk of the motor whipped the air as a man, wearing a "scream suit," tethered to an OH-58 Kiowa Warrior helicopter above, began his daring decent. His official titles included Sergeant with the Butte County Sheriff's Office, Liaison between the S.O. (Sheriff's Office) and Butte County Search and Rescue, EMT (Emergency Medical Technician), and HRT (Helicopter Rescue Technician). His unofficial title was "Dope on a Rope." The terrain was inaccessible by vehicle. He was on a "short haul;" slowly, carefully, the man and his K-9 partner, suspended on a 100 ft. line eased into the canyon. Man and dog. Later, I would learn that his name was Chance McLane, and his partner's name was Mercy.

"Mercy! Track! Track!" he commanded the dog as he released them both from their mechanical restraints onto a narrow sandbar. The beautiful German Shepherd held her nose high as she cast about for scent, and then raced to the end of the bar. Chance grabbed his gear and hurried after her.

Without breaking stride, she leaped into the torrent of churning water and immediately vanished, sucked under by the surging river.

"Mercy! Mercy!" Chance called from shore, his heart pounding, beating in time with the throbbing current.

Resurfacing some twenty feet downriver, the great dog fought to gain a foothold, pawing at floating debris that had piled into the narrow channel and shot from beneath her like slick soap on wet tile.

Undaunted, unerring instincts providing an internal navigation system as Mercy dragged at the rope attached to her harness, gained her footing and scrambled from the icy water. She moved toward the motionless, half-submerged figure trapped in a logjam in the middle of the river. Mercy knew her job. She was a living extension of her master and they worked in a coordinated rhythm achieved through their years together. Through trial and error, with a willing heart and almost worshipful desire to please Chance, Mercy would go anywhere, into any circumstance at his command. Their relationship was similar to that between man and God. For Mercy, it was all about *trust.* For the rest of us, it is called *faith.*

Over ten years of search and rescue work, five with the US Army Special OPS recovery, and five doubling as Investigations Sergeant, SEU— Special Enforcement Unit—with Butte County Sheriff's Office as a liaison between the search and rescue volunteers, Chance was the man for this dangerous undertaking. Off a cliff, into a river, down a dark tunnel or under a collapsed building, he and Mercy made headlines going into dangerous places under extreme conditions where others dared not. More than fearless, more than drawn to danger, Chance was a rescuer by nature.

Chance belayed his ropes into a network of pulleys and anchor points, calling to Mercy to "Hold" as he traversed the stream, finally reaching his mark.

Maybe it was the icy water dripping from her muzzle or the rough feel of her tongue. Maybe it was her eager whine of concern—or possibly it was the stranger's warm lips pressing onto mine as he performed mouth-to-mouth resuscitation. Whichever it was it was, it was heaven sent.

"Miss? Ma'am?" Water dripped from his hair as he worked, bent over me. "Look at me," he directed, pointing to his eyes. "You're going to be okay. I am with search and rescue and I am going to save you. I need you to trust me."

And I did.

I didn't remember falling at first, but the details that had stored in my memory surfaced over the days and nights that followed like bits of flotsam in the wake of a sunken ship. I recall the feeling of drifting through layers of soft white light thinking perhaps an angel had caught and carried me, sheltering me in the river. In those dreams, I rose up to touch heaven. Then came the night-terrors of being sucked into a watery hell of churning, suffocating force that assured me I was nowhere near heaven.

The high-action drama of me falling off a cliff and Chance leaping from the helicopter set the stage for us to *fall* in love and *leap* into a relationship. Five short months flew by. We found ourselves together almost every day.

Sprains, cuts, and bruises healed. My fractured leg and torn tendons were finally free from its burdensome cast. The attraction between Chance and me was dynamic, and it wasn't just physical. Each of us was impressed by the other's career choices, and I was drawn to his declaration of Christian faith. Before I knew it, Chance had proposed and we were boarding the Tahoe Queen, bound for all the romance and problems that come with a second marriage.

"What do you think, Sunny?" Chance asked as the ship pulled away from the dock. "We could jump ship and still make it to shore." Chance's eyes turned violet in the first colors of the deepening sunset. His gaze reflected a love so powerful that it almost frightened me; his voice had teased, yet rippled with a vague undercurrent of sincerity.

Hair blowing wild and free against the untamed backdrop, I put my lips to his ears and whispered, "Don't even think about it. I waited my whole life for you!"

Hearts beating recklessly, Chance's arms enveloped me and we held tight to our love and our dreams.

"Forever, Sunny," he promised. "I will love you forever."

Rounding the inlet of Emerald Bay, the paddleboat steamed its way through the crystalline waters of Lake Tahoe. Captain Leo Sun, *that was his real name*, was the official who married us. I became Sunny McLane. All the signs were there: full moon coming up on the left side of the bay, lightning flashing on the right, thunder booming over the distant snow-capped peaks. The ship's whistle pierced the air following the "I do" moment, and we kissed going into the curve.

All our friends were there: Ashley and Shane, Gayle and Rex, even our bosses, District Attorney Jack Savage and Captain Mark Anderson of Search and Rescue with his new girlfriend, Paige. All those people, yet somehow, Jesus—the One who had made it all possible—did not make the guest list.

I guess ours wasn't exactly a marriage made in heaven in spite of its fairy-tale beginning. We probably should have extended our engagement and spent more time getting to know each other. Chance seemed the 'perfect' Christian. He didn't cuss, seldom drank, and he loved going to church. He was honorable. Somehow... we managed to wait to tie the knot before doing the deed. God knows it was a close call, but I was confident that I earned extra celestial brownie points for my restraint. After all, this wasn't a first marriage for either of us, and our hormones were raging. Lord knows we had a great time making up for "lost time" on our honeymoon.

It all seemed picture perfect. Too good to be true.

ഌ ⅌ ൙

My baby died in our eighth month of pregnancy. It would be years before I understood that while my daughter was lost to me, she had not been lost to God. We would travel by different roads, my unborn child and I, but our destination was the same. Our lives—the baby's and mine—are eternally bound.

I looked at Logan through bruised and swollen eyes as he sat near my bed holding a single yellow rose. There was something different about him. It took a minute to register through the brain-fog of medication; a deep red gash extended from the bottom of a gauze covered eye to his newly bruised jawbone.

"Three freakin' dollars. What a rip-off! I can't believe they wanted three dollars for one stupid flower," Logan said as he stared out the window at the landscaped hospital grounds. "Crap! I could have picked one outside for free."

Okay, I knew this part. This was Logan's idea of an apology. *Been there, done that.*

"I rode the hog. You'll have to see if the neighbors can give you a lift home. Local calls are probably free," he carried on as I rolled over, turning my back on him.

The sound of boots and chair legs scooted across the tile as Logan moved closer to my bed. Lowering his voice, he whispered, "I tried to catch you, Sunny! It's not my fault you tripped. I got tore up pretty bad trying to hold on to you, but you were too heavy with the kid and all. I know it doesn't feel like it, but this is probably for the best. I love you, Sunny. You got to know that."

Cold tears tracked their way across hot, swollen skin, getting lost in my chopped-off hair as I wondered which of his buddies had punched him in the face so he'd look like a hero instead of a suspect.

"Excuse me." A nurse popped in, breaking the tension. Crisp, smiling, young. "I'm sorry. I need some private time with Sunny," she apologized.

"Nothin' I haven't seen before." Logan shined as he took an appreciative sniff of the fragrant rose. He always shined for other women. He was a good-looking man in a dangerous sort of way. Tall, muscular, dark eyes, dark hair, dark spirit. His mustache was black, his leathers were black, and his Harley was black. He wore a "Hells Angels" tattoo inked under their red and gold winged death head logo on his right forearm. A tattooed pair of two-headed snakes wrapped around his huge biceps where most of his friends had tattooed strands of twisted barbed wire, and HELLBOUND was emblazoned across the back of his neck. He fairly radiated "I'm BAD" pheromones with the opposite sex and a testosterone-driven *"What're you lookin' at?"* attitude with men. Bad girls flirted openly with him and good girls peeked at him with lively curiosity.

It was hard to believe that I once wanted this man. Now I just wanted him dead. As dead as our baby that he had killed.

℘ ℽ ℘

Logan seemed like a lifetime ago. Life was everything I had ever hoped for after becoming Sunny McLane. Living in God's County, I liked to imagine that my marriage to Chance and life in our beautiful home was tangible proof of God's love for me.

Butte County is a land of astonishing beauty, but not without occasional perils. Over 1,600 square miles that include the western slopes of the rugged Sierra Nevada Mountains with national forests and rural-remote towns around 3,000-foot elevation with colorful names like Feather Falls, Toad Town, Ragdump, Nimshew, and Inskip. During the winter residents enjoy the solitude of being snowbound for weeks at a time. But recreationists have been known to lose their way and freeze to death in the wilderness.

The forest spills down over lower foothill communities like Yankee Hill, Concow, Cherokee, Black Bart, Helltown, and Paradise, thick with wildflowers and wild turkeys every spring, and wildfires that consume thousands of acres short months later. These hills, in turn, flow down into the valley, fragrant with orchards, rice, hay—and medicinal marijuana. The valley is mostly populated with cowboys and farm workers, college students and bikers. Fishermen and jet skiers, campers and picnickers dot the 167 miles of shore containing the inviting blue waters of Lake Oroville, where people sometimes drown and dead bodies have been known to surface unexpectedly.

Oroville is the county seat, Chico is the university town, Gridley is home to lots of farm workers, and then there is Paradise, a charming community with a quaint town hall. Paradise is mostly home to retired folks who live on streets with congenial names like Bambi Lane and Sesame Street. Billboards on the Skyway read "Eat right, Exercise and Have Fun," followed by another that offers "Memorial Crematorium Plans" in case you ignored the first one.

It isn't hard to distinguish mountain folks from other "Buttants." In winter, they are the ones with the snow on their cars. The more snow on the car, the "cooler" the driver. In the summer, mountain people are the ones with an inch of dust on their cars.

Some people live in the mountains because they like the view. A few find personal satisfaction in looking down on everyone else. Some prefer the anonymity of illegal lifestyles, like outlaws and drug manufacturers. Others, like me, were born in these mountains and enjoy the peaceful solitude, away from the stresses and activities of city life.

Many foreigners, those not born in California, tend to confuse Northern California with Oregon, and Southern California with Bay Watch. They envision NorCal, as we call Northern California, as cool redwoods with ocean breezes. I admit that's an accurate description providing you live along the north coast in the redwoods. But anyone harboring those profiles for the entire state has probably never visited California's vast interior that bakes throughout summer in the ninety-degree-plus range and then heats up to a broiling 100-115 degrees for several weeks. I tell people, only half-joking, that the real reason we are called the Golden State is that everything green dies in the last week in May, leaving the landscape in various shades of gold until the rainy season returns around October or November.

Having worked in Criminal Division for nearly three years, my co-workers and I tend to see the world filtered through the lenses of our experiences. Criminal Division sees a different Butte County than the happy tourist does.

We see meth labs and marijuana plantations hidden deep within our beautiful mountains. If someone stumbles onto a cash crop while fishing the creeks and streams, they might not come out. Travis, my work partner, says "The foothills aren't good for anything but marijuana and jackrabbits." To which I replied, "They are also good for outlaws and keeping battered women hostage until their cuts and bruises heal."

Bored high school students call in annual bomb threats, a teacher hit-list was confiscated by police, gang activity has spread like a bad case of nail fungus from the towns near the migrant farm worker housing, and emerging Asian gangs are filtering in from Sacramento. Chico State University, once touted by Playboy magazine as "The Number One Party School" in the nation, requires additional law enforcement from nearby towns to haul out-of-control students to jail by the busload every Halloween. Those are typical events in any big city. Little country towns get big-city backwash.

In spite of the contrasting elements—or perhaps because of them—throw together the Chico State wanna-be-hippie-liberals, plenty of red-neck rodeo cowboys and cowgirls, and some good ol' white long-haired and Native American steel-toe-booted loggers on a Saturday night dance floor, and we call it... *home!* It's a place where the logging trucks, hybrid cars, and Harleys share the road, and their drivers mostly live in peace next door to each other. I love Butte County and can't imagine wanting to live anywhere else.

CHAPTER 2

೩೦ 🕊 ೧೪

The rumble of the Harley grew louder as the rider drew near, pulling into the parking lot wearing his usual church attire. Wrapped in black; helmet, leather coat, chaps, and boots, Pastor Mac Masters had recently arrived in notorious Concow—a small, remote mountain community that blends seamlessly into my home in Yankee Hill, bringing with him both the gospel and his testimony.

Chance and I stood on the porch of the charming little whitewashed, historical, one-room schoolhouse. The good people in the area—and they are abundant—banded together to rescue the aging building from its original location in Melissa Valley, some twenty miles away. They restored it right down to the white picket fence and cast iron school bell, adding flowerbeds that explode each year with the vibrant colors of spring. The building serves as a community center during the week and Calvary Chapel Concow on Wednesday nights and Sunday mornings.

"Mac is a Godsend. There is no other explanation for it. It's like he's a divine appointment or something," said Chance with honest admiration. I knew he meant it because the odds of Mac preaching barely a mile from our home fell somewhere between slim and none, especially if you factored in the close relationship they had shared through the years. They had first met when Chance was seventeen.

Chance has participated in the opening day of hunting season since he was in diapers. He claims his first toy was a plastic gun and that his Dad spiked his bedtime bottle with "just a drop" of Jack Daniel's to help him sleep at night.

If that was true, then I guess Chance's father probably finished the rest of the bottle. Michael McLane literally drank himself into an early grave trying to raise Chance and his younger sister, Crystal, by himself. Possibly he'd done so because Casey McLane, Chance's mother, had hated country life and left him to return to the excitement and sophistication of the big city. But more likely, it was the death of Tennessee Dave; Michael's best friend, that tipped the scales. Anyhow, Chance's dad and the boys were doing what they always did on opening day—getting hammered on whiskey, telling each other outrageous lies—and shooting their guns. Michael had drilled into his son a million times to "Make every shot count" and was repeating this admonishment while grabbing for Chance's rifle, causing it to accidentally discharge and wounding Dave who died later of complications.

Pastor Mac had been the volunteer police chaplain on duty at the hospital the night Dave died, ministering to another person. On his way out he spotted a young man sitting alone, crying. That is how they met, Chance and Mac, and Mac continued to take a personal interest in Chance through the years, remaining his friend as Chance partied his way through high school. Mac finally led him to the Lord on the same day Chance boarded an airplane for Ft. Leonard Wood, Missouri, where he would begin his basic training in the U.S. Army.

"Morning, Mac," I called out. "Great day for a ride, huh?"

"Thank the Lord! It's a great day to be alive," Mac shouted back over the roar of the four motorcycles that pulled in behind him. More would follow.

I am sure there were days when Mac Masters second-guessed his calling to preach to this once very dark community. Concow had a long-standing reputation with the child abuse investigators for its unusually high rate of cases. No doubt, the violence linked to the even higher rate of meth production and consumption.

But every Sunday, Mac brought the word of God and the testimony of his own life as an outlaw biker, alcoholic, and womanizer, to Concow's flock. Through his many trials he had done a 360 and given his life over to serving God. Concow welcomed his honesty, his humility, and his integrity. Chance greeted his 'savior,' friend, and mentor.

"Hey, buddy." Mac dismounted and bumped fists with Chance. "Glad you two are here. I want to talk to you about something."

Mac opened the door for the others and then led us around the corner to a quiet space. "Hope you two have a minute because I'd like to run something past you." Mac tugged at the corner of his mustache and rocked back on his heels. "I'm kind of in a jam, between my work here at the church and the chaplaincy ministry with the police department. I am over-extended, trying to staff the other P.D.s and keep up with the church, so I've been thinking about the Wednesday Night Bible studies, and I think I need a man of integrity, like you," he said, gesturing to Chance, "to lead it. Now, you don't need to make a commitment right this minute or anything. It's just something I'd like you two to talk over and pray about."

I was so excited that I missed hearing most of the pastor's sermon. It was hard to take my eyes off my husband long enough to follow Mac's reference's in the Bible. I am one those people who take just one Bible for us to share so I can cuddle under the arm of the sexiest man in church while hearing the word of God. I knew people watched Chance and me as we looked long and deep into each other's eyes, exchanging volumes of wordless thoughts. I knew they envied our hugs and stolen kisses as we sat in church—and I was positive we were pleasing to God. I was proud to be a role model, believing we were the perfect example of a perfect marriage, and it was my constant joy to remind Chance that I thought so. I wanted my husband to realize he was my American Idol and that there was no competition. I adored him.

After the service we found ourselves standing outside on the porch near our usual spot at the usual corner with a great view of the mountains and easy access to the coffee and cookies. "Are you going to do it, Chance? Are you? Huh?" I fairly bounced up and down next to him, beaming with more pride than a wealthy neighborhood's Christmas lights in December. "You have to admit, it's an incredible opportunity. Not that *we* are exceptionally qualified," I added, thinking that I had yet to read the Bible in its entirety. "Still, we should do it."

Somehow, Mac's request to Chance had morphed in my mind from *he* to *we*. Unlike me, Chance had developed a thorough, comprehensive knowledge of the Bible and a rare gift for rendering it into simple terms that apply to everyday real-life situations. I knew my husband had the heart of a preacher and loved to share the Word, whereas my enthusiasm probably stemmed from pride and need to control and lead. Not that I am domineering. Just independent.

Chance has a long history of leadership. He is the strong, quiet type that men instinctively follow in a tight situation. He is a natural leader who prefers anonymity but frequently ends up in the spotlight due to his dedication and courageous actions. Then also, his six-foot-four and 220 pounds of well-placed muscle make him stand out in any group. He is the guy who left football coaches drooling and high school girls dreaming. Still, Chance is more of an easy-going country boy than a hardened mountain man like his dad. He comfortably interchanges his rock-climbing boots for his cowboy boots and running shoes.

Chance frowned for a moment and then smiled his slow, easy smile. "Nope!" he said with conviction. My shock reflected in his mirrored sunglasses.

Okay. That was direct, but unexpected and out of character.

"Why not? It sounds like something you'd love. You're *always* preaching," I said with my perfect pout. Bottom lip pushed out, head tipped down, sad eyes up. I like to think Chance was defenseless against such a face. "We could do it together," I coaxed with a suggestive finger tracing the buttons down the front of his shirt." We hardly have any time together anymore."

One thing about mirrored sunglasses; they are easy to hide behind. Chance hung his head, frown lines deepening along his forehead as he shook it back and forth. "Um-hum," he confirmed.

I paused to study him, thinking I must have missed something. What

I saw was California bronzed skin with a rugged, outdoorsman toughness to it, untamed hair, and a hint of a mustache that perfectly framed sensual lips that drive me crazy. Today he wore a blue dress shirt, denim pants, and tan cowboy boots, looking like a poster boy for a Marlboro ad; although today his cowboy hat was sitting in the truck next to his baseball cap. Hidden behind those Oakley sunglasses was a pair of baby blues that seem to turn purple when we make love. However, when I tried to read between his frown lines, I came up empty.

I have been told that we look like a "pair of bookends," except I don't have a mustache yet. Maybe after menopause. Or maybe it is our character projecting through us that that people see as similar. I am a young thirty-two, size ten, and my best friend Ashley labeled me a "hottie." That probably means my character reflects my famous jalapeño poppers—*they go down easy but are a pain in the butt.* Okay... well, if not a "hottie," I like to think I at least rate "not-bad."

Chance is four years older than I. He is a man of stark contrasts in that he is determined and quiet, manly but sensitive, battle-hardened, yet tenderhearted.

So, we really don't look like bookends. It is just that we might have been fished from the same gene pool. I am tall, but he is taller. I have long "dirty dishwater blonde" hair, which doesn't sound all that sexy, and he has rough-cut dark blond hair that the sheriff is always reminding him to cut.

Not to be deterred, I continued, "So... is that an *'um-hum maybe'* or a *'um-hum no-way'?"* Guy grunts can be hard to interpret sometimes unless you are a guy. Kind of like men trying to figure out why women cry.

"I don't think so, hon," he said, pushing out his jaw and shoving his hands deep into his jeans pockets. His tone had an unfamiliar an edge. Rough words slipped out between tight lips." I don't really want to talk about it."

Really? When a woman says *I don't want to talk about it* to a man, they are cool with that, which women usually interpret as *he doesn't care.* When a man says *I don't want to talk about it* to a female, he may as well wave cape in front of a bull.

"Why not?" My voice raised an octave and face scrunched, adding to the frown lines that are such a turn-off in old age. "How do you expect me to understand you if you won't talk about it? Say something already!"

Piles of cookies and a ginormous pot of coffee graced a table on the porch after the service. Usually, this repast compensates us for us skipping breakfast, allowing us to sleep in on Sunday mornings and still make it to church on time.

Chance reached over, picked up a cookie from the tray and stuck it in my mouth. I was horribly offended and would have said something unchristian if it hadn't been one of those fabulous shortbread cookies that look and taste like a pound of snow-white lard blended with a sack of sugar, hidden beneath a trench coat of rich dark chocolate. The argument melted in my mouth with an "Umm" of a different kind. The cookie was sinfully delicious, and I savored the moment while making a mental note to continue our dispute at a more opportune time.

My friend Ashley had been browsing through the cookies, choosing a healthy oatmeal one to go with her cup of herbal tea as she moved closer to us. Ashley has the ears of a feral cat, the eyes of an eagle, and the heart of a newborn babe.

"Wow, Chance, I hear you're going to be leading Bible Study," she said.

"I never said that, Ashley." Chance removed his glasses and flicked his eyes on high beam, tightening his expression in annoyance.

Undaunted and perky as ever, Ashley admonished, "Well, you should, you know. How can you say 'No' to God?"

"I'm not saying 'No' to God. I'm saying 'No' to Mac," Chance countered.

Shane joined us with coffee in hand and tale-tell crumbs in the dark beard that tickled the top of his leather vest. The four of us share a love of God, motorcycles, and cookies.

"Hey buddy, good to see you," he said to Chance with a fist-bump to Chance's arm.

"Back at you."

"What did you think about Mac's message today?"

Chance's countenance softened, welcoming the diversion. Mac's message had been about our identity in Christ. To Him alone, we should give honor, as opposed to putting ourselves on a pedestal.

"It was good, but kind of tough," Chance said thoughtfully. "You know, it's really easy to get caught up in our daily work. People generally hate me as a law enforcement officer, then call me a saint when I save their lives." His comment sounded a lot like people's relationship with God.

"Yeah," Shane agreed, "women practically fall at my feet in idol-worship." They laughed in mutual guy understanding. Shane owns the Harley shop in Chico and has his own fan base.

Chance paused thoughtfully. "I hate to admit it, but I can't imagine doing anything other than what I do. It's hard to see myself apart from it. I like the rush and the danger, but I confess, I like the hero-thing too. It's like a natural high."

"What do you say, little Miss Sunshine?" Chance asked, turning to me. "You're in the hero business."

Flattery will get you everywhere," I said. "I think you're still my hero. Three years of picking up your socks and underwear from under the pedestal I've put you on, and I'm still crazy about you." True enough. I loved this man more than anything and everything in the world. In fact, I owed him my life.

Pressing against his hard body, both arms wrapped around his neck, I fully embraced him in front of God and everyone.

"Gross! Get a motel! Don't you know children are watching?" Shane always makes us laugh.

"Watch and learn," I quipped.

"Hey, how about lunch? Ashley suddenly exclaimed. "Anybody hungry for something besides cookies? How about something healthy? We could barbecue some veggie burgers," Ashley offered as Chance's fingers responded, tapping out a "NO!" on my back. Ashley and Shane live just up the hill from us.

Barbequing is more than a way of cooking. It is a lifestyle. However, Shane and Ashley—okay, mostly Ashley—has gone Vegan. Barbecuing veggie burgers seems like a perversion to a great American tradition. It just feels "wrong," although we occasionally indulge because we love Ashley and Shane.

"Veggie burgers on organic wheat buns with alfalfa sprouts and soy milkshakes. You guys can't say no to that!"

Oh yes, we could.

Ashley smiled. She was a beautiful woman inside and out. "You need to eat better," she declared. "I bought you guys a cookbook called *The Vital Vegan.* You're going to love it."

Poke-poke-poke. Chance continued to tap his finger into the small of my back.

"The cookbook is really thoughtful, but I promised Chance to help him—uh... um..." I said weakly.

"... give Mercy a bath." Chance was so helpful.

"Yeah... right. She smells like a dog. Besides, Mercy and Chance are having their pictures taken for *Search and Rescue Magazine* tomorrow. You know what they say. 'Look sharp, be sharp.'" I interjected, not even feeling guilty for lying as I reached for another cookie.

"Oh." Ashley was clearly disappointed. "Too bad. The contractors finally got the new barbecue installed. I really wanted you to see it."

I must have looked confused. "Contractors? You need *contractors* to install a barbecue?"

"You know the one. I emailed you a picture.

"Ashley, you sent me a hundred pictures," I reminded her.

"The one with two built-in brick ovens? The sink with a worktable on the side? Gaslamp overhead? Matching fire pit?" She gave up trying to explain which picture. "It looks great next to the fountain."

"Bet you'll get some air miles on that one," said Chance, looking at Shane sympathetically.

"I paid for it myself." Ashley glowed. "Did it with my last sale on eBay!"

Ashley is the Queen of eBay. She can sell *anything* and usually does. And I mean, anything. A "power seller" with an online store called Ashes for Roses, she started out selling pinecones some ten years ago. Really! We were burning them while she was selling them. I guess you just have to know your market. But she has moved up in the world to high-priced items like the sale of a rare, mint-condition 1929 three-speed Harley-Davidson

JD. Of course, it didn't hurt that Shane owned a Harley dealership.

More prodding from Chance. He was anxious to go, causing a thought to flit through my mind. I wondered if he was eager to escape veggie burgers, Mac, or just eager to get home, get naked, and get in the hot tub. I was hoping for the latter. We hugged Shane and Ashley goodbye with promises to get together another time. Ashley whispered into my ear, "You guys need to pray about the Bible study."

I jumped into the Dodge Ram thinking; *Boca Burgers on a barbecue costing thousands of dollars.* "Life is so unfair. They don't even need the money," I mumbled to Chance, feeling jealous. Shane was born into money and owns the largest motorcycle dealership in the North State. He always rides the latest, greatest cruiser. We had all bonded from the day we met. Shane is always trying to sell us motorcycles, but it's not the right time. Not now. Maybe not ever.

Chance loves bikes, but I was glad he had to sell his hog long ago as part of the traditional California divorce settlement, where he lost everything but his boxers to his ex-wife, Megan Shaughnessy. His had been a typical small town story where the head cheerleader married the golden boy quarterback right after high school graduation. Less than two years later, she gave up her job as an aerobics instructor at La Spa Massage and Sports Club and ran off to San Francisco with Chance's sister, Crystal. We don't talk much about Crystal or Megan.

Mercy never did get a bath, but Chance and I did manage to pour some sparkling mineral water into some wine glasses and climb into the hot tub long enough to enjoy the view of the Coastal Range mountains. I let go of the argument that started at church for enjoying the moment.

Both of our lives revolve around our cell phones and the stand-by status of our work. We both make a living out of rescuing others. In a way, our jobs reflect the fundamental differences between men and women. For the most part, Chance rescues the external and I rescue the internal. His clients are literally at the end of a rope and mine are figuratively at the end of their rope.

In our spare time, we tend our mountain home, sharing it with Mercy the Magnificent and Kissme, my dizzy blonde Pomeranian, enjoying all the benefits of life in Northern California. We boat, we fish, and we fish and we boat. Well, at least we used to.

Chance was my forever hero. No doubt about that. I believed he was my heavenly reward, God's way of assuring me that I had done something right in my life. Lord knows I have made mistakes. But coming down off the mountain to rescue me from the river that day, when I looked up into his face, I was certain he was an angel sent by God. It was so different having a man in my life that I could trust with my heart. I had never felt safer, happier or more complete than I have these past three years of marriage. It feels like heaven after surviving many years in hell.

෨ 🕊 ෬

"And I will always love youuuuuu." The theme from *Bodyguard* came out of our pants pile. It was our simple tribute to the memory and angelic voice of Whitney Houston.

"Hey babe, they're playing our song." Chance untangled from our intimate embrace, pulling away, he stood, dripping, steam rising from his bare body as he climbed out of the hot tub. It wasn't one of our smarter ideas to have same phones with identical ring tones—cute, but not smart. We never knew which of us was getting the call until we traced it to the red or black phone.

Red phone. I knew I'd be heading to the hospital. A woman gets battered every nine seconds, and three out of five will be sexually assaulted at some time during her life. The oldest rape victim I knew of was a ninety-eight-year-old woman in an Australian nursing home; the youngest was only eight days old. There is never a safe time in the life of a woman.

I let out a long, dual-purpose sigh; some genuine feelings for my victim and a lot of pity for myself. I made the call to Rape Crisis. I guess there is never a convenient time to be brutalized. Butte County averages close to 1,000 domestic crisis calls a year. Most of the serious ones seem to occur on weekends and holidays—specifically, *my* weekends and holidays. I had the fire of desire for my husband, but lately, it never seemed to get stoked.

Dressing required one more glance in the mirror. Satisfied, I picked up my keys then paused for a quick moment to inhale the fragrant essence of the latest bouquet my sweetheart had bought me that brightened our table with a promise of romance. It calmed my flesh and deepened my appreciation as I walked out the door, counting myself the luckiest girl in the world to have such a thoughtful husband.

CHAPTER 3

၏ ❧ ೞ

Hunkered down in my Volkswagen Beetle, I cannonballed down the mountain as fast as my TDI could go without getting caught to Oroville, the county seat. I love my car, bought in part with insurance money from the Great Harley Barrier Reef that now lay corroding beneath the Feather River. My bike had become a safety barrier for the little fries to hide behind, even as it had once shielded me from my problems. Riding a motorcycle had been therapeutic. It had been my vain attempt to regain control over my past—which is an impossibility, and also my future—which is just as futile.

The road to town winds down out of the mountains and past the district attorney's office perched high on a hill. Not by coincidence. The county buildings are laid out like the feudal system of old: the Welfare Department on the bottom of the hill, then Juvenile Hall with its counterpart, Child Protective Services, at equally low levels on the opposite sides of the hill. Midlevel is the Sheriff's Office and adult jail. Next up is a modern, imposing two-story building built around a large open atrium, housing County services that include the Auditors, Recorders, Taxes and Voting on the bottom, which is eye-level with the Probation Department and Mental Health stuck out in left field. Upstairs is where the heavyweight's reign—the County Supervisors and Criminal Division of the District Attorney's Office, including my little corner office, with a window facing the atrium and my name on the door. *Dreams do come true.* I sit level with the top of the hill crowned with the Judgment Seat, also known as Superior Court.

It takes twenty minutes to drive to work, barring road construction, logging trucks, RVs, and the highway patrol. Tonight I made it safely in fifteen. With just about five minutes to go before reaching Oroville Hospital, I called to check with today's referral source, Rape Crisis.

"Hi, Serena. What are you doing on the Crisis Line on a Sunday?"

Love my hands-free car phone. California is cracking down on no seatbelts, no phones, no texting, and no dogs in your lap in a continuing effort to save us from ourselves. Any day now they will outlaw watching DVDs, changing clothes, putting on makeup, polishing your nails, and eating meals while driving. Not that I have ever done those things. Much.

Serena, the Director for Rape Crisis, hacked up phlegm-ball on the other end of the line.

"*Ugh!*" I exclaimed, instinctively reaching for the Germ-X on my console.

"Sorry," Serena croaked in between sniffles. "Everybody's sick with the flu, including me, but somebody had to come in."

"Aw... you poor thing. You should be home with Eli feeding you chicken-noodle soup," I said sympathetically.

"Ugh! Don't even mention food. I am so sick! You on your way to the hospital?" Serena asked.

"It sounds like *you* should be. I'm almost there. What do you have?"

"The sheriff's office called," Serena replied. "I think 'Crazy Bob'"— whose real name is Deputy Robert Martel—is waiting for you."

Crazy Bob is an officer who is hated by almost everyone but me. Maybe it is because I don't have to work in the same agency with him, or maybe it is because I see him as being in a state of perpetual crisis. Some victims wear uniforms.

"Who's the victim?" I asked Serena.

"Chelsea Nielsen. Nineteen, married, pregnant. Umm..." she paused. "I don't know how far along she is. Last I heard, Dad—that would be Gregg Nielsen, took off with their two-year-old girl." Serena always knew how to break it down and give me "just the facts."

"And Rape Crisis is calling me instead of the Sierra SAFE (Stop Abuse For Everyone) House because there's a spousal rape involved?" I guessed.

There was silence followed by a soft sigh. "That too, Serena said, stressing "*battered*, pregnant, and raped."

I caught my breath, sucker-punched by the memory of a raging Logan who had pushed me off the upstairs deck, sending me falling and bouncing off a massive ancient oak stump that stood twelve feet tall beneath a tangle of wisteria branches before rolling, unconscious, to the ground. I recovered from broken ribs, but not the broken heart. My best friend—the unborn child inside of me—had died. The born I had talked to, dreamed with, and sang songs to as it drummed along with its tiny feet and heartbeat... was gone. With it went the hope of future children.

"Sunny? Hello? You still there? Darn cell phones!"

"I'm here, Serena. I drop a lot of calls driving in the hills," I said trying to refocus on the task at hand. "Is the baby alive?"

"Last I heard it was. The sheriff's office asked if you would field this one. Sorry. It seems she is beyond uncooperative. They'd really like to get this guy and so would I, but *you didn't hear me say that,* " Serena added empathically.

"Say what?" I could feel her sad smile. "Thanks, Serena. I'll give you an update when I leave. Meantime, you should keep trying to find someone to cover your shift. Maybe Marne could come in early."

I heard some huffing and mumbling from Serena. No love lost there. Marne never would have called me out. Marne has what is called "old school" thinking that typified advocates' negative attitudes toward law enforcement back in the 1960's and '70's. Today, those dinosaurs not only hate me because I work with "the enemy" law enforcement, but also because branding me a traitor to the liberation movement of our sex.

There is a dividing line in my job. While narrow, it is razor sharp and cuts deep. On the one hand, I am a Victim Advocate. One of my shortcomings includes a profound lack of political correctness. Like the story of *The Emperor's Clothes,* I just call it as I see it, and I see a significant number of Rape Crisis and Domestic Violence Advocates that are hard-core man-haters. Which isn't to say they don't have husbands or boyfriends—or justified reasons. But I work for the District Attorney, which in the world of *them* and *us*, makes me one of *them.*

Old school advocates still remember the grassroots development days of the women's advocacy movement. They recall the days when police could not respond to a spousal rape or wife beating call because the law still regarded such incidents as private matters. Even if they wanted to intervene, their hands were legally tied. Many women misinterpreted this to mean the cops were condoning male violence, which wasn't necessarily true. I admit some cops are wife-beaters, but there were, and still are, real men who do their best with the resources they have.

Law enforcement is still a matter of apples and oranges. Family Law (apples) and Criminal Law (oranges) are two completely different things, although most people don't understand that. They think the police can enforce anything relating to law. What they don't know is that cops who try to intervene in family law matters can be personally sued. When that happens, they usually lose their jobs, their homes, and almost always their families by the end of the lawsuit.

Back in the day, the law declared a woman crying at the door with a black eye could not *prove* that her husband was the one who punched her, even if his knuckles were bleeding. There were no eyewitnesses except for the wife who could not testify against her husband in court. But that was then, and this is now. A lot of things have changed since OJ murdered his wife... or whatever you choose to believe. The ugly truth remains: beatings still happen and sometimes they result in death.

"Hey Crazy... *what's happening*?"

Bob looked up from his seat in the hall. He looked physically bankrupt and totally lost in thought. It took a moment for him to tune in. "Montana. I'm moving to Montana—a thousand miles from everybody," Bob proclaimed, looking miserable.

"I'll try not to take that personally." I laughed, putting a supportive hand on his sagging shoulder. "You look exhausted. Out chasing bad guys all night?"

"I just got back from a week-long seminar on sexual assault." He shook his head. "Sick... and tired of it." Have you talked to Chelsea?" he continued.

I shook my head no.

"I figured you could talk to her first. All I know is that she is about six months pregnant and bad-dad is both father and perpetrator. He is also bio-dad to their two-year-old daughter who is with him... somewhere. We did a drive by and no one was home.

"He supposedly took off to go fishing." Bob snorted, shaking his head. "We have an APB out and Fish and Game has a heads-up at the lake."

"Thanks, Bob." Moments passed, both of us deep in thought. "And Robert." He looked up. "I hear the hunting is terrific in Montana."

I left him smiling as I headed down the empty corridor, my shoes echoing a sad, steady refrain to the private SART Room, located away from public eyes. Devised by the Sexual Assault Response Team, a collaborative effort between advocates, law enforcement, and medical providers, the SART Room is isolated from the ER, designed to protect victims' privacy and provide specially trained nurses in the use of equipment necessary to gather and preserve forensic evidence

Chelsea was one of the 25-45% of battered women who are pregnant. Abusers, who are control freaks by nature, resent that attention is taken from them and directed toward the unborn. Additionally, like Logan, they may resent the expense or inconvenience of a child. Mostly, the belly is just a target with a tempting bull's-eye.

Sadly, more babies are born with birth defects from their mother being battered, than from the diseases and illnesses for which they were immunized.

There's only one kind of "shot" that can protect the mother and baby in a case like this—and it doesn't come from a hypodermic, I thought.

I knocked, and the SART nurse opened the door. We exchanged greetings as she let me in. She was bound by HIPPA's patient confidentiality, but she raised her brows and whispered, "Good luck," while giving me a *go-ahead* tip of her head and pointing to the patient with her eyes.

Moving past the nurse, I saw two knees shaking under a draped flannel blanket and carrot-red hair fanned across the pillow. The victim's face turned toward the wall, the silence broken only by the rhythmic, reassuring beep of a fetal heart monitor. I moved to the bedside.

"Chelsea? My name is Sunny. I am the Advocate from the District Attorney's Office, and Rape Crisis has sent me to talk to you." I began in as soothing a voice as I could muster.

A swollen face with two angry green eyes with bruises the color of wine-stains turned to glare at me. I mentally winced. I am a pro at concealing my feelings from victims. Her tears had pooled and spilled onto the bridge of her broken nose. I reached carefully over her bed and pulled some tissues from the box on the table by her bed.

"May I touch you?" I asked. She nodded, and I took her hand in mine while pressing the tissues into her other. Sometimes that's all you can do. The sonogram was completed and the baby was holding steady. Next would be the Rape-Kit Exam.

The nurse explained to a practically catatonic Chelsea, who was listening without hearing to what the procedure would entail. The nurse picked up a swab and asked Chelsea to open her mouth, explaining as she worked. "These swabs are to gather possible DNA." The nurse continued with additional swabs to her vagina. "Next, I am going to take clippings from your fingernails and pubic hair. Those samples might provide trace evidence." Chelsea shut her eyes and sniffled. "Now Chelsea, I am going to apply a blue dye to the inner parts of your vagina. Then I will take some photographs with a high-tech camera. The pictures document any lacerations or trauma the dye might reveal."

Chelsea chewed on her bottom lip and swiped at silent tears with the back of her hand.

Not everybody has visible injuries from rape. Not everybody cries. Some people—especially juries—have a difficult time sympathizing with victims like these. That is why I also serve as Expert Witness for the prosecution. I educate people about the dynamics of rape and domestic violence. If Chelsea cooperated, with such apparent injuries, her husband could serve three or more years in prison just on the rape charges and another two or three years for the domestic violence. If the baby died... I added up the possibilities... but they all hinged on the victim's cooperation.

It was possible Chelsea would go sideways and drop the spousal rape charges. This is her legal right and may provide a temporary reprieve for the victim, but it also increases the likelihood that her abuser will go on to victimize more women with a feeling of impunity.

"I just want to know where my daughter is." Chelsea sobbed.

"The police are looking for your husband and your daughter. Do you know where they might be?" I asked.

"Fishing! I already told the cops, he said he was going fishing," she retorted, undoubtedly tired of repeating the story.

The bottom line is, everybody wants to help. The problem can be with varying methods and repetition of the traumatic event, leaving women like Chelsea emotionally exhausted. Some Advocates will intervene at this point to protect the victim's right *not* to have an exam and *not* to cooperate if she doesn't want to. They believe they are doing this in the victim's best interest by supporting her immediate wishes. That is advocacy in its purest sense: to support whatever the victim decides.

I, on the other hand, am there primarily to gain the victim's cooperation and hold the offender accountable. Ultimately the victim has no choice but to fight back or give the abuser a *Get Out Of Jail Free* card. I passionately believe that it is in the victim's best interest to take an active role in the justice process. I had yet to see any victims benefit from running from their past or living in denial. And yet, I was guilty of both.

"Step One" in every recovery program begins with admitting you have an overwhelming problem. At this moment, Chelsea was definitely overwhelmed. She was also vulnerable. I hoped to exploit her weakness and thereby empower her. Sometimes, it is in your darkest hour that you find your strength nger can be a powerful, motivating emotion. The advocates on the other side of that professional dividing line equate my actions as being as contemptible as the abusers. In their minds, my method is a form of revictimization. They could be right.

I held Chelsea's hand, silently praying for her as she went through the humiliation of an intimate, invasive examination of her already traumatized body. As she rolled onto her back, a small tattoo peeked over her shoulder; an ornate cross draped with tiny red roses. That is my green light. I can lose my job for proselytizing or preaching religion to victims unless they initiate the conversation. I am vigilant, careful never to violate the ethics of my job. However, I am just as relentless in seeking every opportunity for God.

"You can get dressed now," the nurse announced.

At this point in the procedure, the nurse would typically offer the victim a Morning-After pill to prevent an unwanted pregnancy. I pondered the emotions of women who have the added misfortune to suffer rape while pregnant. I wondered how she will feel every time she looks at her child, forever and inseparably linked to her agony. Then too, I considered the future of the child, born stained with the sins of the father.

I had been born into a milieu similar to this baby. I knew the hostility and rejection of an angry mother and bore the scars of my father's many sins. Like most victims of child abuse, I accepted my parents and craved their approval until adolescence when I learned that the word "abused" applied to me. Awareness typically births rage, acceptance, or as in my case, a muddy blend of both.

Startled, I looked up to see the nurse securing the chain of evidence; those swabs and vials that brimmed with sorrow and suffering, into a lock box.

"Chelsea. There's an officer outside the door. He wants to talk with you about what happened," I began.

A fire kindled in her eyes. "I don't want to talk about it again. I want out of here. Where the hell is my kid? Why haven't they found her?"

I wasn't put off by her caustic behavior. I but knew that her response was rooted in physical and emotional trauma. "Chelsea, I see by your tattoo that you believe in Christ," I crooned, extending a comforting invitation to the faith option. This was dangerous territory.

"Fuck you and God too! Don't you dare preach to me. I didn't deserve this! Where the hell was God, and... who the hell are you to talk to me? What do you know about being raped anyhow?" Her words were venomous, her manner toxic as she continued her rant. "Like, what? Did you get a degree in 'Rape' in college?"

No, I thought angrily, staunching unexpected tears. I earned my degree from the school of life. Unlike many of my colleagues, my work is rooted in empathy, not sympathy. I didn't read about it in a book. It was birthed through the pain of my youth.

CHAPTER 4

ෛ 🕊 ෬

Motorcycles roared through the woods, engines slowing to turn down the dirt driveway. At least Lefty had made it home for my birthday. I felt like I was sixteen-going-on-twenty-one because I had lived mostly on my own over the past six years.

Lefty tried to stick around after Starla left, but stability just wasn't in his outlaw blood. Lefty was a driven man. He had a hard outlook, was hard hitting and hard riding, with a pack of Vietnam-inspired demons at his heels. He had been more than happy to arrange for our nearest neighbors, an elderly Native American couple, Joyce and Benny Clark, to watch me during the week and him returning home on weekends.

He knew, because of their cultural tradition, the Clarks probably wouldn't call Child Protective Services to take me away, and he figured some money to supplement the couple's Social Security was a fair trade off for allowing Joyce to preach her "Christian crap" to his kid. Lefty didn't know and wouldn't have cared, but Benny was not Christian. He remained close to his heritage. He believed in many spirits—drumming, singing his native songs, sweating in the lodge down by the river, and gambling at the annual Hand Games, or *Tep We* as the gathering is called. Hand Games are where tribal members drink, sing native songs for power, and play a guessing game where they toss and hide small animal bones in their hands. Joyce and Benny always had a hot meal, an extra warm bed, and plenty of love.

Joyce helped me bake a birthday cake. She taught me to cook and taught me about religion. The only religion I had known growing up was the "Jesus Christ!" and "God damn it" that came out of Lefty's mouth when he was dangerously angry.

At least a dozen hogs rumbled down the road onto our five acres surrounded by national forest land, and I was pretty sure Joyce and Benny could hear them from a mile away at their cabin. Most of the homes scattered about Feather Falls were originally brought down on logs from logging Camp One as part of the government's Indian Land Grant provision before I was born.

I looked with despair at my little cake and wished Jesus would multiply it like the loaves and fishes I had heard about. I doubted that I would ever get a bite with all these people showing up. Sighing, I ran out to greet Lefty. I loved my dad. He was just who he was, and he was all I had.

"Daddy!"

"Hey, Princess! Happy fucking birthday!" He swept me up in his powerful bear hug and smothered me with kisses. "How's my favorite girl?"

I didn't struggle, in spite of being laughed at by others watching a fifteen-now-sixteen-year-old dangling from Lefty's arms like a rag doll. I knew most of his Hells Angels brothers. They'd all been regular partiers over the years. Cheech and his "old lady" girlfriend (who was also my Mom's best friend) Sheena, Fugly and Rags, Skunk, Preacher, Sonny with an unknown blonde, among others including a lively redhead who had ridden in two-up, seated behind Lefty with her arms wrapped possessively around him.

Today, colorful bags of gifts decorated the back of most of the bikes. In the midst of all the laughter and excitement, I felt the stranger's presence before I saw him. Tall, dark, intense, about thirty. I felt eyes boring into me and turned, freezing like a deer in a spotlight before my future husband. Black leathers, three-piece patched—meaning he was a full member—and a red on white diamond "1%" patch indicating he, like all Hells Angels, was one of the one-percent of bikers designated as *outlaws*. I wondered why I hadn't seen him before until I noticed the San Bernardino, or "San Berdoo" Chapter patch and realized he was up from Southern California, called 'SoCal' by NorCal natives.

Tattoos that ran from wrist to shoulder told the rest of his story; he belonged to Hells Angels, rode a Harley, was Born to Die and was Hellbound. There were the others, including a pair of SS lightning bolts and twin two-headed rattlesnakes that seemed to coil and slither when he flexed his powerful biceps. Ultimately the ink he had taken into his skin was a mark of the beast, the way a signature on a document shows ownership. Too bad I didn't know how to read contracts at the time.

"Hey, girl, that's Logan. Be nice to him and get us some beers, then you can open your gifts," Lefty said as he gestured to the newcomer.

Logan didn't say a word. The corners of Logan's mouth twitched slightly up. He barely nodded, but I got the message and got the beer.

80 🙟 03

"Mom, is it weird being with so many guys?" I had asked this very adult question of Starla when I was thirteen. She returned for a visit shortly after giving birth to my very dark, kinky-haired, adorable baby sister.

"No, honey." She said, in the same wistful manner she had once read me fairy tales. "It's like a field of wildflowers. Each one is different, and God meant for us to enjoy them all." My dad and the club seemed to share her views—at least about the enjoyment-without-commitment part.

Starla's "god" intended purpose was a lot different from what Joyce, who was very religious, had told me God intended. Joyce said that God's plan deliberately, intentionally, and divinely, calls for one man and one woman, and that, in a married relationship. She also taught me that God made Adam and Eve, not Adam and Tiffany and Bambi and Glow. "And," she reminded me, that "God didn't make Adam and Steve or Delilah and Eve, either." She said homosexuality was an "abomination" to God and unrepentant gay people were destined for hell. Her husband, Kenny would nod in agreement but told me later that he didn't believe in hell.

Lefty made fun of Joyce and Kenny, calling them Jesus Freaks when he was nice and a whole lot worse when he wasn't. God knows that Lefty plowed his way through as many women as Starla did men.

It was my sixteenth birthday, I was lonely, and I thought Logan was a fox—with his tall body, sharp features, dark in a Mediterranean or maybe Native American kind of way. Clean shaven with loose, shining black hair that seemed untamed and free as the man himself. His eyes were the color of dark chocolate with flecks of gold. *Yes*, I thought, *Logan is a fox*. But *wolf* would have been more accurate.

Ⅼ 🦋 ⁝

"Chelsea, you don't have to do anything in the future that you don't want to do, but you won't have this opportunity again." I pressed her. "If you wait too long to make a report, the jury will be less likely to believe you. Right or wrong, most jurors think a victim should want justice and be willing to make a report," I urged her, speaking clearly and distinctly in my most convincing tone. Decisions have consequences.

I didn't go on to explain that one reason jurors don't understand the victim's reluctance, is because the pictures aren't of *their* privates being passed around for everyone to see. And when there is a delayed report, coupled with an absence of pictures or witnesses, they are more inclined to believe an allegation is an act of revenge concocted by an angry woman.

"You don't understand," Chelsea said bitterly. "How could you?"

Ⅼ 🦋 ⁝

"Happy birthday, kid," Logan drawled in a deep southern accent that gave me goose bumps. He was almost invisible as he leaned against the giant oak tree in the failing twilight. There was something terribly insincere and mocking in those words, but they made my heart race. "I got something for you," he said, unwrapping his bandana and holding out his hand. Cradled in his palm were two white tablets with a yin-yang symbol stamped on top.

Blushing and feeling like a kid, I said, "I don't take drugs."

"Really. Well, how about a beer? Got a problem with beer—little girl?" his voice teased, but his eyes weren't laughing.

He thrust it at me before I could answer.

What would my dad say if he caught me drinking? Would he kill Logan? Would he beat me, like he did my mom? There was the beer, right in front of me. I turned to look at the fire pit where everyone was gathered, drinking and partying and breaking open a kilo of Thai-sticks. I located Lefty howling and stumbling with the redhead in tow into the house and no doubt, the upstairs bedroom.

I looked back at Logan. He had popped the top and held it like an offering.

"A little beer won't hurt." He smiled and moved closer, inviting and invading my personal space. I could feel the warmth of his body. So close. My heart kicked into fifth gear and breathing about stopped.

"Logan..." My objection was as weak as watered down lemonade.

"Girl..." he whispered in a husky voice.

I didn't think of Logan in terms of being sexy—I was too immature for that. I thought he was the cutest guy on the planet and I couldn't believe that he liked me and was treating me like an adult. No one had ever wanted me that way!

$$\wp \; \gamma \; \wp$$

"Earth to Bob. Hello!" I waved a hand in front of his face. "Are you okay? You're on. She's dressed and wants to talk to you."

Bob snapped out of his daydream. "Yeah! Yeah, I'm good. Is she dressed?"

I am probably the only advocate around who recognizes officer burnout when I see it. Other people call him "Crazy," but I'd say "Toast" was more like it. I also called him "friend." Maybe it's because he reminds me of a one-eyed Chihuahua or a one-handed man. Part of the whole is damaged, but there is still plenty left to love. Rumor has it Bob holds some political cards in the deck that keep him from being fired. Like others, I thought he should have retired long ago.

"She's dressed and waiting for you in the visiting room," I repeated.

Bob rose from his chair. "Good. They picked him up on Nelson Creek. Looks like he really did go fishing." Bob shook his head. "Oh yeah... Gina from CPS is on her way over now. Meet her in the lobby?"

"No problem." This was good news.

I picked up a container of ice cream from the nurse's station on my way to the lobby. Within minutes Chelsea's daughter was sitting quietly between Gina and me, eating her ice cream and wearing a chocolate mustache. Her little face was blank, but her eyes were filled with questions. I wondered about the things she had seen and heard—and if she would ever be able to forget.

ℴ 🦋 ℛ

Logan told Lefty the next morning that I had said, "I wanted it."

Did I say that? Did I even know what "it" was, that I was supposed to have wanted? It was hard to remember that night. I recall Logan leading me out into the woods. I told him things about my life and private thoughts I hadn't even revealed to myself. I giggled a lot. I guess I wanted Logan. At least I wanted him to like me in the way an adolescent child dreams of flirting with a rock star.

I sure didn't know that "it" was going to hurt so badly. I had cried and begged Logan to stop, but he just kept saying, "You know you want it."

I was still confused; my face burning red as much from the two double-stacks of Ecstasy Logan had slipped into my beer as it was from the burning shame rising up from deep inside. Pins and needles were jabbing my skin. I felt dirty. What I really wanted, was enough water to drown in. I was dying of thirst wanted to die. Drowning seemed like the perfect solution.

"Well..." Lefty's eyes fixed onto Logan like a King snake on a rat. "Now you had my baby girl... you bet your ass you're gonna marry her."

Everyone laughed, but tension crackled beneath the surface. Nobody crossed Lefty. Nobody. So, Preacher put down his breakfast beer and everyone gathered around as Logan and I were married biker-style. I don't remember saying "I do." It was more like "Okay," because nobody crossed Lefty, and that included me. I had no desire to end up like my mother on the south end of his northbound hook.

ℴ 🦋 ℛ

By the time Officer Bob finished taking the preliminary information, Chelsea had transitioned from tears to anger to extreme fear.

"They arrested Gregg?" She cringed. "Where will I go? I can't go home. God knows what he'll do when finds out I talked to you." Her responses to our questions were typical. "*No*, I don't have anyone to stay with. *No*, I don't have any money. My name isn't on any of the checks or credit cards."

The door to the Visitors Room flew open. In stomped Marne with more attitude than Angelina Jolie taking on a hoard of enemy combatants.

"You don't have to answer any questions... you haven't done anything wrong. I'm Marne, from Rape Crisis. You have the right *not* to speak with law enforcement."

I sighed. Just my luck. Why Marne, when Rape Crisis had so many other nice, normal advocates.

Gray-haired, square-jawed, butch-cut, red-faced, with a noticeable mustache on her upper lip, Marne. Marne, who hates men and looks just like one. I personally disliked her for *who* she was not *what* she was, although I failed to see the difference between employing a lesbian-who-thinks-she-is-a-man as opposed using a straight man to work in female victim services. It is kind of like putting a wolf in a pen full of wounded lambs. Temptation abounds.

Chelsea looked confused. "I don't understand. I thought Sunny was from Rape Crisis."

"Hello Marne," I said, with a mental eye roll, waving fingertips in feigned politeness before turning back to Chelsea.

"I am. But I also work for the District Attorney."

Marne glared at me and said to a very distraught Chelsea, "She's *not* your friend."

Officer Bob intervened. "Ma'am," speaking to Chelsea, "you have a right to do what you think is best. I am taking this information now and you can decide later on whether or not you want to press charges."

"I'm tired. I'm tired and I'm scared. Who is going to protect me when Gregg gets out of jail? He's beat me before." She lowered her voice and folded the paperwork in her hands. "Next time he'll probably kill me."

Bob stepped in. "He will be arraigned in court tomorrow morning. He may be held in jail without bail or he may be given an opportunity to post bail. If he posts bail, one of the conditions the court will impose is called a *Stay Away Order* in the unlikely event he is released," Bob flat-lined the refrain like a Miranda Rights advisement.

"You'd let him go *free*?" Her accusation followed by a few demeaning curse words.

"Ma'am. I have no authority..."

"He will kill me. Don't you get it?" Panic flashed through Chelsea's sad eyes.

"I am sorry, ma'am. If I had it my way, I'd..." Bob fingered his gun.

"Thanks, Bob," I interjected and grabbed both Chelsea and her Oroville Hospital take-home bag. Guiding Chelsea by the elbow, I propelled her to a heartfelt reunion with her daughter and then toward the exit. "I'll take you and your daughter by your home to get some things and then drive you to the SAFE House in Chico. I'll call you from the court in the morning and let you know what happened."

Marne growled as she followed doggedly behind, "You can do whatever you want. You don't have to go to a shelter." Ironically, Marne would have referred Chelsea to the same shelter if I hadn't been there. What Marne really objected to, was the time I would have with Chelsea outside of her sphere of influence. Too bad. Chelsea had decided to come with me.

Bob talked with me privately as we exited the building and walked through the parking lot. "This is the reason I decided on Montana... but maybe Montana isn't far enough. Maybe Alaska..." he muttered, as he nodded farewell and climbed into his patrol car.

80 ❧ CR

It was late by the time I drove back up the hill. Abuse calls are always difficult, but in a way, my work helps me make sense out of my screwed up childhood.

A question I am frequently asked (and occasionally ask myself) is, "Where was God when I was a helpless kid?"

Sometimes I say, "He was right there. He never left you. Life can take you down, but God can lift you up."

Other times I simply don't have an answer. Sometimes abuse is too terrible for words. It is pure evil. Part of living in a fallen world where people are free to make choices and sometimes, directly or indirectly, die as a result. I guess I will have to ask God to explain everything to me some day. The path I have chosen is not called a Faith-Walk for nothing.

Sleep was slow in coming in spite of my exhaustion. I curled up in the warm protective shelter of Chance's arms. "I love you, Chance," I mumbled as I reached up to kiss the soft skin that covered the inside of his strong arm. Finally, in search of peace, I let go, drifting away into the night.

Chance, however, did not sleep very well that night. I was running from demons in my past, but his were very present, lying in our bed and delighting in tormenting his nights.

CHAPTER 5

ॐ 🕊 ॐ

"And *I* will always love *youuuuuu.*" The familiar tune belted out from within last night's clothes heaped next to the bed just ahead of the alarm clock. The good news was that it was Chance's pile and not mine. The sad news was, I had spent the past ten minutes trying to rouse my husband in more ways than one.

"Great," I mumbled, resenting that he would come to life for a phone call, yet lie there like a dead thing while I ached for sex.

If sex was ever good with Logan, the memory remains vague. I mean, *nobody* in a fiery car crash remembers that they were on their way to Disneyland. While there were good times with Logan, I have shelved them along with the bad to make way for new.

Relations with Logan were usually fear-based experiences with a high expectation of performance, getting angry and abusive with anything short of an Oscar performance. Logan's fantasies were mostly fueled by alcohol, ecstasy, cocaine, porn, strip clubs, and notorious Hells Angels parties.

Loving Chance was so incredibly different. I had waited all my life for a love like this. I wanted so much to meld into him that I lightly told him, "When I die, I want our ashes 'shaken, not stirred' together." But unless lightning hits us in one form or the other in the next few minutes, the merging probably wasn't going to happen today.

Chance pressed the phone tightly to his ear, eyes narrowing as he listened intently. I sighed and handed him pen and paper. "What? No." He frowned. "We didn't watch the news. Yeah, right. Wow!"

"Hey, Sunny! Turn on the news!"

More talk. "Umm, yeah, okay, I can be ready to roll by noon."

I had known before he hung up that he would be leaving on assignment. The situation had to be far away or he would have been out the door in minutes, not hours.

"Katrina," he said solemnly. "Got the go-ahead from CalEMA. I'm headed for Louisiana. They say the levees broke last night and the city is flooding."

CalEMA is California's version of FEMA's disaster relief coordination. I watched the news, feeling awful for the people in Louisiana. However, I was feeling sorrier for myself. Chance must have noticed because he took me in arms and said, "I love you, hon. I'm sorry I've been so distracted lately. I've got to go, but babe, I'll call you every day."

Then we prayed together, hand in hand, which was something we have done religiously every day for the past two years. We prayed for the people in Louisiana, the rescue teams, and their safe return. Then Chance prayed for me—for my safety and good health. His words lacked something I needed to hear, but I couldn't quite figure out what it was. Then he was gone with a happy Mercy who was just as eager as Chance to be off doing what they loved best.

They fired up the monster truck, the Ram, and disappeared in a cloud of dust down our driveway and out towards Highway 70. I couldn't blame them for being eager. I like the adrenaline rush when responding to a crime scene. Rescue and advocacy are both serious business, but they are also exciting and rewarding in their way.

Hello guilt, thinking God must see me as selfish and petty. Then I took a deep breath, finished gathering my things, put Kissme in her pen, and followed them down the hill to work.

&० ੴ ੨

Paige was there before me. I saw her car in the parking lot. Like her, it was hard to miss. Paige drove a candy-apple-red BMW Z4, a cool 50k sports car with a bumper sticker on the back that read IT'S ALL ABOUT ME, which might have been funny, except that it was true.

Paige was currently a paid Advocate intern whose name first appeared on a list of potential candidates from Community Legal Services, a social service program connected with the university. Pretty, perky, naturally blonde, and at least a hundred years younger than me. She calls herself a progressive liberal and is guided by a different moral compass than mine.

Sometimes her vibrancy is downright annoying, but the men in the office were drawn to her like matches to fuses on the Fourth of July. Then again, a man would have to be blind or out of Viagra not to take in the short hair, short skirts, long legs, and enhanced breasts. She had pulled a few strings close to home to gain this very coveted position. Paige was dating Mark Anderson who was Lieutenant at Butte County Sheriff's Office and acting Captain of Butte County Search and Rescue.

Mark is a great guy who also happens to be Chance's friend. Small world. One thing led to another and changes followed. Mark used to go fishing with us on Chance's beloved 1934 Chris-Craft Custom Runabout, so beautiful that we entered it in the Concourse d' Elegance at Lake Tahoe the year after we met. With friendship came changes. As Mark and Paige became a regular item, the guys dropped a 350 hp V8 engine into the boat, and fishing poles were traded in for water skis. Fishing became flashing.

The heightened activity was reminiscent of our younger, carefree college days and easily enticed us at a time we thought we had grown mature and more sedate. Fall arrived, and we would gather around the chiminea on the deck for hot dinners on cool nights. Paige and Mark had no interest in talking "religion" and always deflected the conversation on to other, lighter topics. One of those topics included asking me to get Paige a position in the DA's Office.

I really liked Paige at first. She was fun and funny, and we got along well. I had always been an outsider going through school; friendless, withdrawn, and radically different from everyone else. It was easy to see that Paige had been the most popular girl on campus. I still felt shy around her lively, extroverted personality, and sadly accepted the fact that we would never reach girl-friend confidant status. My history was awkward and embarrassing. I hid that I had grown up without electricity, daughter of half-hippy half-biker parents who worshiped drugs, guns, and Mother Earth. Then too, there were seamier parts of my life that I was still trying to forget.

When Chance would eye-ball Paige, I concluded that it was petty jealousy on my part. After all, Paige looked like a cover girl for *Seventeen Magazine* and was a pretty sharp thinker when she wasn't doing her dumb-blonde routine.

"I have a POST Certificate," she assured me when I hesitated at the guy's request to help place her in the DA's Office. Mark lit up.

"Why not apply for a position as an enforcement officer? I'm sure you'd be great," I lied with an encouraging smile. She might have passed the Police Officer Standard Training courses, but I shrank at the thought of Paige with a gun.

Paige had winced at Mark's sudden interest, and mumbled something about "sexual harassment" that sounded a lot like, "I slept with the training officer."

I admit Paige makes me crazy, always flirting with Chance and every other male between the ages of ten and dead. But she did possess a lot of training that could make her a valuable asset to the unit. I didn't realize until later that while she had a working knowledge of the law, she knew very little about victims and their issues. Paige had majored in criminology, and I had majored in victimology.

ဆ ⚥ ര

"Wow, you look terrible!" Paige greeted me.

I paused for a second, taking a mental time-out. Okay, it was Monday, and I hadn't slept very well. I gravitated to the coffee machine for another cup. "Yeah, I got called out on a rape yesterday. Keep your eyes peeled for a police report in the intake box for a Gregg Neilson."

"Who's the victim?" Paige asked.

"His wife, Chelsea."

Paige's right eyebrow shot up. "His *wife?* She filed a complaint?"

I sometimes wonder about Paige and my stupidity in hiring her. I am pretty sure that dumb-blonde jokes were written with her in mind. I roll my eyes when men in the office tell them, and she takes pride in not getting the punch line. I know she's not stupid so I find it irritating that she works at perfecting the empty-headed ditzy image. Sometimes, *most of the time*, I am embarrassed that Chance and Mark ever talked me into recommending her. I figure she majored in Sleeping Your Way to the Top 101 with a Double-D Doctorate.

"Yeah," I tried to explain. "Rape of a spouse is a crime. Wives get raped the same way other women get raped—forcibly. They have a long history of domestic violence. Now she's pregnant, and he's raped and beaten her."

Paige looked thoughtful. "Huh. I'm surprised she reported it. I wonder what she did to make him so mad. Probably stopped having sex with him because she was pregnant."

"The rape wasn't her fault. Rape isn't about sex anyhow. Rape is a guy beating a woman with his penis instead of his fist." Paige wrinkled her nose in disgust. I continued, "And what if she did start the fight? She still didn't deserve to be raped and beaten. No one deserves that."

Paige stiffened at my remark. "She should have left him if her marriage was that bad," she said with a disparaging attitude.

It occurred to me that while Paige might be a genius on a computer, that her talent ended there. She was less informed on the subject of domestic violence than most of the jurors I instruct.

Drumming my fingers on the desk, I was losing patience. It's a good thing we had an old friendship to fall back on. Also, I wanted to make Chance proud of me for training Paige, so I made a mental commitment to be patient and tolerant.

"Let me list some possibilities for you. Try pregnant, no job, no money, no car, family hates her, and she has a child to support. Anyone who beats you half to death and says he'll kill you is a high risk for doing it. She's terrified, Paige."

Her eyes snapped. "Well, I wouldn't let anyone do that to me! I'd leave him first," he said.

Okay, my commitment to patience had lasted about thirty seconds before vaporizing in a nanosecond. I rose from my chair and leaned into her. "She didn't *let him!* Anyhow... don't you have something to do? Make coffee, dump the trash?" I wanted her to go away so I could work.

I spun around to find myself toe to toe with Travis Winslow, the newest investigator in our vertical prosecution team that was comprised of a prosecutor, an investigator, and an advocate. I only avoided throwing coffee on him by splashing it down myself instead.

"I hate it when you do that!" I glared at Travis who laughed as I tried in vain to wipe brown splotches from my new white shirt. I don't know if he works at sneaking up on me or if he is always in stealth mode.

Travis is as handsome as Paige is sexy, only he doesn't look like Ken compared to Paige's Barbie-Doll image. Travis looks more like the action figure, GI Joe. There is a reason for that. Reyna in Personnel had told me everything. A fountain of gossip, she said that Travis had served in the Intelligence Division of the Army during the Gulf War and did two stints in Iraq. Furthermore, he was hired by ATF before the ink was dry on his discharge papers.

I suspect there is a military story behind the thin, pale scar that peeks out just between the collar of his dress shirt and his sandy brown hair. He is about Chance's age, has a pair of intriguing green eyes, is average sized with muscles that press nicely in all the right places, and he is always chewing gum to release surplus energy. Travis embodies all the maturity and discipline that screams military background.

Only God and Jack Savage, our District Attorney, knows why he is in our neck of the woods working for us. He seems like a career guy who would have been more at home in the Intel Division of the Pentagon instead of replacing our former Investigator, Davis Martin. Davis had been transferred out of SVU and into BNTF, the Butte County Narcotics Task Force. It was a coveted promotion for Martin and Travis had slid into Davis's spot much to the dismay of other seasoned applicants in line for the job.

Travis pulled a tissue from the box on my desk. "Let me help." He smiled and started dabbing at my breast.

"I've got it!" I said, huffing and batting his hand away.

"Have it your way. Got a special delivery for you," he said, giving me the file in his other hand.

"Oh my gosh... how did you get this so fast? How did you know?"

"This is just Chelsea's statement. Deputy Robert Martel, uh... Crazy Bob, said he would hand deliver the full report when he's done."

"Thanks, Travis. You're the best!" I went from scowling to grinning faster than Paige's BMW does zero to sixty.

His green eyes teased. "Yeah, I know. Got to get to court." And he was gone.

"Nice buns." Paige followed his exit with predatory cat eyes, or possibly they were glinting with jealousy. The thought made me smile.

"What about Mark?" I asked.

"What *about* Mark?" She smirked. "He has nothing to do with other men's behinds."

"Oh, that's real loyalty."

"Oh, yourself! Get real." Paige raised her voice. "Men window shop all the time and it's no big deal. Men are nice for just *one* reason. Sex is all they *really* care about. Besides, you act all churchy now, but you must have been hot once with—what was his name? Morgan?"

"Logan. His name was Logan, and the concept you're searching for is called *self-control*."

She knew Logan's name and that he was a member of Hells Angels. Her eyes had widened when I told her a little about him. She had pumped me for all the gritty details, but I never shared the dark stuff—the rapes, the baby, the beatings. Since Paige started work for the DA, our relationship had not only cooled, but chilled. I began to build a familiar, impenetrable wall. I was a master mason when it came to building walls. I had no intention of telling her the secrets I had so carefully withheld from my husband.

Paige smiled sweetly. "Whoops! I must have let my membership with Club Christ expire."

I was used to Paige's increasing sarcasm as our relationship devolved, from friendly-friends to worker-supervisor. She increasingly reminded me of my mother who also lives life without boundaries or consideration for others.

"You might want to check your nails," I replied, just as sweetly, presenting the back of my hand and wriggling my fingers, causing Page to do a quick damage assessment of her long, elaborate solar nails. "Your claws are showing, dear."

She became red-faced and defensive. Paige was easy, in more ways than one.

"And *you* still have coffee stains on your shirt," she said, spinning away on her platforms, swishing her way back to the common area.

The phone rang. "District Attorney Office, this is the Advocate."

"Sacramento Airport. This is Chance."

"You miss me and can't live without me! Right?"

"That too." Chance paused, losing his stride before regaining it. "I'm calling to let you know that I left my cell phone at the house." He sounded anxious. "I can't believe I did that. I need you to look everywhere for me and turn it off. If you need to reach me, you can use Mark's number."

"Is that what you're on now?"

"Yeah. Mark's not happy that I forgot my phone, but he can't say much. Last month he dropped his down a toilet at a rest stop and reported it 'lost.'" Chance laughed. "Oh, hey, I think they want us at security. Gotta run. I love you. And Sunny, don't forget to shut it off, okay?"

"No problem. Love you too. Have a safe flight."

$\wp \, \vartheta \, \alpha$

I looked at the stack of cases, about ten deep, with a small groan. Every month Victim Witness sends me data sheets that rank Domestic Violence as the number one violent crime in the county, making up about one-third to one-half of all violent incidents. No big surprise to those who know that Butte County gets about one-thousand domestic-related calls each year.

As the population goes up, so do the calls. I know that the violence is not based on socio-economics, race, gender, income, education, or motorcycle type. People of all colors, backgrounds, and income levels commit interpersonal violence. Offenders always think they have a justifiable reason for striking out; blaming their problems, their pasts, and their addictions. But everybody has problems, and Lord knows that I know everyone has a past.

As far blaming addictions for violence, alcohol and methamphetamine are simply fuel for the fire. Addictions don't *cause* violence, they enhance it. I have been assaulted by Logan both drunk-and-high and clean-and-sober.

Some say alcoholics only hurt themselves—physically. Adults are expected to make choices and take responsibility for their behavior. Unless, of course, you are a progressive liberal like Paige who gives more weight to *blame* than *accountability.*

The file-pile is usually larger on Mondays. Probably due to the weekend increase of recreational substance abuse as much as the office being closed on weekends. "Mia Vang. Where do I know that name?" A mental challenge since Vang is more common than Smith in the local phone book. I sipped my coffee, and the caffeine pumped directly to my brain.

Got it! That's it—the Mental Health referral. A frail woman in her mid-forties who looks more like she is in her mid-eighties. Many people have never heard of "Hmongs." They were a simple mountain tribe who befriended Americans during the Vietnam War and were later brought to America to keep them safe from political retaliation when we withdrew. They are refugees who, while dispersed throughout the nation, have a significant population and a remarkable talent for growing the best strawberries in Butte County. Mental Health offered special services to accommodate their cultural transition into American culture.

Poor Mia! During a women's group encounter at Mental Health, Mia disclosed that she had been hemorrhaging for several years, since the birth of her fifth child, leaving her body ravaged from a hormone imbalance and systemic drain on her health. She lives in a perpetual state of anemia and exhaustion and her husband will not allow her to have a much-needed hysterectomy because his friend advised him, "It makes them"—women— "dry down there." Heaven forbid that her husband should be denied lubrication! The group session had also revealed that Mia's husband had assaulted her.

"Tong Fong Low's—what do you say?" Travis suggested. He was back from court and didn't look happy. Court is always a hurry-up-and-wait affair.

I reevaluated my pile. I had finished reviewing the new cases and prioritized them, not by date, but by possible lethality; bumping those victims most likely to end up dead to the top. I was unable to reach Mia on the phone and was not surprised. I doubted that her husband allowed her to use it.

Her husband had showed up to the preliminary hearing with about fifteen other Hmong men. One man tried to enter the courthouse with a live chicken in a burlap bag. "We will take her behind the courthouse and kill the chicken," he explained to the bailiff. "Mia must drink the blood. If she lives she is innocent, if she dies, she is guilty." But that wasn't nearly as shocking as his Defense Attorney advocating for their right to follow this cultural tradition.

"Isn't this supposed to be America? With American laws?" I whispered in court to the prosecutor, Amanda Cross.

The man with the chicken had to leave, but much to everyone's amusement, *someone* put a rubber chicken in the defense attorney's discovery box for him to find the next morning. The attorney squawked about it, but the DA only laughed.

The trial date was set and Mia had left the courtroom shuffling along three feet behind her husband staring at the floor, not daring to make eye contact with anyone.

"We call it Chow Mein Charlie's, not Tong Fong Low's," I corrected Travis. Locals still call the place Chow Mein Charlie's.

"Would you mind stopping by Mia Vang's after lunch? Hopefully, her piece-of-crap husband will be off with his girlfriend or losing his butt at one of the casinos."

Paige poked her head into my office, hands on the doorframe with the practiced moves of an exotic pole dancer, tossing her chin and looking hungry for more than food.

"Lunch? I didn't realize it was so late. Mind if I tag along?"

"No problem, Paige... but you'll have to take your own car." Travis glanced my way. "Sunny and I have some follow-up investigation to do before I have to beat it back to court."

Paige started to pout. "I'm supposed to be an intern. Why can't I tag along? I've learned everything there is to know here in the office."

I saw that flash of jealousy again.

Travis raised his eyebrows and tucked in his chin. "Really? I'm impressed. How long has it been now? Three months?"

"Almost four," she argued. Did she not know sarcasm when she heard it? "Besides, it's Sunny's job to train me."

I was out of arguments to prevent Paige from joining us and told myself it didn't matter.

Travis slid into the booth next to me. We ordered our food, and Travis asked, "What's so special about Chow Mein Charlie that this place kept his name?"

"Oroville has a rich Chinese heritage from the gold rush days," I said, warming to the topic. "The original restaurant was half this size. It used to have a row of booths along that wall," I pointed, "and each booth was draped with dark red velvet curtains. The people inside had total privacy. Very mysterious! You know—secretaries and their bosses, shady politicians, opium dealers."

"Sounds perfect," Travis lowered his voice suggestively.

Pretending to study the menu, I found myself wondering where Chance was now. I also wondered about Travis's lack of a wedding ring as he studied the menu. Travis ordered Chicken Chow Mein, Paige ordered a Lite Stir-Fry Special and I already knew that I wanted flaming Mongolian Beef. Travis doesn't *feel* married, I thought, and Paige was on that, like white on rice.

The egg roll appetizers and won ton chips arrived and I bowed my head in silent prayer over my food.

"Why do you do that?" Paige interrupted my prayer. "It's so embarrassing! Don't you know people are looking?"

I finished my prayer without a flinch before asking, "Do what?"

Paige rolled her eyes to heaven. "Act all holy in public."

"Because the Lord said 'Do this in remembrance of me,' whenever you eat Chinese. Think of it as a Post-It Note to God."

"What's it say?" she countered.

"I remember." Duh!

Paige smirked. "That's lame. 'Chinese!' Anyhow, it shouldn't be a public freak show."

Travis intervened as the server returned with platters of food. "There is a simple solution," he advised Paige.

"Yeah, she can keep her act at home where it belongs."

"Or," said Travis, taking up his chopsticks, "you can always eat with different company."

"And miss yours?" she cooed with familiarity. "No way!"

CHAPTER 6

౫ ⚲ ಶ

The stop by Mia's house had been futile. Her husband opened the door about six inches to advise us that Mia wasn't feeling well and that she was sleeping. I looked over his shoulder saw nothing more than a calendar with an Asian pin-up girl and a Coca-Cola clock on the back wall of the entryway.

Crazy Bob was waiting with the report on Chelsea's husband, Gregg Nielsen, by the time we got back.

"Thanks, Bob, this is great. What are the charges from your end?"

"Sexual battery and misdemeanor domestic violence."

"What happened to the spousal rape charges?"

"Not gonna happen. The vic clammed up, the kids won't testify, and..." Bob made pincher motions with his thumb and forefinger, "there are no other injuries besides the Dalmatian spots he left on her body."

"Didn't the hospital send the kit results?"

"They did, and we sent them up to you guys this morning. The pictures aren't the problem. She's refusing to allow the sexual assault photos be admitted into evidence and says the bruises are from her scratching mosquito bites. I hear Amanda's filing a 273.5 as a misdemeanor."

"*What?*"

"Uh-huh. Seems Mia's new friend Marne talked her out of pressing the rape charges."

"I guess that's it," I sighed, thinking maybe Bob had the right idea about retiring in the outback of no man's land.

౫ ⚲ ಶ

An hour later I made my way across the parking lot to the courthouse. I always feel like a moving target when negotiating the parking lot. Most criminals resign themselves to being sentenced after breaking the law. But at least half of the Family Law attendees exit the building enraged. It's one thing to take away a man's freedom and another to take away his kids.

The criminal courtroom was overflowing. Travis sat next to Amanda, the prosecutor of our vertical prosecution team. Amanda Cross is an unforgettable two-hundred and fifty pounds of African-American tigress. A remarkable, sophisticated woman who can hold her own on any courtroom floor, and probably on any bar room floor if needed. Her trademark is her broad, sweeping, colorful hats and turbans that tend to intimidate both defense attorneys and the sternest of judges. As long as she keeps her professional demeanor, she is free to express her heritage with her colorful attire. And she does just that.

I edged my way toward the table and managed to grab the last chair as the next case was called. Judge Pack might have been sitting on his gavel from the pained look on his face. The room went silent as the judge established eye contact with Travis and motioned him to the bench.

Travis paused and pointed to himself. "Me?"

"Now!" the judge fumed.

Travis got up and made his way to the bench where Judge Pack leaned forward and whispered something in his ear. Travis, however, walked away looking totally confused. Halfway back, Travis paused and turned back toward the bench. "The gun? The *gun?*"

Judge Pack dropped his head in despair. "The *gum*. Get rid of the *gum!*"

The courtroom erupted in laughter, and I was the worst.

Bam! "Order in the court."

Travis pulled himself together. "Thank you, Your Honor, for not embarrassing me in front of the court," he said, throwing the judge a winning grin as hysterics broke out again.

80 🕊 ⅋

An hour later I borrowed Travis's personal camera, offering him a pack of gum as payment. I left him laughing and headed out to meet Chelsea who had returned to her home in the agricultural town of Palermo, just south of Oroville after the court issued a "stay away" order against Gregg on her behalf. For now, the house was hers, and Gregg was staying with one of his sisters in Oroville.

Bruises deepen in color over time. Yesterday's red is today's black and blue. Convictions should be commensurate with the full extent of the injury. Most injuries are scarcely visible in the first few hours, so I try to get follow-up pictures over the next two-five days to strengthen the prosecutor's case.

Sure enough, Chelsea's eye was Welch's grape juice purple, and she had fingerprint-shaped bruises on the inside of both thighs below her shorts. She was depressed and still disagreeable. Her daughter's laughter wound its way down the hall, and her giggle was a breath of fresh air as she watched cartoons from her bedroom. We had a window of opportunity for privacy in the front room. Chelsea lifted her tank top over her rounded belly. I reached out and lightly touched it with a kind of reverence and awe.

Variegated shades of red and purple crossed her breasts and stomach. "Let me take some pictures, Chelsea. The jury has a right to see your injuries at their worst."

"No," she said. "I went through this before when we lived in Portland. Gregg was arrested for pushing me out of a moving car. All he got was an anger management class that he didn't even complete." Despair seemed to engulf her. I didn't know all the details of how he had slipped through the cracks in *Oregon*, but I made a mental note to follow up.

I was drawn once again to the tattooed cross on her shoulder. "Chelsea, are you a Christian?" I asked.

Amazing how God opens doors. It's understandable that people get angry at God after they have been victimized. But given time to process their anger, ninety-nine times out of a hundred they leap with hope at the opportunity to approach their circumstances through the door of faith.

Before leaving Chelsea, we said a prayer for healing and understanding that God had not forgotten her. She may be despised by her husband, but she is loved and precious in the heart of God. God does not make trash, and God did not beat her. Neither did he design his daughters to be punching bags. Chelsea needed to understand that she had been the victim of another person's free will.

Travis wasn't around when I stopped by to return his camera. Probably still in court. I could have left the camera on his desk and walked out, but I thought I should leave a note about Chelsea's decision not to use the sexual assault pictures taken at the hospital. Okay, the truth: I was curious, and wanted to snoop into his private life. So I looked around at a completely sterile office. No pictures, no plants. Not even a calendar. I've seen more inviting prison cells. *He probably wouldn't mind if I peek in his desk.*

Nothing of interest in the middle drawer, unless you call a pack of gum and a Swiss Army knife exciting. *What is it with men and their pocket knives?* And they criticize women for their purses! These guys pack one or more handguns, a rifle, and canister if mace in their cars and they still need that little red knife to complete their outfit.

Hmm? *Probably find Post-it Notes in a side drawer.* Wrong. No Post-its, but there was a photograph of a beautiful woman and two children; a girl about four years old that looked just like Mom, and a miniature Travis who looked around seven. It was signed on the back; *Love, Christy and the kids.*

"Excuse me. Can I help you find something?"

It was Paige.

"No."

"I want to see," Paige said as she snatched the picture from my hand. She studied it, and a smile played at the corner of her mouth.

"Hmmm. Looks like Mr. T's married. Cute kids. Very sexy."

I have no idea why she thought being married made a man sexy. Then again, maybe she thought his wife was sexy. You never know these days.

"I was looking for... um, paper," I said.

"Sure you were," she mocked, with a derisive laugh. She flipped the picture on the desk, spun around and sashayed her way back to the common area.

80 🕊 ○3

Home feels empty when Chance is gone, but Kissme, my almost three-pound blonde Pomeranian is always there, spinning in circles with abundant joy and endless wet kisses. Dogs are distinguished in their various talents. I stared in contemplation as I watched Kissme turn six full circles as she trotted down the hall. Unbelievable!

My childhood neighbor and caretaker, Kenny, never had to teach his Siberian Husky to pull. From the first time he harnessed Matushka to a sled, *Whoosh!* She was gone. Another neighbor raised a Collie named Chief. That crazy dog spent every day of its ten-year life trotting out to the pasture right after breakfast, dutifully barking and herding the same two horses around the pasture all-day-every-day of its life. Put Chuck's hound, Little Bit, on a bear trail, and you could watch it follow the bear to the ends of the earth... or until it is treed the bear, whichever came first.

What was God thinking when he designed a dog to alway spin in one direction? If I took Kissme to Austrailia, would she turn in reverse, like the water in an Austrailian toilet whirls in the opposite direction of ours? I finally concluded that Poms must be living proof that God has a sense of humor.

At least with Chance gone, I imagined sleeping in. I had early meetings in Chico and would drive straight to them.

I moved between comfortable, warm, slippery sheets, softly moaning. I could smell Chance's strong masculine scent and feel his twenty-four-hour five o'clock shadow brush across my breasts as I woke. I lingered. *Oh please don't let this dream be over. I am so ready!*

I never fantasize about other men, preferring instead to daydream about my sexy husband. Chance would be pleasantly shocked at what we have done and where we have done it in my imagination. I missed Chance and ached for him alone.

Kissme gave me a rude reality check, standing on my chest and bumping me with her wet nose, demanding that I get up and take care of business. Sighing, I let go of the vision, pulled off the sheets, grabbed my robe and let out the dog before heading to the shower.

"And I will always love youuuuuu."

Hugging a large towel, I dripped my way down the hall to answer my cell, flipped it open and got the dial tone. So I poured an oversized cup of coffee and shuffled back to the bathroom. I don't function without coffee.

"Beep."

Blonde, sun-streaked hair tumbled from the towel as I stood in front of the mirror shaking my head.

"Beep."

I turned on the blow dryer thinking if I ignored the sound, it would go away. It didn't.

"Beep."

I hate that sound. The one that comes at o'dark-thirty when I am sound asleep, telling me my cell phone's battery is low. I got up and checked my phone before remembering that Chance had forgotten his and asked me to look for it. It should be just short of dead by now.

"Beep."

I narrowed the field. The phone was either in the trash, the hamper, or the toilet.

"Beep."

Found it! Black cell phone in the inside pocket of Chance's dirty work shirt. "Huh." The *New Text Message* symbol was on the screen. Being the dutiful wife, I figured I would forward the message to Mark's phone.

I didn't know Chance's password, so I experimented by keying in my best guesses; "Sunny" and "Sunshine." No go. I keyed in "rescue." Not good. Okay. I hated to admit it, but maybe I am not his first love. I keyed in "Mercy" and Bingo! I was in.

The text message included a picture from allaboutme and read, "Hey baby, meet u @ casino @ 3. got r room!"

My jaw hit the floor.

It didn't take a plastic surgeon to figure out whose silicone snow cones I was looking at.

CHAPTER 7

ℬ 🕊 ℛ

Sweat ran into my already fried eyes, fueling the burning caused by the thick dust and exhaust from the half-million bikers traveling at two miles per hour as they funneled into Sturgis.

As sure as the geese fly south every winter and the salmon run in the fall, Hells Angels trek to Sturgis, probably the largest motorcycle rally and flesh fest in the free world.

Booze was on the menu—breakfast, lunch, and dinner.

Login drank himself drunk at every stop along the way, like he was pigging out on appetizers before the main course at the end of the trail.

We probably would have wrecked if it wasn't for the crank he snorted following the rounds of beer.

Wasted bikers have an internal autopilot that functions most of the time, and they seem to be okay with that.

I had just turned seventeen, and although I was used to the drunken debauchery that took place at least twice a month at the cabin growing up, I was still a stranger to big cities and large crowds.

I had never been in a bar, attended an outdoor festival, or even been to the Bay Area.

My life was in the mountains, and Sturgis attracted more people to their annual motorcycle rally than the entire population of Butte County. And all of them were bikers.

Since this was my first trip to Sturgis, or anywhere else for that matter, I was ecstatic in spite of my fears.

Logan kept me close to his side from Frisco to Colorado and on to Custer, South Dakota.

About seventy miles out of Sturgis we met up with several other Hells Angels chapters arriving from coast to coast, now totaling over one-hundred motorcycles in our pack.

I clung to Logan in fear while taking in the wonder of it all.

Hells Angels were different from the other bikers.

Although Sturgis is attended by the most powerful biker gangs in America, we were the most famous of them all with chapters from across the country and around the world.

Outlaw biker clubs are made up of soldiers, and chapter presidents might be kings of their turf, but Sonny Barger was Emperor of the Angel universe.

Oakland ruled.

Our president rode out in front of the entire procession.

We were like gods—or maybe more like locusts—depending on your point of view.

Honda Gold Wings had taken up the parking in front of Gunner's Saloon.

The Honda Gold Wings were like a row of Cadillac's, luxury-touring bikes typically associated with retirees. But they weren't there for long.

Sonny immediately broke the biker's cardinal rule of *never* touching another person's motorcycle, by dispatching his *prospects*—those club initiates who were still in the process of earning their patches—not only to touch the bikes, but move them to the parking area in the middle of the road.

At first there was a lot of cursing and honking from backed up traffic as enraged Gold Wing owners ran out of the bar. But the melee ended as fast as it began.

The Gold Wingers' hot tempers did a quick chill as Hells Angels colors came into focus. They proceeded to mount up and ride off without further commotion, leaving us plenty of parking in front of *our* bar.

Other riders waited for the road to clear, the near riot ended like the flick of a switch as sodden brains lit up with recognition.

Hells Angels ruled.

I didn't think of myself as a victim with Logan there.

I felt safe, surrounded by such powerful men.

I knew they would protect me from all of those crazy people.

🕉 🕊 ☪

Some people wake up to the sounds of traffic, honking horns, and the steady hum of city life.

Looking out my kitchen window, I almost always count my blessings that I wake to the sounds of mountain life: cattle lowing down in the valley, my neighbor's obnoxious rooster, Canadian geese honking their way back home, and the wind sighing in the pines.

This morning, however, the magic of the moment dimmed in light of the music playing on Chance's cell phone in the palm of my hand.

"Hello? Hello?" Whoops! Wrong phone. I picked up my phone and proceeded with caution.

"Good morning, beautiful. It's almost 10:00 o'clock here. How is it going?"

Chance's voice always made my heart beat faster. Usually with love. But today I was practically in cardiac arrest from hurt, anger, and confusion.

Still foggy with sleep, I wasn't sure where to begin.

"Sunny? Can you hear me? Hello?"

"Hey, Chance. Where are you?"

"We are in a staging area outside of the city. Man, this place is unreal. People are actually shooting at us if you can believe it."

"Shooting at you? Why?"

"Looters, probably," he speculated. "One of the rescue boats was hijacked by a gang of teenagers. You have to see it to believe it. We flew in over downtown New Orleans—and we are talking a major disaster here. Looks like half of the state is under water. Probably is. Dangerous. They say there are about sixty-thousand people still trapped. Pray for us, Sunny."

Pray for him? Is he for real? I'll pray an alligator bites him in the crotch—

"Hey Mercy, knock it off."

"What's she doing?"

"She's got her nose in Mark's butt."

I could hear men laughing and joking in the background, but it seemed like a million miles away.

I tried to organize my thoughts.

"Babe, did you find my phone?"

"No." Lying is a sin, but I *wished* I had never found his phone.

I wonder if that's another negative point on my celestial scorecard?

I wasn't ready to face the truth and all of its consequences.

"Shut it off for me when you find it, Okay?"

"I'll put it on the charger for you."

"No! Uh... not necessary. I'm going to be here for a long time. Just go ahead and turn it off."

"I can forward your messages to you." My eyes narrowed in anger.

Silence for a couple of beats.

Chance rarely raises his voice. He made an exception. "Turn it off, Okay!" His stress stabbed at my already wounded heart.

My unasked question had just been answered.

"Right! I gotta go. Have a good one. I don't know when I'll be able to call again. I love you, Sunny."

Really? "Yeah, okay."

"Bye."

The full moon was faint, riding low over the valley, reflecting yet another golden feature of our beautiful state—turning the drought-ridden landscape to a pale flaxen gold until the rain returns, six months from now if we are lucky.

I drove down the hill with the windows down and the heater on with just one thought in mind—*Starbucks.*

I would sort everything else out after that.

The weather was pleasant enough to leave Kissme outdoors in her "gated community," a twelve-by-twelve foot pen under a black oak inhabited by two large gray squirrels that were bigger than her.

I am pretty sure they won't harm her, but I wouldn't be surprised if they spend their days laughing and using her for target practice with their acorns.

I thought about coffee. I thought about my dog. I thought about living on the moon and wondered if Kissme would be happy there.

I thought about everything but Chance, the dreadful text message, and how my life was about to change.

Those thoughts, or *absence* of thoughts, were a skill I had developed early in life, or perhaps I should call it a *gift*.

It is called *dissociation.*

Victims of constant abuse know it well.

When circumstances overwhelm, the mind dissociates; thoughts pack up and take a vacation, leaving the rest of the world behind.

ജ 🕊 ଔ

If Logan was anything, he was familiar; "Little Lefty," some called him. That should have been frightening, but it wasn't—at first. After all, I was Daddy's Girl.

I remember after one nightmare Lefty had kicked a drunken bimbo out of his bed and onto the floor for the night so I could crawl in and curl up next to him.

He had whispered in my year, "Got to toughen up, baby girl," kissed me on my head, and held me close until we fell asleep. Even my nightmares were afraid of Lefty. But I wasn't. So it never occurred to me as a teenager to fear Logan.

Okay, sex was really scary, even painful at first. But hormones kicked in as my innocence faded and I started to miss my husband during the week and look forward to weekends differently than when I was a child.

Logan vanished for two weeks following our impromptu marriage, and I had missed him and wondered if the events had just been a dream.

No one talked about him, and I was too embarrassed to ask.

Then there came the time almost a year later when he showed up riding with a beautiful girl who was older than I was.

I grew up really fast then.

Everyone—except her—laughed as we rolled around in the dirt in my first real cat fight, complete with scratching, biting, and pulling hair.

Logan slept with her that night but somehow ended up in my bed on the next one. I was furious when he tried—but failed—to get her into bed with us.

They rode off together with her on the back of his bike giving me the "California salute" with her middle finger as they turned up the driveway.

Like Lefty, Logan usually got what he wanted.

Lexi Krauss looked a whole lot better before her nose was broken.

While there is never an excuse for domestic violence, some women have a natural talent for driving their man to the brink of sanity.

Lexi's husband, Roland, was a hardworking man. Maybe he worked too hard.

Maybe he should have spent some of that overtime on his wife instead of saving it for their retirement.

No matter.

Roland had come home after working a double shift at a freight distribution center. The kids, ages seven, nine, and thirteen, were all watching TV and giggled when he asked, "Where's Mom?"

He found Lexi in bed, *their bed,* with another man.

First, Rollie punched out Lover Boy. He might have stopped there if not for the hurtful remarks Lexi was screaming in his face about the, uh— how do I say this kindly? —*The limited endowment of his manhood.*

Okay, that is too wordy.

He had a dinky-winky, which is in no way a reflection of his masculinity.

I mean, guys think size is everything, which is why Lexi used it as a verbal rocket launcher to blast a hole through his ego. But a real woman measures a man by the size of his heart, not his penis.

If men really understood this, there would be fewer divorces and a lot more happy marriages.

But Roland's actions constituted a felony and Roland would have to pay the consequences.

What was exceptionally sad was that while Rollie was in jail, Lexi would probably get divorced, get the kids, and he would have to continue working those double shifts. Only this time, all of his money would go to child support and he would be coming home at the end of the day to a house that was as cold and empty as his wife.

I wondered as I closed out her file if my mother had been like Lexi; if my dad had worked hard to provide for her, but for whom *enough* was never *enough.*

For a person whose life's mission was all about *peace and love,* my mother had done an awful lot of complaining and arguing.

CHAPTER 8

ဆ ❦ ෬

"Logan, I'm tired and I'm hungry. Can I have some money? Please? I'm starving."

In fact, I was famished. Riding across the country had been fun, but the food stops had been few and far between. The heat was intense even as night fell. I wanted food and water, not beer, whiskey and cocaine. I never took drugs, except for the spiked goods Logan would occasionally slip me for laughs.

We had arrived at Sturgis and set up camp.

"What the fuck! You want money, you earn it." I knew exactly what he had in mind but I was more concerned with my stomach than what lay a few inches below it, so I did the cry-baby thing; whining and pleading with tears welling up in my eyes. Logan got mad and fired back with "I don't need you to get some!" Then he was gone.

Sturgis is all about sex, sex, and more sex. Okay, it is sex-fueled to radical heights by mountains of drugs and oceans of alcohol. Where else can you throw up on the bartender and still get served another drink?

The yearly gathering at Sturgis is not really about motorcycles. Motorcycles are just the vehicle of choice. Great bikes are on display at thousands of cycle shows across America every summer. Sturgis is about sex, and the attendees happen to be bikers. They rally around the bikes, but they don't come to see the bikes. They come to see naked women walking around and naked women riding mechanical bulls, frequently two at a time. They come to get wasted, get into rubber wading pools with naked women and whipped cream, get more wasted, look at more naked women, and hopefully   score with one or even two at a time. Angels never have trouble in that department. Beautiful, young, spun-out women are always eager to brag that they had sex with multiple members of Hells Angels.

I don't know what time Logan returned to our tent, but he was next to me when I woke up. We did our mating ritual and he got up and dressed. Looking around, I realized my clothes were gone. I mean *really* gone. In their place was a red thong, a scanty red-leather string bra top, and my black leather chaps.

"Get 'em on and we'll go get breakfast." Logan smiled at me like a sinister kid grinning at a butterfly speared to a mat.

"But Logan... where's my stuff?" Panic rose in my throat. I wasn't allowed to sleep with clothes on when I was with Logan. He had advised me early on in our relationship to grow up and lose the jammies. I grabbed his bag, and he slapped my face.

"Don't *ever* touch my bag or I swear to God, I'll break your neck." Eyebrows squeezed together over eyes that burned like coals in the dimness of the tent. I knew he meant it. Evil was behind them. Back then I thought the evil was drugs and alcohol. I didn't know about evil spirits and demons. I didn't know that drugs can break down spiritual defenses and leave a person wide open as an empty house with an unlocked door.

"Hurry up and get dressed. I want the guys to see what I got." His eyes glittered with predator excitement.

"No Logan, I won't." I protested.

Logan grabbed my face and pinched until I squirmed and cried in pain. "Suit yourself," he hissed, sending a spray of spittle across my face. He shoved me back on the sleeping bag and stormed out.

ഇ 🕊 ൙

Campfires burned throughout the campground, mingling the essence of food with a chorus of wood smoke, unwashed bodies, and exhaust fumes in a Sturgis harmony that hummed across the strings of an evening breeze.

Wearing a pair of Logan's pants and my leather vest from the bottom of his forbidden bag, I followed my nose through the wild, hard-core partying. Past naked women and toxic men. Past the Bandido Nation camp, where men leered and called out obscene propositions until they saw my vest with PROPERTY OF HELLS ANGELS embroidered on it. Most of the gangs try to keep Sturgis a neutral turf and avoid all-out war, so the harassment was just verbal.

Log had tried to force me into tattooing PROPERTY OF HELLS ANGELS across my back and shoulders, but I am terrified of needles. Amazingly, it was Starla who came to my rescue.

My mother returned to the cabin no more than five times after she walked out when I was ten years old. She had shown up as unannounced and abruptly as she had left, looking for something she had forgotten—and it wasn't me. She arrived in the middle of a huge fight between Logan and me. Shaky Jake, Logan's tattoo artist buddy sat on the sidelines as Logan cursed and threatened. I wouldn't back down and stubbornly refused to let his friend touch me with tools that looked like torture devices belonging to a dentist serial killer.

"What's wrong with just putting it on a vest?" Starla asked Logan. "I

ॐ ☥ ☪

used to wear a vest."

"Because it's a new millennium Starla, not the fucking sixties," Logan said, his words dripping with sarcasm. "Nowadays, people get tattoos."

"Yeah, Stupid. And people are getting hepatitis and HIV from using dirty needles."

"So?" Logan could care less if I got those diseases as long he looked cool with me tattooed on the back of his motorcycle.

"*So?* You are such a jackass," Starla declared as she stood there with her hands on her hips.

I was stunned. I had never seen my mother talk to Logan like this. No one spoke to Logan like that without a fistfight.

"That means *you* can catch hepatitis or HIV from *her.* Idiot!"

Argument over. The next time Logan came to the cabin, he brought me a vest proclaiming that I was the official Property of Hells Angels.

80 🕊 ଔ

Driven by hunger and fear, skirting the party crowds, I moved toward a camp with a banner reading CMA, the Christian Motorcycle Association. Their patch's rocker, the curved parts that identify the club's home, declared "Riding for the Son," and the center emblem was a Bible topped with a cross and a pair of praying hands. I didn't know much about Christian bikers, but I felt safe entering their camp. The people were warm and friendly and food was offered before I could ask.

A pastor's wife introduced herself as Katie and put her arms around my shoulders. "Honey, you shur look like you could use a hot meal," she said.

"You're not afraid of Hells Angeles?" I asked.

"Oh my, no!" Katie lightly laughed. Her Southern accent made me think of ripe Georgia peaches, home cooking, and lemonade. "We marry 'em and bury 'em" she said, "and some give their lives to Christ and become an eternal part of our family. Lord, bless 'em."

That night I discovered that they were not a just bunch of religious nuts. Katie was right. Many CMA members and other Christian biker groups had members who had been outlaw 1%ers before coming to Christ.

I finished a hot tri-tip sandwich and an ice-cold Pepsi, pretty sure I had discovered a bit of heaven in Sturgis when Logan found me. It wasn't the first time Logan beat me, but it was the last time he did it while Lefty was still alive.

It was the middle of the night when I woke alone and in pain to the presence of evil. Something sinister. Something large. Something so terrifying, that reality hung in the balance during those fragile seconds between nightmare and waking. My mind stampeded like some wild thing alert to danger, my body paralyzed by the proximity of a predator. A malevolent force whose presence set my heart pounding.

A dirty hand clamped over my mouth, foul breath reeking of alcohol bit my body as he ripped away my clothes. His body was massive and unyielding. He took me with force and violence.

I struggled against my rapist. And the next one. And the next one. Some were brutal. Some not. One was apologetic. I lost count. Through the night and stink of battle, the coppery smell of blood, and the searing agony of being torn in half, I knew that my attackers weren't from our club.

At first, I tried to protect myself by fighting viciously; biting, kicking, twisting, scratching. I tried to kill my attackers. I wanted them dead. Later, as my strength failed and theirs did not, I had begged for death to escape the agony. Finally, came surrender, and the blessed state of unconsciousness.

Morning dawned and melted into day. Noon hit its zenith, and I woke up alone. I spent the rest of the day lying in the tent, feverish, in too much pain and too much fear to leave. Nobody bothered me; nobody cared. I looked around the tent and found was an empty whiskey bottle. I gripped it by the neck with what little strength remained and swore I'd kill the next man who walked in.

I was sick with thirst, hunger, searing pain, and undeserved shame by the time the night fires were lit and the partying intensified. No Logan. No Lefty. No strange men. I crept out wearing the same pants I had stolen from Logan's pack and wrapped a blanket around my shoulders leaving my vest on the floor of our tent. A vest is like an envelope with your name and address on it, and I didn't want to advertise my presence. Walking in a wide circle, I staggered in by way of a path from the back of the CMA camp on legs as shaky as a newborn colt.

Katie appeared from out of nowhere then stepped back. "Oh, my Lord!" she started, clamping her hands over her mouth as if to suppress her shock and horror. She reached for me. "What happened?"

It was a simple question. Katie's eyes, so unlike Logan's, were lit with an inner fire that radiated genuine care. She looked at my face, swollen and purple, lips caked with dried blood, body shivering with cold in spite of the heat. "I'll get mah husband, Brandon. We'll take you to a doctor," she urged. "You need a doctor!" She hastened to assure me, "You needn't worry 'bout the money. We'll pay."

"No! No doctor. No cops. Please! I just need water and a little sleep. Somewhere safe."

Katie led me to a different tent on the far side of the CMA camp. "You'll be safe here," she said, taking me inside and sitting me on a cot. Katie brought a bowl of warm water, a washcloth, and towel. She helped wash away the filth and blood from my battered face, breasts, and thighs. A short time later she returned with a cold drink and a plate of hot food, accidently brushing against me. I jumped at her touch like a spark plug, triggering another wave of adrenaline coursing through me and to my horror, dropped the plate of food in the dirt.

"Don't worry about that," she said sweetly, hurrying to pick up the spilled food. "I'll bring you a fresh plate." And she did.

We talked as I gulped the water and gobbled food.

"My husband thinks you should speak with the police. He says they would protect you." She dropped her gaze. "No matter what happened, you didn't deserve this." Tears glistened on her eyelashes when she looked up.

My words trembled. "My husband, Logan, would kill me if I did... and you know it. I just want to go home."

Not only was I terrified of Logan, but I was raised to believe that cops were enemies of bikers. If I couldn't trust the club, who was my family, who could I trust? I started to cry, and like a fractured dam giving way, I sobbed on Katie's shoulder. Her loving arms cradled me, and she gently rocked me, pulling the blanket on the cot close around and crooning sounds of love and comfort that mother would make for her child.

"It hurts so bad." I wept a river of tears.

I never told anyone what club I belonged to, although Katie had seen my vest the first time we met. Knowing who I rode with, it was a bold decision on her part to help me. Being taken in by a rival gang could easily trigger a war.

The last thing I remembered was Katie reading from the Bible: *"Peace I leave with you. My peace I give to you; not as the world gives do I give to you. Let not your heart be troubled, neither let it be afraid."*

Two days later I woke up. It was morning, and the sound of silence filled the air. I peeked through the tent flap and saw that the camp was nearly deserted. The party was over until next year. No one had found me, not even my dad, although it was hard to guess what lies Logan might have spun. I felt strong enough to start worrying about how to get back to California.

The little CMA tent had become an island in an ocean of trash left behind by the crowds. A couple of people moved about, jabbing at the refuse with pointy sticks and stuffing it into black plastic trash bags that hung from their shoulders. I wondered briefly if they were inmates in a work alternative program and shuddered at the thought. They made me think about the bond between outlaws, and I feared that Logan might have them looking for me.

Stomach rumbling, head throbbing, I turned to face my angel, Katie. She stood there with long brown braids framing her glowing face, balancing a platter laden with a bowl of hot oatmeal, a sweet roll, half a banana, a can of orange juice and bottle of water.

"Good beautiful mornin' to you. I thought you might be awake and hungry." Katie set the food down next to the bed and prayed over it, asking God to give me strength, comfort, and healing. "Easy, now. You just take yor time. There's more food where that came from," she said with the lilting tones of a dulcimer on a misty Appalachian morning.

Then she handed me a large towel wrapped around some clean clothes, toiletries, and a toothbrush. I felt a warm rush of gratitude, overwhelmed that a stranger should be so kind and generous. Katie was beautiful. Not that her features were remarkable or memorable. I think it was the peace that enveloped her every move; like soft clouds drifting through the heavens on a spring day. That was Katie's beauty.

"Katie," I asked anxiously, the spoon trembling in my hand, "did anyone come looking for me?"

She lowered her eyes in a moment of thought—or prayer—sat next to me and replied, "A couple of guys came 'round. I think God must have been watching out for you since they only asked our members who honestly didn't know you were here. Everyone has gone home. Yor safe now. You mustn't worry. Enjoy yor meal and then join us when yor ready. There's someone I'd like you to meet."

She stood, reaching out with a tentative hand, waiting until I nodded. She brushed some hair away from my face and softly patted my cheek in a gesture that spoke volumes. "You just take yor time," she repeated, before slipping through the door of the tent.

I ate, found a bathroom and cleaned up. Bathing took all my strength, but it was refreshing to wash my hair.

When I was done, I found Katie who walked me down the slope towards her husband, Brandon, a CMA chaplain and pastor in their hometown of Trenton, Georgia. Next to him stood a tall man in his fifties; a hardened biker by appearance, dressed in the standard black leathers and with bushy eyebrows and a long white beard that reached to his waist. He and the chaplain were laughing softly with a younger couple over by the bikes. Their attention shifted to me as I approached.

"Hello, Sunny," Brandon greeted me warmly. "I'd like you to meet Tim Heartwood. He rides with the Iron Horse Apostles in Northern California."

The older man nodded and removed his dew rag in place of a cap and held it respectfully to his chest. "Hello, ma'am."

Ma'am? No one had ever called me "ma'am" before. I was barely seventeen. I smiled and yet, with that single word, knew I had found safe passage home.

Tim rode a Harley—what else? Sixteen hundred miles we traveled together, and it was plain that Tim was not in a hurry. In fact, I am pretty sure that Tim saw our ride as a mission trip. We started late and stopped early. In between, he asked me at every break if I was okay and if I needed to rest. Many times we would stop for the day, just to take in the wonders of God's creation.

I slept in his tent, and he slept in a sleeping bag next to his bike. We had long evenings together that changed my life forever. No alcohol, no drugs, and he didn't try to "do" me. When I woke up screaming, reliving the violent rape, sweating in horror, his soft voice would always comfort me, reassuring me that I was safe. Then we would sit by the campfire and talk about God until the sun came up.

Tim said that God loved me and had a plan for my life. "You'll find your way when you find your purpose," he said. "And until you do, make peace with your journey."

"Tim," I asked, "why would the God of the universe care about a beaten, raped, worthless thing like me? I am the daughter of a whore and an outlaw. Is God punishing me?"

"Sunny." Kindness danced in his eyes. "God loves you, child. He is far more interested in where you are going than where you have been. And," he added, "try not to judge yourself or your parents too hard. I'm sure they did the best they could with what they knew. No matter what you've done, God loves you, and God loves them too. It's not who *you are*, it's who *he is*."

Some nights I could hear Tim singing softly under the stars. I had never heard praise and worship songs before. Some of them made me cry.

We traveled south to Denver, and the fresh green fragrance of the Rocky Mountains reminded me of home. Then we headed back north and west, making southern detours to cross through the magnificent natural monuments of Bryce and Arches, carved out of the flaming red Utah desert.

I could have gone on forever feeling safe and genuinely loved as a sister by this kind man. Maybe I was affected by Tim's songs. Maybe I got a new perspective of God's Country. Maybe it was the days I rode behind Tim looking at the CMA patch with the praying hands and Bible that touched my heart. I'm not sure. But somewhere along the way, I found the Lord and asked Him into my heart. From that moment on, I never felt afraid. Until we crossed the California state line.

I was new in the faith, and some things—like Logan—still seemed bigger than God.

ℰℴ 🕊 ℭℛ

It was almost 2:00 p.m. and I was chewing a fingernail, struggling to keep my personal life from intruding on my work when Travis came through my door carrying a white paper bag from the Subway shop.

"Hey, Sunny-one. You eating fingernails today or are you doing the Annie-worship thing?"

A lot of teenage girls are proclaimed followers of Annie, the goddess of Anorexia, and Mia, the goddess of Bulimia.

"Not today," I said, shoving my work aside. "I follow Fatso," the goddess of fast food."

I hadn't realized how hungry I was until I sank my teeth into a meatball and mozzarella sub. Travis laughed and was wiping marinara sauce from my face when Paige walked in.

She was wearing a short purple spandex skirt—spandex being all the rage—that left the guys praying she'd need something from a bottom file cabinet, strappy white three-inch heels, a white tank top, purple nails and a matching purple thingy in her hair. She zeroed in on Travis, who sat there and patiently answered Paige's endless questions about everything and nothing.

It was nearing 2:30. Time to make my move. I excused myself and slipped away and headed for Gold Country Casino on the far side of Oroville. Parked with a clear view of the front door, I sat, waiting and watching. Security drove past me twice and I knew they would stop to ask questions on the next lap. What was I supposed to say? *"I'm looking for a mystery woman who is having an affair with my husband?"* The little security golf cart headed my way with a driver who looked like a bouncer.

The Native-American security guard called out from his cart, "Excuse me, Ma'am. Can I help you?"

There was that "ma'am" thing again. I wondered what the official dividing line is between ma'am and miss. It was a bad day and a wrong time to suggest I was an old-lady.

"Do I look like a ma'am? Do I look like your mother?" I snapped.

I hoped not because this guy was only about fifteen years older than me.

"Are you lost?" he shouted over his engine.

The mental light bulb came on. *Oh, my gosh! That's it... I'm lost!*

What was I thinking?

The annoying casino commercial that airs every morning on the local news jangled in my head, but not for *this* casino. I was about fifteen minutes away from Feather Falls Casino, which is not located in Feather Falls but on the other side of Oroville, some forty-five minutes away from its namesake.

Angry with myself, I turned the key and gas'd the car, nearly running over the man and his cart as I peeled out of the lot and raced across town. Sometimes I feel like the Queen of Stupid.

Feather Falls Casino always reminds me of a big, fat, XXX plus-size gaudy hooker. And so she is. Voluptuous and seductive, the building towers above everything else the city has to offer. She is designed to lure you in, give you a quickie thrill, take your money, and turn you out—just another John. All anyone has to do is look at the multi-million dollar get-up to figure out where the money comes from to pay for it. Casinos aren't all that appealing to me.

I pulled into the lower lot next to the casino-owned bowling alley and parked off-center, but still in sight of the main entrance to the casino.

Maybe I was too late. Maybe she had left when Chance didn't show. Maybe Chance had called her last night from Mark's phone. Maybe... *no way!*

I didn't want to believe it, but there she was, pacing back and forth glancing impatiently at her watch.

Lord! Why me?

CHAPTER 9

သ ⁘ ଓଃ

Paige tossed her hair and heaved a big sigh, glanced at her watch with visible irritation. The scowling drama queen could not conceive that anyone would be late to meet her. After all, solitary men were openly checking her out as they entered the casino, and men with female companions were sneaking peeks from behind their sunglasses. Like bees drawn to honey, like the tide rising to meet the moon, or in Biblical terms, dogs returning to their vomit, men just couldn't resist.

Chance has a similar effect on women. He is a man's man and women just can't help but stare at his masculine physique and virile good looks. It is something I have learned to live with, possibly something I have taken for granted, and now find painfully undeniable. Dwelling on the male-female physical attraction brought all of my insecurities surging to the surface.

I sat in the car like a chicken on a rotisserie doing a slow roast, fully absorbed in watching Paige rummage through her Gucci handbag, pull out a phone and punch in numbers with hard little jabs.

Good thing she didn't look my way—she would have seen me bolt upright as Chance's phone, now fully charged, belted out Whitney Houston's sad song. I searched through his phone's message menu thinking how I had romanticized *The Bodyguard* as being a song about two ill-fated lovers. I sat corrected as I realized it is really about two people who love their careers more than they love each other. If Chance's betrayal had been a shot in the heart, I now rifled through his messages looking for Page's bullet to my head. A sudden rap on the car window and I jumped, tossing the phone in the air and banging my head on the visor. Travis's goofy smile peered through the passenger window.

I stared. Shocked. *What the hell?*

Travis pointed at the lock and I hit the release switch. Climbing in, he closed the door and turned to me with one brow raised, turning his face into a question mark.

"What do you think *she's* doing here?" Travis whispered in a conspiratorial voice, pointing in Paige's direction.

"What...? What are *you* doing here?" I stammered in confusion, barely aware that he had placed his hand on my arm.

"That was my next question." Travis's eyes darkened as they locked onto mine. "One minute I'm talking to Paige, and the next minute she looks at her watch and goes tearing out of the building like it's quitting time saying she had to find you. So"—he smiled—"I followed her. The million dollar question is, what are you doing here and why is she looking for you at a casino?"

"I don't know." Long pause. I am a lousy liar, always pausing to consider plausibility. My father used to tell me that my eyes always gave me away; something about them rolling around. "I don't know why I'm here."

It wasn't a complete fib. All I knew was I felt like a gunshot victim— and I pulled away from Travis to keep from bleeding all over him.

"No, you don't. Not happening." Travis had no intention of letting go. "Talk to me Sunny. What's going on?"

The force of his voice, the depth of his concern, and the touch of his hand held me fast.

"I don't know what's going on. I only know that I'm going home! Sign me out when you get back. Okay? Travis... please," I pleaded.

"No. I mean, yeah, sure, I'll sign you out. But I'm not letting you drive away like this. Come on. Let's talk to Paige and find out what's going on."

Sickened by the very idea, I froze. No one must know about Paige and Chance. I would die of shame—again. It felt like a rerun of my life's story— faithless men and faithless women. I silently swore to God I would never trust anyone again.

"No Travis. Don't! Promise me, whatever else you do, you won't tell Paige I was here."

"Don't have to. She's leaving," Travis observed as Paige stalked to her car looking like a cat that just had a bath.

Panic gripped my insides tighter than Travis's grip on my arm. Stomach acid torched the back of my throat as Paige cut through the lot walking behind us, got in her car, and drove away.

"Sunny." The voice grew distant as I disassociated from the situation. Travis got out and walked around, opened the car door and pulled me out. He drew me gently toward the stream of people dropping off their kids at Tyme to Bowl before they slipped away to gamble. "Sunny, come on. Let's go where we can talk," Travis said as he guided me indoors through an air-conditioned blast of coolness and through the darkness of the bowling alley.

The *thunk* of the bowling balls rhythmically hit the hardwood floors and rumbled down the lanes sending pins exploding in every direction, followed by subsequent "oohs" and "yeahs!" that followed us into the coffee shop. I was burnt, Travis was warm, and the cokes were chilled. "It's complicated," I said at last, "but it's not about work."

"Really? Then what is it about?" Travis leaned into me, inviting me to open up.

"I'm not sure yet, but Paige *can't* know I was here," I said, looking into Travis's hunter green eyes.

"Okay. No problem. I'm here for you, Sunny. You know that, right?" Travis reached over the table and covered my hands with his, fingers sliding between mine like a lover's hand-hug.

"If you need to talk, I'm a pretty good listener."

No doubt. Travis had felt like an old friend from the moment we met. He not only listened to what I said but had a knack for hearing what I didn't say too, frequently discerning my thoughts before I could put them into words. And who else would make sure I ate a healthy lunch? I was attracted to Travis—*but not like that*, I hastened to assure myself. I couldn't allow myself to think of him like that. I was a happily married woman. Or I used to be. We sat quietly amidst the noise as Travis gazed into my soul.

"I hate casinos," I said, looking around with distaste.

"So... why are you here?" He looked perplexed.

"Travis." Silence filled the noisy space between us. I took a deep breath. "Two days ago, everything was good. Today my world is falling apart. I can't talk about it right now. I have to think about it first, and I am having a hard time sorting it out. I just need some time."

"I've got time. All the time you need. I want you to know that it's okay to call me at home. Whenever, wherever. I care about you," he said. His eyes had kindled and face tensed, but his voice warmed and drizzled butter and honey.

Uh-oh. Better go. Rising too fast, I found myself dizzily clinging to Travis who rose with me. He was a life raft about to be severed from Titanic, only I wasn't ready to jump ship. I allowed myself to be comforted for a moment, then pulled away and headed out. Glancing up at the giant digital billboard that overshadowed my car, I felt an unexpected stab of vindictive satisfaction. It looked like 'allaboutme' had been a loser in today's *High-Stakes Gambling Tournament.*

ℬⱷ☙

Too depressed to eat, I settled for a glass of wine out on the deck as I watched the sun deepen from gold to orange, then purple to black. The first stars came out to bless and dress the night sky. The second glass of wine seemed like a good idea. Followed by another. And another.

So, Paige really was the other woman. Just my luck. How long has Chance been seeing her? I wondered. In taking Paige, he had betrayed both me and his good friend Mark. *How rotten is that? How stupid am I?*

I mulled these questions and more as I resigned myself to loser status.

"Words have power." Pastor Mac frequently reminded us that God spoke the world into creation and holds us accountable for our words. Mac cautioned us never to speak sickness or defeat into our lives.

But positive energy was more energy than I could muster. Tired of the endless scenarios spinning in my head, I reached for the comfort of my faithful Kissme.

Well, okay, she isn't all that faithful either. She tried to run off with the propane man last time he filled the tank, jumping up and down on his leg trying to get into his truck. That hurt. But she was warm and affectionate tonight, hoping no doubt that I might actually eat dinner at some point and share the leftovers. *Sigh*. Somehow my relationship with Kissme sounded painfully like my relationship with Chance.

I didn't know what to pray for and wasn't sure it would do any good anyhow. The floodgates of doubt were wide open: *How could God...? Haven't I been a good Christian? Why would God answer my prayer for a good man and then trash it? God hates me. There is no God.*

The brain-train rumbled through my mind only to be startled by the incessant ringing of the phone. Instinct told me it was Chance. I stared at the phone, tired, spent, and possibly drunker than a wine vat. I had nothing left to give, and the room was starting to spin. I lay down on the couch. Okay, I *passed out* on the couch as Chance redialed, this time on my cell phone. The intrusive *'and I will always love youuu'* iTune began, but all my tired brain heard was the disillusioned, fateful lyrics that followed: *"... and we both know... you're not what... I need..."*

My head hurt. I cradled it in my arms and stared into the night, my imagination running loops of Chance doing Paige. I wept. Not wanting to sleep in our bed, I opted to stay on the couch. Tossing and turning, I drifted in and out of dreams and memories.

၈၀ 🕊 ಜ

When I was twelve years old, I stepped out the back door down to the steps that led to our Japanese bathhouse. The bathhouse was a small log cabin-style out-building the previous owner had built to honor his wife's heritage. I froze, my foot poised in the Karate Kid's crane position just inches above a rattlesnake that stretched across the entire width of the porch. I almost didn't make it to the toilet in more ways than one. My world stopped in midair; no breathing, no thinking, no heartbeat. Time slipped into slow motion for me, but not for the snake that coiled up in a heartbeat to rattle out its death vibe.

My return from Sturgis felt like a rerun. Climbing off of Tim's motorcycle and stepping onto the walkway that led to the front door, Lefty was standing on the porch, his arms crossed over his chest. He stood there, staring long and hard at the cuts and abrasions that had scabbed over on my cheek. Then he scanned me from head to toe, taking in the fading bile colored bruises that still splotched over one eye and trailed down my arms.

Lefty gave off a death rattle in his throat and amazingly, never once asked me what happened, if Tim Heartwood had beaten me, or even if I was okay. He just got on his Harley, hooked a doughnut around Tim and shot up the driveway, leaving us standing in a cloud of dust and probably setting a new land-speed record back to Oakland and Logan. Whatever had happened to his baby girl, he knew that Logan had left me behind in South Dakota and failed to protect me.

I doubt if Lefty had a problem with Logan making the return trip with a new girl on his bike, nor did he care that I had returned home riding behind another man. But ultimately, he held Logan 100% responsible for my safety and well-being.

Six long months had passed before I saw Logan again. I silently hoped he was dead, but my mother's best biker friend, Sheena, hinted something about "reconstruction" and an extended stay in the hospital. Hospital stays are rare for an Angel, who, after being subject to retaliation, is usually dead or under arrest. But no one talked about what Lefty had done to Logan, and I stopped asking.

The next few months were spent with Joyce and Kenny, being loved and ministered to by this amazing couple. Joyce taught me that God was like a potter, and although I felt as though my life had been shattered beyond repair, she said God was more than able to make me whole again, ready to be used for his purposes. While that might be true, I opted out of joining her at mass. I knew I wouldn't fit in. I didn't belong. I didn't know the chants or Bible stories and was pretty sure I'd be a social leper if the parishioners knew the truth about me.

So I worked in the garden that summer and occasionally tried to decipher various passages in the Bible. I liked to sit in the shade with Joyce's Bible on my lap, close my eyes and say, "Okay God, teach me what I need to know." Then I'd point my finger like a divining rod to my daily dose of insight. All I wanted was answers. The last thing I needed or wanted was another relationship.

I had just finished reading Revelation about the End of Days when Logan found me. His nose was a bit left of center, but the scariest addition was the black patch over his left eye and its fractured socket.

"We got six long months to make up for, sweetheart," he had said with a leer. The "Beast" never left any visible marks on me again. It wasn't just the highs and lows that typify the Cycle of Domestic Violence; where an intense buildup of tension is followed by an explosive release of violence. Then comes the honeymoon phase; "Honey, I am so sorry..." and some romantic, repentant behavior—until the tension builds again.

Logan's behavior was compounded by a mental disorder called bipolar, a condition characterized by dramatic shifts of euphoric, energetic highs followed by sometimes dangerous, depressive lows. Not every bipolar person is violent, but for Logan, it was a contributing factor. Logan liked the roller coaster ride and refused to take stabilizing medication, swearing loudly, "It's not *my* problem."

Logan had mental health issues, but he wasn't stupid. He replaced physical beatings with emotional abuse and spousal rape. There were times he would tenderly declare that he loved me and frequently told me I was the most beautiful and smartest woman he had ever known. He usually qualified "love" by adding, "If I can't have you, no one can."

I lived on the mountain and finished high school. I was in my last year and I had no friends, no family, no job, and no car. For some reason I thought my life would change and I would be free when I graduated. At school, kids talked about going to the prom; picking out their formals, their dates, and Grad-Night. Normal stuff.

My normal was marked with guns, drugs, Harleys and intimidation. That realization brought tears that slipped out in secret one night as Logan slept with his vice-like arms holding me tight.

ℬ 🕊 ℭ

It was strange going to church without Chance, although it wasn't uncommon for us to be separated when duty called. Ashley and Shane slid into the seats next to me. When the worship music ended, Ashley leaned in. Said, "Where's your Bible?"

Bible? Oh yeah, Bible. "I thought I'd use the use this one," I lied, reaching into the pocket attached to the seat in front of me.

Ashley shook her head and frowned. "You should have brought your Bible. I always carry my Bible. It's special to me," she said, implying that she enjoyed a relationship with the Lord that I did not.

I thought I had the Spirit of God in my heart, but sometimes she makes me wonder. The Bible says that God keeps a lot of books. Sometimes I imagine him like Santa Claus, making a list of who's naughty and nice. If God does keep score, Ashley's "nice" column is probably filled with happy faces. She would make a fine Sunday school teacher.

Today, I was surprised that she didn't send me to the corner. For all that I love her and appreciate her kindness and company, she has an overbearing way of making me feel insignificant in matters of faith. If faith were a horse race, Ashley would see herself as crossing the finish line with me—and probably the rest of the world—in the backstretch. I really love my friend, but sometimes I think it is people like her who make the world hate the Christian "holier than thou" attitude. Truthfully, Ashley has led many people to Jesus, but I wonder how many others she may have turned away with her religious arrogance.

It was hard to sing. My lips formed empty words that rose from a hollow heart. I lifted my hands, but my heart remained somewhere under my feet. So I gave what is called "The Sacrifice of Praise," meaning: you're not in the mood to praise anything, but you do it anyhow because God deserves it. Lacking passion, I defaulted to obedience as I faked my way through the rest the service.

After church, I went through the motions of, *"Yes, I'm fine... Yeah, I really miss Chance when he's gone... Okay, I'll tell him you said hello."*

I felt abandoned, desperately lonely, and angry. I was mad at Ashley, nearly suicidal about Chance, and disappointed in God. All I wanted was to go home when Pastor Mac accosted me at the door.

"Hey Sunny, mind sticking around a few minutes? I need to talk with you."

Oh, Lord. Is my hangover that obvious? "Sure." I gave him my professional smile, an entry level requirement for public servants. It's all about the smile.

I tried to make myself invisible as I avoided Ashley, ate too many cookies, and prayed everyone would go home so I could too. Finally, it was just Mac and me.

"Sorry, we didn't get back to you, Mac. Chance is in Louisiana. That's why he can't do the Bible studies." Mac waited patiently while I rambled. "He should have called you," I said with more anger than intended.

"He did." Mac's voice was soft. "I am so sorry."

"Well, maybe another time," I continued lamely.

"Sunny. Chance told me about the affair."

How could he? My head swam with humiliation, embarrassed that he had already told Mac his shameful secret. My stomach clenched. Would it make headline news on the next prayer chain?

"What do you say we talk?"

"Mac," was all I could choke out before the tears came.

There was no feel-good sermon forthcoming from Mac. Just unconditional love. And that was just what I needed.

"Let's pray for him, Sunny."

"I don't want to pray for him," I said coldly. "I don't care what happens to him."

Mac eyed me. "I know you feel that way now, and it's okay. I'll pray for both of you. How about we meet here on Thursday? I'm free after the AA meetings."

"I don't know," I replied. "I don't think I believe in God anymore." Then I went home.

I was a wounded creature, spiritually snapping at the hand of God and his servants.

℘ 🕊 ℭ

As a child, it never occurred to me to question where Lefty lived during the week or why he never took me with him when he left. For that matter, I never wondered if any of the Angel family had homes, jobs, or families. They were bikers, and Lefty was my dad. I guess I thought they all lived the rest of the week riding around on their motorcycles, which probably wasn't far from the truth.

It wasn't until years later that I discovered my father had another home and family down in Oakland. It wasn't until years after that, I considered the possibility that Lefty might not even be my dad. After all, Starla had been the Johnny Appleseed of Hippyland, planting kids all over the place and then moving on.

Hells Angels typically reject bureaucracy except for hiring an attorney when they need one. But calling an attorney is different than making a police report. So, odds were against anyone calling Child Protective Services when Starla left me behind and headed off into the sunset in search of herself.

Childhood was confusing at times. I loved my dad, although there were times when I'd hid under my bed while he slapped my mother around. She would lie on the bed above me and cry herself to sleep without bothering to check on me. She didn't look for me in the mornings either. More often, I would look for her and find her, wash the dried blood from her nose or hold a cold washcloth to her eye or cheek. I loved my mom, but she never had much time for me.

Starla was convinced that she deserved what Lefty dished out. After all, she had been drunk and flirting with the guys, or had failed to buy food because she was too wasted from getting high. Even worse, were the times Starla had screamed every curse word she could think of at Lefty in front of his brothers. Not smart.

Much like Paige in my present life, Starla could have put a bumper sticker on her van declaring that life is "All About Me" and been ahead of her time. Not that Starla's behavior justified Lefty beating her. After all, Lefty could have stayed in Oakland. No one made him come back.

I think in part, the beatings were fueled by expectancy from Lefty's biker brothers who witnessed Starla's tongue-lashing and cutting remarks. After all, Lefty had a reputation to defend. He was a Hells Angel. The MC was his protection, his suit of armor, and one day, it would be his downfall. Like Roman Emperors of old, someone—usually family members—were always looking to take them out.

There were things Starla loved. My mother loved her garden, her books, and the stars. She loved the mountains, yoga, meditation, playing the recorder, and Lefty. I was more on par with Frito, our one-eyed Chihuahua. Something to be fed and tended and sometimes petted. Like most children in a home where there is domestic violence, the child takes on the role of the adult, and the adult becomes the helpless child.

I learned to take care of myself and I learned to take care of my mother. I fixed her food and sometimes brought it to her in bed.

How could I love someone who hit my mom? In part, I am certain I loved Lefty because he never hit me. Lefty gave me unconditional love and attention whenever he was around and he wasn't wasted. Maybe Lefty gave me the love he couldn't give my mom. Or maybe he just had a soft spot for strays like me and Frito, and himself.

CHAPTER 10

కు 🕊 ౪

Evidently, Travis had a problem reading the "Do Not Disturb" sign I'd hung on my office door in an attempt to avoid contact with both Paige and him. But then, for a Starbuck's triple shot venti latte, I would have opened the door for Jack the Ripper.

"Good morning, beautiful. Thought you could use a little pick-me-up."

"You can't read?" I snarled while chugging the coveted latte.

"You're welcome. I take it you're not a morning person," he quipped.

Travis smelled good. *Umm.* Maybe even fantastic. Was it him, his body wash, or his deodorant? Best not to dwell on it. Whatever it was, he exuded a warm masculine fragrance that was so inviting I found myself sampling it before I caught myself—but not before Travis caught me.

"You like?" Travis's eyes darkened into pools of liquid jade. He smiled and narrowed his eyes, probably the same way he had peered through his sniper scope during the war.

I felt a slow heat rising and averted my gaze.

Ring-Ring. *Thank you, Lord!* The sound of the phone shattered the sexual tension of the moment.

Jack Savage is a tough DA. His hair is salt and pepper, a little heavy on the salted top with a striking pepper-colored mustache that makes him look like the career politician he is. Good looks blended with intelligence and charisma kept reelecting him District Attorney for so long that people were hard pressed to recall the name of his predecessor. It might have been Moses or some such. As much as Jack likes to joke around with his people, when he cracks the whip, we make the trip. Next thing Travis and I knew we were scurrying across the atrium towards his office. Jack may be friendly, but he is not a patient man.

Two federal agents rose to greet us as Jack ushered us into his conference room. They seemed to know Travis on a first name basis which only added to my partner's mystery.

Two hours later, Travis, Paige, and I were on our way to Feather Falls to meet with Keira Gilman and her two young daughters—who were also her sisters.

ଽୠ ୪ ଔ

I kept my eyes on the police report and tried not to look at Travis who kept glancing at me. He was avoiding Paige who was watching him.

"This is so disgusting." All of our cases are disgusting to Paige. "I'll never understand incest cases. I mean, how can a woman have *two* children by her father? I can understand her being molested as a helpless child, but she's almost twenty for God's sake. The oldest kid is nearly four! Wouldn't you think she would have told the police or a teacher or family member, or someone before this?"

I clenched my teeth. I didn't want Paige to come with us, but then didn't really have a choice because I didn't want to be alone with Travis. To my thinking, Paige was toxic waste and Travis a box of chocolates when you're supposed to be on a diet. Travis kept glancing at me expectantly as if waiting for me to answer her questions.

"Probably fear of her father who has always controlled her," I reluctantly volunteered. "She's been brainwashed and threatened. Being a victim is probably her *normal* at this point. Then again, maybe she doesn't want him to go to jail," I added, thinking of my dad. "Maybe she was too young to know she was a victim when it happened and doesn't hate him for what he did. Anyhow, she did go to the police when he started messing around with her, uh... sister-daughter. The three-year-old."

Travis glanced again. "Read on," was all he said.

"Hmm..." I skimmed the investigator's report looking for specifics we hadn't covered in the meeting. "It says here they started having sex after her mom ran off with another guy. She was about eight or nine. Dad drove her to Southern California for an abortion at age twelve and again at fourteen. Then she kept a child at sixteen and gave birth at again at age nineteen." I flipped the page.

"OhMiGod." Paige paled at the information. "How sick is that?"

"Dad would drive her up to Reno," I continued, "and pimp her out to truckers across the state line."

"That's what the Feds said," Travis added. "When was that? How many years?"

"Uh, ages fifteen to eighteen. This is what happens when Planned Parenthood breaks the law," I interjected. "I hate people who think their personal agenda is above the law."

"What law did they break?" Paige hurried to defend Planned Parenthood. "In case you didn't know, this is why the law says girls can get an abortion without their parents' consent." She snatched the report from my hands.

"Thanks for making my point, Paige. No one cares about the kid! In case *you* didn't know, the law also says medical practitioners are mandated to report child rape. But they don't. It's more profitable to go on running their little abortion mills, making billions of dollars every year off kids and their dead babies. Oh, but it makes headline news whenever the SPCA uncovers a puppy mill."

"But it wasn't rape," said Paige, "or she would have said so. It says here she agreed to it. That is called *consensual* sex."

"That's it! I am asking Jack to transfer you to Animal Control or maybe Environmental Waste," I fumed. I'd had more than enough of Paige for more reasons than this.

"Why? Because I am more progressive than you?"

Travis laughed heartily and handed me a stick of gum. Paige just sniffed.

"So the case still falls under the statute of limitations," said Travis.

"Which is?" Paige demanded.

Totally blonde. I rolled my eyes, not in disbelief, but sheer amazement. How was it possible that she worked for the district attorney and didn't know about the statute of limitations? H*er bra size and IQ must be the same.* I blew out steam.

Travis looked in the car mirror before answering Paige. He seemed to study her for a long time and I felt a pang of jealousy as I imagined some flirting going on between them. But then, I have grown used to the fact that all things male stare at Paige.

"It's the amount of time a prosecutor has to file a case. The amount of time varies, depending on the nature of the crime. Some, like murder, have no time limit; others have a very short time."

"Knock it off, Travis. I'm not stupid. Paige huffed. "I know what the statute of limitations is. What I want to know is how long is it in this case?"

Travis and Paige again exchanged verbal eye contact in a language I couldn't decipher before he continued. "A rape case has to be prosecuted within ten years. But if the victim was a minor child, or if the act happened more than one time, or if it included the use of a weapon, oral sex, sodomy, or other variables over the years"—he caught his breath—"the filing time can be extended. The number and types of charges can all impact the filing time and length of the final sentence."

"Well, I hope he gets a life sentence because that's a rotten thing to do to your kid."

My eyes narrowed, and lips pinched. *Speaking of rotten... What about what you did to me? Me! The one who got you this job.* I tried not to think about poor Mark who had been dumb enough to love her... the way I had loved Chance.

Paige and I reached a new level of antagonism. It seemed incredible that we'd ever had a relationship, even a superficial one. Yes, Paige had tried to extend the girlfriend-tells-all thing, but I had kept my distance. Not only because of my past but because we are polar opposites. Sort of like the difference between cats and dogs, or maybe butterflies and scorpions. Instead of girls-day-out at the mall, I liked to imagine ripping her hair out and jabbing a finger in her eye. Lucky for her I exercised restraint.

Keira's mobile home screamed "quarantine." It was little more than a rust bucket tucked behind a tall fence that barely contained two large pit bulls lunging at the gate that was guarded by a Rottweiler—that was not behind the gate.

"Where is my Glock when I need it?" I smacked my forehead with my palm as the Rottweiler jumped against the car door. Okay, it *lunged* at the car door slinging drool everywhere. Paige was screaming, freaking freely in the back seat as she fumbled to power up her window.

"I got a gun," Travis threw me a dazzling smile. He loved this stuff.

"Good. Shoot the bitch, will you?" I said, gesturing towards Paige, who was scrambling to get behind Travis in the driver's seat, "then I can deal with the dogs." Paige wouldn't stop screaming and Travis couldn't stop laughing, so I rolled down the window and called the dog.

"Hey, Stupid! Come here, boy!" The Rotty, who had been circling the car, spun around and took a short cut over the hood, unaware that I was having a *really* lousy day. I rolled the window up before he could reach me and kicked the door open with both feet, sending him yelping, head over paws, across the road and into an irrigation ditch. As if by magic, it was suddenly quiet—except for Paige, of course.

"Shut up!" Travis and I yelled in unison. Paige's mouth hung open, but no words came out. I slammed the door shut and waited. A minute passed, and I figured it was safe to move. Hopefully, I hadn't killed Keira's dog.

"Shuger... Honeee... come here, babies." A soft voice called from the porch.

Sugar? Honey? Not Blood and Guts or Smith and Wesson?

"Come on babies."

Babies?

The voice hastened to assure us; "Dan't worry. They won't bite chew."

Dang! I hate it when they say that. It's like a nurse saying, "This is only going to hurt a little."

Keira stood on the porch with an adorable little rag-tag waif clutching her leg and a tiny baby in her arms. With luck, she hadn't seen me Frisbee her dog into the canal. It wouldn't make for good rapport.

"'Bout time someone took a hand to that dawg. It skeers me haf to death," she said as she let Shugar and Honee, her "babies," into the house.

Keira was wearing a sheer shift held up by an embroidered stretch band. Her wild, tousled, mousy brown hair piled on top of her head. Bare feet, bare face, and naked eyes. I liked her. She reminded me of the gentle, wild animals that inhabit the forest.

"Your dog scares you to death?" I asked her with a laugh.

"Not my dawg," she explained. "Folks jus drive up here from Or'ville and dump their pets so they don't have to pay pound fees. Por' things just go wild."

Keira's face lit up when she saw Travis come through the gate. I knew by her look that Keira hadn't turned lesbian from her sexual abuse. Most women understandably do double-takes on Travis. He exudes a masculinity that is different from Logan or Chance.

It's hard to explain. Logan is lean and dark. He radiates "bad boy looking for a good time" and comes across murderously dangerous. Chance, on the other hand, emits a sexy contrast of physical toughness tempered with sensitivity. He is a man's man as it were. You know: the rugged, battle-scarred soldier tenderly holding a newborn baby in his arms. That is a perfect picture of Chance.

But Travis? I would say that Travis is more like Michael, the Archangel. Clean, with an understated presence of power. A force for good. An enforcer of justice. Under his clean, athletic exterior, he exudes the inner calm and intense focus of a Samurai warrior. He's definitely someone a bad guy would not want coming after him. I guess one could say that Travis feels like a lethal weapon.

Travis and I made our way indoors, through the maze of toys and piles of clothes and what-nots. I tried to avoid thinking about the what-nots. Shugar and Honee took up their posts as sentries in the hall and kitchen doorways, eyeballing us like steaks on the barbee. Travis wisely remained standing while I sat on a sofa with a huge wet spot. *Oh Lord, don't let that be what I think it is.*

"No, thanks," we chimed to Keira's offer of something to drink. Travis took the lead with a series of investigative questions that went smoothly until Keira popped out a boob to feed the fussing baby. The Samurai lost his cool for a nanosecond and then continued.

The little girl, her long hair tangled and dirty face shining with curiosity had been studying Travis. Venturing away from the security of her Mom, she made her way toward Travis and reached up to touch the gun under his coat. "S'at?" What is it about this man that inevitably attracts females? And how is it they know something special is under his clothes?

Travis didn't respond. He just moved out of her reach. I thought for a second how Chance would react in Travis's place, and knew that he would pick the child up in his arms, call her by her name, and tickle her until she squirmed with joy, helping to her forget all about the gun. Children love Chance and Chance loves them.

A car door slammed and we all jumped. Okay, Travis didn't jump. Samurais never jump. All eyes turned toward the living room window looking out at the county car. Paige finally felt it was safe enough to make her way up to the house.

"I'm gonna go on Dr. Phil." Keira beamed. "The world wants to hear my story. Least that's what they tell me." She blushed. "I'm gonna be famous."

A shriek pierced the air and grew louder as Paige broke into a sprint, ran up the walkway and crashed through the front door, tripped and went sprawling into a pile of dirty clothes heaped on the floor. I guess the Rottweiler wasn't dead after all.

Not missing a beat, I redirected my attention back to Keira.

"Keira, I'd like to work with you regarding the TV show. I think the audience would like to hear the *whole* story. You know, so it's not just a tease? Maybe it would be a good idea to postpone your appearance until after sentencing." Travis smiled at my strategy. "Then everybody will get to see how the story ends."

Shugar and Honee bolted from their posts toward Paige, who took one look at them and scrambled madly back to the door she had just come through, pit bulls in pursuit.

Keira continued to suckle her child, looking thoughtfully at the door as the pits collided into each other, snarling and bickering as the screen banged shut in their faces. "She sure is a nervous one," Keira observed as Paige doubled back to the car.

We smiled and nodded in agreement. I had just started talking about preliminary hearings when screaming broke out again. We all moved quickly back to the living room window. Paige was almost to the car, having slammed the gate behind her only to find the Rottweiler closing in fast. Yanking at the car door, 'Cujo' latched on to her coat sleeve. Paige managed to lose the blazer and jump into the car, leaving her smartly tailored pant leg caught in the car door for the dog's newest amusement.

"That dawg don't seem right in the head," Keira observed. "I do believe he was bred a little too close to kin."

Stunned by the remark and considering the circumstances, Travis and I exchanged uncertain looks. As in so many of our cases, there are times when you don't know whether to laugh or cry.

I wrapped things up, referred Keira and her children to Victim Witness Services and gave her some brochures and my card. Keira packed her boob back in her dress and we said our farewells to her and the "babies," Shugar and Honee. The little girl approached me shyly and offered me a piece of candy, spitting it into her grubby hand and holding it forth like a treasured offering.

"Thank you, sweetheart," I said, taking it from her. "I'll save it for later, after lunch, okay?" Travis and I stepped outside when I was hit with the realization that I too, had started life as a ragged waif of an abused mother just about ten miles farther up the mountain from where we stood. The thought raised a lump in my throat and an ache in my heart. I felt sorry for my mom. She didn't deserve what my dad had done to her. I could see why she had left me. But suddenly, with a substantial measure of guilt and an overwhelming ache in my heart, I missed my dad more than words could say.

The Rotty sat to one side watching the car. He turned to smile at me, ears perked, wagging his stump. I tossed him the candy and slid in the car. Paige was crying in the back seat, mascara running down her face.

"That went pretty well, don't you think?" I asked Travis.

He popped a fresh stick of gum in his mouth. "Yeah, I thought it went pretty good."

We drove back in stony silence, each of us lost in our private thoughts.

I thought of Lefty. Travis looked like he was thinking of Paige as he kept an eye on her in the mirror. Paige was probably plotting murder. Her face smeared with a mixture of dirt, tears, snot, and mascara, she leaped from the car when we finally parked the remote parking lot—livid.

"You can't get away with treating me like this! This isn't what I signed on for!"

Paige looked like she had stuck her tongue in a light socket. She'd returned with with frayed pants, bruised knees, hair like Kramer's on Seinfeld and eyes popping with rage.

"You think this is funny? I'll have your job!" she raved.

Turning, I scanned her deliberately from head to toe. "You stink," I remarked. "Probably the dog poop on your coat." Then, placing a hand on my cheek in mock surprise, added, "Oh... my-bad... maybe it's... *you?*"

Escalating into a shrieking banshee, Page was spitting venom. "You no-good slut! I slept with your husband! How's that for a laugh? And he wasn't all that good!"

Travis stared, speechless, as I exploded with laughter.

Who was she calling a slut?

Catching my breath, I said, "You can keep him, Paige. You deserve each other. He told me *you* weren't any good in bed either."

Spinning away, I sauntered off to my car, confident that my defiant look, carefree strut, and lying mouth had managed to fool everyone. Everyone but me.

ഇ 🕊 ൽ

Logan was back with a few of the brothers after a long weekend down in Laughlin, Nevada. I had begged him to take me with him, but he brushed me off, saying, "You can't come. It's business, babe. I love you," he had added with a kiss, handing me an envelope full of money to buy food and necessities.

Logan was usually generous with the money as long as there was lots of food and beer at the house. He didn't care if I bought clothes as long as he liked them. He made me keep the receipts and return the clothes he didn't like. I accepted this because he reminded me all the time that it was *his* money.

Lefty had done lots of *business* at the cabin. Lefty's business consisted of selling pot, hashish, and cocaine. But Lefty didn't come up much after Logan got out of the hospital. Probably because Logan was promoted to Sergeant at Arms and was wearing the club's TCB—*Taking Care of Business*—patch. It was now Logan's sworn duty to take care of both the club members and their families, which included me and ironically, a sworn responsibility to take care of Lefty, too.

Logan's business was different than my dad's had been. Logan dealt meth and guns—lots of guns. And it was probably gun business that took him to Laughlin. I wanted no part of Logan's business dealings.

I pouted when the guys took a second "business trip" without me, heading back to Laughlin just two weeks later. But I ran downstairs to greet them when they returned, pulling up next to the cabin in a cloud of dust. Logan arrived with Skunk, Matt-the-Rat, Fast Freddie, a guy whose patch told me he was a brother from a German Hells Angel's MC, and to my utter amazement, one Mongol and one rider from the Bandido Nation.

Crossing club lines was a very dangerous thing to do. It was as shocking as looking at a herd of wild horses and seeing a zebra and a camel running in the mix. Sure, they all have four legs, but that is where the similarities start and stop. It just isn't done between one-percent gangs.

Rushing out to greet them, I could hear Logan raging over the roar of the engines.

They shut down their machines and Logan carried on as the riders dismounted and followed him indoors.

"They're dead. The dirty S-O-Bs just gunned them down. They are *so* dead! I'm gonna kill 'em... all of 'em!" Logan shouted, waving his arms in the air.

"Who's dead? What are you talking about? What's going on?" My words jittered inside of me like the staccato rapping of a woodpecker tapping on a rotten log.

The men remained silent, grim, and tense.

"Who's dead?" I shouted.

Panic gripped my heart, dread nipped at my heels as I trailed a furious Logan who continued to blaze his way through the cabin, slamming doors and kicking over furniture.

No way! Don't let it be...

"Lefty and Digger. Popped Lefty twice in the head and shot Digger in the heart."

Logan turned his back to me as he dug through the refrigerator and tossed beers to the boys. "Don't worry, Sunny," he said, turning around and finally making eye contact. "I'll kill 'em for ya. I swear it! Every damn one of them!"

Time stood still, the world went sideways, and all the demons in hell partied as I dropped to the floor in a dead faint.

Chapter 11

꧁ 🕊 ꧂

"… and more rain is expected to fall across the already flooded regions of the Ohio Valley, Indiana, and Mississippi today. In New Orleans this morning, levees are reported to have broken, flooding the city as the already swollen river…"

"Here Kissme," I called to my little dog who spun in a circle before taking the proffered toast. A dirt bike screamed past my road and I looked out the window to see a thick cloud of dust rolling in like a fog bank along a beach.

It was a petrified-bone-dry 105° degrees and the dirt road to the highway was two-inches deep in pale ivory dust. Ghostly white footprints trailed indoors and out. The South and Midwest were flooding, and California was in its tenth year of brutal drought. I looked wistfully at the clouds drifting in from the north. The morning weather report included the possibility of showers and thunderstorms, but I shook my head in disbelief. The reporter must be from out of state because everyone in California knows that thunderstorms and lightning might happen, but rain isn't on the menu this time of year. I get a more accurate forecast by looking out my kitchen window across the valley.

A storm was building both outside and in. Being a strong respecter of privacy rights, not to mention Logan's training, I never went through Chance's personal items before coming across the message on his cell phone. It was time to stop being stupid and start ferreting around. The temperature soared to a fever pitch as I tossed the bedroom closet, desk, and all his other phone messages—not without results.

It didn't take long to find damning evidence; a condom in the pocket of his tan suede shirt, multiple cash withdrawals at the casino's ATM, Paige's phone number in his contact list along with a couple of nude pictures of her privates. There were three other text messages Chance must have kept to stroke his ego; one self-proclaiming "nasty-girl," the second, "you're sooo sexy," and the third and worst, "does she know?" I wondered how Chance answered that one.

꧁ 🕊 ꧂

The house phone rang, and I didn't need Caller ID to tell me it was Chance. There was no use putting him off. If I didn't pick up, he would be sending out the cavalry. He left me no choice.

"Hey, Sunshine. I've been trying to call you for three days. I've been worried sick about you. Where have you been? Is everything okay?"

And then. I lost it.

I let loose with, "I know about you and Paige!"

He countered with "Let me explain," followed by something about being *"So sorry"* and *"Please don't leave me."*

Someone yelled, "F-You! I hate you!" I am pretty sure it was me. The Bible says "out of the mouth comes issues of the heart," and my heart was blowing like a geyser—or perhaps a broken sewage main for a major metropolis.

I tried to change. Honestly. I'd given up swearing so I wouldn't sound like Logan and company who can't communicate any other way. The new me never-ever swears. Except when I do.

Then came a flood of tears on both sides—shattered trust and receding dreams—the sound of something dying. A sound as old as the ages.

ℴ ₮ ℞

One-one-thousand...Boom! One-one-thou...Boom! One-Boom! Boom!

I lay in bed hugging a trembling Kissme, counting the seconds between flashes of lightning that lit the bedroom like a newborn sun. A mysterious cold front from Alaska had crept down to battle with the sweltering valley heat, casting towering pillars of clouds like so many siege towers against the impenetrable Sierras.

Boom! Boom! Boom! I wanted to die. *Boom! Boom!* It was so hot. If only it would rain.

"An unprecedented lightning storm has hit northern California. Simply amazing that the storm lasted as long as it did. Five to six thousand lightning strikes" said Del Walters, assistant regional chief of the California Department of Forestry and Fire Protection. *"We are finding new fires all the time."*

The morning news went on to report there were over one thousand active fires burning; seven hundred just in our area. Where would they find enough firefighters?

"It feels like the end of the world," I told my dog. And for me, it was, the end of *my* world."

Kissme seemed to understand as she licked the tip of my nose, or maybe she just wanted breakfast. The news was all bad, both personally and locally. The fire burning at Concow Lake was just five miles away. It could be here in an hour if the wind shifted. Two more fires were burning to the east, up the canyon by Scooters Café and to the north near Jordan Hill.

Another bloomed in the south, near the community of Berry Creek. I made the usual coffee and shared my toast with Kissme.

"Girl," I said, "we are surrounded by fire on three sides." She turned in a circle and didn't look too worried, so I tried to feel the same.

The local news preempted regular TV programming: *Our most critical lightning events often occur in late July or August, and we have no expectation that this season will be different."*

Great... just great. It was the end of May and hard to believe there would be anything left to burn by July or August.

I carried the phone with me out on the deck to see smoke rising on the other side of the valley, just below Paradise Ridge. I swallowed hard. That would be west, completing the circle. I needed to call work and give them an update.

"District Attorney's Office, this is Gayle."

"Hey, Gayle. Just calling to check in with you."

The wheels of justice never stop, even when faced with acts of God.

"Oh Sunny, are you okay up there?"

"Yeah. I'm okay, but we're on standby evacuation. I won't be coming into work today. Got to pack—*again.* The news is calling it a *firestorm."*

"You're not alone," said Gayle. "We have dozens of people calling in. Jack knows what's going on. Don't worry about work. Is Chance there to help you?"

"No... Chance is still in Louisiana doing rescue work from Katrina. He probably hasn't heard about the fires up here."

"I'm sorry. Rex and I want you to know that our home is open to you and your animals if you need us. We have it all figured out. We'll put all the dogs in the yard and all the cats in the garage."

A montage of images tripped through my brain: Mercy, the Queen of Destruction, returning from Louisiana and using Dinky Dog, their miniature doxie, for a squeaky toy. Then there was Chance's collection of some six feral cats from various rescues along with their cats—all bouncing off their garage walls in the Ultimate Cage Fight.

"Thanks, Gayle. I love you guys. I'll let you know how it goes and keep the offer in mind. Give my love to Rex."

I wasn't ready to tell her about Chance's affair. X-rated images of him with Paige kept running through my head.

I stayed home but didn't pack. *Let it burn.* I didn't care. No loss in this world could hurt half as much as the one I was going through.

I spent the day sailing with Captain Morgan, hoping to drown in a six-pack of Cokes. First feeling sorry for myself at first, escalating to rage as the day progressed. Logan popped into my head to say something about revenge tasting sweetest when served up cold. So I indulged my imagination, which is fertile soil for action. How to get even with Chance. How I'd pay back tear for tear and hurt for hurt. Not very Christian, but it felt good.

৪০ ভ্ ৫৩

Evacuations are an annual occurrence, sometimes more than once a year. I was still on stand-by and Kissme sleeping in my car. I was back at work and Paige wasn't. The DA thought I was home and sent her along with Travis down to the bay area to pick up evidence or something. I was relieved that she was gone and didn't care why. I was holding my own in spite of my 8.5 on the Richter-Scale headache. I was sorry Paige hadn't quit her job and mildly surprised that I still had mine.

Office talk was all about the wildfires when the call came. From that moment on, the topic of fire would never be the same.

It is a tragedy to look at a home reduced to ashes, another to experience the flames of anger in your soul, and quite another to respond to a victim whose body has been charred by her boyfriend.

৪০ ভ্ ৫৩

"Tamika?" I held my breath and tried not to gasp. One of the keys to being a professional advocate is a great poker face. Never give away your real emotions. I steeled myself as a young black woman, wrapped in a coat of white bandages and looking like a freshly clubbed baby harp seal, turned two brown eyes toward me. Sad eyes. Pain-filled eyes. Glazed, innocent eyes.

"Tamika, my name is Sunny. I am an advocate from the district attorney's office. Can I talk with you?"

She turned her head back to the wall. Looked a lot like "No" to me. Deputy Martel, a.k.a. Crazy Bob, had gotten the same response when trying to interview her earlier.

Deep breath. I prayed, *Okay Lord, I can use some help here.*

"Tamika, I'm here to help you. I thought you'd like to know what's going to happen with your case. Marcus is in custody. He's being held without bail. He can't hurt you anymore."

Not all of her fire was extinguished because flames shot out of those sweet little eyes as she turned back to me.

"What the fuck do you know? Marcus loves me! And now he's going away forever. I might as well be dead."

This is why my job exists. This is the head-banger for juries; someone sets you on fire and you resolutely declare, "He loves me." I mean, if that is how this guy shows love—and I'm sure a jury would agree—I'd hate to be on his bad side.

I pulled up a chair and sat next to her. I had an idea. "I'm sorry. I was wrong. I can see that you love him. So... what's Marcus really like? Tell me about him."

She attempted a smile. A hint of an upturn at the corners of her mouth and I knew I was in.

"We've been friends since diapers. Our mamas were best friends. Never had a daddy. Marcus is the only one..."—she started to cry—"it's my fault... all... my... fault. And now..."

I waited. What could be more tragic than looking at someone with burns over most of their body, yet dying of a broken heart? How could she excuse him? "How is it your fault, Tamika?"

Her lungs had been scorched from breathing the flames. Her words tip-toed like frightened children.

"I was screamin' in his face. I know he hates that. I know it. But I just went on screamin' and cussin' at him, and then... and then... he just..." Her eyes rolled to the ceiling as she relived the memory. "I begged him not to do it. I begged him and begged him..." she gasped and then slept.

The State had affirmed my qualifications as an expert witness on the subject of domestic violence. Years of specialized training, hundreds of victims, and countless hours qualified me to educate juries. If Tamika lives, she will be an enigma to a jury.

The average person would expect Tamika to be enraged and eager for justice. I shuddered at what the jury would think if I wasn't there to explain the dynamics behind her words.

As long as Tamika believes the incident was her fault, she retains some control and understanding of Marcus's egregious betrayal. If she were to let go of that belief, she would have to admit she had no control over the past or her future. She would have to accept that someone who swore he loved her, had, without remorse, doused her with gasoline and set her on fire.

I sat in my car, reeling with feelings of guilt that I dared compare my own trauma to Tamika's. I had lain awake last night wondering what I had done to make Chance cheat on me. If I could only figure it out, I could change it. I finally concluded that *guilt* is a lighter burden on the heart than *hatred*. Guilt requires acceptance. Hatred requires action.

ജ 🕊 ൙

Large drops of salty wetness tracked their way along my hairline before trickling into my eyes. The heat was relentless. Ugh! I never sweat. Why didn't I put on waterproof mascara this morning? The combination of salt and mascara fried my "smoke-smuggered" eyes.

Day five of the crisis. The Concow Fire merged with the Empire Fire and was devouring everything in its path as it headed my way. Just seven miles down narrow twisting Concow Road lies the small subdivision of Camelot—just right of the Concow Campground, and left of nowhere. It was a combat zone complete with exploding propane tanks and homes that melted before the raging inferno.

Lines of weary evacuees headed for the highway. Trucks came, overloaded with tools and toys, hauling trailers that bulged with household goods and treasure boxes filled with memories. Cars teeming with amped-up kids, frazzled parents, weary grandparents, blankets, cats and dogs. People walked for miles, leading their horses up the road past exhausted firefighters that were driving in to relieve an even more exhausted night shift.

Everyone headed for Highway 70, then past the barricades set up by the highway patrol. Once passed the checkpoint, there is going back until evacuation orders are lifted. No one can force people from their homes, but once they leave, the authorities *can* and *will* prevent them from returning. By evening the entire region was a ghost town except for the few residents who remained and the random patrol sweeps made by law enforcement.

"Air quality districts from Bakersfield to Redding have issued health advisories through the weekend, urging residents to stay indoors and limit their exposure to the smoky air. Air pollution readings in Northern California are two to ten times the federal standard for clean air," said Dimitri Stanich, spokesman for the California Air Resources Board.

The local news repeatedly advised staying indoors and not running swamp coolers that would only funnel more smoke into the house. The result felt like being trapped in an oven with the kitchen on fire. As hundreds of fires continued to rage across the North State, thousands of firefighters began pouring in from across the country and from as far away as Australia.

The alarm buzzed. It was 5:00 a.m. when I opened the curtains to let another day seep in through gray shadows of smoke-laden air. Delicate flakes of soft swirling ash fell like the first snow of winter. The only difference was, these flakes carried fire instead of ice. The air was thick and oppressive, weighing down the spirit as well as the body. I looked around for my cleanest dirty shorts, made a mental note to do laundry and pulled on a white tank top.

I let Kissme outside to do her business and filled her dish with venison and sweet potato kibble. She was tired of the roasted duck and wild rice from the gourmet dog bakery. Kissme thinks she is a fearsome huntress—her ego being vastly bigger than the rest of her. I put her in the master bedroom for her morning nap, turned on her fan, and headed out to meet Ashley at the local Grange Hall.

It was a short drive *above* the CHP roadblock, so they couldn't keep me from returning home. I drove past the Arson Reward posters that go up every year. People watch for suspects like scratchers on a lotto ticket. I thought God might be the arsonist this time although that kind of thinking probably wouldn't net me any heavenly rewards. But I wasn't in a forgiving mood, and hell's flames didn't scare me half as much today as the ones burning in Concow.

Biscuits and gravy, home fries and scrambled eggs, and lots and lots of fresh hot coffee was prepared for over 200 hungry, exhausted, but very grateful firefighters. Both my work and life has taught me that the best cure for *depression* is *expression*. So I focused on something besides myself and volunteered to help cook and serve breakfast to these brave men and women.

My heart filled with gratitude for our local firefighters who had worked around the clock with an army of 3,000 other firefighters. Just two weeks ago they had labored around the clock battling a 23,000-acre fire protecting the town of Paradise. Sixty-six homes were lost in that fire, and they had been nothing short of heroic in their super-human efforts to control the blaze. Now here they were again, bone-weary but determined, and back on the line.

"Good news, Sunny," said Ashley, already up to her elbows in flour kneading biscuit dough. "One of the fire captains came in for breakfast and said the fire is now ten percent under control."

"I love you, Ash, but has anyone ever pointed out that is the politically correct way of saying the fire is *ninety percent* out of control?"

Ashley paused to think about it. "Haven't had your coffee, huh?"

I frowned. Was it that obvious?

"Chai?" She waved a tea bag at me that she'd pulled from her shirt pocket.

"Gun?" I offered.

"O-kay. No problem." She shoved the tea bag back in her pocket, leaving white flour smudged across the front of her shirt as I stalked to the coffee pot. I do not function without coffee.

"Have you talked with Chance?" No reply. "When's he coming home, anyhow?"

Maybe he'll drown, and I won't have to think about it. Sweet Ashley. We share everything... except this. This one I intended to work out alone. Just talking about Chance was unbearable, so I dodged her questions and comments with all the grace of a matador trying not to get gored in front of a crowd.

"The biscuits are done," I said, pulling some trays from the oversized oven. "I'll run them out to the service area. They're waiting." I grabbed a tray and headed out. I figured as long as I don't think or talk about Chance, I'll be okay. Maybe. At least until I get home.

I found myself staring at the backside of a firefighter eating his breakfast as I dumped the biscuits into the warmer.

"What does that say on his shirt?" I asked Ashley.

I was impressed by how far many fire crews had traveled to our little neck of the woods.

Ashley squinted. "Napa City."

I carried over a pitcher of juice and couldn't resist asking, "What are you guys doing here? Napa Valley is burning, isn't it? I heard evacuations are in progress. Aren't *your* homes in danger?"

The entire crew pointed to a young man at the end of the table with sunglasses on. "His house could go any minute," said an older man as he passed around a platter of bacon.

"Yeah," the young man said thoughtfully between bites. "It doesn't look too good." In a heartbeat, he was my new hero. I touched him on the shoulder. "I'm so sorry." I couldn't say more.

Hours later I sat down in front of the fan with a home-made cookie I had brought back from the Grange Hall, contemplating Chance and our situation. I wondered about the young firefighter and if he had someone waiting for him back home. I resented Chance being away, rescuing others when I needed physical and emotional help preparing for my own evacuation. Maybe Chance was someone's hero today, back in New Orleans, or wherever the heck he was now, but he sure wasn't mine. I wanted to get even, and at the same time, I missed him. Go figure. Maybe I was crazy. Maybe I was more like Logan than I wanted to admit.

℘ 🕊 ℛ

"Start talking!" Ashley stood on my steps, chin pushed forward and both hands on her hips. It was the following morning and Ashley, not usually an early riser, still had her slippers on. Her shoulder-length tawny brown hair, naturally shot through with shades of blonde and silver, was hastily tucked behind her ears. "Chance called us at 4:00 a.m. this morning. He's worried sick about you. He said you won't answer his calls."

Sigh. "Chill. You want some coffee? I'll make some." I still had my jammies on and felt like I had an axe buried in my brain.

"Coffee would be good. Thanks. You look terrible." Ashley is known for her double-barreled honesty.

I grunted, shuffled to the kitchen, started a pot of Rocket Java coffee and set out a pair of oversized mugs. Ashley popped some English muffin slices in the toaster without so much as another word. The sun was coming up, and we hauled breakfast and Kissme outdoors.

The wind chimes resonated in vibrant hollow tones, like the soft toll of a distant church bell, although church bells were historically used to sound warnings as well as calling the faithful. The breeze was the morning diurnal air current that blows up the canyon in the morning and downhill in the late afternoon. Like so many things that feel good, those breezes can also be bad. Our momentary reprieve from the smoke also fanned hungry flames. We seized the moment, perhaps appreciating it all the more because we knew it wouldn't last.

We sat in silence for a long time, as good friends are able to do; not feeling obliged to make small talk. Then I was ready.

"It's Chance," I said, staring over the rim of my mug at the first light of day, spilling over the mountain tops and running down the slopes. Fire meets fire. "He's been having an affair with Paige."

Ashley froze, dropping half of her English muffin onto the deck much to Kissme's delight. The old adage: *One girl gathers what another girl spills* seemed to work for Kissme as well as Paige.

"Sunny?" She whispered my name. "Are... are you serious? I can't believe..." Her beautiful gray-green eyes brimmed. "Are you sure? How long?"

"Yes, I'm sure. I don't know how long."

Ashley's brows furrowed as she reached over and touched my arm. "Do you want to pray about it?" It was more of a directive than a question.

"No. I don't think so." Another sip of coffee. We listened to the tap-tap drilling of a woodpecker hard at work on a black oak down below and watched a blue-belly lizard do push-ups on the deck rail.

I sighed again. "I'm not sure which hurts most, Ash, the unfaithfulness of my husband or the unfaithfulness of God. At least Chance has an excuse. He's a pig, and I hate him. But God has really let me down—again." I settled deeper into the chair, bracing myself before continuing. "I don't think I believe in anything anymore. I think I hate God."

I waited patiently for Ashley's sermon. I could always depend on her to chastise and correct me in all matters of faith, but she kept silent for a long time, staring off at the encroaching clouds of smoke, seemingly lost in thought.

Finally, having reached a decision, she took me by the hand and looked me in the eye. "You have to forgive him. It's not easy, but you have to forgive Chance, and then ask God to forgive you."

"Oh, Ashley! Can't I just shoot him?" I asked. She smiled sadly, and we laughed at the absurdity of my remark. Then she rose quietly and held me as my laughter dissolved into a stream of tears.

CHAPTER 12

ജ 🕊 ൙

I stared in wonder at the ruby-throated hummingbird as it hovered, sipping its cocktail from a scarlet bottle in front of a blood red sunrise. Why it didn't drop dead from smoke inhalation, I had no idea. It was day ten of the firestorm. The sun and moon had become a perpetual reflection of the inferno below. Nothing more than diurnals had stirred in all that time. It was like having a campfire inside of a tent. The air had grown heavy; dense smoke deepened from haze to fog, to near-zero visibility. The hummer darted about as I coughed and sniffled. My eyes watered in an attempt to rinse out the grit.

People were now evacuating from more than their homes. Many were leaving Northern California altogether in search of fresh air. Others stayed behind with the less desirables: those people who had evacuated with their pit bulls, meth-lab equipment, and sound systems all crammed into old school buses. They refused to go to evacuation centers and chose instead to camp behind the Dome Store, a colorful self-descriptive survivor of a building trend that was California's answer to earthquakes back in 1970-1980's. The Dome Store, whose original name is seldom remembered, is a local mini market that specializes in tobacco and alcohol, bread and milk, lures and live bait, over-priced gas and riff-raff.

Our fires aren't like the massive fires down in San Diego—where refugees gathered in the Charger football stadium and taxpayers brought in live bands and deli food. Got to love Southern California! By contrast, ours was more like a meth-fest with looting and home invasions happening in broad daylight.

I sat, glued to Chance's scanner, horrified as reports came across of "shots fired" at the firefighters battling a section of the blaze that had worked its way down into someone's pot plantation. Some patches are known to be booby-trapped with trip wires and shotguns.

For a moment, I was glad I wasn't a firefighter, and then realized that my job held similar risks. I risk getting shot for helping a woman like Tamika escape a meth-fueled gun-toting fire-burning woman-beater.

ഇൗ ℘ ඥ

"Marcus is out? How is that possible?" Fear and anger flooded me.

Crazy Bob fell silent. For a heartbeat, I thought we had been disconnected. "I'm sorry Sunny. The jail said it was a clerical error." I could hear him wince. "He was SWAP'd out."

SWAP stands for Sheriff Work Alternative Program. The recent trend was to SWAP out the misdemeanor domestic violence cases along with other eligible misdemeanors. Too many offenders, not enough beds, and always—budget cuts. Inmates in the program report for roadside cleanup work instead of serving time in jail. Dangerous offenders remain held. Penal Code section §273.5 says domestic violence can be charged as either a felony or a misdemeanor.

What were the authorities thinking when they let Marcus out on SWAP? *It's a family matter? She probably did something to piss him off? A guy has his limits?* That was old-school, average-Joe thinking, and had probably influenced the decision to let guys like Marcus out to pick up litter along the highways with the other misdemeanor offenders; like shop-lifters, DUIs, and people who failed to appear in court to pay their traffic fines. Somehow, dangerous felon Marcus Kane had been let out with the misdemeanor offenders and now he was on the run.

I packed Kissme, her bag of treats and a pillow into the county car along with my makeup, credit card, and a change of underwear in case I couldn't get back through the CHP roadblock. I also packed an extra NP 95 smoke-filtering facemask. These masks were flying off the shelves at hardware stores. I left Kissme with Ashley who lived like me, far enough from the fire and close enough to the highway not evacuate at this time. Shane was staying in Chico, living in his office at the Harley shop.

"Would you like to pray?" Ashley asked.

"No time," I apologized, as I backed out of her driveway and zoomed off to work.

ഇൗ ℘ ඥ

"Amanda, what can we do?" I took my frustration to our fearless prosecutor Amanda, who huffed and gave me a frustrated, helpless look. A tigress in the courtroom toward defendants, her attitude towards a victim was always soft and tempered with compassion.

"The jail has its own policies, Sunny. There isn't anything I can do about it. They made a mistake."

The tigress was a puss, so I tried the DA. "Jack," I said, "this is unacceptable. Marcus is out. He could kill Tamika." I didn't respond to the proffered chair. Standing in front of his desk, the DA, much like Amanda, was sympathetic but unable to do much about it.

"There isn't enough room to hold everyone in jail. Decisions have to

be made. This was clearly an oversight, but I'll talk to the Sheriff about it."
There was finality in his tone. He had to "take a call," and I was dismissed.

He might have been finished, but I wasn't.

Some outraged, anonymous somebody called the *Chico Enterprise-Record* about a homicidal maniac who had escaped from SWAP.. The bad news is, the newspaper leaked it back to the District Attorney "for comment," stating that the information had come from "a woman working inside the district attorneys office."

Next thing I knew, I was on "administrative leave."

ℰ 𝒴 ℰ

The county car is my standard mode of transportation, but "leave" included leaving my car, and Travis volunteered to give me a ride home. He flashed his badge "on business for the DA," and we were able to slide past the angry citizens who were trying to get past the CHP roadblock. Amazingly, the CHP kept the good citizens out but were unable to remove the evacuee-squatters camped just a few hundred yards inside the barricade. Bureaucracy at work.

"Are you sure you want to stay here?" Travis looked skeptical. "You'd be safer on the boat." Travis couldn't help but admire Chance's boat parked next to the house. "Want me to tow you to the lake? Could be fun," he teased suggestively.

I smiled. I loved this guy and thanked him for making me laugh as I headed up the steps.

"Sunny." Travis reached out to clasp both my arm and my attention. "Be careful," he admonished. "Call me if you need me."

I nodded.

"I care about you," he added with a tender look. He released his hold and left.

ℰ 𝒴 ℭ

In California, we pack to evacuate like other people pack to go on a family vacation. We have learned to economize, frequently blending both events into a two-for-one special. Another summer, another fire, another holiday. Unless you left the state, there really wasn't anywhere to go, except Southern California where the residents can't tell the difference between serious smoke inhalation and just another day in SoCal. Southern Californians are a unique population that has learned not to trust any air they cannot see. So, many people evacuated from Northern California because the air was bad and headed for Southern California where air pollution is normal.

Over the years, I have learned to downsize and prioritize. In the past, I packed everything we owned in every vehicle we had and then crammed the animals in the remaining air pockets. Later, I learned to abandon the county car for my VW, stuffing it to the ceiling with my computer, laptop, electronic devices, camera, TV, Blue Ray player, pictures, bedding, and all of my clothes. I wouldd wedge Kissme, eyeballs pressed to the window, on the dashboard. Last year we narrowed the list to dogs, guns, Bible, and the birth control that I didn't need, but kept for appearances.

I always planned to tell Chance about the baby and Logan's assault that left me damaged and unable to have children. The longer I held on to the secret, the more difficult it was to let go. I was starting to realize there is never a good time for bad news.

This time, I went to the Dome Store and stocked up on food. This time, I wasn't going anywhere.

଼ଡ଼ ৺ ଔଓ

Ashley made us Zucchini-Quinoa Lasagna for dinner, and it smelled good as she dished it out alongside the salad I had brought. Eating together was better than eating alone. We typically solve the world's problems a couple of times a week, so we chatted while we ate.

"I guess you missed the local news today, huh?" Ashley was good at keeping informed about current affairs.

"I just caught the weather. News Flash: Hot and smoky. What else?"

"There were three gay 'marriages' in Chico the day before the fires started; one performed by a secular person and two by men who call themselves Christian Ministers. People are saying it's God's judgment on us because the firestorm hit three days after California's first gay marriage." She chewed thoughtfully. "What do you think?"

"Don't fall for that, Ashley. Don't believe it for a minute." I was surprised that my friend would even consider such a thing. "Look at Hurricane Katrina. There's some Rabbi in Israel saying God is punishing America because people in New Orleans didn't study the Torah. Then Al-Qaeda says it's 'God's answer to Muslim prayer.' Oh yeah... and Louis Farrakhan says "God is judging America for racism," even though black people are suffering and dying right along with the whites," I huffed with disgust as I scraped my plate into Kissme's bowl. She sniffed, turned in a circle and barked once. "And Kissme says it happened because you left meat out of the lasagna."

Ashley laughed. "Poor Kissme," she said, reaching down to give her a sympathetic pat on the head.

"Really, Ash, I could be wrong, but I am pretty sure all this stuff happens because we don't live in the Garden of Eden."

"Yeah. I guess you're right." Ashley sounded disappointed. It has always been a struggle for people to understand natural disasters. Why one home burns and the neighbor's house remains untouched. Why one side of a street gets demolished by a tornado while the other remains unscathed.

There must be a reason behind the unfairness.

I guess in my heart I was feeling the same way about my marriage. Hadn't I felt that my relationship with God would result in a kind of divine protection from the evils of this world? Didn't I think that my faith would make me bullet-proof? I guess the truth is, life isn't fair.

Pastor Mac would say, "When in doubt, drag it out," So after dinner, we sat in the living room, and I thumbed through Ashley's Bible to the Book of Luke. I read the story about a construction accident in Babylon where a skyscraper collapsed and killed all the workers. Did all the workers deserve it? When asked about the accident, Jesus said the tower fell on "both the good and the bad" workers and that "rain falls on the saved and unsaved alike."

It sounded a lot like Logan's *"shit happens"* explanation for everything. That was about as philosophical as Logan ever got.

"So, disasters and blessings are impartial. They happen to everyone," I concluded. The major difference between Christians and non-Christians is that godless people are trapped under the crap when disaster hits, but God can make good things grow out of manure for believers. That is our hope and our blessing."

Ashley still looked disappointed. She was another soul looking for justice in an unjust world.

"It feels like end times," Ashley concluded with a sigh.

Indeed. Now, there was something we agreed on.

ഇ ᾿ �

I got back home, and the phone rang. I didn't recognize the number on caller ID, but I knew it was Chance.

"I don't want to talk to you!"

Okay, so why did I answer the phone when I knew it was Chance, just to say "I don't want to talk you"? Maybe what I really meant to say was, "Bring it on! Let's do this!" My heart raged and lips quivered with emotion.

In grade school we had a science project where we froze marbles, then dropped them in a pot of boiling water and watched, mesmerized, as they shattered inside while the outside remained smooth and polished. I wondered irreverently if God was entertained by watching a human version of this experiment as I locked horns with Chance.

The call went as expected. A lot like our previous fight but this one ratcheted up the animosity on both sides as we dueled to the death.

"How could you? I trusted you! I thought... I never... you promised..."

"I'm not your damn angel, Sunny. I'm not perfect. I'm just an ass..."

"And don't bother coming home!"

"Fine! I won't!"

CHAPTER 13

ಱ 🕊 ಒ

Two weeks into the fire, five days into my time-out, and eighteen hours after my break up with Chance, I pulled every shade in the house down to keep wandering stragglers from peeking in and to keep the blistering heat out, turning indoors into twilight. A strange way to use my administrative leave, I thought. More appropriately, it was a *leave of absence without pay*.

My situation could have been worse. I could have been using vacation time or comp time. I could have been fired. I was one of the thousands of people kept away from work because of fires and dangerous smoke levels in the air. All in all, my leave was working out for the best. I would rather be ice fishing in the Arctic, but for now, with no swamp cooler, I was contemplating a nap next to Kissme on the kitchen floor, where the granite tiles felt were cool and refreshing.

Short shorts and a shorter tank top, I was still hot, hot, hot. 106° degrees outside—about 200° indoors—and more thunderstorms predicted for the weekend.

The tribulation had arrived, and I hadn't been raptured. *Sigh.* It figured. If I were in line for the Rapture given my present scorecard, God would surely take me sideways. Everyone else would go straight up, and I would be taken *Ooh-Ow-Ahh-Ouch, Wham-Blam*, through every building, bridge and mountainside.

I pulled off my white tank top and held it under the kitchen faucet, wrung it out and waved it in front of the fan. Put it back on, then almost jumped out of it again as someone knocked on the door.

I opened the door with my Glock in hand.

"Travis? What in the heck are you doing here?" *wearing jeans and a dark green dress shirt and oh my, oh my. . .* an unexpected, much-welcomed shiver danced along my spine.

His emerald eyes took in all of me, making my heart skip a beat. "I came to get you out of here. I thought you could use some help evacuating."

He looked pointedly at the gun. "Were you expecting Chance?"

I rolled my eyes. "You're letting in smoke. Get inside."

"It's nice in here." Travis laughed softly as he stepped indoors. "Well, you know, compared to out there." He moved in closer.

"I'm not leaving."

"It's mandatory."

"We both know they can't make me leave. We don't live under martial law. Evacuation is my choice."

"Are you doing this for Chance or for you?" He paused. "What? Do you think he'll love you more if you die protecting the house?"

Maybe. The thought flitted through my head before catching myself. "I don't care what he thinks or feels. We're separated," I said with determined anger. "I can do what I want." I spun away, dismissing him with a wave.

Travis reached out, catching my arm and gently pulled me back into a tight embrace. His free arm slipped behind me, fingertips running up through my hair and taking hold with a soft grip. The other arm wrapped around, pressing, closer... closer. Tipping my head back, he pulled my gaze up to meet his and waited for a heartbeat for the protest that did not come. Moving in, his lips covered mine, drowning out the anger that had been poised on the tip of my tongue. Completely engulfed in the shock and passion of his embrace, I only faintly realized that at some point, I had been literally swept off my feet. Cradled in his strong arms, he continued working wonders with his mouth as he carried me to the soft embrace of my bed.

I had a sinking feeling that had nothing to do with the mattress. Warning bells went off from somewhere in the back of my mind, then quickly faded into the fantasy world of Neverland.

Is this what being unfaithful is all about? The thought flitted through my mind. *Getting lost in forgetfulness? God knows I want to forget!*

Right or wrong, I made the choice that most women make when the "other woman" is discovered. As Logan would say, "If it's good for the bull, it's good for the heifer." Crude? Yes. But, payback was standard biker-justice. The kind of justice I had grown up with. It was second nature. "Don't get mad. Get even."

What a way to get even.

"Oh, Travis" I whispered, breathing in his essence. "Make me forget."

Shirts came off slowly, in an enticing, sensual dance; button by painful button, kiss by painful kiss, uttering sharp little cries and moans that sounded oddly like my dog when she's begging for treats, perhaps even stranger still, that I named her Kissme. Go figure!

I hungrily unbuckled Travis's belt and removed his pants, fingers trailing every inch of his strong, muscular legs. The bra slid from my shoulders, and he sent the matching thong shimmering down my thighs. Travis stood over me, poised for an agonizing heartbeat as we gazed at each other in breathless, painful expectancy for one splendid moment.

Bang! Bang ! Bang! Someone was at the door. Not possible!

"Don't answer it," whispered Travis. His mouth was on the move. The incessant pounding faded further into the distance as Travis worked his way down.

Again, bells went off, only this time they were certainly not in my head. The piercing scream of the smoke alarm shattered the moment like a tsunami siren obliterating the tranquil bliss of a tropical beach.

Was it divine intervention? *Oh Lord, I hope not.* God was watching, and I was naked as Eve.

The door went from banging to rattling as someone tried to force their way into the house. Kissme howled like a wolf on a full moon as decibels ricocheted through her head. Travis ran off to silence the shrill blast of the smoke alarm. The dream morphed into a nightmare.

This isn't happening! No! No! No! Go away. "Go Away!" I yelled, taking mere seconds to leap back into clothes that had taken long minutes to remove.

Bang! Bang! "Sunny! It's Mark! Get out of there!"

80 ⅋ ⅃

Panic!

"Hang on a sec," I shouted, stuffing my other leg into my shorts and hopping down the hall. Travis had silenced the alarm and disappeared. Kissme stopped howling and began barking hysterically as I opened the door to an exhausted-looking Mark. Right behind him was an equally fatigued fire engine pulling up to the house.

"Spot fire down below," he warned. "Get Kissme and get out!"

Ignoring him, I turned and ran to the deck. A wall of flames was sweeping up the hill, hungrily devouring everything in its path. To my amazement, Travis was already dressed and spraying water on the deck and roof with the garden hose.

I could hear the escalating rev of the fire engine as the pump engaged, and a crew of firefighters rounded the corner with their hoses to take over for Travis who dropped his hose and swept up Kissme.

"Come on!" Travis pulled me back as black fingers of smoke reached out, sounding like a fiery demon cracking trees like dry bones and chewing leaves with a crackle and a hiss. Behind the smoke, flames propelled forward from their own microclimate of self-generated wind.

"Stop! Sunny, wait!" Mark shouted behind me as the deck began to shudder and windows rattled, sounding like a train bearing down on us even as it elevated to a deafening roar.

"Down! Everybody down!" Mark cried out, yanking me flat on the deck as the firefighters dropped to the ground and covered their heads.

"Oh God!" I screamed, face down, covering my ears as the roar and shaking redoubled. From over the house and just above the tree line a borate bomber roared past, overshadowing us as it released its blood-red payload of fire retardant on the encroaching flames, missing the house by mere yards.

The flames were immediately suppressed by the air attack and the firefighters hurried to hold the line. Another engine pulled into view from

Ashley's hill, and I could see its crew running into the fray, beating back the remaining flames into the burn, where they would die from lack of fuel.

ഔ ℘ ൽ

Mark swore, then exhaled. "That was a close one," he said, standing up to wipe the sweat that poured from beneath his helmet.

"You all right?" asked Travis, getting up and pulling me with him.

"Yeah. I think so," I replied, hanging on to a traumatized Kissme who continued to rattle long after the plane receded into the distance, winging its way back to Chico for a refuel.

The crew advanced downhill in tandem with the team that was working its way down from Ashley's side of the hill into the burn zone, effectively squelching the last of the sizzling hot spots.

"Mark! Where did that come from? I gasped. "I thought the fire was still miles from here."

"I don't know, Sunny. Maybe the tan oak. The oil in the leaves gets hot and propels 'em up. Sometimes the wind can carry them for a mile and start a whole new fire." He wiped his brow again. "That's one possibility. I'm just guessing. But I intend to find out," he added.

He turned to eye Travis as if seeing him for the first time. Travis stood there, his clothes still clean, not a hair out of place, looking confident and relaxed.

"Uh, Travis this is Mark, Chance's boss. Mark, this is Travis. We work together. I think I introduced you guys on one of your drop-ins at the office to see Paige.

Mark paused, his eyebrows drawn, penciling black lines across his sooty forehead

"You guys know each other?" I asked, voicing the obvious.

"We've met," Travis interjected, reaching out and shaking Mark's hand. "Inter-agency pow-wow."

They nodded, making polite acknowledgments to each other, but the air had become tense from more than one near crisis.

Mark scanned me briefly and I prayed I hadn't left my bra in the bedroom or put my shirt on backward. I could only imagine what I must look like.

"You should be okay now. These guys got a handle on things. I need to go check on this from the bottom of the hill. I'll be back later," Mark said with a candid look at Travis, who turned and placed his hands on my shoulders. Travis looked me in the eye, unafraid and completely unintimidated by Mark's presence.

"Will you be okay?" His face filled with concern. "Should I stay?"

I noticed the muscles in Mark's jaw quiver as if working to hold back anger.

Oh, God. He knows! Is it that obvious? My phone rang providing a temporary reprieve.

"Hold on, Ashley. I'm okay. How about you? Yeah, the plane freaked me out too. Listen, Mark's here with half of the fire department. It was a spot fire, but it's been contained. They're mopping up now. Let me call you back. Better still, how about coming over here? Good. Bye."

"Sounds like you're in good hands. I have to go, too. But don't forget," Travis added as a soft smile played on his lips, "if you need anything at all, call me." And Travis was gone.

How does he do it? Travis was different from anyone I knew. Always calm, always *au fait*, on top of his game.

Mark grunted in farewell, his eyes narrowing as he watched Travis depart through the house.

"I'll be back," Mark repeated, kissing me on the forehead. "I'm glad we saved the house."

"Thank you, Mark," I said with genuine affection and a hug.

I felt more than guilty. I was blanketed with shame. I had come dangerously close to making an irrevocable decision. Only fate, or God, had interceded on my behalf keeping me from acting exactly like the people I judged as immoral. What a time for Marne to pop back in my head. Like her, I had almost become the very thing I resented. I was no different from Chance, Paige, Logan, or my parents.

Mark was gone. I tried to come to terms with myself. After all, this wasn't the first time a husband had cheated on me. All those years with Logan should have prepared me for this. But somehow, it hadn't.

My new life was supposed to be different. We were Christians and I wondered what happened to my "blessed assurance;" believing I would never again be sad, sick, or have to suffer. *Be careful what you pray for,* I concluded, recalling that I no longer pray for things like *patience* and *strength* because patience is born through trials, and strength through temptation. Recently I prayed for growth, forgetting that growth begins with birth, and birth always starts with agonizing pain. Now I pray for things like a raise.

Another disruptive knock at the door. I knew it was Ashley this time and greeted her with a loving embrace.

"Oh Sunny, I was so scared," she said with a warm hug. "It's absolute insanity out there. I was worried about you all alone over here," she said, as she took my hand and made our way outside to survey the damage.

The trees on the slope were still smoking beneath the deluge the firefighters continued to pour on them. Other crewmembers stirred pockets of sludge using mattocks and Pulaskis, the tools of their trade.

"Mark just left. He said he'd be back soon. Let's go back inside."

I poured us ice water and we talked about the fire and borate bomber. I was carefully avoiding any mention of Travis when a blaze of fur blew past. Kissme had found a new treasure and was burning off adrenalin as she played her favorite game of keep-away. We both smiled as she pranced and spun around, showing off... *what is that?*

"Is that what I think it is?" Ashley inquired.

Men's underwear. More specifically—Travis's underwear. The chase was on. Kissme had more moves than a rock star. The more I tried to grab them, the more she gleefully dodged about, flaunting a pair of black silk boxer shorts clamped in her jaws.

Ashley shook with laughter, catching her breath before catching Kissme as she cannonballed around the sofa for the third time. Her eyes widened in joyful speculation.

"Hmmm? Chance in silk boxers? Nice! I should get Shane some of these."

Red-faced and puffing, taking Kissme from her, I finally wrenched the boxers from Ashley's grip and walked back, tossing them on my bed where pillows remained scattered and sheets rumpled.

"He sleeps in them," I lied. I suspected Ashley was mentally adding up the number of days since Chance had left.

"Are you sure you're okay? You look a little flushed." Ashley observed. *Only a "little flushed?"*

"Ya think?" I answered sarcastically as I led her away from the scene of the crime. "Considering everything we've been through today, not to mention chasing my stupid dog."

"Where were we?" *Please let it be "goodbye,"* I thought.

Lies are like that. Like having your dirty underwear dragged into the open.

Ashley rose, removing the glasses from the table. Walking to the kitchen, she asked, "Have you talked with Chance?"

"No. I fought with Chance. We broke-up."

Ashley's mouth twisted in skepticism. "You *break-up* when you're dating," she said meaningfully. "Marriages end in *divorce*. Have you been praying for him?"

I had studiously avoided prayer. "Sure," I said.

"You need to keep praying for your marriage—without ceasing." Ashley admonished.

I would like to eat ice cream without ceasing, lie on a beach without ceasing. I could even fish without ceasing. But I really didn't want to give Chance another thought, let alone another prayer.

"When Chance gets back, you guys will work things out," Ashley said confidently.

Or *not*, I thought. At this point, leaning more towards the *not*.

"Anyhow, I understand if you don't want to talk about it," she continued lamely.

"Good. I don't." My tone was hurtful, and I thought it was a good thing that friends can't read each other's minds. If Ashley could read my thoughts regarding Chance—or my fantasies about Travis—she would not approve.

I figure God sure knew what he was doing when he made Eve. Sex is the greatest blessing in life. It is the glue that strengthens marriage, a mini-vacation for the tired, mental health for emotional pain; always a blissful escape from brutal reality.

But I also knew that sex could be the greatest curse. Rape, child molestation, sexual-addictions, perversion, and a weapon for revenge "served up cold."

Sex is two people melting into one. Sex is the absolute ultimate, intimate gift of giving and receiving—or stealing and deceiving—depending.

ဆ �ﾟ ଔ

It was almost dark when a haggard-looking Mark returned to give me the initial results of his cursory investigation.

"Dave-the-baker"—a neighbor who lives below me and makes manna-quality bread from grains that he grinds, and then bakes in wood-fired brick ovens—"said he saw a motorcycle parked off the side of the road. He didn't see the owner and figured he was piss—uh, relieving himself in the bushes somewhere. Could be a coincidence, but it's enough to justify an arson investigation."

Mark didn't know the details of my life with Logan. Withholding information now was intended to protect both of us. But to be on the safe side, I suggested that he investigate Tamika's boyfriend, Marcus Kane, who had walked away from the SWAP detail on the first day of the firestorm.

"Where is Chance now?" I finally asked, trying to seem indifferent as I brought him a glass of ice water and sat next to him on the sofa, touching his arm in friendship. Mark looked uncomfortable as he held the glass, swirling the ice around with his finger and then almost knocking it over when he set it down.

"Chance is fine. Don't worry about him. I sent him and Mercy down to Baton Rouge a couple of days ago. He asked me if he could come back so he could be with you, but I really needed them there. The world is falling apart with disasters. I came back to California because he made me promise to help you evacuate.

It was surreal to be talking about floods in light of today's experience.

"The Army Corps of Engineers says it will take almost three months to pump all the water out of New Orleans *after* the pumps have been repaired. I came back here because of the fires, but I am... um... sending some replacements so Chance can... uh... come home."

Mark was acting weird. "So, how is Mark?" I asked him about himself with genuine care.

"Sunny. I don't know where to start. This is tough. I'm not exactly an emotional guy." A bitter chuckle escaped his first line of defense.

"And...?"

"It's about Paige. Well... actually..." Prolonged pause. "It's about Paige and Chance."

Imagination usually exceeds truth, but I didn't want to hear the truth. I already knew it. My breath stopped, my heart stopped, and time stood still.

I was in a car once with my neighbor Kenny driving us down from

Feather Falls, when a deer launched off the mountainside sending its hindquarters through the front windshield. I never saw the deer, but the resulting explosion sounded as though someone had blasted Kenny with a shotgun. The car seemed to whirl through space and time. A soft white fog of shattered glass rolled in as we spun across the bridge. Time slowed as we continued to turn around and around. Fragments of glass suspended in space. I don't know why God would slow time in that way unless maybe he is giving us one more chance to accept Him as Lord and Savior before we are catapulted into eternity. But the five-second spin-zone had felt more like five minutes.

I could see Mark's lips moving, but I didn't hear a word he said. Stranger still, I had no idea how long he had been talking.

"What?" I interrupted.

"Yeah... that's what I said. I couldn't believe they would do this to us. I really love her, Sunny." A tear slid down his weathered cheek, making a tender contrast to the hardened lines on his face, "and I know how much you love Chance."

I shook my head to focus. Oh, boy! Of course, I knew about the affair before Mark arrived, but life had been more promising just a few days ago. Glaring suspicion had been one thing. It left a comfort zone of doubt and hope. Hearing the truth again took me beyond despairing, all the way to hopeless. The Bible says "Truth will set you free," but I didn't feel free. I felt crippled. Being shot is one thing—being shot in the heart is another. One is a serious wound—the other is fatal.

෨ ༀ ൝

I woke up screaming in the dark. Flames licking the walls and Kissme licking my face. I stumbled to the bathroom thinking, *I really need a Xanax*, and then used the toilet and went back to bed without one. Nightmares were a regular part of my life. Nightmares without Chance to rescue me were the worst.

The Xanax came when Logan began stalking me, and my dreams had taken me captive, revisiting the night terrors of my youth. The difference between a nightmare and a night terror is that dreams are remembered, and night terrors are not. Both leave you drenched in fear. When I asked the doctor for sleeping pills, he had prescribed Xanax instead. Great stuff. Too good, really, so I try to take as few as possible.

Back then, I had Chance to hold me, and he would chase away my fears with his great strength and his great love. Or so I had thought.

Okay, let me think this through. *My life is ruined, the world is on fire, and I am having a screaming nightmare. So, if I don't need a Xanax now... if this isn't stress...*

Kissme started spinning in circles, doing her strange Pomeranian-thing on the bed and barking her head off. Kissme isn't really the yippy-type, so I needed to make a quick decision. Grab the gun or grab the Xanax.

I heard the distant rumble of a motorcycle coming down the driveway and opted for the weapon, which in this instance, was better than Xanax.

I can shoot Logan, go back to sleep, and call the cops in the morning. No regrets.

Opening the bedroom blinds, I peeked between the slats, making a mental note to dust them if I was still alive in the morning. The motion lights went on, lighting up the front porch. He was here. Black bike, black leathers, black helmet. My heart hammered. Drawing back, I kissed my dog in case I died and never had another chance to say good-bye.

Moving fast, I retrieved the Glock from my sock drawer, chambered a round and took a deep breath. It didn't matter that I wasn't the world's best shot. It's not as if I was planning on wounding him. My plan was to fire every one of the fifteen rounds in the clip right into his worthless heart, with a few pointed south for good measure. I doubted if he even had a heart. Besides, it only takes one bullet to do the job. I felt confident that I could probably land at least one round out of fifteen.

The tile was cold under my feet as I made my way into the front room, a sharp contrast to the sweat breaking out in my armpits. I picked up the phone and dialed 9-1-1. The doorknob rattled, then shuddered under a couple of hard shoves.

"Nine-one-one. What is your emergency?"

Bam! Bam! Bam! I fired at the door. Three down, twelve to go.

"Sunnnneeee! What are you doing???!!"

I dropped the gun and it fired once more, nearly hitting Kissme who was cringing on the back of the couch as the bullet whizzed over her head, through the French doors, over the deck, and possibly across Highway 70. Yikes!

"I'm sorry! Honey... please, don't kill me!"

"Nine-one-one. What is your emergency?"

Chance was home.

Ω 🦋 ℧

I opened the door, or what was left of it, to a white faced Chance dressed in black leathers.

"Hello. You're back." I stated the obvious, certain I was dreaming.

"Yeah." Raising his eyebrows, scanning the room left and right for booby traps. "Is it safe to come in?"

Now there was a thought. Only minutes before I had been aching for my husband. Now I had a loaded gun just inches away and let my imagination run amuck. Walking back into the living room, I picked up the phone and informed 911 that the call had been a mistake. Wordlessly, I stomped to the bathroom and took a whole Xanax, then grabbed my still-trembling dog before slamming the bedroom door and going back to bed.

It was Saturday morning and I thought I was dreaming again when I woke to the smell of bacon and waffles. Chance was home. I tried to burrow deeper in the bed, but Kissme pitched a fit and kept head-butting me. It was her not-cute way of forcing me to get up and let her out to go to the bathroom. Probably the smell of bacon had gotten her attention too. Such a demanding, bossy little dog! I reached over and kissed her furry head when my mental light bulb clicked on.

Oh my gosh. Had I really shot at Chance last night? I flew out of bed and hurried to the kitchen. There was Chance, stirring batter in a mixing bowl. He had slept on the couch, using a black leather coat for a pillow. Dang! I wished he didn't look so good in the morning... tousled blond hair over hopeful, big sky-blue eyes, shirtless, wearing only a loose pair of cotton drawstring pants and holding out a fresh, hot cup of coffee. He was such a rat, playing on all my weaknesses. I simply can't say *no* to coffee.

"Good morning," Chance said. His expression transitioned from hopeful to cautious as he extended the peace offering.

I took the coffee, took the dog, and paused to inspect the shattered front door on my way outside. *Ouch! That's going to cost a bundle to replace.* Kissme took her own sweet time as I checked out the gleaming Honda 1800 VTX sitting in the driveway.

Okay. It definitely hadn't been a dream. Apparently, the motorcycle-gun-thing had actually happened. I went back in. The Glock lay on the breakfast bar with the clip out.

Chance held out a plate of food. "Are going to shoot at me again?"

My eyebrows narrowed as I considered the question. Taking the plate, I piled butter and syrup on a steaming waffle.

I thoughtfully chewed a piece of bacon before replying, "I should! Anyhow, I thought you were Logan. And where did the VTX in the driveway come from?"

"The vet. I bought it from Craig down at Look Ahead. He's treating Mercy."

Panic gripped my heart. "What's wrong with Mercy?"

"I think it was Papite's Alligator Jambalaya from the farewell sendoff dinner."

"What's a Papite?"

"Not a *what*, he's a *who*. He was our Cajun cook."

"Huh! Where'd the alligator come from?"

"Uh, I shot it. That's why I'm home. Pending review for disciplinary action. Anyhow, Mercy ate the leftovers and then threw up in her airplane crate on the trip home. You wouldn't believe the stink! Mac picked Mercy and me up from the airport and insisted that she smelled like death and said I should take her to the vet. So we dropped her off on the way home for a checkup and a bath." He buttered and syrup'd be his waffle.

"You *shot* an alligator?"

"It was already dead. Who knew? Long story. So," he continued eating his breakfast, "my truck is at Mark's. Craig gave me a deal on the bike since it was the middle of the night and since Mac wanted to get home... It's a great bike."

I eyeballed the Glock with a rising tide of anger that he could be so lighthearted after putting me through hell.

"Sunny, you don't look well. You're all red. Do you need a Xanax?"

Good thing tomorrow was Sunday and I would have the whole day to repent for what happened next.

CHAPTER 14

෪ 🕊 ෫

Chance's things were packed in the back of his truck. Amazing how men can fit everything they own into the back of a pickup truck, and a buddy will help them move for a six-pack. By contrast, women typically require a moving company with a big-rig, a crew of men to do the heavy lifting, and a credit card to cover expenses. We probably deal with emotions the same way. Men can stuff a lot of emotions into a small space, leave them there, and move forward over a beer and a ball game whereas a woman might require a therapist, a support group, a dozen self-help books, and a bottle of wine never hurts.

"Sunny. Please. Let me say something before I go." Chance moved next to me. Sunlight and shadows played across his rugged face as we stood on the front porch. He didn't flinch or look down but searched my face as if looking for something he didn't want to forget. My eyes narrowed in self-defense, and I pulled back, folding my arms over my chest to protect my heart. Chance drew in a ragged breath and poured out what I assumed was a rehearsed speech.

"I am ashamed of what I've done to you. I have spent the past six years of my life rescuing strangers, but I let the most important thing in the world—our marriage—die. Even worse, I killed it myself." He stepped back, dropping his gaze and shoulders in a quiet gesture of defeat. "It's all my fault. You're everything to me Sunny. Everything I ever wanted or dreamed of." His voice echoed the same anguish in my heart. "I hope you'll forgive me someday. I pray that you'll meet a man who deserves someone as special as you."

"Nice speech," I said sarcastically.

"I wish you would let me explain," he pleaded.

"Then explain this!" I spat out the words as I threw the foil pack containing the condom that had been in his wallet. "Tell me, Chance! How many times have you pretended that I am someone else while having sex with me? Well now you're packed, and you can go shack up with your whore!"

Apparently, this wasn't turning out the way he expected. Chance poured out his heart and I slapped his face. The muscles in his jaw tightened as he struggled to control his next words.

"Oh yeah, I almost forgot! *You're* perfect! You've never made mistakes," he retorted with a tortured look in his eyes. "Right? right!" he demanded. "You're too good, too righteous to forgive me. No one has ever given *you* a second chance. Am I right?"

I wasn't sure if it was a question or an accusation, so I kept silent until the quiet was too much for either of us to bear.

"I'm staying at Pastor Mac's until I can get into my old place if you care to know," he said, stepping back and turning away.

"Mercy, come!" he called to his dog and walked off with head held high, as he strode to the truck. Mercy whined in question, then jumped into the seat next to Chance. A huge lump formed in my throat when she turned to watch me through the rear window as they drove away.

I have never cheated on him! I told myself, struggling to maintain a sense of self-righteousness. An unwelcomed memory of a glowing, naked Travis intruded in my thoughts. *That was different,* I hastened to reassure myself. *Nothing happened. Besides, Chance didn't just cheat—he lied to me!*

And then, I was hit with another tidal wave of guilt, convicted over the volumes of secrets I have kept from my husband. Even I knew that withholding the truth is the same as a lie.

₧

Sunday arrived. Shane left Ashley to go on a benefit motorcycle run. Chance was picking up Mercy's doghouse and then moving a few larger things from the house into a storage unit. I didn't want to be around to watch the fabric of our lives unravel, so I went to church with Ashley.

Mac probably wrote the sermon with me in mind. It was all about the power of forgiveness. To say the least, it was more than I was prepared to do.

"Morning, Sunny. I was hoping I'd see you today," said Mac.

"Chance is missing church?" I queried, knowing full well he was at the house, but taking grim satisfaction in pointing out the fact that *I* was at church and *Mr. Bible-Study Leader* wasn't. *God scores one-for-me and minus-one for Chance,* I thought, feeling smug.

"Yes, I know," said Mac patiently, refusing to take the bait. "He will begin teaching the Wednesday night Bible study I offered him next week. It's *you* I want to talk to. When is a good time?"

When hell freezes over, I thought bitterly. Apparently, all you need to do is commit adultery to get a promotion.

"Thursday? Here? Before the AA meeting?" Mac was solid as a storm door in the face of a tornado, but all I felt was the emptiness of having failed at a second marriage. I nodded yes.

"Great, I'll see you then." Mac paused. "I'll call to remind you this time," he added as an afterthought.

Yeah, great. I visualized yet another heavenly black mark against me for having a bad attitude and sighed. *Oh hell, what's another checkmark?* I figured God was probably running out of space next to my name by now anyhow. Then I caught myself. I did a quickie repent for my blasphemous thoughts and superstitiously followed up with a hasty "Sorry, God" to avoid being struck by lightning.

Escaping to the refreshment table, Ashley and I decided on a trip to Chico. The air had become less smoky as the Butte County fires slowly came under control, although tall columns of smoke still billowed from the northwest toward Mt. Shasta and Redding. We agreed to take two cars so she could grocery shop on the way home.

After a second last-cookie each, we headed out, stopping to pick up lunch from a little deli close to our destination. Ashley had a bean-thing wrapped in something green, I ordered a chicken and bacon wrap with ranch dressing. She had Sun Chips, and I had yellow fingers from digging into my Cheezy Puffs.

"You hit him with *what?*" Ashley was aghast.

"A fully loaded waffle," I replied as we hiked up beautiful Yahi Trail into upper Bidwell Park in search of Big Chico Creek.

"Was that before or after you shot him?" she asked, her expression incredulous.

"I didn't kill him, just shot *at* him! Besides, I thought he was Logan. Chance doesn't own a motorcycle. At least he didn't have one when he left for Louisiana."

"I'm glad you didn't shoot Shane."

"Shane wouldn't ride up unannounced in the middle of the night." I paused to reconsider. "He'd call first... right?"

"Well, he will now!" Ashley was a gentle soul. Some of her gentle ways reminded me of Starla, except Ashley didn't have to "find herself." She knew that she was a child of God.

"Watch out for snakes," Ashley called as she jumped from rock to rock, safely crossing the creek's cold, rushing water. You have to watch for snakes this time of the year. Rattlers are drawn to water.

We found a shady place and dove into our lunch. Ashley was thoughtful. "I don't know which is weirder. Mark still speaking with Chance, or Mark wanting to make up with Paige. Mark must really love both of them." Ashley commented.

"Mark heads Search and Rescue. Those guys are both married to their work. They'll get over her. Maybe. I mean, I still have to work with Paige. I don't like it, but I love my job more than I hate her. I'm not giving up my career just because... because..." I faltered, pausing to take a long drink of water, choking down the words that stuck in my throat. "Anyhow, they don't *love* her. They *lust* her. They all *lust* her. She looks like a porn star."

Ashley laughed her carefree, musical laugh. "She isn't any prettier than you."

"Really?" Breadcrumbs spilled from my mouth.

"Absolutely. Besides, what good are great looks if you're so self-centered, you can only love yourself? I think I feel sorry for her."

"Ashley! I thought you were my friend. How can you feel sorry for that nasty, home-wrecking skank?"

Ashley was unmoved. "Think about it. Seriously. Men just use women like her. She'll never have a man's heart unless she repents."

Ashley could afford to be kind-hearted. She was married to a saint.

Who wants a man's heart if the rest of him is being spread around? I mused.

"At least now I know why Chance turned down Mac's offer to lead Bible Study a few weeks ago. I can't believe the nerve of him accepting the job now." My tasty lunch was turning sour. "Like, God is going to forgive him just because he's do-gooding. What a hypocrite!"

Ashley nodded sympathetically. She was such a dear friend. My heart filled with gratitude.

We finished the wraps in silence and turned our attention to the remaining chips.

"Sunny, can I say something to you... *as a friend?*" she asked tentatively.

"Anything, Ash. You know that." Something in the *friend* word didn't sound too friendly.

"Okay. I know this will come as a surprise to you, but you have deeply hurt my feelings."

"I hurt your feelings? What... how..?" I was surprised.

"Do you know what today is?"

"Sunday?" I was pretty sure it was still Sunday.

Ashley rolled her eyes. "Do you know what *month* it is?"

"I think it is still June." Probably. Most likely.

Ashley threw up her hands. "It's June eleventh."

"And...?" I shrugged.

"Duh! Sunny. How could you forget? June seventh is my birthday."

My tired brain tried to compute.

"You really hurt my feelings. You're so insensitive. I *always* remember your birthday. I *always* get you something nice."

Silence. Shock.

"Aren't you going to say something? Aren't you *even* going to wish me a happy birthday?"

My world was falling apart. My husband had cheated on me, and I had almost cheated on him. The mountains were still smoldering, and my just-in-case evacuation bags were still packed, waiting patiently by the front door. Here I sat, in need of comfort, getting a tongue-lashing and a guilt-trip from my best friend. *Just shoot me!* My life is in crisis, and Ashley is thinking about balloons and bows.

"Hmm... I don't know what to say." I was still stunned. She was borderline angry and 100% offended. I handed her the rest of my bag of Cheezy Puffs. "Happy birthday, Ash."

Annoyed, I stayed behind after Ashley left. I needed to be alone to think, and home was feeling more like a house these days. "I am lonely, Lord. But I would rather be lonely forever than forever hurt by the people who are supposed to love me."

Are we not Christians? Didn't we just finish sitting together in church for an hour listening to Mac talk about forgiveness? Ashley can't forgive me, and I can't forgive Chance. What a sorry bunch we are. This Christianity thing isn't at all like I thought it would be. I thought we were supposed to be blessed. At the moment, faith felt like a burden. It seemed unfair that the rest of the world could party-on, happily cheating, sexting, and indulging every form of lust, while I was tormented with guilt.

I had believed that Chance was my blessing from God after years of Logan's abuse. Now I worried that God would punish me for almost having sex with Travis. I settled back, sliding into the black hole of depression. Today I had lost my two best friends.

Another huge sigh escaped as I cradled my head in my hands. I didn't know the human body could hold so many tears. I knew I could walk away from Chance and Ashley. But if I walked away from God, where would I go?

ဆ ɣ ca

I gave myself some time. It felt intrusive to look at people's burned-out homes too soon. I didn't want to catch families wandering amidst the ashes and ruins in shock, or worse, weeping in each other's arms. Two weeks after the fires were officially out, I took the five-mile drive past Concow Lake.

Living in a forested community that has been ravaged by fire, is something like waking up to find yourself trapped in an Alfred Hitchcock movie. Hitchcock was the master of horror back in the days of black & white TV—before Stephen King was around to paint gruesome in living color.

All the mountains, trees, and charred earth, as far as the eye could see were dressed in black and white and every shade of gray. The smell of smoke and ruin lingered, having permeated everything organic and the very air you breathed. The landscape was surreal. Naked trees looked like ghosts rising from the ashes, jutting fingers into an opaque sky. The death of homes, along with their owners' dreams and history. Dead. All dead.

The once cheery little creek that had danced beneath a canopy of green now choked with burnt matter and strangled all life. What struck me the most was the crazy, haphazard pattern of the fire. No wide swaths. The fire had snaked its way along in a branch-lightening pattern, striking homes here, partial properties there, and skipping others entirely.

The whole effect weighed on my heart as I drove back toward the church and my meeting with Mac.

Mac was there, and I was relieved to discover that Chance wasn't. But then, Chance would be teaching on Wednesday nights and this was Thursday, about a half hour before the church hosted AA meetings. I opened up our conversation by telling Mac about the drive to Concow and what I had seen. I knew he dealt with trauma survivors all the time and he wisely reflected, "One thing I am sure of; some people will come out of this hating God. They'll ask, 'What kind of loving God would do such a thing do me? Why me? Why not the druggies next door? I am a good person! If that is God, then I don't want him.' Other people will draw closer to God and say, 'Thank you, God, for sparing our lives. Thank you for all the days that you gave us in our home. It hurts to lose our home, but we are grateful in the certainty that you will provide for us.' Same problem – two different choices of how to process it."

"And God can make something good come of this?" I asked.

"The Bible talks a lot about dividing," he explained. "Wheat from weeds, sheep from goats, family members from each other. I think it's not so much what happens to us in life, but what you do with what happens that counts. People will either grow from their problems or be eaten alive with bitterness."

"I guess the same could be said for my marriage." It just slipped out. Mac looked at me kindly. "I've been talking with Chance almost every day since he first left for Louisiana. I guess you could say, I knew about the affair before you did," he confessed.

My head spun. "Does everybody know?"

"I don't do business with *everybody*. I do business with God." Then he went on to talk about the fall of man, temptation, and sin. He assured me that forgiveness is "not about letting someone get away with something, but letting go." Laying your burden of heartache at the foot of the cross.

The session concluded as Pastor prayed over me and my marriage. I figured that God might have heard Mac's prayer, but he was flying solo as far as I was concerned. None of that *"Where two or more have gathered in my name"* for me. Mac's prayers and exhortations fell on deaf ears. I blamed both God and Chance for my predicament. The hour was late. I said "Good night," and we would "talk again soon."

I was a vessel overflowing with resentment. *Hadn't I been punished enough in life? Hadn't I loved Chance more than anything?* In fact, hadn't I loved him more than *everything*. I had loved my husband more than... well... more than God himself.

God might forgive him, but I never would.

CHAPTER 15

ജ 🕊 ൙

I sat in my car and pondered the difference between *humility* and *humiliation*. I suppose that *humility* is a choice, and *humiliation* is something forced upon you.

It's about the same difference as great sex and forcible rape. So there I was, sitting outside of the lab, waiting for blood tests to see if I have HIV, Hepatitis, or some other sexually transmitted disease.

How many men has Paige slept with? And how many diseases have those men caught from other women (who had other men) and passed along to her? The math was frightening.

"Sin," it seemed, was a communicable disease. I wondered how many women my lying-cheating-no-good rotten husband had slept with?

Lord, I miss him. My heart twisted before I could correct myself. What I missed... was the feeling of love that I thought we shared.

I reminded myself for the hundredth time that I had been faithful. I already decided that Travis didn't count. I mean, we didn't actually do the deed, so technically I was still a faithful wife by default. And, it wasn't for lack of opportunity. My job frequently took me out of town to conferences for days at a time, usually in the company of sexy DA Investigators. Investigators who lost their wedding rings on day-one and mysteriously found them on their way home.

Feeling wounded and soiled in places that cannot be reached except by death or salvation, I waited for the hospital lab to finish off what was left of my pride. Crying in the sanctuary of my Volkswagen, I realized that if I had been bleeding in the flesh instead of the spirit, my car would look like a crime scene.

I didn't know where I was going, but I knew it included getting away, fast. I soon found myself rocketing through the mountains to the winding narrow road that leads down to Dark Canyon and the Lake.

ജ 🕊 ൙

What... Not possible... Crap! I slammed the brakes. Great plumes of noxious black smoke filled the air as I screeched to a stop. I'd mistaken the largest snake on the planet for a fallen tree branch.

"I hate snakes!" My eyes narrowed. "You are so dead!" I flipped a dangerous U-turn on a blind corner and headed back down the road, eager to put the snake out of my misery.

Visualizing Chance, I paused to take aim—then charged like a pit bull protecting a cash crop—pedal to the floor. The snake never knew what hit it. It was like flying over a Wal-Mart speed bump doing sixty.

Looking back, I wasn't even certain it was a rattler. We have bull snakes that look just like rattlesnakes, minus the rattles. I braked for a closer look. Good Lord... it was still moving! I flipped another U, driving like a crazy woman going the wrong way in the wrong lane, launching airborne over the snake again; crying out in grief this time, instead of rage. Not grief for the snake, but for myself. I wanted it to die—*but not really.* Swerving back in my lane, I was stunned to see all six feet of the snake in motion, slithering across the road: Snakezilla!

Giving up, I drove back up the road feeling bad for the snake I had probably left with a permanent limp. Pulling into the empty parking lot at the Grange Hall, I wept bitterly.

After the snake incident, I realized I was moving into a new phase of my pending divorce. It had begun with shock, denial, and complete immobilization while Chance was in Louisiana. After Chance had moved out, I felt an overwhelming emptiness. No hope or light; just a void in my soul.

There'd been a day when I heard a wounded animal wailing in the distance, before realizing it was me.

Now I entered into phase three; righteous anger. Mt. St. Helens had nothing on me after the drive down Dark Canyon.

I drove back home, pretty sure if Chance coming the other way on his bike, I would be flattening my second snake of the day.

ⅎ 🕊 ⅍

I hadn't returned any of Chance's calls since my check-up and close encounter with the alien snake. I needed to know first if Chance had infected me with a life-threatening disease. We needed to talk, but I didn't know what to say, so I screened my calls and ignored everybody:

"Sunny, this is Travis. Pick-up." Nothing more. Click.

"Sunny, this is Chance. Pick-up." Nothing more. Click.

Sunny, this is God. Pick up. Nothing more. Click.

In blocking communication with others, I had severed my connection with God. He was so distant! Or maybe it was me.

The plate of leftovers sat cold and uninviting before me as my thoughts drifted to soul food. Having been betrayed by my friends, I was left to reconsider the One True Friend. The One *who cannot lie*. The One who is closer than a brother. The One who will never leave me or forsake me.

"Maybe, God's is the only love I need," I told Kissme, who watched me expectantly, "except for you. For that matter, maybe God's is the only love worth having."

I scratched her head. She didn't look too worried. I turned to Isaiah 54:5. "Your Maker is your husband, and Lord Almighty is his name." This was an eye opener. Who needs more than one husband? What a concept. I could have an intimate, one-on-one romantic love relationship with God himself.

€ ȿ ¨

Paige smirked as I passed her on my way into the office. She looked like a cat in spandex that had devoured a low-fat canary. The eyes of the secretaries tracked me as I carved a path into the refuge of my office. I imagined everyone thinking, *Sunny must have been a lousy lay.* As if it were my fault Chance had been unfaithful.

I always hungered for Chance's touch, could never get enough of his love. Maybe because touch was the only expression of love I had ever known. I thought that touch was how men show love, and if he wasn't demanding sex all of the time, he didn't care about you. That had been my experience.

"You have a one-o'clock coming in."

Startled at the sound, I looked up to see Paige posing in the doorway. I took a deep breath and counted to four. It wouldn't look good to be seen rolling around on the floor yanking each other's hair out.

"Paige, I expect you to knock from now on." Being nice to her in the past had only gotten me where I was this morning: miserable and broken hearted. "Who is it?"

"Courtney Hill. You know... *Silicone Woman?*" she smiled, flexing her brows suggestively.

"Thanks. You can leave now."

"But..."

"I said, you can leave. Now!"

I can be a cold-hearted b-word and still be professional. "I'll take it from here."

In spite of my misery, I was curious about the woman that the male Investigators called Silicone Woman. However, I was in for a big disappointment. Meeting Courtney Hill only confirmed my suspicion that I will never understand men.

I expected a pair of monster chesticles, but hers didn't look any bigger than mine. Well... she didn't look any bigger than Paige's silicone job. But Courtney did fit the California-blonde stereotype; her bleached hair highlighted with wild, kinky multi-toned strands, oversized hoop earrings, a pair of tight short-shorts, black suede ankle boots, a white tank top that showed off her studded navel ring, and enough cheap perfume to gag a horse.

Maybe she wasn't a natural bombshell, but it was evident that she *thought* she was. And maybe that is what men pick up on—attitude. Maybe that is what Chance detects when he is around Paige, a pheromone attraction.

No, I had to admit, Paige *really is* younger and prettier than I am. But then, so are a couple of other women at church who peek at Chance when he isn't looking. The thought only added to my confusion and depression.

"Hello, Courtney. Why don't we talk in my office?" I brought her some coffee and she sat on the sofa, pausing to gaze at the small table fountain that highlighted my relatively small room. Investigators design interrogation rooms with discomfort as their primary objective. They even shorten the front legs on the suspect's chair to force them to lean forward. The intent of my office is to soothe trauma victims by creating an atmosphere of safety, tranquility, and peace.

Courtney sipped her coffee and summarized her story.

"I got back from Thailand about ten days ago. I was Army trained and did two tours in Iraq. I am an expert with MWD's—Military Working Dogs—as a handler. In my last year of service, I met Reilly, my current boyfriend, who just came back from Afghanistan. He was a specialist on the base, an instructor in advanced hand-to-hand combat. Reilly was discharged about eight months after me. About three weeks later we got an offer from the Thai government to come over and do some training with their troops; me working canines and Reilly teaching hand-to-hand."

This is good. I always appreciated something a little different on the work menu.

"We were only in Thailand for a week when Reilly hit me for the first time. He punched me right here," she said, pointing to her left cheek, which made me note that he was probably left-handed. "It just got worse." She started to cry and I handed her a box of tissues. "Pretty soon he was hitting me all the time. So I ran off. I came home, but I know he's coming for me."

"How do you know he's coming?" I asked in a soothing voice.

"He left a message on my phone that he was on his way." Sadly, she had erased the message. "I need a protective order *now!*" She didn't know that emergency orders are rarely issued during daylight hours. Courtney sobbed. "I have this baby-blue convertible Corvette, and I just *know* Reilly or his friends are going to see me driving it around town."

Duh! "Have you thought about getting a less obvious car?" *One with a hard top?* "Maybe dying your hair?" *Maybe putting on some clothes?*

She looked at me like I had completely lost my mind. "Are you serious? No way! I love my car."

Do you love living? I nodded.

"I'm freaked out. Reilly's bringing in guns."

"What do you mean 'he's bringing in guns'?" The warning light between my ears began to blink.

"I mean guns. He's smuggling guns in from Thailand."

Ooh, boy! "Excuse me for just a minute while I get my partner, Travis."

We spent the rest of the morning sorting out the details of Courtney's story. Basically, we had a highly trained killer who beat women. He was flying into Texas tomorrow in a quasi-military aircraft with some private contractors, bringing with him several crates of illegal guns he had purchased in Thailand. Reilly's plan was to transport them in a U-Haul up to Reno and then cut over into California and head for the Bay Area, hoping no doubt to swing by for a quick visit with Courtney on the way.

I shuddered, recalling the guns and the kind of men who dealt them when I lived in Feather Falls.

After Courtney had left, Travis and I walked downstairs and out to the roach-coach. It was my first day back following my leave of absence and I was feeling painfully awkward as I avoided eye contact with everyone.

Travis paid for both of our coffees over my objections, saying, "You owe me now. Let's talk." Reluctantly, I trailed him back to his office where he promptly closed the door without a second thought to office gossip.

His office was as sterile as ever, except for his warm masculine scent that shadows him wherever he goes. Travis, who never missed a thing, studied me a moment and then continued to speculate about Courtney.

"She got to you, huh? You seem... disturbed by this case." I pulled the guest chair off to one side of his desk, and he rolled his over, close to mine. Reaching out, he asked, "Memories?"

"Yeah," I confessed. "My ex had a thing for guns." It was tempting to talk with Travis about Logan.

"Tell me about it." Travis prodded.

I needed to trust somebody.

"I don't know," I hesitated. "As a friend or a cop?"

"I think we're more than friends, babe," he said with a grin. "Don't you trust me?"

Blushing, I was surprised to feel more than embarrassed. I still felt guilty. Even ashamed.

Before I could turn away, he laughed lightly. "Sunny, are you blushing?"

My face heated like a blowtorch as he caught my arm. "Come on! Babe. It's all good. It's no big deal. What's wrong?"

No big deal? No big *deal!* I almost had sex with him and he thinks it's *no big deal?*

I sputtered, "Travis." *Okay, I'm off to a good start.* "I'm sorry." *Progress.* "I made a mistake." *Maybe.* "I'd like to forget what happened at the house." *Never.* I squared my shoulders and looked up in time to catch a glint of gold flashing through the green of is eyes.

He gave a slow tight smile, his brows tightened. "Okay," he said slowly. He gave a little shrug. "You can forget if you want, but I'm not likely to. However... I respect your wishes and even apologize for my... unchivalrous behavior. Boy Scout's honor," he added crossing his heart.

His answer rang as hollow as the beat of a wooden drum.

He's making fun of me. The thought hurt.

"Seriously," he said, "we're friends. I don't want to lose that."

Hope renewed, I smiled as we toasted the truce with cups of coffee.

"So where did you and Paige go when Jack sent you guys to the Bay Area?"

Travis froze for a nanosecond, then thawed and exploded into laughter. "Are you jealous?" he laughed. "You had me going about *just wanting to be friends.*" He laughed again, wiping a tear from his eye in hilarity.

I huffed. "Knock it off, Travis. I said *friends* and I meant *friends.*"

The now-composed Travis repented. "I'm sorry to hear that." His forehead wrinkled in thought. "So, let's talk some more about guns."

Carrying around the burden of my past, the mess that was my present, and the fears I imagined for my future was exhausting. I was tired, and something was encouraging in the way he patiently waited. I desperately wanted to trust Travis, and ultimately, it wasn't our brief moment of lust, but his willingness to set lust aside that helped me take a tentative step.

I took a deep breath and told him briefly about Logan and the other bikers who had buried money and stashed crates of guns in the bathhouse.

Travis's eyes burned with interest. "Are they still there?" followed by a rapid-fire line of questions and digging for details: Who? What? Where? When? Why and How? Travis would have made an excellent journalist.

Once a cop, always a cop, I thought sadly. "I don't know. It was a long time ago." Being in command of my own inner-galactic starship, I raised my deflector shield and radically changed course.

"Travis," I said, dropping my gaze and softening my tone, "I only have a few more minutes, and I have a weird guy-question I'd like to ask you. It's about Silicone Woman."

"Fire away," he said, his eyes fairly danced with amusement.

"Well, to tell you the truth, I was disappointed when I saw her. She didn't exactly live up to the label."

"And?"

"And... well, what is it that guys see in women like her... and Paige," I added.

Travis didn't hesitate." Paige is *hot* and Courtney is *easy*. Uh, let me rephrase that. Courtney is *easy,* and Paige is *hot and easy,*" he added in jest.

I studied my cup. "Is that what it takes to get a guy?" I looked up for an answer and to see a shadow of sadness fall across Travis's handsome face.

"Usually," he said. "Men are pretty easy, too," it was his turn to stare thoughtfully into his drink, "but it takes more than sex to keep one."

Travis shook off his mood and returned to the subject of guns, pressing me again until I became upset.

"You said I could talk to you as a friend, not a cop, remember? Men are all alike." I rose and huffed my way out. I escaped the interrogation but not the terrible memories the day had resurrected.

80 🕊 03

Logan and the boys laid low for over a week before they decided to take action. Logan was super-saturated with adrenalin, spending his evenings smoking crack cocaine before heading to bed to torment me for the orgasm that the drug kept him from achieving.

"What's wrong with you? Get with it Sunny!" he roared.

I imagined my face burning in the dark knowing that every man in the house was lying downstairs listening to Logan thrashing and raging.

"Logan, stop. You're hurting me!" I pleaded in a desperate whisper.

"You think that hurts? We'll try this..." Each night the rape started and sex finally completed. But that wasn't all that began that week. Deep inside my womb, a tiny seed was planted. Sown in pain and watered with tears, a child, sweet and innocent was conceived.

Then they were gone, back to Oakland. A few days later Logan returned with two men that I recognized even without their colors, as the Mongol and Bandido riders that had ridden back from Laughlin bringing the news that my dad had been killed.

Driving a pickup truck with a camper shell, they stayed long enough to bury a metal ammo box full of money in the woods and haul about a dozen oblong crates into the bathhouse. Later, Logan would get his MC brothers to help move the guns down into the bomb shelter.

"Where did you get all those? What are they?" I asked, curious but frightened by the men and their sense of urgency.

"That's money, honey. M-16s. Fully automatic assault rifles, each one capable of firing 750-900 rounds per minute," Logan answered with arrogant pride. "Now shut up and take this." He left me with some cash and an ominous warning. "I wasn't here, Sunspot, and don't ever forget it!" Then he kissed me and left.

80 🕊 03

Gayle had been a guest when Chance and I married. When she invited me to lunch, I couldn't say "Yes" fast enough. I was tired of Paige's catty looks and avoiding the halted conversations between secretaries whenever I walked into a room. I was also avoiding a disappointed Travis, telling him over the phone that I was meeting Gayle for lunch.

We met at Checkers, a little nearby restaurant run by high-school students learning the hands-on trade in a program called Careers in Food Service. We made small talk as plates of chicken parmesan and pasta arrived with garden salads and breadsticks on the side.

I couldn't wait any longer, so I blurted out, "What's everyone saying about me, Gayle? It's killing me. I'm probably on next month's cover of

People magazine."

She laughed lightly, reminding me of my mother's laughter and the sound of delicate wind chimes. "It doesn't matter, Sunny. They're just a shark pool looking for the next victim." She smiled sweetly and tenderly touched my arm before continuing on a more serious note. "I know you're going through a tough time. I just want you to know I'm your friend. If you ever need someone to talk to, I'll be happy to listen. You know, Rex and I love both of you."

I choked up. Real friends were rare these days. I told her about Chance's affair with Paige and that he had moved out. I told her that I still loved Chance and missed him, but I simply couldn't forgive him. We finished our meal and Gayle listened, giving me support without criticism.

"Call me if you need anything, and don't worry about the secretaries." She smiled confidently. "They'll find someone new to talk about soon. They always do."

℠ ❦ ℛ

I spent the afternoon working on Courtney's temporary restraining order. The paper wouldn't stop her boyfriend, but it gave the police authority to arrest him without a warrant if he came within two hundred yards of her.

It turned out that she never needed the TRO. Travis had an almost supernatural way of cutting through red tape. He told me the next day that he had Reilly picked by the Feds outside of Las Vegas.

And Silicone Woman? She hit the road in her baby-blue to avoid being subpoenaed to testify at Reilly's hearing.

I admit that a huge part of me envied her ability to keep her identity, and just drive away from her problems without looking back.

Chapter 16

ಖ 🕊 ಛ

Logan was a dangerously handsome man when he smiled. There were good times. In fact, there were some great times. When Logan was happy, everyone was happy, and life was good. I especially loved the times he when he would come home, pick me up and swing me around in circle calling me his "Sunny Girl." This affectionate display reminded me of my dad and happier times. And in a strange way, I felt a familiar sense of safety when he was around. Men feared Logan, even as they had feared my father. But Logan was not Lefty.

"I did it, Sunny Girl! Wahoo!" he sang out, radiating joy as he dismounted and lifted me in his arms, kissing me.

About seven mounted riders pulled up behind him and slid into a precision line, looking like a row of Storm Troopers standing first at attention, then at ease. There was a festive charge in the air. Everyone was happy and looking at me expectantly.

"You told them?" I asked excitedly. I had told Logan the previous weekend that we were going to have a baby. I knew he was shocked and upset at first, but was confident that given a little time, he would love the idea. I knew we would be happy; he would settle down, maybe live full time at the cabin and be a great dad.

"They already know. That's why we're here!" Logan said with a squeeze and another kiss. "Guess what?"

I was confused. "I give up," I answered with a shrug of my shoulders.

He pointed with pride to yet another tattoo—fresh and painfully new— located just below the twin lightning bolts were the words *Filthy Few*. Those words are reserved for killers.

"We blew up the Mongols' Club House!" he rejoiced. "I told you I would get the guys that killed Lefty." And he kissed me again. "I did it all for you, babe. God, I love you!" he exclaimed passionately, then turned to the other riders with a war-whoop shouting, "*Par-ty!*"

ಖ 🕊 ಛ

The light blinked like a beacon of hope on my message machine. "You have two new messages," the automated voice told me.

"Sunny, this is Chance..."

I skipped over that one with a drawn-out sigh. It was too early in the evening to put myself through an emotional wringer. Let the answering machine blink. Next, I returned Ashley's call.

"Guess where Shane is?" It was Ashley on the girlfriend-grapevine.

"Duh... at work?"

She made frustrated noises, and I smiled. She is an easy tease.

"He's helping Chance move from Mac's place back to his old house. The rental."

Now, this was news. The "rental" is located about fifteen minutes' walking time, five minutes' driving time and just a couple of beats as the crow flies from what is now "my" home.

"What happened to the renters?" I asked.

"Pastor Mac paid their first month's rent to move downtown so they could be closer to her elderly parents. I guess they aren't doing too good. But Sunny—I hope you don't mind my asking—I've been wondering. How come you guys bought a new house instead of moving into the one Chance inherited or the cabin where you grew up?"

I was silent for a moment. Ashley's question was a weighty one.

Chance was moving into the "rental," which was the same house he had grown up in and been living when his mother moved back to the city. It was his home when the terrible accident took the life of his father's best friend. It was where his dad had died while he was in the Army. And later, it had been the house that he and Megan Shaughnessy—make that Megan McLane—had shared during their short marriage. I once asked Chance the same question; *why we don't we live there?*

I had my own history and unspoken reasons for not wanting us to make our home up at the cabin.

So I repeated Chance's simple answer for Ashley. "Too many ghosts."

₨ 𝔗 •℞

I took my time changing out of my work clothes, pausing to do an in-depth, critical self-evaluation. I studied the stranger in the mirror and I hated her. I always look at my clothes, check my hair, and inspect my face for blemishes—but rarely look at my body or peer *into* my eyes at the risk of seeing my naked soul.

I wonder when those white hairs happened? Old lady squint lines had formed in the corners of my eyes since the last time I looked. And I didn't need to step on the scale to know that I've kept the five pounds I gained over last winter's food fest.

I suddenly felt old, considering I was still relatively young, and could only guess at how I must look to Chance. Somewhere along the way, I must have become undesirable and uninteresting when I wasn't paying attention.

Feeling wretched and aching with loneliness, I poured a glass of wine and sat down at my desk and began the depressing task of filling out divorce papers.

ഔ ᯤ ଔ

"When are you gonna stop wearing those stupid clothes and start lookin' like a *real* woman?" Logan drawled with contempt.

That phrase would haunt me for years and became a pet insult of Logan's all because I fired back, "What's that supposed to mean? *A real woman?* What am I, huh? What?" My fury fueled Logan's delight.

I glanced down at the tie-dyed t-shirt Starla had made me under girlie overalls that were trimmed with the lace and embroidery so popular with girls my age.

"And you oughta cut your hair. You look like a freakin' hillbilly." This, coming from a man who always needed a haircut, a shower, and a shave.

Love turned to hate. I learned to keep my mouth shut after the beating Lefty had given him and his resulting stay in the hospital. Logan was drunk and giving me "the look" that always preceded trouble. I wished with all my heart that my dad had finished the job and killed Logan before Logan killed me.

"A fat freakin' hillbilly." Logan doubled over as if he had cracked the funniest joke in the world. But the *fat* in this case, was our baby in my eighth month of pregnancy.

"Lose it," was all Logan had to say when I'd told him I was pregnant. I was two months along at the time. "We got enough problems without adding a rat. I'll drive you to the clinic in Chico tomorrow. Hey, don't worry girl, we got money to pay for it."

That night I ran down the dirt road to Joyce and Kenny's for comfort and guidance. Joyce had given birth to nine children in her life, five of whom rested deep in the woods in the tiny Feather Falls cemetery, almost hidden under the dense foliage of tangled morning glories that always threaten to overtake the graves. Three of her children died before age three, one died of meningitis when she was seven, and her son, drunk at age fifteen, had slipped while hiking with friends above Feather Falls and plummeted some 640 feet from the brink of the falls to his death. Yes, Joyce knew about losing children.

"When you abort a baby," she told me, lovingly holding my hand in her sturdy wrinkled brown one, "you do much more take a life. You also destroy God's plan for that child." Joyce was wise. "You might be killing the person who would have found a cure for cancer. Every child has a destiny."

"If women don't want their kids, they should give birth and then abort themselves," Kenny blurted from his recliner. "They had their shot at life. If death is good enough for the baby, it should be good enough for them."

While Kenny's observation was both shocking and politically incorrect, it wasn't without merit.

I stayed at Joyce and Kenny's house for the night and hoped Logan would be sober by the next morning. He was. But he didn't change his mind.

"I'm not going and you can't make me! It's a *baby*, Logan. It's *our* baby." I stood my ground and refused to go to the abortion clinic, although Logan would eventually get what he wanted. He always did.

Months passed and his visits home grew few and far between. We continued to fight and the abortion issue escalated when Logan pressed me to have a late-term abortion. That night, I told him I would die first, and then, I almost did. I woke up the next morning to discover that Logan had cut off my hair while I slept. I stood staring in shock and horror at almost two feet of braid lying on my pillow like a dead thing. The little cabin echoed with my screams until Logan walked upstairs, punched me in the stomach, and pushed me off the balcony.

ဆၣ ϓ ౧

I kicked back on the overstuffed Lazy Boy with a bowl of Cheerios topped with a freshly sliced peach. Kissme wasn't big on peaches but stood guard in case an O missed the mark. Stroking her head, I glanced at her "diamond" studded black velvet collar. I knew she wasn't perfect enough by American Kennel Club standards to compete in dog shows. Her jaw is slightly undershot and she has a funny little kink in her tail that can't be seen, but a judge would feel. In spite of her flaws, she will always be Best of Show and Grand Champion of my heart.

Distracting her with a milky O, I reached over her silky head and hit the play button on the message machine.

"Sunny, this is Chance. *Please* don't delete this without listening."

Now there was a thought! Responding to a power surge, I deleted the message without listening. "There." Kissme cocked her head and whined. "Not you," I said, kissing her on top of the head. "You are all I need."

ဆၣ ϓ ౧

Years would pass before I would return to the cabin where my baby died. When Logan left the hospital, I rolled over and threw the single rose he had given me into the trash can next to my bed.

My milk came in that night; bitterly reminding me of the child I would never hold in my arms, or nurse at my breast. Hope died along with my baby. I had dreamed of innocence and love. It had to be a dream because I hadn't seen either of those things in life. Maybe I had read too many children's books from the school library that were set in more innocent times... like *Little House on the Prairie, Swiss Family Robinson* and *Call of the Wild*. We rarely watched TV because of the limited power supply to the cabin and because Starla said it would brainwash me. We used a tired old generator that would chug through the dinner preparation while pumping water into a holding tank and then turn it off when we lit the kerosene lamps. I read a lot of books, and they fed the dream of having a "real" family in my young girl's heart.

I wanted to be normal. My dream family would gather to celebrate holidays and milestones, sharing our tears and triumphs. We would sing in church on Sundays and go on family picnics. There would be doting grandparents, children who would grow to become loving parents, and rambunctious grandchildren who would fill the house with laughter. Husbands were strong, honorable, and passionately romantic. Wives were beautiful, smart, and happy with their roles in life.

Talk about a dreamer! There was certainly nothing in my life to support such naive fantasy. But those dreams birthed a great determination to escape from Logan and break out of the prison that had been my home.

ॐ 𝔜 ൠ

"If I can't have you, no one can. You're mine, Sunny." But of course, I wasn't.

I was the child who had raised herself. The one who could build a fire, tend chickens, work in the garden and orchard, and shoot a gun by age ten. I got myself up and walked to school in the rain, snow, and blazing heat. I enjoyed hiking in the forest, doing my homework, and reading library books. My straight-A grades pleased my teachers, my father, Joyce, and Kenny, and mostly, me.

While my independence assured Lefty that I could take care of myself on one level, he was, nevertheless, a realist and a warrior.

"Hey, sweetheart, Daddy got you something." My ten-year-old eyes glistened expectantly. Every gift from my father was a treasure. Lefty didn't give gifts lightly. "It's not a toy," he admonished, as he produced a small .22 caliber pistol for my very own. "Let's take it outside."

I followed him dutifully and we spent a warm, happy day together in the orchard, laughing as we shot at beer cans and fresh eggs from the chicken coop. I was a pretty good shot at the end of the day, filled with happiness and basking in my father's praise. Then Lefty grew quiet and serious, falling into one of the moods he had brought back from the war.

"Over there," he said, pointing to the numerous birds that raided our cherry tree this time of the year. "Aim steady, Sunny. I want you to shoot a bird."

"No, Daddy. I don't want to. I like birds."

"That's why I need you to shoot one," he said solemnly. "Do what I say. I want you to shoot a bird."

Animals were my friends. Besides Frito and the chickens, the wildlife; birds, deer, mountain monkeys (that's what my Dad calls squirrels), and raccoons were my friends. Eyes moist, hands trembling, I tried and missed, sending birds exploding from the tree like a flock of startled quail from under berry bushes.

"Try again. Steady, girl. I want you to focus. Pretend they are beer cans in a tree. Keep your eyes open and squeeze. Don't jerk on the trigger."

It wasn't long before a beautiful robin that had moments before been full of life, song, and cherries, lay bleeding and flopping beneath the tree.

"Pick it up, Sunny."

Tears ran down my face like twin leaky faucets as the lovely creature twitched and died in my hands.

"Now bury it."

I did. And when I was through tamping down the dirt, I looked up at my father to see what I should do next.

Lefty reached down and planting a lingering, loving kiss on my grubby, tear-streaked face said, "I know that was hard for you. But you needed to learn two things. One is that using a gun has consequences. Things can die when you shoot them. Two is that you know you can take a life if you ever need to, and it's okay. This gun is a tool. Never use it lightly and never shoot just one bullet. If you ever have to pull the trigger, don't stop until it's empty. It's okay to practice but I want you to keep the gun clean, keep it full, and never put the safety on. And baby, never tell anyone you have it."

℘ 🕊 ℭ

I never shot Logan, although I thought about it. I did as my father told me and kept the .22 both loaded and secret. As much as I grew to hate and fear Logan, I didn't want his blood, like the robin's, on my hands.

Looking back, I would call what happened next *divine intervention*. After my baby died, Joyce and Kenny picked me up from the hospital and took me to their daughter's house on the outskirts of Oroville. I spent an uncomfortable month there healing from the "miscarriage" among strangers who lived in a residential housing tract. It was always noisy. Joyce's daughter, Jerusha was kind, as were her husband and four children. The TV was always on in the front room and a riot of noise spilled out from the kids' rooms. I thought of them as kids, although the oldest wasn't much younger than I.

The neighbors had a band that met in Jerusha's garage several times a week and the jam sessions would rattle the windows until my head hurt. At night I listened to the wail of an occasional ambulance or police car out on the highway instead of coyotes hunting in the woods. In my heart, I longed to go home.

It was Joyce who brought the news, along with Frito. Kenny had seen two sheriff's cars turning down the driveway to the cabin and followed them. He watched quietly over hateful glares from Logan as he was cuffed and taken into custody, along with a large quantity of methamphetamine and some lab equipment he had stored in the bathhouse. Fortune, God, or both had smiled on me. Logan had purchased the equipment from an undercover agent. I was going to be free for a long time—but not forever.

With Joyce and Kenny's encouragement, I left the cabin behind and moved to an apartment in Oroville. I got a job at a local car wash during the day and an after-hour job in the evenings sweeping up hair and doing laundry for a salon. It wasn't much, but eventually I saved enough money to buy a used er reef

beat-up motorcycle; a 1985 Harley Wide Glide.

Cheap rent, cheap gas, an application for a PELL Grant at the college, and I was on my way. Logan had always called me stupid, leading me to believe I wasn't smart enough to get into college. But there I was, staring at my first-ever parking ticket on my first day of school, issued by Butte College Campus Police. Late as ever, I had raced from my apartment in Oroville to the beautiful sprawling college nestled in the soft, rolling foothills and pulled into the last remaining parking spot—in front of a fire hydrant.

I figured I was as good as dead whenever Logan finally got out of prison, whether I returned to the cabin or started school. It didn't matter anymore; dead or alive. That was the state of mind necessary for me to make my break for freedom. I was willing to risk everything, knowing at least I would die free.

଼ ⁂ ଼

"What does the term 'domestic violence' mean to you?" The district attorney leaned back in his plush leather seat behind a rosewood desk, hands folded across his chest and his eyes assessing my every move and word.

I swallowed hard, racking my brain. I wanted to say whatever he wanted to hear. This internship meant everything to me. "Umm..." *Good start, Sunny,* "ah... it means a physical assault by one spouse or intimate partner upon another... resulting in an injury?" When being interviewed for a job, one should *always* sound confident, even when you aren't. I could tell the DA wasn't impressed by the implied question mark in my response. That was a mistake I would never repeat.

He studied me, and I silently hoped he was focusing on my potential rather than my shortcomings.

"We're starting a new internship position here with a focus on domestic violence. You can have it if you'd like. You would be answering directly to me. Are you interested?"

My brain was screaming, "Yes! Yes!" and I had to restrain myself from giving him a high-five and doing a Happy Dance on top of his desk. I kept my poker face and began an award-winning career that included the DA spending a small fortune on my training—back in the days when California had money.

Two years later my job evolved into a paid position when I wrote the grant that funded the first Special Victims Unit in California. I would be an

Advocate and my clientele would be victims of domestic violence and sexual assault.

We were called the "Vertical Prosecution Team," which meant that all three team members would take our cases from beginning to end instead of the usual passing them off to other attorneys for various court proceedings. SVU consisted of Deputy DA Amanda Cross, Investigator Davis Martin, and me—the Advocate.

Later my job would expand to include my role as Expert Witness for the State on felony DV cases, Davis would be transferred to the Child Abduction Unit, and Travis, the man of mystery, would appear from out of nowhere to replace him. Travis, a man from all appearances without a past or present, and never talks about the future.

"How can you stand your job?" curious people would ask. My answer is always the same: "I love my job." But as I recovered from the motorcycle accident over those first weeks on the job—in fact *on the very day* that marked the sixth anniversary of my moving out of the cabin—the nightmare returned.

CHAPTER 17

ဆ ✣ ႘

My past caught up with me the morning I found myself grabbing my lunch and keys, headed for the county car—*my* county car. For a short time I had relied on public transportation, stumping my way to the corner bus. Then came the full-time use of a brand new county car.

Pausing to kiss Frito on his little apple forehead, I opened the apartment door, a cheap, dented metal door that usually sticks. It popped open with a whoosh and I stepped out and down onto some ghastly—*something* that crackled, snapped, and crushed like a bag of bones. Hurling myself backward, I grabbed for the doorjamb, missed and landed on my butt with a cry loud enough to wake my neighbor. I sat there with my feet pointing at a dead thing. Frito yapped hysterically as the neighbor rushed over and helped pull me back up. Hot adrenalin surged through my racing heart.

"Okay. Not to worry. I'm alright," I said to calm both the neighbor and my dog. At my feet lay a dozen very dry, very dead, blood red roses wrapped in a shroud of black tissue paper and neatly tied with black wire ribbon. Nothing more.

Time warped, slowing and stretching until I had no idea how long I stood looking at the corpse-bouquet in my hands. The world faded to shades of gray. The neighbor advised me to find a new boyfriend and returned home. I knew Logan had found me. Worse still, I knew his intentions. The message was clear.

The hall was quiet, but the sound of banging rose up from below. I peered over the guardrail to see our maintenance man, Jorje Gonzales dumping trash into a bin at the edge of the parking lot.

"Hey, Jorje! Jorje! Hey... *Buenos dias!*"

Jorje smiled, his gold fillings flashing in the morning sun as he waved.

"*Buenos dias.* Hola, Soleda!"

"Did you see anyone on a motorcycle this morning?" He frowned, confused, so I tried Mexican, which is a homogenized blend of Spanish-

English phonetics. *"Mo-to-ci-cle-ta?"* Okay, so I'm not bilingual. But you can't live in California without picking up the important stuff, plus a few extras that aren't on the menu.

"No, gracias. Adios."

Gosh, doesn't this guy speak Spanish? Frustrated and scared, I double-checked the locks on the door before leaving.

Frito felt extra good when I hugged him after work. He has been my constant companion for most of my life and an endless supply of unconditional love. Frito lost his right eye in a fight with a cat as a puppy. I think that's why Lefty brought him home. Lefty understood losing body parts. Now Frito has a cataract on his good eye, he's deaf, and incontinent. Much to his disgust, I tie a maxi pad around his waist at night to prevent flying-out-of-bed with wet feet and trying to get back to sleep on a cold couch. Frito was my buddy through thick and thin.

"Quit faking... you are *not* dying!"

Frito dragged himself across the kitchen floor doing his dying dog act as I heated leftover chili beans for dinner. He rolled onto his back and stuck his legs stick straight into the air, looking like three-day-old road kill.

"Yeah right, Frito. That's how I feel after breathing your dog farts all night. No more chili for you." Defeated, he rolled over and headed for his bowl of crunchies.

Ring!

"Must be a call-out," I informed my little beggar as I picked up the phone.

"Hello, this is Sunny. Hello?" Heavy breathing. "Hello?" Silence.

Click!

ॐ ℘ ॐ

Every day I come in contact with dangerous men. Bust a major drug dealer, and he will usually take his punishment "like a man." No surprise there. Men know there are consequences if caught committing a crime. But influence the outcome of a custody order that keeps Stupid away from *his* wife and *his* kids, and it becomes personal. I run the risk of being run over by a ticked-off wife-beater every time I cross the parking lot between the courthouse and my office. These men are very dangerous, but they are not in the same league with Logan.

Logan is a killer. He wore the club TCB patch like a medal of honor and confessed to killing people over business. He also bragged his Filthy Few tattoo after blowing up the Mongols' clubhouse in retaliation for Lefty's murder. I knew the bombing had started a gang war that led to more deaths. I concluded that Logan must believe that I know too much.

ॐ ℘ ॐ

Allegra Pesci had a sad but steady look behind moist eyes. She was a dark, classic Italian beauty in her mid-thirties with full lips, thick chestnut hair hanging over her shoulders and large liquid brown eyes. She wore a print cotton dress and a matching pair of strappy Esmeraldas. Her voice never wavered, although she swallowed hard and spoke through dry, trembling lips and gripped the armrest on the office sofa when she announced, "He murdered John Taylor."

I read the signs of fear and nervousness but believed she was telling the truth.

"I hear you, Allegra. We both know that Vincent is on the run. He's made phone calls from..." I scanned the activity sheet inside of her file, "six states now. We've alerted law enforcement and we are going to catch him." I spoke with confidence that belied an underlying uncertainty.

Allegra chose tea over coffee and started to relax. Victims are seldom aware of the soft background music that permeates my office, but it helps to defuse the stress of asking them to relate and relive their worst memories. "So, tell me why you think Vincent killed John? John is still listed as a missing person."

Assessing victims for credibility is part of my work. There is truth in the old adage about eyes being windows to the soul, but there are other indicators as well. Body language, for example, speaks volumes. Allegra leaned into me without tipping the chair or fidgeting. No defensive posturing; crossing her arms or legs. Neither did she roll her eyes or stare at the ceiling when answering difficult questions. She was open and her gaze straightforward, just like her answers.

"Vincent thought John and I were having an affair. I'm sure of it. But we weren't. Anyhow, John was just helpful. You know; he jump-started my car once and helped me pick up and unload a new refrigerator. Man stuff." Allegra choked up with gratitude as she recalled the kindness of her forty-something-year-old neighbor. John's country home was visible from the far corner of her small orchard. Walking distance, for sure. "So I'd take him some cookies or some cherries from the orchard. Little things. I know Vinny killed him," she said, clenching her fist. "Vincent always thought I was cheating on him. He's a control freak. It's the Italian in him."

There may have been a degree of truth to her "Italian" comment. No race is more violent than another, but some cultures are more tolerant of domestic violence, and still other cultures treat their wives with less consideration than their livestock.

Vincent Pesci had jumped bail after throwing Allegra through their sliding glass door. She had not been sliced and diced, so the court reasoned that Vincent, being a homeowner and having held a job for almost six years at Discount Plywood, was not likely to go anywhere. They issued a Stay Away Order and a warned him that he would be arrested if he tried to contact Allegra in any way. Vincent was also ordered to surrender his guns to his father who lived in Marysville. Somehow the guns never made it to his dad's house and now Vinny was on the run with his weapons.

The UPS man discovered John Taylor's body some two weeks later. Taylor had been shot but the bullet casing was missing, and the living room, where the crime was committed, had been sanitized. This case was going to be a tough one.

"Let me get Travis, our investigator, before we go any further," I told her.

Like most women, Allegra smiled at the mention of Travis's name. Travis had done the follow-up investigation on the domestic violence when the case first came up from the sheriff's office. Neither of us had been happy about Vincent making bail, but his father was a prominent businessman in Yuba County and more than able to put up a cash bond. Sadly, I suspected he might also have put up flight money for his wayward son. For all anyone knew, Vincent could be on his way to Sicily—or on his way to Allegra.

⊗ 🕊 ℣

There are several indicators to look for when doing a lethality assessment. The evaluation is a flow chart without any guarantees the perpetrator will go with the flow. He could skip some of the steps and head straight to murder. While I teach about lethality all the time as an Advocate, it didn't hurt to do a review for my own protection. I pulled out two of the *Stalking* brochures I had written for the district attorney office, one for Allegra and one for me. Flipping to the back page, I considered each question:

1. *Has your partner threatened to kill himself, you, the children, or family members?*
   Sigh. "I wish he'd kill himself," I thought aloud, before answering the question. "Yes." He killed my father and our baby. And he's almost killed me.

2. *Has he told you his plans for carrying out his intention? How he will kill you, where he will hide the body, or what he will tell the police?*
   Okay, I knew the answer to this one. I had a client whose husband was a farmer with a plan to plow her body into the rice fields. Then there was a man who taught his little boy to point the remote control at Mommy and say "Bang! Bang!" Several months later, the father replaced the remote control with a loaded gun. Logan had threatened me with several variations of hiding my body in the woods and sinking it in a lake. He had yet to update me on his newest plan since the finding dead flowers.

3. *Does he have a weapon or the means to carry out the threat?*
   A hard chuckle escaped. Logan had guns, knives, bombs, drugs, two hands, and teeth. I guess that's another big "Yes."

4. *Has he committed prior acts of violence?*
    Let me see... numerous beatings, spousal rape, and at least three murders. Yup!

5. *Is he depressed?*
    I rubbed my forehead knowing that he dwells in the "black hole" whenever he is not riding the up-side of his bipolar roller coaster.

6. *Is he using drugs or alcohol?*
    Do bears poop in the woods? Yes to both. Heavily.

7. *Is he prone to rage?*
    Is he ever any other way?

8. *Has he killed an animal or pet?*
    My heart clenched in fear for Frito. He is my best friend.

9. *Have you left the relationship or threatened to leave?*
    Ouch! This is so not-good.

10. *Are you being stalked?*
    Long sigh... I am so dead!

CHAPTER 18

ॐ 𓅃 ॐ

Some stains are almost impossible to remove: spaghetti sauce on your white shirt, dog pile jammed in the crevice of your shoe, cigarette stink from a smoker's home, and a stalker from your life.

After circling the apartment complex twice, I parked and headed upstairs feeling depressed and worried about which kind of weapon to buy. A Taser? Mace? An Uzi? Maybe one of Logan's surface-to-air-missiles he probably has squirreled away somewhere at the cabin. Not that I ever advise my victims to buy a gun. Typically, I suggest a small, indoor dog that isn't familiar with the abuser's scent, a large can of pepper spray available at most sporting goods stores, and a video device can be useful for recording drive-bys—as long as you're not standing in the road with your stalker is behind the wheel. I remind them of the utmost importance of saving "gift" items and recorded phone messages as evidence for court.

Like most of my victims, I made the wrong choice to trash the dead flowers, acting on emotion instead of good sense. Too bad Frito knew Logan's scent. Logan made no drive-bys, and his phone messages were always hang-ups. I was pretty sure I could shoot Logan with the gun Lefty had given me. I just needed to get up the nerve to return to the cabin to get it. But going back for the gun seemed riskier than living without it.

ॐ 𓅃 ॐ

"Frito? Baby, I'm home. Frito!" I called, kicking off my shoes. "Frito? Hey, buddy, wake up! Frito? *Foooood!*" Silence.

Frito was either dead or gone. There was nobody in sight, so I searched the apartment. The familiar adrenaline rush returned in a burst of fear and fury before asking myself, *How does a dog vanish from a second story apartment?* The windows were still locked and the door had not been pried open. I headed for the manager's apartment, then stopped short at the sound of a lawn mower.

"Hola, Sunnee. Soleada." Jorje's golden smile gleamed. He was my favorite maintenance man and was looking up and waving. "Hey... I see your, uh... *su novio...* boyfriend. *El montar.* You know... *una motocicleta.*

He had seen Logan! "*Donde esta?* Where is he?"

Jorje paused to think. "*Él es ido...* he *adios...* bye-bye."

"What about Frito?"

Jorje shrugged. "*No sé.*"

"Follow me. *Rapido... ándale...* whatever! Come on." I motioned crazily.

Racing downstairs, heart flip-flopping in my chest, Jorje hot on my heels, we headed for the manager's office. On a good day, the discussion that ensued might have been delightfully entertaining. Today, as I listened to Mussarat Hardeep, the manager's wife, shouting and gesturing in her Punjabized English and Jorje responding in Spanish-English, I was not amused.

"My apartment. Did you give the key to my apartment to anyone today?" I asked her.

"What? Chiu needa key?" Mussarat's face furrowed with concern. Her husband was away and she didn't usually get involved with tenant issues.

Jorje started making motorcycle noises. "Rrrrummm, rummm. *Motocicleta.*" He volunteered.

"Big guy," I said, throwing my hands in the air to indicate *big*. "Biker. Did you give him my key?"

She smiled blandly. "Out, yes? Needa key, no?"

"Frito. Did someone take Frito?" Tears welled up in my eyes.

"*Perro.* Arf! Arf!" Jorje started to pant like a dog. "*Frito.*"

Mussarat's eyes shifted back and forth between us suspiciously.

"Thanks, Jorje. That was good."

Mussarat's face visibly brightened in comprehension. "Ohhh." She grinned. "To-day. No? Eh, nasi brudder. Yeah, yeah, leetle Free-to. Yes, gone. Dog-tor." (*Dog-tor? Doctor? Vet?*) Mussarat looked pleased. "Back, yes?"

"Back, no!" I started to cry.

"*Soleada...* Sunnee, Jorje help," he said, handing me a red grease rag caked with lawn clippings to blow my nose.

"I'm calling the police," I sobbed through the grass stuck to the snot on my face.

"Dun call da po-lice I tell you! No tanks!" Mussarat was waving her hands in the air.

"*Policia? No es necesario!*" Jorje took off at a lope. He'd probably misplaced his green card.

Gestures seemed to be our primary form of communication. "He's a killer," I yelled at the frightened woman, forming my fist into a gun and thrusting it in her face.

Mussarat exploded into a panic-stricken torrent of terrified Punjabi as she ran in circles, yelling "Po-lice" over, and over, and over.

After the police had left my apartment, I called every vet and animal shelter in Butte and Yuba counties. My little friend was gone. I reported that an unknown man had taken my dog from my apartment. I hadn't actually seen Logan, but they noted him as a person of interest in the report along with "No forced signs of entry," and a recommendation that I "get a good night's sleep" and see a doctor if my anxiety persisted. "Perhaps some Xanax," they offered.

ℰᴖ 𝒴 ℭℛ

"Why did I hear about this from dispatch instead of you?" Chance looked hurt and confused after hearing about the Frito incident at work. "This wasn't a break-in, and the police report suggests possible harassment, not stalking. It doesn't even mention the dead flowers. Sunny, Logan is *stalking* you which is a major crime. You know how dangerous he is. You have got to make another report, babe."

Chance's eyes were blue-hot and I thought could melt into them. I huffed and grunted as we moved the recliner I'd picked up at a yard sale upstairs. "It's the right thing to do," he said without breaking a sweat," and your options don't look good."

We had been dating for almost three months, ever since the motorcycle crash. Chance knew about Logan. Well, he was aware of *some* things about Logan. Other things were too painful to share, and I didn't know if I could trust Chance with the whole truth. Deep down, I saw myself as nickel, and Chance worth a million dollars. That is how much I valued him and how little I respected myself. After all, I had a history that included drugs, sex, gang rape at Sturgis, plus all the illegal activity in Feather Falls.

Then, there was the baby and the secret knowledge that I could not get pregnant. Maybe there would be a "right time" to tell him everything one day. I worried if Chance knew who I *really* was, he would not—could not—love me anymore.

Aren't I property of Hells Angels? I asked myself. *Can I ever be anything else?*

Chance reached over from the new chair with a reassuring touch. It was evening. Dinner was finished, the lights turned low, and a soft breeze drifted in through the open window carrying the sound of kids playing little league ball over at the park.

"If you won't report the stalking, you can at least talk with your DA.

"I know, Chance. You're right. It's just... well, I'm afraid of Logan."

An unwanted avalanche of painful memories slid through my mind. Logan's assaults, the black eyes, punches, hair-pulling, the rapes. The rapes were the worst. I shuddered, wondering again where Frito could be and started to cry.

Chance got up and sat next to me on the love seat. Although we were still getting to know each other, he made me feel safe when he wrapped his arms around me.

"I love you, Sunny. You're smart to be scared. That's not a bad thing. And you're not defenseless. You're a strong woman. In fact, you're the strongest woman I've ever known. I'll help you." He continued. I'll write the report myself. I'll have Logan picked up and charged with stalking and a dozen other offenses for the DA to bargain with. They'll send him back to prison for a long time. However you want to do this, I'll be there for you. And you know, I would die protecting you."

Chance's eyes deepened to midnight blue as he gazed into mine. I knew he wasn't joking. I knew he was capable of killing Logan, which brought its own set of worries.

Just because Chance dedicated his life to rescuing people didn't mean he wasn't a trained killer. Not only was he an officer in the sheriff's department, but the army had also fully equipped him to do what needed to be done. Chance wasn't afraid of Logan, but I was afraid for Chance.

"You can't always be with me, Chance. Promise me you'll let me handle this my way. Trust me."

I was afraid to tell him about the murders—afraid to file charges, too. Mostly I was afraid to testify. I only had favor with Oakland Hells Angels because I was Lefty's kid. Now Lefty was dead and Logan had moved up in rank. Logan had been promoted to Sergeant of Arms and it was his duty to carry out the dictates of his newest tattoo—*Taking Care of Business*—and I had no intention of becoming his next order of business.

Chance took me to Nice Shot gun range a few days later and presented me with a Darth Vader-looking 9mm Glock.

He placed it in my hands. "Kiss it," he said.

"I am not going to kiss a gun. That is the corniest thing I've ever heard. Why would I kiss a gun?"

"Because you're a woman," Chance said, stating the obvious. "A man can become friends with a gun just by holding it, but a woman needs to have a relationship with it. She needs to trust it. Trust me. Kiss the gun."

Lame or not, I kissed the stupid thing and, *wham*, he was right! My weapon instantly became my protector. I was no longer afraid to lock and load.

In my heart, I knew I was not the same person that I had been back in Feather Falls. It is true that I am afraid of Logan, and as Chance observed, that was smart. But Logan was not afraid of me, and that was not so smart.

80 🕊 �

It was just an old shoebox. Stained, crushed on one corner, mummified under layers of filthy duct tape. It sat in the driver's seat of my car, parked in the lot below the courthouse. It had baked all day in the blazing sun. I beeped the car open with the remote. The handle was hot enough to burn my fingers, yet the presence of the box pierced me with a chill so deep, I shivered. The box smelled of death.

My heart hammered erratically, and I morphed into a full-scale panic attack. I fought back the scream that clawed its way up from my throat and lay trapped like a wild thing behind clenched teeth. I slid in, timidly moving the box to the passenger seat while holding my breath. Still being relatively new on the job, the last thing I wanted was to attract negative attention with a scream.

Run! It's what I do best. *Run!* Don't look back. *Run! Run!* "I can't. I can't. No. Oh God, I don't want to do this! I can't," I told myself.

Drive! Okay, I was pretty sure I could drive. *He's watching me.* My instincts rocketed to code red. I could feel his eyes boring into the back of my head. The smell! *Sweet Jesus, save me from the smell.* I turned the key and slid the moonroof open. I kept the tinted windows up and eyes straight ahead to avoid eye contact with anyone. Driving out of the lot, I looped down to the sheriff's office and parked, hoping to throw Logan off my trail.

Ten minutes later found me merging into the five-o'clock employee migration heading north on Highway 70. I kept my eyes on the rearview mirror and cracked the window, partly to let out the smell and partly to listen for the sound of Logan's motorcycle. Away from my apartment, up the canyon and then turned sharply towards Cherokee and the sheer cliffs of Table Mountain. Pulling off the road and pausing at the intersection, I waited five minutes and five million heartbeats to see if I'd been followed, then continued to the top of the mountain. Terror, outrage, and dread churned deep in the pit of my stomach.

Dear God who controls all things, please don't add to the smell. Please don't let me vomit inside of my car.

Wheeling the car into a fenced parking area, I jumped out and lost it: lunch, tears, and all. I was alone.

After wiping my mouth and drying tears on my shirtsleeve, I took the shoebox and cradled it my arms like the precious treasure it was. Walked across the flat surface of the mountain, weaving through the tangles of yellow and purple wildflowers. Followed a fragile stream that wandered through the meadow, then gently tumbled downward until at last, it spilled over the sheer cliff in a glistening ribbon to the valley far below.

There, at the edge of the world, I clutched the box to my heart. "Frito," I cried. "My little dog. My dearest companion. When I was alone, abandoned by my parents, you comforted me. When I was afraid, you made me feel safe. *I am so sorry.*"

A little thing in the eyes of the world, he had meant everything to me. It is no small wonder that d-o-g is G-O-D spelled backward. His enduring love, unconditional forgiveness, and unbridled joy were such God-things. Frito never hurt anyone. He was just a little dog with a big heart. He was my friend, and I laid him to rest beneath an undercut in the bank, enclosing his tomb with rocks to keep out predators. I picked some wildflowers that grew nearby, placed them next to the entrance, and watered them with fresh tears.

I never opened the box. I couldn't bear it. But in my nightmares, in the dead of night, the box sometimes opens to the grotesque and macabre: Frito, half-mutilated, half-alive, whimpering in pain, trusting me to rescue him, or riddled with maggots wriggling through dismembered parts. Hideous. Horrible.

"My friend." I would wake sobbing, "You never let me down. I let you down. I couldn't save you. Please, please, forgive me."

ℬ 🕊 ℭ

Chance screeched down the road, leaving three feet of skid marks in front of my apartment. He jumped out with clenched fists and thunder on his brow. I had called him at work and told him about my dog. Now he wanted to avenge his fiancée, the love of his life.

"Babe, I don't want to wait any longer. Let's go to Reno. We can be married in just a few hours. I want to take you home and protect you," Chance said earnestly. "I can't stand around waiting until Logan does something to you. Please, Sunny. Make a report. And if you won't do that, then marry me, for God's sake. Marry me now." He swept me into his arms kissing every bit of resistance away. "Yes." I caught my breath. "Yes. I'll marry you."

Not exactly the romantic circumstances and proposal a girl dreams of, but it was sincere. I wanted him badly, but not because I needed his protection. I wanted Chance because the thought of marriage was both right and proper. I wanted this man for my husband, forever.

We didn't get married in Reno, but we did move the date up about six months, trading in "The Biggest Little City" in Nevada for the tranquility of nearby Lake Tahoe. Lying awake in the dark, I would wrestle with old demons. These were more than pre-wedding jitters. I needed to make a decision, and it was a tough one.

I *really* wanted my mother to attend the wedding. With all of my heart I wanted her there to see me beautiful, happy, and on the road to success. Isn't that what parents want for their child? Then again, I was afraid of what Chance might think. I was overwhelmed with what-ifs. What if Chance is disgusted or thinks I will end up like her? What if Starla gets drunk and tells Chance about Hells Angels business or the baby? What if she totally ruins my wedding?

ℬ 🕊 ℭ

I still had some time before the wedding. Unable to sleep, I decided to call Sheena, my mom's old biker friend. Maybe she would know where Starla was staying. I hadn't heard from my mother in years, but if anyone knew where she was, it would be Sheena.

"'What do ya' expect from the daughter of a crack whore?' His words,

Sweetie, not mine." Sheena apologized sympathetically as she made her way through Johnny's Bar so she could talk privately out on the sidewalk. The club was drinking it up at 1:00 a.m. at the ever-popular biker bar in Hollister listening to Logan rage about my mom and me.

"According to Logan—*if you can believe anything he says*—he heard Starla got arrested right here at Johnny's because she wouldn't stop dealing drugs on the job." Sheena laughed as if we shared an inside joke, then caught herself. "Ahem," she cleared her throat. "Sorry, Sunny. Your mama had a awful habit to support. She sent me a letter saying she has a parole hearing coming up soon and wants to stay with us when she gets out. Cheech about flipped out. Can you imagine those two under the same roof?"

My mother was in prison? My head spun until Sheena asked, "How you doin' girl?" We talked for a time, and I asked her to call me when my mother had a release date so I could meet her at the bus station. She said, "No problem," then promised not to tell anyone we had spoken.

Like so many of the hippy generation "in search of" themselves and the purpose for their lives, Starla had spiraled downhill from LSD and dancing in the park with flowers in her hair, to narcotics, cuffs on her wrists, and prison garb. Her other three kids, only one of whom I had ever met, had been taken from her early on by Child Protective Services in the Bay Area and placed in foster care. Starla only cared about herself, always putting her needs and desires above everyone else's.

ఈ 🕊 ల

In the end, no parents attended our wedding. Starla was still serving time in Chino Women's Correctional Facility located in Southern California. It turned out, as so frequently happens, that I ended up losing a lot of sleep worrying about something that was never more than fanciful imagination.

Chance's mother and new husband had been two of the people on the Bay Bridge that fateful day in 1989 when a 6.9 earthquake caused the upper level to collapse, killing sixty-two and injuring almost four-thousand others. The tragedy had significantly influenced Chance's decision to commit his life to search and rescue. And his father, Michael McLane, had committed suicide-by-alcohol, one day at a time—one drink at a time, after his wife left and friend, Dave had died.

As to absent siblings; Chance's little sister, Crystal, wasn't invited because Chance didn't want his ex-wife, Megan—who was shacking up with Crystal—to show up. As for me, I never had contact with my siblings who, like their fathers, had vanished off the family radar.

We invited a few close friends from work and our new neighbors, Shane and Ashley. Mark was Chance's best man and Ashley was my maid of honor. Captain Leo Sun gave a beautiful secular service aboard the *Tahoe Queen*.

I guess it's one thing to say that Jesus is Lord of your life, and another to live it. It takes practice to incorporate the spiritual into the physical on a daily basis. Like dieting or exercising, spiritual insight is a process, not an event. Jesus didn't even make the guest list at our wedding. We were so filled with each other that we never noticed his absence until it was too late.

Joyously honeymooning in a beautiful cabin nestled under an aspen grove with a magnificent view of the lake for five wonderful, fun-filled, romantic days, we jet-skied, rode horseback, hiked, and dined—when we weren't making up for six months of sexual restraint.

ℰℊ 🕊 ℭℛ

Chance was first to move into our new house, making the place ready for his bride. He laughed and I cried for joy as he swept me off my feet and carried me across the threshold into our new life together. I returned at last to the quiet tranquility of my beloved mountains. We walked out on the deck holding hands, and I spoke with a kind of reverent awe and wonder. "Oh Chance, it's a view of eternity." And it looked bright.

There was the Coastal Range, all dressed up in winter white, glistening across the vast valley like a bride on her wedding day. The scent of pine filled the air bringing brought back pleasant childhood memories, the quiet of the woods broken only by the occasional tap-tapping of a red-headed woodpecker, an occasional squawk of a blue jay, and the chatter of mountain monkeys.

Chance brought out soft pillows and cold champagne. We nestled together, waiting for our first sunset. Dusk brought the inevitable chorus of insects and the lonely echoing cry of the *who-who-me:* the Concow Indian name for night owls. Breathtaking beauty. Our lips met and we made slow, sensuous love that transported us through the cosmos and back again under a canopy of stars. I knew I was home.

The next morning Chance insisted on going back to my apartment alone for the last load of boxes saying, "I got this, babe."

"Hurry home," I blew him a kiss.

When he returned, Chance emerged all smiles—holding a swaddled infant tucked in a pink baby blanket. "Honey, it's a girl," he announced, handing me the bundle.

A little black nose poked out, followed by a tiny pink tongue. Kissme had arrived.

PART TWO

Chapter 19

"And there will be wars and rumors of wars... earthquakes and hurricanes... and these will be the beginning of sorrows." —Jesus of Nazareth

I woke up bleary-eyed having weird dreams from the Bible, inspired in part by a double-pepperoni pizza and staying up to watch a movie called *Armageddon.* Doomsday movies are my favorites: an asteroid heading for earth, flesh-eating virus devours New York, a mega-volcano unleashes in the heart of L.A.

I don't completely understand the attraction, but I have always had it. I guess it is my version of a thrill-ride; like the Kingda Ka roller coaster that goes straight up for 456 feet then drops down at 128 mph, or bungee jumping 708 feet off the Bloukrans Bridge in South Africa. There's nothing like experiencing cataclysmic danger from a recliner. The appeal does make sense in a way. After all, I was raised in the shadow of impending disaster, living in the "Safe-House" in Feather Falls.

Starla and Lefty were part of the great back-to-the-land movement of their generation. It wasn't just a feel-good migration motivated by a desire to commune with squirrels and eat organic food. It was also fueled by copious amounts of paranoia-inducing drugs and the resulting compulsion to escape the city and Big-Brother government that was *coming to take our guns* at a time when people felt they needed them most.

My parents had been taught to "duck and cover" in school. Scheduled air raid sirens would scream across the city on the first Monday each month, and the children were told they could survive a nuclear bomb by diving under their desks and putting their arms over their heads. Their teacher's would caution them not to *"look at the bright light"* or it would burn their eyes out.

Lefty's Uncle John had a real bomb shelter in his back yard. The neighborhood kids would play in it during the hot summer months because it was always so cool down there, in every sense of the word. When he was young, the bomb shelter served as a boys-only club, but when he got older,

Lefty started taking girls down there and telling his buds to get lost. Buying a cabin in the outback of Butte County's Sierra Nevada Mountains and putting in a bomb shelter was the one thing my parents agreed on.

After Vietnam, when Lefty got out of the hospital and earned his patch with Hells Angels, the cabin quickly became a refuge for members with arrest warrants or who were lying low after a major drug bust. I was too young to understand what was going on.

Years later, during one of her rages, Starla told me about Lefty and the Altamont shoot-out at the Rolling Stones concert. According to Starla, Lefty's participation had resulted in one person's murder and the accidental deaths of four other people. When I came to my father's defense, yelling *"My Daddy never killed anyone!"* she had replied with cold calculation, "Don't be stupid, Sunny! He was in the army. He killed lots of people. Probably even women and kids your age." She let that sink in, and when I started to cry, she added, "But he felt awful about those concert goers."

By contrast, Logan, who had also killed people, typically slept with his gun at night and would run out the back door into the woods whenever strangers arrived at the front gate.

It was Lefty, not Logan, who explained survival to me. Lefty always thought the world was coming to an end, unlike Logan, who thinks he is going to live forever.

ഇ 𝔙 ന

Harriet Johnson, a thirty-four-year-old short, exceedingly obese woman who required a power chair to move her bulk parked in front of my desk. She was shabbily dressed with tangled hair that hung to her shoulders. Harriet had broken blood vessels in one eye and emotional pain that glistened in the other.

I had read the police report first thing in the morning, hand delivered by Crazy Bob from the sheriff's office. This wasn't the usual method of delivery, but I was pretty sure Crazy liked me as a person and maybe even had a little crush on me. Maybe because I was one of the few, if not the only coworker who liked him at all. And I did like him. Crazy was a bit of an outcast, like me.

The report stated that California, AKA "Cal" Johnson, had been married to Harriet for almost four years, was about six-foot-two, and weighed in at 135 lbs. Cal liked to drink, and he liked to go on an occasional meth run.

Harriet loved to eat—lots. This is not an uncommon arrangement in Butte County and elsewhere: couples enabling each other in their own addictions. Cal paid the rent and married Harriet, getting her three beefy kids as part of the deal. Harriet spent his money on fast food and groceries. She bought cases of soda, prepared junk food, lots of beer and sometimes, cheap whiskey. In return, Cal got great sex, adoration, an okay housekeeper, and didn't feel like a loser without a family of his own. He commandeered the TV remote at night while she lived life vicariously through reality shows and soap operas during the day. Harriet kept the boys out of Cal's way, never complained about his drug and alcohol binges, and Cal never told her she was fat or undesirable.

That arrangement worked out just fine until she caught him bouncing between the sheets with her trim little sister. Harriet flipped out, screaming at the top of her lungs, and Cal had silenced her with a punch. The sister took off in tears and ran back to her boyfriend's house, demonstrating a classic pattern of codependency, frequently interwoven throughout the fabric of domestic violence.

Harriet was a person I would suggest try a Codependents Anonymous (CODA) class along with making appropriate referrals to Victim Witness and counseling through the SAFE Program. There are many wonderful counselors in the world, but figuratively speaking—just as I would not refer a person with hemorrhoids to a brain surgeon—I do not recommend family therapists for domestic violence. I prefer to send participants to specialists who are excellent at what they do.

ဢ 🕊 beta

I thought I was different from my clients and never considered that I might fit the "codependent" profile. At least, not until I told Ashley that I had an interesting CODA case.

"Have you ever thought about attending a codependence class? You should try it."

"Ashley!" My friend had deeply offended me—*again*—although we had made up with a trip to Java Juice and an *"Oh, you're so sweet. You didn't have done that!"* belated birthday present. "What would make you say such a thing?" I asked defensively.

I hate it when Ashley or anyone else tells me what I should do. The minute I hear *should*, my heels go down and walls go up. I referred women to codependent classes several times a week but was stunned to consider the possibility that I—*the one with all the answers*—might have issues of my own.

Ashley and I had launched our kayaks in the upper waters of the Feather River that morning and thrilled to an exhilarating ride through perilous foaming whitecaps as we thundered down the river to a point where the river slows, above Rock Creek Power House. Dragging the kayaks ashore, we tied them to some shrubs. Tired and hungry, we collapsed in the shade of Sandy Beach. Ashley dug out her lunch contribution of falafel and cucumber pita pockets with yogurt sauce, and I added jalapeño-lime potato chips and Oreo cookies.

I lay back and focused on the spillway, quietly remembering the motorcycle accident that had taken place upriver, my near-death in a watery grave and Chance coming to my rescue.

Ashley shrugged her shoulders as she opened the bag of cookies. "I went to CODA meetings for about a year after Shane and I were married."

Wide-eyed, I slow-mo blinked my disbelief. "You? You're both Christians. Why would you need counseling?"

"Shane's biker roots. Not gang related, but he was pretty controlling the first year we were together. I found myself saying 'yes' to things he wanted to do when my heart said 'no.' He would want to go places or do things that I didn't feel good about. I blame myself, not him, and figured a little therapy couldn't hurt. So I checked it out."

"And?" I was aghast. Their marriage seemed so sweet.

Ashley laughed, tossing her hair back, gray eyes dancing. "Shane thought it was wonderful. He said he liked an independent woman who could think for herself. We just got... better." Ashley went back for thirds on the Oreos. "I've got a book I'll loan you."

I groaned silently before conceding. Ashley had only heard the vanilla version of my childhood. I had never dished out the bitter truth.

"Just read the first chapter," she said. "If you don't like it, give it back."

୨୦ ✝ ୦ଓ

Jimmy Hendrix once wrote a song called "Purple Haze." And while he was almost certainly singing about the colors dancing through his drug-drenched mind, there is a real purple haze that adorns the mountains at twilight in the latter part of summer. I sat on the deck with Ashley's book in my lap, lost in the beauty of lilac skies and magenta-streaked clouds hanging over the coastal range, watching them diffuse into deepening shades of lavender and casting an amethyst glow on the trunks of pines and firs. This fleeting moment of tranquility is not unlike the "golden hour" that blesses the twilight hours in spring the same way "purple haze" graces the final weeks of summer.

Knowing Ashley would require a book review, I opened the book and began. The prologue left me in tears. Kissme sat in my lap licking the back of my hand. I was stunned that someone had written a book about me.

୨୦ ✝ ୦ଓ

"You have one new message and three saved messages," the phone responded to my touch on the button. Bored and lonely, with nothing of interest on the 600-plus TV channels, I listened to the messages. It was the beginning of another lonely weekend and Chance's voice resonated in the hollow places in my heart.

"Hi, Sunny. It's me, Chance. The weather is perect. I thought maybe I'd take the boat out tomorrow. I was hoping you might want to go with me. You know, just for a few hours. Sunny, please pick up the phone. Even if you say 'No,' I'll understand. Just... call me back, okay?" followed by a deep intake of breath. "I think it's time we *talk* or *walk*. It's your choice, and I'll respect it. Okay?" *Click.*

I indulged in a fanciful flight of thought and a nasty feeling of power knowing that I could let him stew and payback some misery. But then again, I *am* an advocate. My life's calling is to end suffering, not feed it. I abhor abuse of those who are vulnerable, and I am not a predator.

෯ 🕊 ෨

The truth was laid out in black and white. After finishing Ashley's book, I made the decision to attend my first Codependent's Anonymous meeting. But first, I needed to talk with my pastor.

God's timing is always perfect, I acknowledged to myself as I met with Mac. I had been doing so weekly. Except when I skipped once—or twice. I always brought questions, and he always let me take the lead, never directing, just guiding.

"Pastor Mac!" I called as he headed inside to lead the weekly community AA meeting. We still had about twenty minutes.

"Hey, Sunny. Nice to see you. If I knew you were coming, I would have got here sooner."

"Thanks. I'm sorry I've been such a flake."

Unlike me, Mac is reliable. He gave me his usual pastoral hug and chuckled, "You're not a flake. You don't hurt me when we don't meet. You only hurt yourself." I sighed, adding a five-pound chunk of guilt to the emotional garbage bag I dragged behind me through life. "Are you talking to Chance yet?" he asked, as we entered the little building.

"Was it you that got him to move back into his old house?" I helped unfold chairs and set up for the meeting.

Mac stopped what he was doing and looked up, breaking through my defenses with a moment of silent consideration. "It's good to face your past. We have to make peace with our past in order to see our future. I'm sure your work teaches you that."

It took a moment for me to digest that. "I was thinking about attending a CODA meeting and wanted to ask your thoughts about secular twelve-step programs."

He had unfolded the last chair before he turned to give me the full weight of his attention. "Well, that depends. Who is your Higher Power?"

෯ 🕊 ෨

The back of the parking lot provided cover as I scanned the people walking indoors. My pride was poised to bolt. Referring other people to these meetings is easy. It never occurred to me that they might be afraid or embarrassed.

As challenging and humbling as it is to admit to a group that you have a problem, the hardest part is admitting to yourself that the problem exists. Denial is the greatest obstacle to success in any recovery program.

It turned out to be a great meeting attended by caring people. I learned that I had given Chance complete control over my happiness. My happiness was dependent on his choices.

If Chance repented... if Chance had been faithful... if Chance wants to keep the marriage... then...

I had given him absolute power over my life and realized that it was time for Sunny to make some choices of her own. I knew I had it in me to make difficult decisions. After all, I had left Logan at the risk of being beaten to death, or worse.

I tried to process the night's CODA message as I drove home from Chico. Moonlight skipped through the car's open moon-roof, peeking in and out of scattered cotton ball puffs of clouds and bathing the hills with a pale yellow light. The warm air was rich with the last-days-of-summer smell of over-ripe, parched grasses longing for rain.

Lord, help me to understand that Step One in every twelve-step program is the realization that I am powerless to change anyone but myself. Help me remember that I am whole, healthy, and complete, I prayed, declaring aloud, "I am cake," imagining marriage as icing on the cake. My stomach sidetracked my brain at the analogy as images of chocolate cake and carrot cake flitted through my holy meditation. I had dropped God for a cake fantasy. I sighed. "Sorry Lord." I visualized yet another withdrawal on my heavenly bank register. I am frequently diverted by worldly things when trying to communicate with God. It leaves me feeling insincere, guilty, and certain that I will never live long enough to become a Prayer Warrior. Prayer Whiner, definitely. Prayer Warrior? Maybe not.

ഉ 🕊 ଔ

My favorite disaster movie has a scene with an incoming nuclear bomb. The entire family is scurrying to take cover in the basement—except for the mother, who is climbing the stairs to make the beds. I loved this woman and thought she was the only sane one in the house. Then again, maybe she just shares my propensity for disassociation.

I stared dully at the phone, mesmerized by the blinking light until Kissme jumped on my lap and called me back from another dimension. What to do? I needed a safe house, but not like the one in Feather Falls. Not even a bomb shelter could protect me from myself.

So I sat staring at the answering machine while considering my options. How was I going to spend my weekend? I could stay home and put on some country *he-done-me-wrong* songs, or maybe pull a blanket over my head and get sucked into a black hole. I could be my own best friend and invite myself to a pity party. Or—*my personal favorite*—I could devour an entire carton of Ben & Jerry's Chocolate Chip Cookie Dough ice cream in one sitting without regret. Then again, I thought wistfully, I *could* call Travis... probably best not to dwell on that scenario.

Okay. I could listen to Chance without forgiving him, right? And too, I missed being out on the water. The peace, the freshness, and okay, I guess I missed Chance a little bit too.

"Okay, Lord. What am I supposed to do? CODA says I can't change Chance. How can I ever trust him again?"

"You can't," came the firm voice I had heard while hanging on the side of a cliff.

"Then, how can I make him take responsibility?"

"You can't," came another strident word from God.

"Then how can I ever feel safe again?"

"Trust Me." This time the voice was a soft whisper, as soft as a feather on the heart.

After an hour-long discourse with God, I still couldn't get the Creator of the Universe to change his mind. I finally conceded that I couldn't change God and I was powerless to control my husband. Whatever Chance decides to do... he will do.

I was starting to accept that the only thing I have any control over in life, are my own choices. I may not have control over an event, but I have complete control over how I respond. So, I could slide a little farther down that slippery slope of despair, or I could spend a day on the lake.

I called Chance.

CHAPTER 20

හ ⚘ ශ

Carrie Talbot was a pleasant looking woman, but her charm was lost beneath the swelling on her face and the missing teeth that James Talbot had knocked out. Still recovering from oral surgery, Carrie had the classic black circles under her soft brown eyes, and an upper lip was swollen three times larger than normal. We had spent a lot of time together through her husband's trial that went forward in spite of her recanting and perjuring herself.

Unlike sexual assault cases, the prosecutor always has the final word on filing or dismissing domestic violence charges. The intent of this legal authority is to take the burden off the victim. In theory, it prevents the offender from terrorizing the victim into dropping the charges. However, disaster still happens on occasion because abusers think they control everything, including the law.

Most domestic violence victims don't want their man to go to jail. They just want the violence to stop. More than half of all female victims recant. Some do it out of hope. Some call it love. Some victims just need the car fixed, the rent paid, or help with the kids. Then there are other's—like Carrie and me—who recant out of fear of retaliation. We know that anyone who has half beaten you to death is entirely capable of finishing the job.

Carrie looked me in the eye and began, "We were arguing... tripped and fell on the corner of the coffee table..."

...except your injuries tell me he smashed you in the face... no sharp corners.

In spite of her perjuring herself, the jury found James guilty of Penal Code Section 273.5, felony domestic violence, punishable by three years in state prison. But, it was his first (recorded) offense—and his attorney was the best that James's (drug) money could buy—and his Mama (it's always the mom) stood up and told everyone what a Godsend James was (a real gem)—and that his children needed him. In truth, his children didn't want anything to do with him.

Statistics reveal that his son will grow up to be 1,000 times more likely to be a wife-beater and his daughter will be 67% more likely to be battered than if they had been raised in a nonviolent home.

Carrie thought she deserved her beating. "I started it," she said. "I knew he was upset when he got fired from work at the cannery. He always said his boss was a jerk. I shouldn't have nagged him about the bills."

Carrie had many reasons for blaming herself, but none of them justified a beating. James Talbot was clearly a dangerous man.

80 🕊 ❧

Domestic violence makes up twenty-one percent of all crime in California, with thirty percent of female homicides committed by their intimate partner. An in-depth study was done to assess whether certain contributing factors might increase domestic violence in the U.S. The survey wanted to know if men living in the north beat women more often than men who lived in southern states, or if low-income males battered women more frequently than their wealthy counterparts. It also examined different racial and cultural differences. It was an exhaustive study, and in the end, there was only *one* common denominator. Men who beat women were consistently found to be *"some of the nicest people you could ever hope to meet."* Charisma was the one common denominator. These guys could sell cookies to Girl Scouts.

"Carrie, there was nothing you could have done to prevent this," I said, referring to the latest beating. If you didn't need rent money, it would have been the kids fighting, or the TV too loud, or burning dinner." Her eyes widened as if I were a psychic reading her private life.

Blaming herself was easier than blaming James. She could always change her behavior and self-blame seemed a safer option than accusing him.

James was almost twenty years older than Carrie when they met, but Carrie didn't care. James was the sweetest man she had ever met, and besides, "he wanted to make a baby" with her. Carrie knew this was real love; and as much as it upset James—*and he did get angry*—she insisted on saving her virginity for the wedding night. So, they kept the mandatory appointment with a counselor, proclaiming undying love for one another, and then appeared before a superior court judge. Her mother, slightly sloshed, also appeared to give parental consent for her minor child to marry "this excellent man."

After a quick marriage before the County Clerk, they went back to James's house where she was promptly raped, beaten, and thrown naked out the front door with James locking the door behind her. Terrified and shivering, she had desperately banged on the door begging to be let in.

Late that night, Carrie grabbed a t-shirt from the rag-bag next to James's show car, put it on and ran three blocks to her girlfriend's house. The girlfriend had a party going on. "Yeah, come on in." There was plenty of pot and beer for everyone.

There was also a sweet boy, Hector Sanchez, who was more than happy to comfort her—all night long. Hector left in the morning, agreeing to meet Carrie around noon at Bedrock Park, located along the river below the dam. Carrie had borrowed her girlfriend's clothes, unaware that as she did do, James was walking up the steps to the sheriff's office with a .38 Special tucked in the back of his Levis. James tried to report Carrie as a *runaway minor* but was told that he couldn't since they were married. He could, however, file a *missing person's* report, but they would not investigate it until the person has been missing for forty-eight to seventy-two hours.

James went back to his car and started cruising around Oroville until he spotted Carrie walking into the park. It was Easter Sunday and there was Hector, all smiles, sitting on top of the bleachers—until he saw James striding through the crowd of happy picnickers with a gun in his hand. Hector dove for cover, but not before a fatal shot hit him in the chest.

Carrie sent divorce papers that were hand-delivered by the prison C.O. on Third Watch, but no one told her that James had promptly set the papers on fire and clogged the toilet by flushing the remains.

From then on, every Easter James sent Carrie a handmade greeting card with a sketch of the park; including the bleachers where Hector had died and an ominous trash dumpster off to one side. They were lovely cards depicting birds singing in the trees, butterflies and flowers, the river sparkling—and always, a rainbow that stretched from the bleachers to the dumpster. His therapist loved the cards and thought they showed an improvement in James's character, but Carrie was terrified.

James was out of prison in less than three years due to an error in jury instructions and went home to live with his wife.

They created two children over the next five years, offspring of conjugal visits during his return trips to prison for domestic violence and possession of methamphetamine. His PO also found firearms, which are illegal for parolees and anyone convicted of domestic violence. James regularly committed both crimes, choosing the fast-track revolving prison door over compliance.

Carrie grew increasingly terrified of leaving him. She reasoned that being a punching bag was better than being a corpse. James had always found her: when she had moved to her aunt's home Indiana, when she moved to Las Vegas and got a job, and even when she moved with a coworker to Alabama. James always found her and always collected his property, which was how he viewed his family. Each time he hauled them home to Durham, a little farming community just south of Chico.

I had repeatedly advised Carrie between James's stints in prison, but ultimately, I was not responsible for her choices. I could give her the best advice in the world, but only she could decide what to do with it.

૪૦ ૐ ૦૨

Travis sped up to the Fed Ex box located in front of the Board of Supervisors, then slowed, popping the door locks so I could jump in the car with an empty envelope that served as a prop. I was only pretending to mail some papers. Laughing like school kids at having ditched Paige for lunch we sped away from the county buildings. I noticed two box lunches on the seat between us from Schlotsky's Deli over in Chico.

"Is this lunch?" I asked, peeking in the closest one.

"No, they're body parts. I'm dropping them off at the morgue," said Travis in all seriousness. "Crime scene stuff."

"Nasty case," I said, sniffing appreciatively. "Looks like the victim was a chicken. Chicken fingers, to be precise."

"That's chicken *strips*," said Travis with a suggestive lift of his brows.

No matter how bad my days were, Travis could always make me laugh.

I felt the bite of curiosity, like an itch that needed scratching, so I asked; "I know why I dislike Paige, but what's your story? How come you seem to be the only man at work that isn't under her spell?"

Travis laughed, but the look on his face contradicted humor and his hands tightened on the steering wheel.

"What makes you think I am impervious to Paige's charms?"

"Oh." I felt a warm flush of disappointment rising. Travis glanced at me before adding, "Okay, she can play up the blonde sometimes. The same good looks that can take her to the top will probably be her downfall. But she's not a bad person."

My eyes narrowed as I studied him. "What's good about her besides typing a hundred words a minute on a keyboard? She's a horrible person."

Travis pressed his lips into a tight line, frowning at my remark. "You used to like her, didn't you? Wasn't she your friend once? I thought you helped hire her."

I blew out a jet-stream of frustration. I had never told Travis that tidbit, so I guess he must have learned it through private conversations with Little Miss Wonderful.

"*That* is the problem," I said. "I thought Paige was my friend."

"Come on now, admit it," Travis lightened up, "other than having great office skills, she can charm information out of almost anyone. And you have to admit, she is cheap entertainment."

I laughed in spite of myself. He had a point.

Travis continued. "I know you have good reasons for feeling the way you do, but truthfully, almost everyone likes her—except you."

"Do *you* like her?" I asked pointedly. The man who never loses his cool seemed to squirm at the question.

"*Like* her? She's okay. We don't have much in common, but I'm sure she has a story. She probably has reasons for acting the way she does."

My turn to squirm. I wondered how much more Travis knew about Paige's life than I did. I had thought her too young to have much of a past, so I'd never asked, and now I could care less.

We drove on in silence to the fish hatchery located a couple of miles beneath the dam to watch the salmon run. Parking on the upper level, we took our lunch boxes down to the benches at the observation area that overlooked the spillway. Gathered below the fish ladders, waiting for the doorway to their destiny to wrench open, the salmon sometimes converge by the thousands in schools so thick you can almost walk across them to the other side of the river and never get your feet wet.

"There!" Travis pointed to a three-foot long salmon. We watched in awe at the drama before us. A streak of silver gathered fantastic speed as it darted through the mass of fish before going airborne with a mighty leap up the wall of water, flailing his powerful tail, propelling his way up the spillway, only to fall short and slide back, beaten down by the relentless torrent of cascading water. He was magnificent.

I grew thoughtful. "What do think of salmon?" I asked Travis.

Travis chewed thoughtfully on his lunch. "I love fishing for them. I love getting into the icy water and hooking a big one. They're tough. Good fighters. I guess I respect them." Travis paused and tipped his head as an irresistible look flashed like a shining lure across his handsome face. "They're especially good when grilled with fresh lemon juice."

I laughed, making a mental note to ask Chance his thoughts about salmon.

"And you?" he asked me in between bites.

It was my turn to smile a slow, secretive smile. Travis instantly perceived the deeper question behind our light-hearted wordplay.

"I love the salmon! Watching them is like looking into a mirror," I said sadly. "I identify with them. If you want to understand me—you have to understand what drives the salmon."

Travis eyed me skeptically and then followed my finger that pointed to another tenacious fish launching its body through space as though its life depended on it.

"Did you know that they are about three years old when God calls them home from the ocean?'"

I don't know what drove me to say such a thing. I guess it must have been the Holy Spirit.

"Think about it, Travis," I said, enthusiastically. "They were little fingerlings when they entered the ocean. Just kids, like I was when my mom left me. They go through horrible pain as they transition from fresh water to salt water when they enter the ocean. They have to fight to survive three to four years there, lost at sea until God calls them home." I stared for some time at my bag of chips, trying to compose my thoughts. "They almost kill themselves getting back. Their lungs nearly explode making the reverse trip from salt water back to fresh water. But nothing stops them! They aren't fingerlings anymore." I felt the sun glowing on my face. "They starve, they suffer, get mauled by animals trying to eat them, and then... they end up here, more dead than alive. They go through all that—just to lay their eggs and die."

Travis was genuinely surprised. "And you admire this suicidal mission?"

My eyebrows pinched, like narrowing the beam of a flashlight to illuminate a path. "It's the ultimate sacrifice, the essence of faithfulness. They die so others can live." Looking Travis in the eye, I earnestly repeated, "I love the salmon."

€∟ €

I find great comfort in simple routines, like going to bed and getting up at the same time. When I grope my way to the coffee pot, Kissme understands this is priority-one. Next, I either turn on the heater or open the French doors to the patio. Then it is time to chaperone my crazy dog as she drops her morning stink-bomb on the lawn. *Why the front yard when there's a million miles of national forest?*

That leaves just enough time for a quick shower before the news. I always turn on the news to see if the world has come to an end and also to follow the budding romance between the sweet blonde newscaster and weatherman, Scott Sanders, and his pet pig.

You have to be from the country to appreciate Scott and his pig. Scott used to live just down the road from us, and we appreciated the detailed weather reports for little Concow. Then, rumor had it that Scott's pet pig was caught having an affair with a wild boar. That is possibly just another wild Concow legend, or perhaps, the reason Scott moved on.

My cereal was still bouncing in the bowl when—*News flash*—the world did come to an end, at least for one person. Sadly, it wasn't the first time I'd heard a name from my caseload make headlines.

"Shocking news out of Durham this morning where forty-five-year-old James Talbot shot his estranged wife, Carrie Talbot, before turning the gun on himself. The Talbot's leave behind two children, ages fifteen and twelve."

I heard the bowl shatter before realizing I had dropped it—a sad tribute to shattered lives.

The phone rang and sounded like it was coming from another planet. I guess in a way, it was.

"Are you okay?" Travis's voice was tender and anxious. I wondered for a heartbeat how he knew to call me just seconds after the news broke, but didn't dwell on it. Travis was always reading my mind.

"I'm still at the scene," said Travis. "Gina will be calling you."

"Yeah, I like Gina," I pulled it together. "She's really nice. She'll be interviewing the kids, right?"

"Right. And Sunny... this wasn't your fault." Travis was close, but he missed the mark.

My job is to keep victims safe, and I used to feel responsible when someone died. But these feelings changed as I grew in my faith. It was a new twist on the old concept, choosing to either play God or trust God. I learned that giving God control doesn't leave you out of control. It only means that you acknowledge God is smarter than you.

Some of my colleagues have been devoured by guilt over the death of a client. Their careers devolved into mental health treatment as they became depressed and suicidal. Other advocates quit because they saw themselves as incompetent. Today I was heartbroken, but not depressed; filled with sorrow, but not despair or guilt. I know I am not God. I am an advocate and a pretty good one.

"I know," I said. "Oh, and Travis? Thank you. You really are a good friend."

"I care, babe."

ℰ 𓅨 ℛ

As the SVU Advocate, I sit on the Butte County Death Review Team whose objective is to deter and prevent deaths caused by domestic violence. This month we would be asking ourselves how Carrie's death might have been prevented.

I was thinking that I needed to talk with Ashley. I have always found that when you need to vent, there is no substitute for a girlfriend. But good advice can only come from people who have the whole picture... and I made sure that nobody had the whole picture. I never told anyone, especially Chance, the embarrassing private details of my life with Logan. I never told Ashley that I was being stalked by Logan or my sexual attraction to Travis. I didn't tell Travis that I was talking with Chance again and planning a day on the lake together. And I sure didn't tell Chance that Travis gives me hot flashes whenever we are alone together. So their opinions were basically useless, but I asked them anyway, which shows I am a California blonde after all.

The dogs were barking as they raced along the lake, splashing and flinging mud. Kissme wriggled in my arms until I relented and let her play with the big boys, Ashley's dogs. Thrilled but inexperienced in the great outdoors, she spun a few circles, barking first at them and then at me, until I reached down and picked her up again. A lot of things look like fun, but only from a safe distance.

"She's so weird." Ashley reached over and patted Kissme's head as we continued our walk along the shore.

"What will happen with the kids?" Ashley was wondering about Carrie Talbot's children.

Since Carrie was dead, there were no confidentiality issues to breach.

"They'll be living with Carrie's alcoholic mother. As bad as that sounds, I think she is a better choice than James's mother, who thinks Carrie brought everything on herself."

Ashley winced at the thought. "That's got be a tough one for the grandparents. It must be hard to take on a pair of teenagers at a time when you're ready for a nice, quiet senior park."

"Yeah, that's real love," I said. "I admire people who willingly make that sacrifice. I can't imagine raising grandchildren in my old age."

"What about raising kids in your young age?" Ashley asked. She laughed as she threw a stick for Kobi, the Queensland Heeler who never broke stride as she flew into the lake after it.

"I would hope... if I were old, that I'd be like Kobi there, and just do what comes naturally without stopping to think about it. If I thought about raising grandchildren for too long, I would probably reconsider," I joked.

Never one to let things go, Ashley asked, "Do you *want* children? We do! Shane and I..." She let it hang there. A pregnant pause if there ever was one. Color rose in her cheeks. "We want a big family."

"Hmm, I don't!" Jealousy stabbed my self-worth, right to the heart of my womanhood. Ashley's remark felt like another unexpected betrayal. I was hurt that she could have babies when I could not. "Kids are a waste of time for people with *real* jobs." I snapped with a bite, finding perverse satisfaction in the pain that flickered through Ashley's soft, searching gaze. "Thank God I don't have work, kids, *and* a cheating husband."

Ashley remained thoughtful, letting my angry remarks pass as she threw the stick again, this time for Roca, her red Aussie.

"But you don't *have* a cheating husband, Sunny. Chance isn't doing that anymore."

Point taken. Biting my lip, I let it go, along with Kissme, and dove into the warm water. The dogs barked, making a joyful noise as we splashed and swam our troubles away. There is something cleansing and refreshing about being dunked in water and washing away the bad.

CHAPTER 21

ಲ 🕊 ಜ

Amanda, our dynamic SVU Prosecutor, hustled down the hall targeting me with the accuracy of a hypersonic cruise missile and strategically intercepting me after my lunch with Travis. Flamboyant as ever, she wore a fabulous deep orange and green batik wrap with a matching turban.

"Sunny!" she ordered, "a minute, please." Her eyes narrowed to spear points. She didn't pause but gripped my arm, swung me around and marched me into my office.

"What's going on?" I asked, thoroughly perplexed and upset with the brusque way she was handling me.

"That's what I want to know." Her brown face pinched with concern. "And the answer is *ugly*! Over six feet tall, needs a shower, wearing black leather and a 'Born to Die' tattoo. White supremacist? Ring any bells?"

I stared into her big brown eyes. Amanda could have been a linebacker for the Oakland Raiders if she had been born a man. She was fearless and aggressive with moves the opposition seldom saw coming on the legal playing field.

Does she know? I tried not to look nervous as I pulled away and attempted to regain my composure. I had no intention of talking about Logan with her.

"What about him?" I asked cautiously.

"Oh!" Her eyebrows shot up and she placed her hands on her ample hips. "So you *do* know him." She raised her voice. "He came knocking at the front desk looking for *his wife*. Gayle directed Darth Vader to me since you were off gallivanting with GI Joe."

My brain kicked into overdrive. "Were you able to help him?"

"He said his wife's name was *Sunny* and that she works here," she said.

"Must be a mistake," I said with feigned innocence. "My husband's name is Chance."

"Uh-huh. I was at the wedding. Remember?"

I was staring down the barrel of a twenty-gauge glare, and she wasn't packing dove load.

"What does he want with you, girl? Is he harassing you? Are you in some kind of trouble?" She lowered her voice and relaxed.

I could see Travis—*make that GI Joe*—through the window as he approached my office. He swung through the door jangling my car keys in his hand. "Hey, gang. What's up?" he asked, tossing me the keys and chewing a piece of gum with boyish charm.

Amanda redirected to Travis in prosecutorial style. "Sunny had some low-life visitor who claimed to be her husband looking for her today. And it *wasn't* Chance," she added, as her eyes shifted suspiciously back and forth from me to Travis.

"Oh... you must mean Logan. Don't worry, Boss." Travis gave her a smile and a reassuring nod. "Everything's under control. Next time he shows up at the desk, call me first," Travis said, patting her on the arm.

"Mmm-Hmm. Now I know you wouldn't try to patronize me with your charming ways," said Amanda, cross-checking us one more time. "It just so happens that I left a meeting with our dear sheriff this morning. He told Andrew, his arson investigator, that they located an eyewitness to the spot fire below your house, Sunny."

A giant lump formed in my throat as Amanda tipped her head expectantly. She paused and continued. "Andrew turned the information over to the Gang Task Force and low and behold, turns out the biker below your house was flying Mongol colors. I didn't think much about it until I saw that not-husband-biker-guy in the lobby asking for you."

I blinked hard in spite of myself but managed to keep a poker face. "Was he a Mongol?" I asked, trying my best to look curious.

Amanda scowled. "No. He was a Hells Angel." She waited for a reaction that didn't come. "All right, have it your way. You can stop by Andrew's if you're curious enough to see an artist sketch, even though we both know the picture won't mean a thing. But Sunny," she said, her tone mellowing considerably, "we're *all* your friends, in case you forgot." With that, she headed out my door and toward the stairs, her gold hoop earrings dancing to the beat of her swaying rhythmic stride. Amanda carried herself like an African Queen.

Travis and I heaved big sighs as we looked into each other's eyes. I knew why I was sighing, but I wasn't sure about Travis.

"Why do *you* care about Logan?" I asked. "Tell me you're not still playing detective?"

He threw me a sexy smile—*I swear he knows how to deepen those dimples*—that never fails to stir me up. "How many times do I have to tell you? I am an *investigator*, not a *detective*." His eyes crinkled at the corners. "You know I'm just looking out for you, babe. That's all." The smile faded as he lowered his voice. "Are you packing?" I immediately understood that we weren't talking suitcases.

"In my car."

"Give me your keys back. I'll bring it to you," Travis paused, "and I'll walk you to court later. You can leave the gun locked in your desk when you need to go through the security screener. Stay alert, babe." He took my keys and left.

The news about Logan's appearance was probably already masticated and digested by the shark pool. Wincing, my thoughts returned to Travis. I found it disturbing that he knew so much about my life. And since when had I become his *babe?*

Trying not to be obvious, I waited until the last half hour of work to visit Andrew. While officially stating for the record that I never saw the man before, I blanched when looking the sketch of the Mongol. I was certain he was the same man who had returned with Logan from Laughlin and later helped unload guns at the cabin—and I was just as certain that my reaction to the sketch was reported to the powers that be.

ॐ ॐ ॐ

In California, it is common to have zero rainfall from May to October, so it was extremely unusual when the forecast announced rain in August. The heat had been rising from the valley floor and thunderheads piled up casting shadows across the mountains for the past week. I thought it appropriate that it should rain today. Maybe it was angels in heaven weeping for a life taken out of season. The clouds drooped, dragging like ragged curtains across the skyline, ripped and torn like the shattered lives that huddled beneath the tear-stained canopies set up by the funeral planners.

I stood in the rain in my black slacks and pumps, sporting a small purple ribbon pinned to the collar of my official district attorney office dress shirt. The sky was black, my umbrella black, and my mood black. Travis was in Oakland and in spite of the small crowd, I felt terribly alone. I watched Carrie's children as her daughter sobbed and clung tightly to her steely, dry-eyed brother. Thunder rumbled and boomed, echoing over the mountains. The storm felt as oppressive as a shroud draped over the stark graveside.

Gina, from Children's Services was there, along with the kids' teachers and a couple of their friends from school. No family members had bothered to attend except for the alcoholic grandmother—reeking of cheap bourbon—that arrived to take custody of the children. The rest of Carrie's family "always knew this would happen," and were not paying their respects because they "had told her so." James had probably alienated his family long ago.

Gina and I gazed at each other across the gravesite for a few sad moments. We were both probably contemplating possible outcomes for the children. Their father had murdered their mother. Such a violent act was bound to impact their young minds. Would the daughter die one day of a drug overdose or rot away in a cloud of alcohol? Would the son grow up and beat his girlfriend because, after all, isn't that what men do to keep control? My tears mingled with the falling rain.

An arm slipped around me lending strength. I looked up and into a pair of deep blue sympathetic eyes. Chance was here for me. My rescuer. My husband. He felt so good that I dropped my guard and fully embraced the sanctuary of his arms. It didn't even matter that Paige was on the other side of the service, sitting under a canopy that was intended to keep the family of the deceased dry, as she angled to position herself in front of the local TV camera. It made sense. The only reason Paige would go out in the rain for a stranger's funeral had to be in hope of making the evening news.

I completely missed the storm clouds over Paige's head and the thunder in her eyes as she glared at the two of us holding on to each other, but the news camera caught it all. *"Advocate's Anger Burns over Lack of Victim Protection"* subtitled Paige's picture in the morning paper. She was thrilled. Too bad it wasn't a tabloid; *"Jilted Lover Dumped for Real Deal."* The thrill would have been mine.

ↄ 🕊 ℛ

"Go for a ride?" Travis caught me as I stepped out of the lobby into the atrium. He was back from whatever business had taken him to the Bay Area. He looked as inviting as his offer, dressed in a brown shirt and Jerry Garcia tie that was splashed in burnt orange and forest green, topped with brown sport coat. His green eyes twinkled his tone was deep and suggestive.

"I'll go," Paige volunteered, materializing from nowhere, her voice eager and breasts heaving like a pair of matched race horses about to explode from the starting gate.

"Yeah, she'll ride you," I mumbled. "I told Gayle I'd walk these papers over to Amanda. She's waiting at the courthouse. I think our victim's children are in Lebanon."

"Paige will be happy to take them for you. Won't you Paige?" Travis stunned her with a wink and threw her an award-winning grin. "You're a sweetheart." That did the trick. He'd called her "sweetheart." Ugh!

She stood there, possibly speechless for the first time in her life. She gave Travis one of those knowing looks that reminded me of looks Chance and I sometimes exchanged, and then she whisked the papers away.

"She'll ride me?" Travis shot me an incredulous look as we headed up into the hills.

"*Sweetheart?*" I fired back. "You called her *sweetheart!*"

Travis smiled, dimpling, "Charm will get you everywhere."

"Dork."

"What?"

"I called you a dork," I said, with a flirty look. Travis couldn't stop laughing. "And where are we going, anyhow?"

"It's a surprise." He had a devilish look in his eyes.

Swell. I found myself distracted by his sharp outfit and the way his biceps pressed against the fabric. Travis was just downright sexy. Maybe it was the blend of smooth skin and five o'clock shadow. Maybe it was his perfectly groomed messy hairstyle, or his firm athletic body, or the muscle that worked along his jaw when he was tense—not that it mattered—but it didn't help that my hormones were surging at high tide. When I finally tore my eyes from him and looked around, I was surprised. "Why are we going to Feather Falls?" He just smiled.

"Hello? What's in Feather Falls?"

"I need a tour guide. Thought you might help me out."

"What are we touring?" Dark clouds deepened.

"When's the last time you saw Logan?" Travis asked, keeping his eyes on the road.

"*What?*" I wasn't prepared for that one.

"When's the last time you saw *Christy and the kids?*" I countered. Pretty obvious he wasn't prepared either.

Travis stared in honest amazement. "What does Christy have to do with anything?"

"That's what I am asking you!" The question felt intrusive, but they say that the best defense is throwing dirt in the other person's eyes.

Travis drove a little farther until we reached the scenic viewpoint overlooking Lake Oroville. Pulling the car off the road, he killed the engine, turned in the seat and eyed me carefully. "I saw Christy and the kids on Christmas, just like I do every year."

Uh-oh, sorry I asked. "Strike that," I said speaking legalese. "Your business. But why do you want to know about Logan?" I wasn't about to give any ground. He held me in his gaze and seemed to be calculating how much I could take.

"I think he's up there," said Travis.

That did it. "Who the hell *are* you? What are you doing getting into my life? I'm *out* of here!" I groped for the door handle and my purse. Travis moved lightning-fast, gently but firmly holding onto me.

"Sunny! *Sunny!*" Travis held one arm, and I lashed out with the other.

"Are you trying to get me killed? Are you out of your fucking mind?"

Shaking. Furious. I threatened, "You're taking me back to the office or I am walking back!"

"Not until you tell me what's going on." Travis remained calm.

I struggled for the latch and he pulled me back again, turning me in the seat and sliding forward. He kissed me hard on the lips, his mouth enveloping mine, warm and incredibly sensuous. WoW. Talk about a diversion! I stopped shaking but was still upset, confused, and more than a little dizzy from the kiss. I had gone from steaming hot to warm and fuzzy in seconds.

"Show me the cabin, Sunny." Travis's voice softened without sacrificing a sense of urgency.

"You're stupid, Travis. You think you know everything, but you're going to get me killed. Logan is Sergeant at Arms for Hells Angels—TCB! Maybe you don't know their motto: *"Three can keep a secret—if two are dead."*

"I won't let anything happen to you." His breath was warm and moist on my face.

"What?" I pushed him away. "You think Logan hasn't killed before? You think I am some stupid, gullible victim? You think I don't know that when Logan is ready to kill me, it's a done deal? I am already dead!" Hot tears spilled down my cheeks. "You're just another liar! You can't protect me. Chance can't protect me. Hell, I couldn't even protect my dog from him!"

"Sunny..." He cradled my face in strong hands, whispering my name repeatedly, I breathed his strong masculine essence until my tears were spent and I leaned against him, drained and vulnerable.

How does he do it? I wondered. *Am I under some kind of spell?* Nothing in the world could have forced me to take him to the property in Feather Falls, but there I was, doing it nonetheless. We drove in absolute silence until I pointed to the dirt road above the cabin.

Dread and acceptance had crept into my soul. I felt as I once had–right before a beating. It was a learned response. I had survived through submission and acceptance of whatever would happen next. Somehow, Travis's kiss had brought back the familiar adrenaline rush of sex, violence, and resignation.

"Down there." I pointed dully. "That's the road."

Travis slowed as we drove past, still holding onto my hand, then turned the car around a half mile later and drove back the way we came. The silence was suffocating. A half hour later, Travis pulled off the road above the lake, stopping at the same place we had parked earlier.

"Babe." Travis's arm stretched across the back of the seat. "I can only imagine how hard this was for you. Thank you." He reached over and kissed me on the cheek; softly, gently. Tenderly. Except this time he didn't light a fire, and I didn't resist. I was confused and angry.

Victims of repeated sexual abuse learn that to survive by not resisting. It is a survival mechanism of the powerless, like a kitten going limp in the hands of a toddler. My professional training has empowered me. I know *why* I react the way I do, but *change* comes much slower than knowledge.

We didn't speak on the drive back to Oroville. Travis never let go of my hand, and I didn't shake him off.

"I still don't get it," I said as we pulled back onto County Center Drive. "I want to know—and don't jerk me around—how did you know that Logan was stalking me?"

Travis pulled in and parked. Turned off the ignition, he turned toward me once more. Calm and self-assured, he looked me in the eye and said, "Chance told me."

CHAPTER 22

శ్రీ 𓅃 ౭

She was possibly the most fearsome female I had ever seen. Not exactly someone you'd want for a cellmate. In fact, she was about to become an inmate's worst nightmare. About six foot three with a Neanderthal forehead jutting out over dark, beady, recessed eyes; she was built like a battleship and just as daunting. Her butch hairdo exposed painful pink patches where she had ripped out fistfuls of her own hair. No wonder the cops had driven past her three times before realizing she was a *she* and not a *he*. It was not my first same-sex domestic violence case and would certainly not be the last.

According to the police report, Neanderthal Woman had caught her young partner in bed with a man. She had broken Lover Boy's arm before chasing her girlfriend down the street with a belt in her hand. The belt remains a mystery, but it did catch the attention of the police as they hunted for a suspect.

There has been a substantial increase in same-sex violence reports nationwide. Perhaps this is because of an increase in homosexual behavior or perhaps it is because people everywhere understand that inter-personal violence is both illegal and unacceptable in any relationship.

Arriving early to court, I located the victim and her parents. Taking a seat behind them, I quietly introduced myself as we waited for proceedings to begin.

My job had desensitized me to many things that would shock the average person, but I found myself increasingly disturbed by little things that other people would consider *inconsequential*.

My bored victim, young Teresa Hurley, doodled in her notebook. She must have been at it for some time because the page was completely covered in an old-English script whose intricate swirls proclaimed multiple variations of "Gay Pride."

No, that didn't shock me. Teresa's abusive partner, fearsome as she was, did not shock me.

It was her little white-haired adoring mother and father that left me stunned. Sitting close, embracing each other as they observed their daughter's artwork, they wore glowing expressions one would normally associate with watching your little girl graduate from Harvard with honors or watching your son score the winning touchdown in the Super Bowl. They were so puffed up that I feared they might explode into a song and dance routine, whirling around the courthouse or leaping down hallowed halls singing "*The hills are alive . . .*" Why Teresa's parents should be so proud of her for getting naked and having sex with other women was perplexing.

But then, I have always been mystified by people who need to "explore" their sexuality. It seems like a no-brainer. The only exploration necessary is standing in front of a mirror and dropping your pants. If it's an *innie* you're a girl; if it's an *outtie*, you're a guy. Not that complicated, unless one suffers from a hormone imbalance. It seemed no more worthy of parades or special laws than any other treatable disorder.

That being said, I did not have a problem assisting Teresa as a crime victim. She was 100% entitled to and deserving of my best efforts, and I made sure that she got them.

80 ϑ ൭

The sun was hot and the day was drawing to a close. The boat rocked gently to the rhythm of the current, stirred by the late afternoon breeze. We had spent the day fishing and making small talk about everything but the elephant in the boat. We talked about the war in Afghanistan, but not the war between us. We talked about the dogs, but not the issues that dogged us. We talked about Chance trying to get Mark to rename his new houseboat *Spanky* instead of *The Devil's Playground.*

I didn't like the Devil name either, but couldn't help thinking Chance was probably jealous that he no longer had the coolest boat among his coworkers. Mark's new toy looked like a celebrity rec-center with plenty of glitz and bling in the bargain. Mark had transitioned from being a mere fisherman with an aluminum fishing boat to VIP status. Guessing he probably mortgaged his home and his soul to finance the ultimate party barge. That's big on the "BAR" part of "barge." I suspect poor Mark was trying to dazzle Paige in hopes of winning back her black heart.

"What's the deal with that anyway? Why are you and Mark always calling each other and that Spanky guy, *gay?* What kind of name is Spanky, anyhow?" I asked.

Chance shot me an incredulous look. "Because he is. Spanky's real name is Spencer, but he has more swish than my ex."

Okay, it's true; Spencer does wear tight pants, a diamond stud in his right ear, and probably gets collagen shots in his lips. I am guessing he weighs about a hundred pounds with his Nomex on and probably wouldn't last the night in prison without becoming someone's new girlfriend. Nevertheless, Spence is a firefighter. Okay, he is a firefighter whose father has rank and used it to get his wimpy son a rescue job.

I decided I'd had enough of the subject and enough dancing around sensitive issues. Since Chance had opened the can of worms, I decided to fish in deep waters.

"Didn't your ex... Megan... run off with your sister?"

Chance cut the engine and I passed out food I'd packed in the cooler. Shadows along the canyon walls deepened, along with the look on Chance's face.

The affair between Chance's ex and his sister had been a nightmare for him. I later learned that it was a taboo topic. I always thought Chance should come out of the closet and talk about it.

Sex is a powerful addiction. It is the least treatable of all criminal offenses. I believed that God can love gay people and still hate sexual sin. . . all sin, for that matter. God would not make someone gay and then punish them for it. I figure homosexuality is either a hormone imbalance or social disorder, and both are treatable. But like my CODA program, recovery starts with admitting you have a problem that you cannot control, then choosing to treat it.

Chance barely acknowledged the relationship between his wife and sister. I felt sorry he had to go through that, and even now I took no pleasure watching him suffer.

Chance grimaced, pressing his lips together. "I wish I had met you back then... back when we were young," he said wistfully. His tanned face showed lines around his eyes I hadn't noticed before.

"Hey! I'm not old!" I protested. "Besides, you can bet Megan wouldn't have liked the idea of *Golden Boy* running around with *Heidi the Goat Girl* from the mountains."

A brief chuckle escaped him in spite of his apparent sadness.

Chance is still a golden boy I thought, watching the wind run its fingers through his blond hair and caress his tanned face that was dimpled into a tight smile.

"It's not just that we might have been happy, you know. It's just..." Chance paused, searching for the right words. "I think you could have saved me."

"*Saved* you? Saved you from what? The most beautiful girl in the state? The girl all the guys wanted... and you got?"

I pulled my sweatshirt higher on my neck and rolled down the sleeves against the cooling evening air. Distracted by the sound of flapping, we turned to gaze as a pair of ducks soared low across the shimmering water, landing a short distance from the boat.

Chance sighed and dropped his gaze as he continued. "Correction. The woman every *man* wanted and my *sister* got." Pain curtained across his face. "You have no idea how humiliating it was." Placing his thumb to his temple, he set his fingers softly rubbing along his brow. "It was too much to handle. There were times I thought about suicide," he confessed. "I had a plan and I had the means. Guys I'd gone to school with—*guys I thought were my friends*—would make jokes about my sister being better in bed with my wife than I was, calling *me* gay. *Me*, instead of Megan and Crystal. They called *me* gay."

Observing Chance, I had a vision of a magnificent animal marred by a bullet that had wounded, but missed the kill shot. A survivor; grand, noble, and terribly scarred.

"My affair with Paige wasn't about you, Sunny. It was never about you. Guess that's kind of good news and bad news, huh?"

Silence.

Oh, look, an elephant!

"I've done a lot of soul-searching lately. I think, part my actions go back to Megan and Crystal." Deep breath and a shrug. "Not that my behavior is their fault. I take full responsibility. Over the years I have had to wonder, deep down inside, you know; *What kind of man has a wife run off with his sister?*" Chance swallowed hard.

Teresa Hurley came to mind. It occurred to me, as painful as it had been when Logan cheated on me with other women, I could not imagine how I might have felt if Logan had been cheating with other men. For that matter, I doubted I would be testing the waters of reconciliation with Chance if he'd had an affair with Travis instead of Paige.

Head down, eyes shut, Chance tried to explain. "I think I wanted to assure myself that I was still a man. That women still found me desirable... sexual... a real man."

It was a déjà vu trigger. Always upset by Logan's *real woman* taunts, I hotly resented the implications of a *real man*.

Law-enforcement training uses traffic-lights to symbolize present-danger awareness. My mental green light blinked straight to red.

"What are you saying? I wasn't enough woman for you? I am not a *real woman*, but Bubble-Breast is?" Chance flinched as I lashed out. "I'm sure it doesn't hurt that she's a plus-size slut with a zero-size butt," I choked on a lump of emotion, "and years younger than me."

Silence filled the air, broken only by the occasional splash of fish leaping for their dinner before falling back into their dark, watery world.

Chance's failure to make an immediate response only confirmed my worst fears. *Now I know the problem in our marriage – I am not a real woman, and my husband is not a real man.* I felt the first tentacles of a migraine taking hold. I didn't know what to say. I was afraid to say anything as I teetered on the brink of a vent-or-die moment.

"Logan used to cheat on me all the time." Just as I had learned not to discuss Chance's lesbian sister, Chance had learned that Logan was off-topic. "I felt dirty and used. He cheated, he lied, and he beat me. He... he raped me... in every possible way... and then told me I wasn't a *real woman*."

I glared at Chance with accusing eyes. "Those words went deeper and hurt longer than anything he ever did to my body." My steam condensed into tears that stung, but Chance did not reach out to comfort me. This rescue was out of his league.

Flesh wounds heal, but when hearts are broken and self-esteem shattered, it can take a lifetime to recover. Children who are raised with affirmations that they are *loved, smart,* and *capable,* grow up to become positive, inquisitive, and confident because they internalized the identity their parents gave them. The dynamics are the same when adults label their intimate partner with words like *"fat, stupid, lazy,* and *worthless."* Emotional wounds always outlast physical ones.

Chance turned his gaze away from me and stared across the lake. A tear formed in the corner of his eye as he worked his facial muscles and clenched his fists. It was as if we had lanced huge emotional boils that had been quietly festering in our marriage. The noxious release of poison brought an unexpected blend of pain and release.

Finally, he spoke. "You never told me. I am sorry. Sorry I put you through this after all you went through with Logan. Sorry I hurt you. I tried to get you to talk about Logan but you always put me off. If I'd only known..."

"Now somehow this is my fault?" I said, stiffening. "If you'd of known that I was a poor little victim of abuse you wouldn't have cheated on me? You wouldn't have told Travis about my private life? Now I have to deal with him on top of everything else."

"I didn't say that!" Offended, Chance grew defensive. "It's just that you're always so damned secretive. You won't let me help you." He tossed the offense back like volleyball pro. "At least I could talk with Paige."

"Right, Chance. I bet you two did a lot of 'talking.' I was always available for sex. You never had to go shopping for it."

We sat in silence for a long time before he reached over and brushed a tear from my cheek.

How could I expect Chance to understand the trust issues that victims of domestic violence and rape battle, especially when it comes to believing men? I had educated a hundred juries, but not my own husband. Longing for intimacy, I had nevertheless kept him at arm's length. Somehow, without ever explaining, I had expected him to understand.

Chance softened. "I'm sorry. I should have thought. I should have known. We could have been so close." He paused and considered his next words. "I guess there's a difference between being *close* and being *open.*"

"And there's a difference between being *open* and being *honest,*" I added. "So tell me, why did you tell Travis that Logan is stalking me? I trusted you. That was private information. You had no right."

Chance looked defeated; his face fell, haggard and heavy with regret. "Because everything has changed. I felt I could protect you when we lived together. Now you're being stalked. You and I both thought Logan started the fire below the house, even before Mark confirmed it was arson. And now we know he's at least tied to it."

Dinner had lost its appeal, but Chance stayed on track.

"I heard you looked at the sketch. Did you ID the arsonist?"

I studied the napkin in my lap. I didn't want to lie, but I didn't want to endanger Chance with what I knew either. I said nothing.

"There you go again! Now, do you get it? You have never trusted me. You won't let *me* help you, so I thought maybe you'd trust Travis. I figured you can't hate me any more than you already do, so I did what I could to keep you safe." He lowered his eyes and dropped his voice. Words tumbled over one another; "I still... love... want... you."

The ducks swam toward us, quacking as they bobbed and plunged in search of food. We had spent the day fishing and swimming, but now, like the ducks, we dove in search of substance, pulling up bits of our past from deep waters.

It was dark when we docked the boat. By then I had disclosed details of my childhood, spilling my heart about the times my mother had left and the guilt I felt for loving my father. I told him about Logan. How we met, the abuse, the gang-rape he orchestrated at Sturgis, and that I had taken drugs. But I didn't talk about the guns—and kept quiet about the baby. Our relationship hung by a thread and I wasn't about to unravel it.

Chance shared the heartache of his mother abandoning him. He told me he loved his little sister and how he hated leaving her with a drunken father when he enlisted. Then, home on leave for his dad's funeral, Chance said he'd rushed to marry his high school sweetheart and quickly moved Megan in with his teenage sister. He'd thought it was ideal: Megan had a job at La Spa Massage and Sports Club and Crystal could finish high school. Megan wouldn't be lonely, and Crystal would have a big sister. Within months of his return, they left him for San Francisco—together.

₧ 𝕟 ₨

Tunneling through the refrigerator for a late-night snack, I closed the door and stood face to face with a magnet entreating: Bless This Mess, but it didn't seem like that was going to happen anytime soon. In fact, I was pretty sure that God would never bless my mess.

Closing my eyes and pointing to a page in the Bible for inspiration and direction wasn't working anymore. I wondered how many more self-help books I would need to buy, teachings I would have to watch, and friends I'd need to consult before finding the spirit of forgiveness.

I once believed that Chance was a gift from God. I had put my husband on a pedestal and romanticized that Chance was my guardian angel—not lowered from a helicopter, but repelled down from heaven above. The painful truth was... he was just a man. And I had expected so much more.

CHAPTER 23

ॐ ☌ ☊

Crazy Bob... make that *Deputy Robert Martel*... was animated as he waved his arms about, dramatically reenacting the story of his encounter with Tamsin Hunter.

"I tell you, Sunny, I never saw it coming. She's bleeding and screaming, 'Help me! Help me!'" he sounded like a shrieking freaking woman. "Then her brain-dead boyfriend gets in my face and forces me to whip out my mace. I tagged that sucker right between the eyes. He's rolling around on the pavement, cussing and calling my mother obscene names, so I jumped him, put him face down in the dirt and cuffed his sorry butt. Next thing I know, I have two hundred pounds of pissed-off—*e'scuse my French*—female riding and spurring me like a mechanical bull, screaming, 'Stop it! Stop it!'"

Bob froze mid-pantomime and shook his head as if I should be shocked; instead of crossing my legs and holding my sides in hilarity.

Crazy's story made my day. "Let me break it down for you." I gasped, swiping the laughter from my eyes.

A woman once accused me of being "completely unprofessional" because I integrated dark humor into my training seminar. Domestic violence is a serious subject, and violent acts should never be taken lightly. But truthfully, if I couldn't laugh, I would probably shoot myself. So I laughed, which is supposedly the best medicine after all.

I tried to explain to Bob. "She wanted both; to be helped and for the abuse to stop, just like she said, and in the order she said it. She wanted your help to control the violence, and once you accomplished that, she wanted you to go away. She didn't want him to go to jail and possibly get released and come home and beat her again for calling the cops."

Bob tipped his graying head, massaging his ear with his fingers as he concluded, "So let me get this straight. Next time Ms. Hunter needs help, I'll tell her to call you?"

"It's complicated," I agreed, as my stressed-out friend glanced down at his watch. "Sometimes it's all about the money: rent, food, drugs— whatever. And lots of women like Tamsin don't want their children thinking them as *the evil mother* who put their Daddy in jail."

He snorted and shook his head. "Okay, *maybe* I get it. But I still think she's still one crazy bitch." And with that, he took his leave.

80 ❧ 08

"Get the fuck out of my face!" Tamsin Hunter had a temper that was perfectly reflected in her fiery red hair and 49ers T-Shirt. Her green eyes bulged, her pierced nostril flared, and a geyser of Shanghai Red started at the bottom of her XXX-size frame and rushed to the tips of her Woodpecker red hair do. Lucky she hadn't broken Crazy's back.

"Okay, whatever," I said, acting bored and disinterested, spinning on my heels (literally) in front of the courthouse and walking away from her. I rated her a ten on my hostile-witness scale of one-to-ten. "I just thought you'd like to know what's going to happen in court today," I tossed back over my shoulder. *If you want to catch the fish, you have to bait the hook.*

"Wait!" Tamsin chased me down the sidewalk. "What *is* going to happen in court today?"

I explained that a preliminary hearing is not a trial. It is the court's way of making sure the prosecuting attorney has enough evidence to take the case to trial, and "yes," she would have to testify.

"Victim Witness has several..." I began.

"Fuck you! I don't need another social worker!" She cut me off.

"That's good!" I countered with an attitude that resembled her own, "because I'm *not* a social worker. If you don't care about *money* and *benefits*, that's fine with me." Again, bait and walk away.

"Hey! You! Come back!" Now Tamsin was worried that I would leave.

And so it went, repeating the bait-and-walk routine until it was time to go into court where she promptly sat with her very stoned, very best friend, who would become one of my client's in later months.

At no time did Tamsin offer an apology for cussing me out. She was angry at the world, and I worked hard not to take her belligerence personally. As far she was concerned, life had dealt her a bad hand and everyone—*other than herself*—was to blame. Then too, she didn't want anyone judging or condemning her party-hearty lifestyle. According to Tamsin, she had that part of her life "under control." However, Child Protective Services had seen it differently and had placed her eleven-year-old twins in foster care, charging her with child endangerment because of her drug addiction and her refusal to leave her abuser.

I sympathized with Tamsin. Really, I did. She reminded me of my mother. In fact, Starla had a great deal in common with Tamsin, and I could relate to her kids. I would never have forgiven my mother if she had put my father in jail. As an advocate, I can see now that Starla was stuck in a lose-lose situation.

Statistics say that women who testify are seven times safer than those who do not. But it's hard when *you* are the one risking *your* life to put a violent man in jail—or alternately running away from everything and everyone you know and love. I knew those choices intimately from my time with Logan. And like my mother and Tamsin, I had chosen to run from my abuser instead of cooperating with the police.

Is it possible, I asked myself as I sat through a series of preliminary hearings, *that I have misjudged my mother all these long years?* The thought rocked me.

Like my father, I pretended that Starla's absence didn't hurt. But it did. Angry as I was with Starla for abandoning me, I still felt sorry for her. I can never forget the times I hid under my mother's bed as she was beaten, sticking grubby little fingers in my ears, trying to shut out her cries as she begged my father to stop. Then I was gone—racing through mountains and plunging across wild rivers, running with the wind on the back of a wild mustang in my childish, dissociative fantasy world.

By the end of court, I was thoroughly confused about how I felt about my mother. But I was not at all confused about my feelings for Lefty. I still loved my dad.

ℰ 𝔂 ℭ

Chained naked to a tree and held captive in the mountains for an entire summer. The story sounded more like fiction than fact. Things like this don't happen outside of a Hollywood movie set, or so I thought. It turned out to be one of those cases that should have made headline news but ended up going nowhere.

It was late in the day when Gayle, at the front desk, directed the woman down the hall and around the corner to my office. Surprised by a knock on the door, I set my briefcase beside the desk and tried to pretend that the knock hadn't startled me.

"Um, hi. My name is Erin Moeller. Are you Sunny?" she asked timidly.

"You got me. How can I help you, Erin?" It was almost quitting time, and I had car keys in hand feeling tired and anxious to close shop. I was hungry and had spent the last hour mentally feasting on the leftover chow mien and pork fried rice packed into cute little cartons and calling to me from the back of my refrigerator.

Erin was middle-aged, medium height, with a plain face and frizzy blonde hair that showed more than an inch of tired brown roots. She looked like she had been around the block a few times. Short skirt, lots of makeup, and blood-red nails the size of small daggers. She stood at my door fidgeting and glancing over her shoulder. My stomach rumbled as dinner plans faded into wishful thinking.

"Come in and sit down," I said, motioning her to the sofa. "Can I get you some water?"

Spotting the keys in my hand, she took a step back. "Oh, no. Sorry, ma'am. I didn't know you were leaving." She turned to go.

"No, no!" I lied. "I just got back from court. Please, sit down." She flashed a tired smile of relief. "How can I help you?"

"Well..." she took a deep breath and swallowed hard—never a good sign, but I was used to it. My job is kind of like working the ER of the legal field.

Erin's eyes scanned the room before locking on mine. "It's my old boyfriend. He won't leave me alone. He just drops in whenever he wants and demands that I give him a blowjob. He doesn't even knock. He just walks in like he owns the place. I'm tired of it and I want him to go away."

Oooo-kay. It didn't take long to lose my appetite as Erin continued to provide the graphic details of her relationship with Kevin.

"Kevin had a thing for the dog. He followed me down here to Bangor, like what he had done to me up in the mountains was no big deal. Then one day I walked in and caught him with the dog. I threw the bastard out." Erin lifted her chin, her gaze as flat as her tone. She continued, "Bad enough he treated me like a dog. Anyways, he just keeps comin' back, dropping in and... pulling it out. I just can't take it anymore. I wish he would go away and die!"

Not good, but her remark was still a couple of notches below, "I'm gonna kill him."

"When did you first meet Kevin?"

"Two summers ago. I met Kev over at Pigg's Liquor in Southside. We hooked up outside in the parking lot." The corners of her mouth twitched in what passed for a smile. "Well, he was hot. Ya know what I mean?"

Again, I offered her a glass of water nodding "yes" and thinking "yeech."

She ignored my offer and continued. "I have two little kids. I'm thinkin' little Jake was 'bout five and that'd make Tyger almost four. I was in love right then and there. Know what I mean? So we picked up the kids from their Grandma's house. Kev didn't care. He said to bring 'em. So we all headed up to his place to party."

"And where was that?" I asked.

"Somewhere in the woods up above Berry Creek. He had a trailer, ya know? He was doing some growin'. Well, we spent the night drinkin' and shit... excuse me... Well anyway, I woke up the next morning and the SOB had chained me to a tree if you can believe it, out behind the shed!" She paused for a long while to collect her thoughts, lips pressed tight, eyebrows pinched into a V deeper than Butte Creek Canyon. "Then he fucked me. I mean, he'd do me whenever he felt like it. Made me do whatever he wanted, whenever he wanted. Sometimes, we did it in front of his friends."

Here it comes, I thought, preemptively handing her a box of tissues.

"Then, you know what? I'd have to do them too." She continued with a flat affect, not exhibiting the level of emotion one would expect from such a graphic and horrific story. She continued, "Sometimes Kev would just take off and leave the kids and me for days. I'd hear the car start, and *whoosh*, he'd be gone, or else he'd take off with his friends." Erin took the tissue and twisted it around her finger. "Jake—he's my oldest—would bring me glasses of water, but he was only five 'n too scared to walk out to the road all alone and get help. B'sides, I was afraid he'd get lost or eaten by a mountain lion."

The crimes kept piling up. It was time to take a break and go get Travis, but I didn't want to break the flow of her story. *When in doubt, wait it out.* Patience really is a virtue. I reached over with an encouraging smile and touched her arm.

"One time, I guess he was gone about three days. He came back and the kids were crying and I was crying. My hands were raw from trying to get the damn chain off my neck and off the stupid tree. Well, Kev, he comes back and just looks at us, and you know what? That monster just laughs and goes in the house. He comes back out with *one* frozen hot dog. He throws it to me and he says, "You decide. Eat it yourself, or give it to the kids.'

I stared hard at Erin, waiting and wondering. I knew that Starla would have devoured the entire hotdog and counted herself lucky that he'd thrown it to her.

80 ॐ ℃

True to her word, my mother's old biker friend, Sheena, called to tell me that Starla was on her way home. She was being paroled back to the county of origin.

I made up my mind to see her. I wanted to hug her, and I longed to help her. There was so much to say, so much to share. I left home at 5:00 a.m. to make the four-hour drive to the Bay Area and the Oakland Greyhound Bus terminal. Once there, I haunted every inbound bus looking for my beautiful flower-child mother. Somehow, I picked her out of the crowd as she stepped off the bus, but not without a double-take. She was barely recognizable.

"Mom? Mom! It's me, Sunny!" I cried out, bouncing on my toes to see over the heads of bleary-eyed travelers who milled about as they funneled off the bus.

Drug enforcement had found Starla living with two of her kids in a meth lab. They charged her with manufacturing, sales, being under the influence, child endangerment, possession of an illegal firearm, and resisting arrest. Due to an unlawful search and seizure, they dropped the manufacturing charge, but she was sentenced on the sales, being under the influence, and the illegal firearm she had kept by her bed. The child endangerment charge was dropped when the children became permanent wards of the state.

"Sunny? Sunny, is that *really* you?" she croaked as she made her way through the crowd. "Oh my God. It really *is* you!"

I gaped, mouth open wide. Surely this creature was not *my* mother!

She looked fifty going on a hundred and fifty; anorexic with sharp, sunken features on her once soft, radiant face. Starla had circles under her eyes and several jail tats on her arms and back of her hands. Her hair was cut short, spiked, and sticking out about two inches all over her head. Her once velvet voice was raspy and hoarse from smoking—everything.

"Wow, I can't believe you're here, honey! You got any money? I'm starving."

She nervously smoked a cigarette as we walked down the street in search of a sit-down restaurant. The least I could do was feed my mother. Starla ordered a hamburger, French fries and a Pepsi for breakfast. I had fried eggs, home fries, and sourdough toast. Stuffing her pockets with sugar packets from the condiment selection on the table, she asked about Frito and Lefty while we waited for our order.

"Frito's gone, Mama," I said, with a tug on my heart. "Lefty's gone too." I told her about the shootout down in Laughlin and all the bikers who had ridden in Lefty's funeral procession; possibly one of the largest funeral escorts in biker history—after Sonny's, of course. Starla seemed to half-listen as she inhaled her sandwich and picked at her order of biggy-sized fries. When she was through eating, she wiped her hands and finally looked up.

"What happened to Frito?" she asked flatly.

Memories pressed down like a pillow on my face, trapping emotions in the back of my throat as I struggled with the gruesome details. "Logan just took Frito and... there was this old cardboard shoebox wrapped with duct tape..."

Tears started from Starla's eyes, but I never knew for sure if they were for Frito or Lefty. The only thing I was certain of, is they weren't for me.

"Mom, are you going to be okay? Do you want to come home with me?"

"Can't." She sniffled, wiping her nose on the back of her hand. "I got to meet my parole officer in the morning. Got to stay in Alameda County. Get a job or somethin'. You got any money I can borrow?"

I dug around in my purse while she stuffed the rest of the toast I was still eating into her purse.

"I hope this helps," I said, pressing everything but toll money I would need for the bridge into her hand.

"Won't hurt." Starla counted it twice before rolling it up and stuffing it into her bra. Maybe she was worried about getting robbed.

"Where will you go? I worry about you, Mom. Don't you know where you're going to stay?"

Starla hugged me. "Don't you start worrying about me now, baby girl. I've taken care of myself this long without your help."

There was something odd in her tone. *Is she blaming me?* It sounded as though her current situation was somehow my fault.

It is hard to find reconciliation when your head is at war with your heart. I knew this was typical addict behavior. Users rarely take responsibility for their own actions. They usually play the blame game. I wasn't prepared for how much her tone hurt. After all, *she* had left *me* when I was just a kid. I was the one who had the right to be angry.

CHAPTER 24

ॐ 🕊 ॐ

We had yet to talk about the kiss on our trip to Feather Falls—not to mention being lured from the office under false pretenses. Dodging Travis wasn't possible, so I put on my best most professional demeanor and managed to catch him on his way back from the sheriff's department.

I advised him that I had Erin Moeller waiting in my office and led the way quickly to where we would spend the next two hours getting dates, locations, and additional descriptive details on other men who had assaulted her. Then we all walked back down to the sheriff's office to use its thermal infrared imaging camera to take pictures of a faded ring of possible scar tissue that was still visible around her neck. Travis told Erin there would be further investigation and we would be in contact with her. I suggested she obtain a restraining order, lock her doors, and call 911 if Kevin showed up.

"Hey, how about some dinner? I'm starving." Travis asked me as we walked back up the hill along the dirt path that led to the parking lot. It was already dark except for the LED lights that bathed the jail in light.

His casual attitude chafed like a thong wedgie. I thought he at least owed me an apology after breaking his promise to maintain a platonic relationship.

"You should be in jail eating baloney sandwiches!"

"In *jail?*"

"Kidnapping is a *crime* as I recall."

"*Kidnapping?*" Travis laughed with delight—and what was that look?

"You're a pig, and I hate you."

Travis laughed harder. His eyes fairly danced. "Okay, I've been called a pig before. What cop hasn't? But I didn't expect to hear it from you," he added with a trace of disappointment.

"I'm *not* laughing," I said indignantly. "You *are* a pig. You forced yourself on me!"

The smile dropped, and Travis tensed. The air between us palpably charged. Eyes narrowing, Travis took me by the arm and pulled us face to face, almost lip to lip. "Which time?"

"I *hate* you!" My voice lacked sincerity.

Travis held on, his body pressed closer. "I think I love you," he whispered fiercely.

Somewhere in the friction that sparked, flames ignited, smoldered, caught; then blazed, consuming and devouring the very air between us. Lips found lips. Hands reached out for that which did not belong to us. We kissed as if dying of hunger and feasting on the sweetness of forbidden fruit.

The sound of distant voices shattered the night. Officers were scrambling to their squad cars and jumping in. Sirens broke the silence, dousing our passion like ice water tossed in our faces—or lower. Strobe lights flashed in bursts of red and blue, lighting the sky as they sped away on their mission.

Was it divine intervention once again? Oh. My. Gosh.

Silence fell between us except for the sound of heavy breathing, sweet and hot, mingling in the night air as we attempted to regroup and figure where we'd go from here.

A different kind of hunger won out. We drove to The Depot and soon found ourselves working on soup and salad, trying to act nonchalant.

"Erin's story hit close to home?" Travis already knew the answer.

It was hard to focus on his question with the candlelight flickering between us, casting shadows that danced across his handsome face and turned his eyes into luminous cat-eyes. They were enchanting, and much as I tried to avoid them, I couldn't resist a furtive glance—or two—as my vagrant mind resurrected images from the escapade at my house. I tried to focus on his words and failing miserably, my eyes slipped to the tiny button that lay nestled in the hollow of his throat.

I stabbed at my salad mindlessly. The food was good, but I had a hard time swallowing as my mind undid the button, reached in and touched bare skin; hard, smooth and oh-so desirable. I recalled his scent and how he'd looked when leaning over my bed in the midst of a raging wildfire.

I swallowed. The real world wasn't nearly as pleasant as my imagination.

"Yeah." I shrugged. "I don't want to talk about Erin," I said dismissively.

"Then let's talk about you. It's your past, isn't it? Let's talk about your past."

I drew back with pinched lips, upset that he wouldn't give me a pass. He kept comparing me to every SVU victim we had. Or at least, it felt like it.

Leaning across the table, Travis ran his hand along my bare arm. "I wish you'd trust me, Sunny. You know how much I care about you. I want you to tell me *everything* about Logan. You know better than anyone that talking about a problem is the first step in healing."

"Stop it! Listen. I took you to the cabin against my will. You got what you wanted, now give it a rest."

Travis leaned back and picked up his fork. "I'd like to give him an *arrest*," he said emphatically, "followed by a substantial stretch in prison. But even if he were arrested and found not guilty, you'd still need to talk about happened between you."

I rubbed my temple, frowning. "Why are you always pestering me about Logan? *Who are you?*' I asked him again.

"I am your friend," Travis assured me, "and you telling me what's going on is the *only* way I can help you. I am an investigator. Think about it. *Please?* Trust me."

We continued our meal in silence. The main course arrived. Halfway through it, Travis checked back in with me. "You all right?"

"I'm still thinking about it," I said irritably, although that wasn't entirely correct. I was also thinking about Chance and the observations he had made only a few days earlier. I concluded that Chance was right. I was a closed book to everyone in my life.

I knew that Chance couldn't protect me. He was right when he'd said we didn't even live together. Chance's idea of helping me would likely result in Logan's death—or more likely—his own. What I needed from Chance was his steadfast faith, knowing that I could tell him everything about my past and he would still love me. What the future held for us as husband and wife, I didn't know.

Maybe, I thought as I finished dinner, it was time for me to begin trusting the same system that I advocate for my victims. Maybe, *just maybe,* trusting *Travis the investigator* wasn't such a bad idea after all. But to do that, I would also have to trust *Travis, the man.* That was altogether another issue. The conflict was giving me heartburn. Folding my napkin with care and setting it to one side, I started talking.

"You asked if I was okay? I don't know how I am," I answered with calm defiance, narrowing my eyes and leaning forward. "It depends on a couple of things. What exactly are you protecting me from? And just how do you plan on protecting me? Do you plan on arresting all two thousand club members? Because you and I both know that is the benefit of being in a motorcycle club of 'one-percenters.' The old one-for-all and all-for-one thing."

Travis leaned forward once again as we prepared to go head-to-head and toe-to-toe. I could see the green in his eyes darken several shades as he tightened his focus.

"They're not above the law. There are a lot of bikers in prison. You know that. So why not start at the beginning?" Travis set the bait, and I snapped it up. He was really ticking me off.

Taking perverse pleasure in his challenge, I pushed back from the table to arms length, kept my chin high and head tipped to one side, eyes and voice level. I began at the beginning. "Once upon a time I was born in a cabin with no electricity and no indoor toilet. My mom walked out on me to 'find herself' when I was ten. My dad brought Logan home for my sweet-sixteen birthday party where I was drugged, date-raped, and married the next morning—shotgun style—to Logan by a biker named Preacher. *Hmmm*. Let. Me. See. What else turns you on?" I demanded. I felt my face tighten and nostrils flare. Anger churned up and boiled over.

"Oh! I know! When I was seventeen Logan arranged for my gang-rape at Sturgis, most likely by a rival gang. Is that the dirt you're looking for? Need more graphic details? My father, to his credit, beat the crap out of Logan and put him in the hospital for months. Sadly, he didn't kill him. Then I turned eighteen we celebrated Logan's happy homecoming from the hospital. That was the night he taught me about sodomy. It left wounds my dad couldn't see.

Then... Logan lured my father into a gun deal that went south and got him killed. You liking this? Taking notes? Wearing a fucking wire?" Shaking with anger, I gave a rude brush-off to a waitress who'd stopped by with a smile and left in a hurry.

Travis looked ready to snap, his face tight, elbows propped on the table with one fist crushed in the other. Eyes unwavering, I could see much of my pain reflected in his. But I didn't stop. I couldn't stop.

"What? You want more? How about torture and recreational rape? You want to hear about my dead baby—asshole!"

I jumped up, threw down my napkin, and stormed out of the restaurant. I waited by the car, shaking, in shock at what I had just said and how I had said it. I dried my eyes, wiped my nose, and kept my head high. Travis came out a few minutes later, visibly shaken as he unlocked and opened the car door for me.

We slid into the car and sat in stony silence before I turned to him with an accusing glare. But Travis wasn't looking at me, he was silently staring over the steering wheel into the night. Streetlights poured through the windshield illuminating the glistening track of a single tear that slid down his face.

"I'm... sorry." His apology came as soft as a caress. He looked genuinely remorseful as he put the key in the ignition.

෫ ♀ ෬

"Mom." We hadn't talked in years, and this wasn't going to be easy. Not your usual mother-daughter conversation. "Don't go yet. Please. There's something I need to tell you."

Starla pulled a pack of generic cigarettes from her purse. Shaking one from the half-empty pack, she fished out a lighter, lit the cigarette and took a long drag before saying, "You're pregnant." She exhaled a chem-trail. "Right?"

That was an ice-breaker. "No, Mom." Long pause. Another deep breath. "I want to talk to you about Jesus... and what He's done for me." Not that He had done all that much lately, but I was trying hard to get back into

God's good graces.

"Really." She snorted. "Is that all?" She leaned back and took another long pull on her cigarette and blew the smoke out defiantly. "Well then, baby girl, tell me—just what the hell has he done for you?"

Okay. Good question. That wasn't so hard. "Well... ah, God has forgiven me for all the bad things I've done in my life," I began lamely.

Starla laughed. "Sure, baby. I'm real happy for you" she said, reaching over and patting my cheek. "Gotta go. I'll call you when I get a number."

Then she was gone, walking down the dirty sidewalk headed for God knows where. It wasn't until somewhere around Sacramento that I realized Starla couldn't call me if she wanted to. She didn't even ask for my phone number.

∞ 🕊 ∞

Travis and I had another undeclared truce as we danced around each other at the office. But nothing got past Paige. She dropped off the morning police reports. "Trouble in Paradise?" she asked with feigned innocence. To my amazement, her snarky comment was followed by a second-thought and a *"Sorry,"* before she left the room.

In return, I passed several cases that required follow-up back to her. She could go with Travis and deal with victims without my supervision. I needed a break.

But Erin was my case. Okay—*our* case—Travis and mine. Over two weeks had passed since Erin had been at the office. When the time came, Travis brought the car around and we drove to Bangor, a rural agricultural community located about twenty minutes south of Oroville.

From the beginning, Erin exhibited behaviors that typically lead to a quick acquittal for the defendant. I wondered what kind of mental health drugs Erin was taking. Statistics report that as much as three-fourths of all domestic violence victims are either on prescription drugs or self-medicating with street drugs and alcohol.

Erin's flat affect and emotional shut down were responsive behaviors. In effect, when the car overheats, you turn it off. Before the tub overflows, you close the tap. The brain works in much the same way. This is a tough concept for juries, and it doesn't endear victims to prosecutors either. They conclude, "If she doesn't care, why should we?"

Travis and I were invited inside Erin's very small, very neat little house. I asked about the children as we walked into the living room and she said they were at a church Summer Fun program. Little Jake was going into second grade, and Tyger would start first grade in the fall. She politely offered us cold drinks.

"No, thank you. Erin, please, sit down." Travis said, gently leading her to the sofa.

"That bad, huh?" Erin said flatly.

Travis and Erin sat down facing each other. "The incidents we investigated initially took place two years ago. We've been up to the property and interviewed the contacts you gave us, but frankly, everything happened so long ago that we're not able to get the evidence necessary to charge Kevin."

Did she even blink? Erin seemed to take the news in stride. "I just want him to stop coming around. Can you make him leave me alone? He just comes in the house and expects me to drop everything and drop on my knees and... I'm tired of it." That was apparent. She looked exhausted.

As far as we knew, Erin had never verbally refused Kevin entry into her home or refused to perform oral sex. Neither had she called the police or made a report before visiting my office. This strong tough-looking woman was emotionally powerless to defend herself. She felt the hopelessness and helplessness that is typical of many survivors of abuse. I have known women who believe their long-dead abusers still have power to reach from beyond from the grave and "get" them. Not even death could stop those monsters.

"Do you have family somewhere that you and the boys could possibly live with?" I asked. "Somewhere far away?"—I hate re-victimizing victims by suggesting that they move instead of their abuser. If anyone should go anywhere, it should be 'Kev,'—and I was thinking High Desert State Prison would be an ideal destination. Although I had helped Erin file a restraining order, it was apparent that it wouldn't be worth the paper it was written on. She would never call the police to have it enforced.

Erin thought for a time and replied, "I got an aunt and uncle in South Carolina, but I don't have very much money."

Three weeks later, Erin and the boys were packed and headed for a small town outside of Charleston, courtesy of Victim Witness and the State of California. I knew she would be safe there and that made me happy, but I still felt sorry for Kevin's dog. Know what I mean?

₞ ⬇ ℛ

"District Attorney's Office. This is the Advocate, Sunny McLane speaking."
"Hello, this is Tom Aural from the State Parole Office in Oakland. I am calling in regards to"—pause—"Ms. Starla Alleyne."

Alleyne? Hmm. Must have been Mom's last husband.

"I am Starla's daughter. How can I help you, Mr. Aural?"

"I am calling to confirm your mother's statement. She says that that you have agreed to co-sign for her apartment. Let's see." I heard papers shuffling. "The apartment is located in the Port of Oakland. She stated that you will be paying the first and last month's rent and the associated utility deposits."

Silence. Stunned, I asked to speak to Starla.

"Mom?"

"Hey, baby girl! Isn't it just too great? Your Mama got her old job back working at Johnny's Bar!"

CHAPTER 25

ဆာ 🕊 ca

"I can't believe I am so stupid. How could I have lived with Howard for more than twenty years and raised three children together? Now, this?"

"Oh Laurel, don't ever be sorry that you love someone. I've never met anyone completely evil." *Except maybe Logan.* "It's like this," I went on to explain as we sat in a worn booth at a local coffee shop. I moved my toast from its small plate onto a napkin. Brushing the crumbs aside, I pointed to the round plate. "I want you to imagine this plate is a pie-chart," I said. "We'll call it *your husband's characteristics.* Each segment in the chart defines a piece of his character." I drew imaginary lines with my finger. "Let's name the parts. Now, not all of these segments will necessarily pertain to *your* husband, but you'll know which ones apply to Howard. Okay?"

Laurel dabbed at her eyes with a napkin and blew her nose before giving me her complete attention. I waited patiently, taking in her fashionably highlighted hair that framed her red-rimmed, pain-filled, forlorn eyes. She was somewhere in her late forties or early fifties and was dressed in an attractive outfit with matching accessories, even at this hour and under these circumstances. She had a refined, dignified manner. I thanked God that tears were the only visible injuries.

I always qualify my illustrations, using similar examples that I tailor for women from various lifestyles and backgrounds; "We'll call this one *Good Father;* he provides for the children and has a relationship with them." (Or he comes home after work and doesn't beat them). "This next one is *Good Son;* his parents think the world of him. He never forgets their birthdays or anniversary." (Even if he forgets yours). "This section is *Good Friend;* everybody's buddy. They like him at work and always invite him to social events." (Or, he gets asked to go bar-hopping and carousing with the boys). "Here," I say, pointing to another section, *is* a *Good Lover;* he makes you feel good." (Or sometimes, "He makes you scream like a porn star," which usually gets a laugh). "Maybe, he's a *Good Provider,*" I say, pointing to yet another segment of the imaginary chart. "He gives you a nice home,

he meets the family's needs, maybe takes the family on vacation." (Or, pays
the rent, goes camping, takes you to the Indian Casino and buys the beer).
"Last, this could represent a *Civic Leader*, like your husband Laurel, a
prominent judge." (Or lead singer in a band, president of a gang, or a local
activist who would chain himself to a tree).

"More coffee? Last chance." A tired-looking waitress topped off my
lukewarm coffee before offering Laurel another cup of tea. It was nearly 5:00
a.m., and she was probably ready for home and bed. I knew I was. But part
of my job includes a willingness to meet the victim any time and any place
they feel safe.

The smell of bacon and eggs sizzling on a griddle made my mouth
water. Blue-collar workers drifted in, joking and ready for another long, hot
day. I paused to contemplate the rough speech and good hearts of these hard
working people as they teased the new shift of waitresses.

"You're not alone, Laurel. Fifty percent of all marriages and intimate
relationships experience some level of domestic violence. There is nothing
wrong with loving the good parts of your husband. Goodness is always
worthy of love. It is a beautiful part of being a woman. But this part—"*(I say
this part to all women)*—pointing at a wedge of toast, "this last part of the
chart is out of control, and that makes him dangerous to you and your
children."

"You don't know Howard. He would never hurt the children. He loves
them," said Laurel.

I wondered which of us she was trying to convince. "You need to know
that children from violent homes are at fifteen hundred times greater risk
for child abuse than children from healthy homes." She paled at my words.

Laurel dropped her gaze and stared into the bottom of her teacup, lost
in thought as she swirled and studied the remnants with all the intensity of
a gypsy searching for answers. "What will happen next?"

I had received a personal 3:30a.m. wake-up call from Jack Savage on
this one. Although Laurel didn't have any injuries, Jack advised me that the
officers found the living room looking "like a tornado hit it," and kitchen
appliances "smashed to pieces," including a blender thrown through the 82"
screen of the judge's beloved, legendary home theater system. Thankfully
their teenage children were at their respective athletic and educational
summer camps for the economically privileged.

"This case will be referred to the attorney general's office so the local
DA doesn't prejudice the case. Laurel, it has to stop now. You need to tell
the truth about the abuse. If you choose to do nothing, then nothing will
change, except the abuse will get worse. A third of all female murder victims
are killed by their intimate partner. A man doesn't usually wake up with a
plan to kill his wife. Tonight your husband threw the blender through the
TV. Next time he might use it to bash your head, and then it's *Whoops! I
didn't mean for that to happen.* And the sad part is, it's true. There wasn't a
plan. It just happened."

I buttered my cold toast and let the information sink in. "I know this feels like the worst thing that has ever happened to you, but it doesn't have to be all bad. This could be an opportunity for a fresh start. If Howard really loves you and wants to keep the marriage, he'll get counseling, and your lives will get better. On the other hand, if he hates you and intends to terminate the marriage, well...," my eyes cut to the elegant gold cross she wore around her neck, "...well, God's plan for your life will never include being with someone who doesn't want to be with you."

Laurel was stunned. "Are you a Christian?" she asked.

"To quote the Bible: 'I am.'"

Laurel laughed softly, shaking her head at my attempt to lighten the conversation. She leaned forward. "Sunny, will you pray with me? Is it okay? You know, with your job?"

I studied my watch with great deliberation just as I had many times before. "Hmm? Okay, I'm off the clock... *now!*" I reached across the table and took her hands in mine. "Seriously, it would be my pleasure."

We asked the Lord for safety, direction, and wisdom. Then we prayed for Howard; that the Lord might soften his heart and give him the courage he would need to admit his faults and ask for help. Lastly, we prayed for forgiveness, which was hard for both of us.

"Laurel," I said, as she lifted her eyes. "I want you to understand that forgiving someone who has hurt you is a *process*, not an *event*. It may take time."

Doctor, heal thyself. The old adage intruded into my thoughts.

"For tonight," I continued, "let's focus on where you will stay and be safe."

Ultimately, every victim handles abuse in the way they perceive best. Women like Laurel usually break out their credit cards and recover in luxury hotels or go on vacation while they heal. Less affluent women frequently stay with family or friends.

Then there are those who have exhausted family and friends, wearing them down through repeated pleas for help, only to return to their abuser against everyone's advice. Out of that rejected group, the fortunate women will enter a domestic violence shelter for a night or a week.

Unfortunate, ineligible women include those with sons over the age of thirteen, who are restricted by policy from many shelters, as are active drug users and the mentally disabled. Of these, some may be accepted into homeless shelters, and a few will be admitted into mental health facilities.

Then there are those without hope. Those who will commit suicide and spend the night in a morgue, and others who will kill their abuser in self-defense or retaliation.

෨ ⅋ ೞ

Early morning sun filtered through the patio umbrella outside of Starbuck's. Staying awake after the all-nighter with Laurel had been difficult, and I couldn't ethically talk about it with Serena, the executive director of Rape Crisis because the case had no ties to her agency. We still had some time before the monthly SART (Sexual Assault Response Team) Committee meeting convened, so we relaxed over coffee taking in the freshness of the morning and tossing muffin crumbs to sharp-eyed little birds that darted about as if they had already indulged in a venti latte.

Serena smiled sweetly over her coffee, gazing and gauging as she analyzed me. Her once dark hair, now white at the roots against her bronze skin, backlit her face like a halo. Serena has a way of looking into your soul. She is one of those sweet, annoying people you can't deceive, no matter how hard you try.

"I am so relieved that you and Chance survived the fires. I tried to reach you at work, and they said you were on leave."

I stuffed a chunk of muffin in my face and nodded.

She continued her surveillance. "Then I tried to reach you at home, but all I got was a message machine."

I explained with a full mouth, "Yeah. The fire." I skipped over the 'Administrative' part of Administrative Leave. "I was busy packing in case I needed to evacuate."

Serena tossed more crumbs, to the delight of the birds and other patrons.

"I tried to reach you on your cell phone, but you didn't pick up."

"Paige was covering for me at the office."

"That's funny!" Serena laughed at my remark. "Sounds like you are the one doing the covering," she said with a knowing look.

I frowned, thinking a polite person should act as though they believe your lie, even if they don't. Now I felt defensive and resented her intrusion.

Completely unfazed by my sour expression, Serena continued. "So how *are* things with you and Chance?"

"There is no *me and Chance*. He's gone." I kept my eyes on the birds, but avoidance didn't work. I could feel her reproving look boring through me.

"Has he gone somewhere other than work?"

Serena had to know that Chance and I were separated. The gossip grapevine is a short one, and ripe shop-talk about me had probably turned to wine by now.

It had been a rough morning, beginning with Jack's 3:30 a.m. call that ripped me from a dream where Chance was undressing Paige. It was just a dream, but it had dredged up insecurities that left me exhausted, crabby, and inclined to blame Chance for wrecking such a lovely morning after such a long night. It was going to be one of those days.

"He moved out, and he can go to hell for all I care."

Serena remained unperturbed. "He's still your husband isn't he?"

My mind flitted around Travis. "I filled out divorce papers a couple of weeks ago."

Serena cocked her head, pinning me with big brown doe-eyes. "Have you filed them?"

"No. Not yet."

"Are you getting counseling?"

"Kind of. But he's the one who needs counseling, not me."

"Why don't you think you need it?"

"Because there's nothing wrong with me," I said, defending my position for the millionth time.

"Sunny, this isn't about fixing him. That's *his* responsibility. This is about helping *you*. You must be hurting," Serena said tenderly. "Are you two talking?"

Sigh. "Yeah, we talk. We talk about work, weather, politics... stuff." *Okay, we talk about personal things too, but that's personal.*

"Hmm... stuff."

How does she make me feel guilty with just one word?

I get through work and manage to keep-it-together as long as I don't have to talk about Chance. Talking about our marriage is like firing a cannon over an avalanche waiting to happen.

Now Serena had fired the projectile, and before I knew it, I was telling her everything. Okay, maybe not everything. I skipped the parts about my close encounters with Travis, but didn't have a problem giving her details about Chance's affair with Paige. *After all*, I thought, *Chance brought this on himself.*

A long quiet spell followed with me picking at a now tasteless muffin and Serena chewing on my story.

Serena wordlessly reached over and covered my fidgeting hands with her calm ones. Hers are praying hands. "Oh, Sunny," she said from the depths of her heart. "*Sunny.*" Serena's eyes shone with love as she turned her gaze to heaven. "God surely does love Chance."

My head snapped up in surprise. *What?* "What did you just say? God loves *Chance?* Just shoot me! You sound like my friend Ashley," I said, jerking my hands away, tired of taking offense from people I love the most.

Serena didn't respond. She was listening all right, but not to me. She was still looking up as if communing with angels.

Sometimes I almost find it in myself to forgive Chance—on my terms of course. It makes me crazy the way everyone leaps to his defense. If I choose to be magnanimous and bestow Christian forgiveness on my husband, I figure that is a plus on *my* heavenly scorecard and hotly resented anyone else forgiving him first. They weren't the ones who had been betrayed. They had no right.

"Forget Chance. What about me! A real friend wouldn't take his side."

Serena turned to me again, looking positively radiant. Glowing. "Just think... God has given Chance another opportunity." It was as if we were the only two people there. Serena seemed to shimmer and glow with love— or maybe something more.

"God has pulled him up from the filth of his lies, washed him off and given him white robes to wear."

This was not what I wanted to hear. I wanted to hear, "Poor Sunny. Chance is a rat and God is going to punish him," not *reward* him. A righteous God would smoke Chance with a lightning bolt or drive him into a sinkhole.

Serena's voice broke through my vengeful fantasies. "Now you have an opportunity for a real marriage. One based on truth. God is so merciful. What a mighty blessing has come to you."

My coffee became as tasteless as the muffin.

"Oh, my dear friend, "Serena said with tears in her eyes. "How can you go on hating a man whom God has chosen to forgive?"

I don't remember the rest of the day. None of it seemed that important after the incident at Starbuck's. I might not always like the truth, but I have never been one to run from it. Sometimes I take it, like a dog worrying over a bone, gnawing on it for days or weeks. But sooner or later, I will digest it.

CHAPTER 26

ಖ ✣ ಐ

As a native Californian, my DNA compels me to create, no matter how strange the creation. So it happened one bright Sunday morning, at my house before church, Ashley and I were busy making dog jerky for Kissme, Kobi, and Roca; mixing turkey burger with variety packs of Wild Gourmet dog kibble.

The labels were vague, leaving me to second-guess the exact ingredients behind the fancy labels. *Salmon* (probably included heads and fins), *Buffalo* (butts) and *Wild Boar* (could be jellyfish, since male jellyfish are called boars). It smelled like a mixture of slaughterhouse scraps and sun-ripened seafood as it whirred around in the blender. Something only a dog could love.

Ashley had read an article suggesting that under all doggy-fluff "beats the heart of a wild animal," or something like that, assuring me that our creation would "bring out their inner wolf."

Yes sir, if my little Kissme has an inner wolf, this will definitely bring it out. Although it smelled more like an impending exorcism. What I hadn't considered was the possibility that the jerky might bring something *up* instead of *out*.

Bad as it smelled, rank-nasty in the blender, it was twice as bad by the time we returned from church. The food dehydrator that was processing the strips had fanned the stench into every corner of the house.

Ashley gasped. "Yeach! Now you know why I'm a vegan."

I wrinkled my nose as we opened windows and took refuge on the deck.

"That is so disgusting! Ugh! That stuff smells like road kill." Ashley pointed skyward. "Are those buzzards circling? Geeze! I bet Shane can smell it all the way up at our house."

Bikers know about the smell of road kill. Looking up, I nodded in agreement. They looked like buzzards all right. "Yup. Pretty sure." Maybe the dog jerky actually *was* road kill. The kibble company didn't exactly say *where* they acquired the meat for their fancy pet food.

Kissme barked and spun in joyful anticipation. I guess there is no accounting for taste. I imagined that my little princess would just as soon roll in the stuff as eat it, but at least she seemed to appreciate my effort. That said, while my little Kissme-girl is easily the *sweetest*, she is not always the *brightest* dog in the neighborhood.

ℂ ❀ ℁

I smelled the coffee before seeing it; opening slitted eyes to see Travis's hand wrapped around a paper cup just inches from my nose. Lifting my head from my arms that I'd pillowed on my desk, my eyes popped open. I sat up, ran my fingers through my hair and shook my head.

"A little something for Sleeping Beauty." Travis smiled. He shut the door and sat on the sofa. "I've wondered what you look like first thing in the morning. I knew you'd be beautiful."

I yawned, rubbed the grit from my eyes and offered a sarcastic "Thank you, Prince Charming."

"Prince Charming got a kiss." Travis arched a brow and threw me a playful grin.

"You already had your kiss—and then some. However, while I want to pay you for the coffee, I am all out of greenbacks. Do you accept change?"

"Oooh, ouch." Travis laid his hand across his heart, but his eyes twinkled. "No, but I do take debit cards," he countered. "A little grumpy this morning? Make that, afternoon."

"I feel like a lab rat in a sleep-deprivation test," I said, sipping the jet fuel, eyes closing again, savoring the moment. "Umm... good. I can't sleep anymore."

I didn't want to tell him that I lived my nights in a hamster wheel, running and rerunning imaginary loops of erotic sex between Chance and Paige. Or that I would lay awake for hours musing: *Did they laugh at me? Did he wear his ring? Are there others I don't know about?* And I would never tell Travis that I lost sleep thinking over his declaration of love. That scared the heck out of me.

"A problem?" Travis took a seat.

"Besides you and your unsolicited invasion of my private life?" Too tired to fight, I changed the conversation.

"What else? Let's see... my dog threw up all night. You know— from both ends? I had to take her out every hour on the hour. It was terrible. The stink was nasty beyond belief."

Travis laughed easily but remained watchful. "That's why I'm dogless. Anything else? You look like you've missed more than one night's sleep."

"Really?" Talk about an understatement.

"I could help you sleep." A devilish smile played at the corners of his incredibly sensual lips, ratcheting up the pheromone level in the room when he winked.

My blush-thing that followed was terribly outdated, but Travis has a way of turning up the heat.

"Try valerian root," he advised. "When I got back from Iraq I had a terrible time sleeping. I kept replaying and rerunning different things I'd seen in combat, and I didn't want psych meds, and I didn't want to go back on pain killers."

Like silhouettes on a wall, pain-filled memories cast shadows behind his green eyes. He understood. "A buddy told me about valerian root; they make Valium from it. It helped." His smile returned. "And if that doesn't work, Dr. Travis makes house calls."

I imagined myself going from blushing pink to smoking red. "Don't you have work to do?"

"Sunny," he said, only half in jest, "you *are* my work."

"Yeah right, cowboy. Whenever you need help tracking down outlaws."

Travis stood, searching, or possibly assessing, me with brows drawn when a loud knock interrupted his contemplation.

₮ 🡭 ℛ

Ashley has only been to my office once since I started work for the DA. She'd arrived one day wearing her "I got it on eBay" grin, with a gift; a weird and beautiful Grecian-style lamp with a bronzed, robed, slender woman holding up a silken lampshade. Today I opened the door to a flushed and anxious looking Ashley.

"Ashley! Wow. What brings you here?"

"Am I interrupting?" she asked, glancing at Travis reclining on the sofa.

"No. Come in. We were just discussing a case we're turning over to the attorney general's office," I lied, thinking of the Laurel Zehetner case we had considered hours ago.

Ashley was instantly all smiles. "You're sure?" She was either having her first hot flash or having one of those primal responses that light up a woman when she meets a gorgeous man.

"No, not a problem. Travis was just leaving," I said pointedly, giving Travis a *the door is that way* tip of the head.

Travis patted the hand still over his heart. "You're not going to introduce us?"

Ashley's face, already an unusual shade of red, accelerated from worried-to-stupid in a nanosecond. I hate that my friend is one of those natural California beauties who never requires makeup or dress up. She is always natural and always pretty. I imagined throwing cold water on her just for fun.

With exaggerated formality, I made introductions. "Ashley meet Travis, who is leaving. Travis this is Ashley, my neighbor." I turned my *"can I help you?"* expression on my friend, but she wasn't looking at me. She was still looking at Travis with that idiotic smile. I expected her at any minute to burst into a Broadway song and dance routine.

"What brings you here?" I asked, somewhat dismayed at the flicker of jealousy that was sparking within. "Ashley? Hello! I'm over here!"

"Oh! Sorry." She blushed. *Guess I am not the only one who still blushes.* "Um... well, I need to talk to you about..." she glanced nervously at Travis then back at me and lowered her voice. "About Logan," she whispered. "Maybe... "

"Logan?" I interrupted.

Why not just take out an ad on prime-time TV? Is there anyone left who doesn't know about Logan? As close as Ashley and I are, I had kept my history with Logan to a bare minimum, mostly alluding to him as an ex-boyfriend who rode with Hells Angels. She didn't know anything about the stalking

Eyeballing Travis, I tried to compose myself and remain professional. "Travis, will you please excuse us?"

"No." He sat up straight and leaned in. "I'd like to hear what she has to say." A determined look settled on his face.

It was that final second—that awkward moment before the grenade goes off, the cat shreds the dog, the gazelle falls to the lion, and the tsunami hits shore—I was about to engage in some serious interpersonal violence.

Jumping up, I pushed Ashley toward the door. "You'll have to excuse me, Ash. I'd rather wait to talk about this until I get home. I'll call you tonight."

Travis beat us to the door, slamming it in Ashley's face before she could exit. "I'm an investigator, and if you are withholding information regarding a crime, it's in your best interest to talk about it now."

Ashley trembled, and I rolled my eyes, exhaling as I prepared for the storm.

"Over lunch?" Travis offered with a charismatic smile.

৪৩ ঙ্গ ୧ଷ

"Dog vomit. Or maybe it was poop. The guy was totally scary. He was cussing and kicking his boot against your house," Ashley began. "I think he must have stepped in a dog pile because it was everywhere and... can you believe he was cursing dogs when I walked up? I was just dropping my carpet shampooer off on your doorstep and thought he was Chance on his motorcycle."

I wasn't hungry and had no intention of eating lunch, but I wasn't about to let Ashley go off with Travis and discuss my life without me.

"He was covered with tattoos. I guessed it was Logan when I saw his colors. I didn't mean to pry, Sunny. I'm sorry, but I thought you'd want to know right away." Ashley looked apologetic as she picked at her salad.

Travis turned up the charm. "It's all right. I'm sorry you were frightened, but I'm glad you came by. You did the right thing. We've been looking for him. Can you tell me exactly what he said?"

"Well..." Ashley squirmed uncomfortably. "As I was walking up he said, 'Who the fuck are you?' which really freaked me out. I said I was a friend of Sunny's and I was dropping off my carpet shampooer."

"Then what?" Travis coaxed.

Ashley frowned in thought. "Then he stepped in a second pile and told me to get the 'F' out. So I came here."

Tension escalated. "Excuse me," said Travis, wiping his face as he pushed away from the table. He pulled out a couple of twenties and tossed them on the table. "I'll send a car for you."

"No, you won't! You can't just..."

But he was already gone.

ℴ ℴ ℴ

"This is going to stop, or I am going to file a restraining order against you." I threatened Travis back at the office.

"No you won't," he said.

Was it confidence or arrogance? "What makes you so sure? I've had it with you."

"I needed to put out an emergency BOLO on Logan."

"A BOLO?" Ashley paled at the word.

"'Be On the Look Out.' It's a police alert," I explained.

"Oh, my! Do you want to stay at our house tonight?".

"No. It's okay. I'll call you when I get home. Love you, Ash." We hugged, and I propelled her out the door. As soon as she was out of hearing, I opened my mouth to protest and—

"I'll tell Jack you're being stalked." Travis cut me off.

"Everybody knows anyhow." I trembled with anger, drawing back my hand as if to punch him, just as Paige walked in.

Startled, she jumped back, demanding, "What's going on in here?"

Furious, clenched fists remained at my sides as I stormed past her. I heard the distinctive sound of the door closing behind me, leaving Travis and Paige alone together as I headed for the restroom and a time-out.

On my return trip, I overheard them arguing and paused a heartbeat outside of Travis's door, burning with curiosity. Unwilling to be caught eavesdropping, I walked on, telling myself that I didn't care. But minutes later, Travis left for the rest of the day and Paige couldn't look me in the eye.

ᔕ ᔎ ᔐ

Chance probably couldn't hear me knocking at the door over Mercy's barking, so I peered through his living room window. Aching with loneliness, I wanted to talk with him, or just be near him.

When I didn't see him in the front room, I walked around to the bedroom window, a bit fearful of what I might see. Nothing more frightening there than a pile of dirty work clothes and several fishing poles in the corner, so I knocked again before walking around the other way and peering into the guest room. I was hungry, and the candy dish was in full view.

Hard muscles glistened with sweat, flexing and straining as Chance worked out on his Nautilus machine. I drew a deep breath as desire coursed from the bottom of my feet to my... navel. A headset pumped music into his head and he sang along with his iPod. Chance loves his work and willingly pays the price, knowing that lives depend on his staying fit.

Breathe. I reminded myself with an exhale that softened into a wistful sigh.

I knew it wasn't enough to love the outer man. What use is a great piece of luggage if it is empty or going nowhere? But then, Chance was neither empty or without direction. I just wasn't sure we were still booked on the same trip.

I finished circling the house, stopping to give a tail-wagging, nose-prodding Mercy a quick hug and kiss before letting myself in with the spare key that Chance keeps under a rock.

I surveyed the front room as I dropped my things in a chair. It was sparsely furnished, even by bachelor standards. A relatively small TV on a simple stand, an overstuffed two-toned recliner and a picture of Jesus holding a stricken young man in blue jeans and a t-shirt centered above the fireplace, right between a picture of me on the right and our wedding picture on the left. Nothing else, except a reading lamp and a plain coffee table that looked like it doubled for a TV tray, holding a small take-out box with rock-hard crusts piled up like a pizza bone yard.

My gaze was drawn to the oversized living room window, past the small front deck to an emerald green yard and mimosa tree heavy with pink powder puff blossoms. Clusters of bright flowers filled raised beds that ringed a blue jacaranda that Michael McLane had planted long ago. The scene melted into endless layers of timbered mountain ridges lit in various shades of green; pine, fir, and oak, that deepened into an ever-changing, shifting, shadow dance of grays and purples as the sun crept toward the horizon.

Yes, I thought, *there is peace here.*

"Whoa, Sunny. I thought I heard Mercy going crazy. What are

you doing here?" I turned from one magnificent view to another. Chance's body radiated power but his countenance beamed with tenderness. His eyes lit with joy as our gazes locked in an unspoken embrace.

Filled with love and longing, I wondered if my flesh would always be at war with my pride and how long I would continue to reach out, only to draw back in fear and uncertainty.

"I thought, you know, we could... talk." Talking was suddenly the last thing on my mind.

"Sure. Can I get you anything?" Chance said as he headed for the kitchen and the fridge.

Oh yeah. Can you drop that towel around your neck? "No thanks," I lied, lifting my head and squaring my shoulders. Things had mellowed between us, but nothing had really changed. "I'm good."

"What did you want to talk about?"

"Paige." *No-no! Delete that! I don't want to talk about her.* Once again I opened my mouth and stuck a trash barrel in it. Nothing to do now but swallow and hope I don't choke. "I saw her at work today." *Duh! I see her at work every day. What am I saying?*

Chance didn't flinch. "And?"

"And... she asked me about you." Which wasn't exactly true.

"I don't care." Chance shrugged as if the topic of Paige was unimportant.

"You don't care? You don't want to know what she said?"

"No, I don't want to know what she says and I don't care what she does. Everything to do with Paige has led to this," he said with a wave of his hand as if he lived in a tomb instead of a nice house. "I'd rather talk about you, or us, or... nothing at all."

Okay, the first shot had gone over the bow. Maybe if I fired another round at the mast...

"Ashley came by the office this afternoon with information about Logan."

That got his interest. "She stopped by my house this morning and saw a motorcycle there. She thought it was you at first, but turns out it was Logan." I waited for the shock to register. It didn't.

"I know." Okay. He won the war with a single shot between the eyes.

"You know? How did you know that?"

"I saw the BOLO Travis issued... and then we spent the afternoon together looking for him."

That did it! Hot anger blow-dried the steamy sex fantasy.

"What is it with you two? Are you both insane? I swear to... to... Ga... Ga... You're both just as sick as Logan! You're both always in my business, always butting in my life. You better listen and listen good," I yelled, poking Chance about mid-can in his six-pack abs. "I don't need your help and I sure as f-ff... f-ff... I sure as sh... sh... I don't want it. I can take care of myself! So there!"

Sometimes trying to be a good Christian makes you sound like a complete idiot. I hate swearing, but it is a struggle to find other expletives that carry the same force and intimidation. I sounded like a stuttering feeble-minded fool. However, I did feel a small twinge of satisfaction at my self-restraint.

"And stay out of my life! I was doing just fine before I met you!" *If you call falling off a cliff and almost drowning "doing just fine."*

Chance was wise enough not to laugh or bring up the obvious. He just arched a brow, turning his face into a giant question mark.

I grabbed my things and headed out the door.

"Wait. Don't you want an answer?" Chance followed me outside onto the porch.

I spun around, slapped a hand on my hip and shouted, "An answer to *what?*"

"Your question. You asked me a question. You wanted to know *what it is* with the two of us butting into your life."

How does he stay so damned calm?—darned calm?

My furrows between my eyes pinched into a skid mark as I exhaled, sounding like a blowout doing eighty. *"And?"* I asked, knowing that no answer would be adequate.

"Simple," said Chance, his ice blue eyes melting into crystal springs. He took the towel from around his neck, casually wiping the sheen that had magnified his upper body.

Oh, boy...

"We both love you, Sunny." His bright water blues deepened to moonlit pools as the sun slipped behind the mountains. "He's a good man. You should be with a good man."

My jaw must have bounced off the porch. For a change, nothing came out of my mouth. I think I stood there with that freshly stun-gunned look on my face.

Are you suggesting that I be with Travis?

No. It felt like much more than a suggestion. It felt like Chance was giving me his blessing!

ℰℐℰ

"It isn't fair! People treat me like a perpetrator and Chance is some kind of victim."

Pastor Mac, who also worked with law enforcement, offered a weak smile. His blue-gray eyes flickered with amusement, but his body language suggested disappointment.

"How come I am the one in counseling every week? I haven't done anything wrong. I hate this. Chance is the one who needs counseling."

Pastor Mac studied me for a moment. "What makes you think he isn't in counseling?"

"Is he?"

He hit me back with legalese. "You know I am bound by confidentiality and cannot confirm or deny."

I know I am not perfect. I was in a whiny mood, and it was that time of the month. I had a half gallon of Rocky Road ice cream at home, and I was missing another episode of Law and Order.

Pastor rocked back on his heels and pursed his mouth as he considered. "Sunny..." He let my name hang there for a moment. "The question isn't about Chance, it's about you. Why are *you* here?"

Completely caught off guard, my mind cast about wildly for something profound and came up empty, forcing me to resort to the truth.

"Guilt." Then added as an afterthought, "I'm here because... because... I don't know why I am here."

"I've got time," Pastor said. "Think about your answer."

I swallowed my pride, my guilt, and my lust for Rocky Road in one big lump before dropping my defenses. "I want to hear someone—*anyone*—say that Chance wrecked our marriage. He is the bad guy. And *nobody* will."

"Okay," said Mac in all sincerity, "Chance is a bad guy, and your separation is his fault. You didn't deserve this. And I mean it. Feel any better?"

I didn't. Not even a little.

Mac continued. "Are you looking for validation or vindication?" The misery on my face must have been apparent as Mac placed a hand on my shoulder.

"We are all messed up, Sunny. I am a bad guy and you are a bad guy. The book of Romans says that none of us is perfect—*no, not one.* Chance made a mistake. A *big* one. A *serious* one. And I was hoping you came here tonight because you don't want to make one too. It's all about choices. We all have problems. It's how we deal with them that sets us apart from one another."

℘ 🕊 ℭ

Drained, I crawled into bed with my faithful little dog. I like laying in bed and thinking. Sometimes God speaks to me in the stillness of the night. It is probably the only time he can get my full attention. Snuggling deep between crisp cotton sheets, I gazed out the window as the first stars made their appearance, reflected on my day and wondered what to wear to work tomorrow.

Once or twice a year, I break down and shovel clothes out of my closet. I meant—*clean* the closet. It is a tedious job that I put off as long as possible. It requires most of the day to try on, sort out, and haul away stuff that is too tight, too stained, or no longer the trend.

Kissme was trying to dig a hole in the blanket when I thought I heard the Lord speaking to my spirit. It had been a long time since we shared a close encounter of the best kind, so I paid close attention.

It seemed that God was telling me to clean out my prayer closet, which was in a similar condition as the clothes closet. In my spirit, I saw rituals and rules as being too tight for everyday wear, and my behavior as either stained or out-dated. God wanted me to separate the things of value from the junk.

"What do I do with my junk, Lord? Throw it in the trash?"

God said, *You've tried that on your own. How's it working for you?*

"What, then? There's so much stuff I need a spotlight and a shovel just to find two shoes that match. I don't know what to do with all my emotional baggage."

God said, *Give it to me.*

"Why would you want my trash?"

God considered. *I call it, Mercy.*

"Are you really going to do my dirty work for me, Lord?"

God smiled. *That's called Justification.*

"But if I throw everything out, I'll have nothing. What will I wear?"

God laughed. *If you let me clean your closet, I'll give you unlimited access to my credit card.*

"No limits? *Why?* Why would You—Lord of all Creation—do that for me? I am far from being a saint. Look at my scorecard. We both know I don't deserve your generosity."

God kissed me on the forehead. *It's called Grace, Sunny. Now rest. I'll see you in the morning.*

CHAPTER 27

ॐ 🕊 ॐ

Farmers in the valley had been harvesting for months. Fruit stands dot Highways 70 and 99 with tempting signs for fresh peaches, apricots, melons, and tomatoes. Fall always ushers in hay mowing in the valley and pot picking in the hills. Thousands of pounds of "medical" marijuana flow from these hills like gold and many of the gardens are managed by illegal Mexicans who can't speak a word of English, but know how to plant, cultivate, and defend their lucrative crops.

"Hello. Good morning." Chance called on the house phone just as I finished my morning makeup ritual that I call *enhanced natural.*

"How can I help you?" I asked.

He paused. "I'm not a phone solicitor. I thought you'd like to know that Logan is still off the radar. We... ah... Travis and I, are still looking. Please be careful."

I skipped over the point. "It figures that Travis would update you first. Just-like-yesterday..." I rolled out the words.

Chance cleared his throat "Actually, it was Shane who told me that Ashley had seen Logan at your house."

"And you didn't think to call me?" I banged my head against the phone with a whump!

"Sunny? You okay?" I imagined his finger hovering above 911 on speed dial.

"I'm late for work. And I have a headache. Thank you for the update. "

I dressed in my last clean pair of tight jeans. Okay, they weren't all that tight when I bought them. They were probably made in China where the population is generally size *small* and *smaller.* Or maybe I had turned the heat in the dryer too high. Anyway, I stuffed myself into a great pair of blue jeans and topped them off with a white dress shirt, tied my hair neatly back with a white elastic band dotted with pretty pearly things and slipped on a new pair of Nike running shoes—just in case. You never know when you might need to run, especially in light of today's destination: Helltown.

Helltown was where Maria had reportedly been held in a pit for a nearly a week while her boyfriend, Ramiro, shoveled dirt onto her head several times a day. When she finally escaped, she chose to avoid the police and get help instead from Migrant Farmworker Services in Gridley.

Maria had good reasons for not going to the police. First, she was an illegal alien and feared deportation, and secondly, she'd left her seven-year-old daughter, Paloma, behind with bad-guy Ramiro. She could only imagine what her psychotic boyfriend might do to her daughter if she jeopardized their marijuana operation by calling the police.

The story she told my colleague was that Ramiro had been drinking one night and caught one of his dope-growing partners groping Maria in the kitchen. Hurling accusations at her, Ramiro had used Maria for a punching bag, then he dragged her through the woods to an old hydraulic mining pit, shoved her in, and repeatedly threatened to bury her alive. Admittedly, he'd tossed down food and bottled water twice a day along with shovelfuls of dirt, but he ignored her pleas to be let out.

Being resourceful, the youthful and agile Maria had used some sharp pieces of quartz to dig at a few tree roots that poked through the walls of the pit, creating steps and handholds sufficient to pull herself up and crawl out. She left her daughter at the house for fear that Ramiro might catch her, and reluctantly made her way down a moonlit dirt road and out to the highway where a horny trucker Jake-braked his way to disappointment. Not unsympathetic, the trucker gave Maria a ride to Gridley and dropped her off at the Migrant Farm Workers Association. There he gave her a twenty hoping for a little appreciation in return, but got nothing more than a grateful, "*Muchas gracias!*"

A social worker named John Palos arrived at work and asked Maria if she needed assistance. Maria's story revealed multiple crimes, so John had called out of safety concerns for Maria and her daughter. About an hour after his initial call, he called me again, this time advising me that Maria had walked away from MFW around ten o'clock. It wasn't hard to figure out that she was headed back to Helltown for her daughter.

Technically, I should have forwarded the information to the sheriff's office, but I was avoiding Chance both at home and on the job, ever since he'd opened the doors for me to have a relationship with Travis. Anyhow, I figured a bilingual advocate from the women's shelter could help Maria file a police report later.

The district attorney would not have approved this trip. My plan was to head for the hills without asking permission. Alone. But God had other plans.

I succeeded in dodging a hundred employees, but I couldn't avoid Travis. When I told him my plans, he insisted on going along to "*cover me.*" What he wanted to cover was most likely my rear—to keep it from getting shot off. There had been recent incidents where "coyotes"—*human smugglers who move illegals over the border from Mexico*—would hold the undocumented person's family hostage in trade for their work on a pot plantation. Travis was playing it safe.

Travis knew I owned a gun, but shooting a target and killing a person requires distinctly different mindsets. I am a fair shot, but neither of us was really sure I could kill a person; unless the person's name starts with L-O-G and ends with A-N. No matter, I chose to leave my gun at work. I didn't want to be frisked by Ramiro and found packing. I just wanted to pick up Maria, grab her daughter, and get the heck to *Casa Segura*, a Spanish-speaking shelter in Glenn County.

Guns are a part of living in the mountains, and most mountain people own them. But generally speaking, the farther out the dwelling, the farther out the gun owner's psyche. Between radical gun-toting survivalist-type folks living in the backwoods and the illegal Mexican gangs that have invaded the woods with pot plantations and meth labs, the tranquil Sierra Nevada Mountains can be a precarious place to navigate in certain places and at certain times of the year. Maria was on her way to one such location.

My plan was to play the gender card and pass myself off as a harmless social worker. Travis saw it differently. I tried giving him the slip.

The key was in the ignition and my seat belt buckled when a white 4x4 SUV sped up behind me and braked, blocking my exit. The tinted window rolled down to reveal a grinning tousle-haired gum-chewing Travis peering from behind a pair of Oakley's. "Thought we'd take the Big Boy since the helicopter is booked."

I wasn't sure if he was kidding about the helicopter. A little reluctantly, I beeped my car shut and climbed into the 4x4, sliding across the smooth leather seat with paperwork in one hand and my shoulder bag in the other.

"You fly helicopters?" I asked.

"Only when I need to."

His reply was a total turn on.

It was another bright California-perfect summer day that invited daydreams about flying away with Travis as we left the county complex and headed up toward the foothill communities of Paradise and Magalia.

Turning off the ridge from Skyway, we left the pavement and began our slow descent into Butte Creek Canyon. The trek led us down twisting and treacherous roads with names like Humbug, Nimshew, Centerville and Boneyard Flat. At last, we approached Helltown. Established in the 1850s, Helltown was one of the earliest mining camps in the area and once had a population of about 2,000 people. Nowadays the place is a health risk for census takers, Jehovah Witnesses, and strangers.

Helltown has never been known for its warmth and hospitality. It is known more for taking pot-shots at firefighters, setting tripwires and booby traps around pot crops, and greeting people at gunpoint. Legend says the town was named by miners one morning after a wild night of drinking and gambling, when they realized they'd been lighting their smokes, striking matches off kegs of gunpowder. I find the story easy to believe.

"Helltown isn't even a community," I explained to Travis as we bounced along. "It's more like a... a location." He nodded, keeping a vigilant eye on the road.

Clouds of dust rolled up from behind, occasionally overtaking us as we slowed for potholes that looked deep enough to eat us for lunch and use the SUV for a toothpick. We finally pulled off to the side of the road, and I watched with apprehension as Travis checked his weapons with calm assurance.

"What?" Travis raised his eyebrows. "You don't expect trouble? You think they'll invite us in for tacos?"

"I was thinking... that I've brought *trouble* with me and you are going to wreck my lunch plans for tacos in Glenn County."

Travis smiled slyly and I had a hot flash, which is pretty amazing since menopause was still light years away.

The used-to-be-cabin-now-shack was set back off the road, and the standard Butte County welcoming committee of three large, nasty looking pit bulls greeted us as we came to a stop. Travis pulled a can of mace from the left door panel and held it low and out of sight while keeping his right gun-hand poised for action.

"Any other surprises?" I asked.

"Count on it," Travis said with a grin that triggered another a hot flash that landed inches below the belt and miles below my brain, "but this one is standard issue." He passed a second can of mace over to me, and I tucked it in the empty holster pocket of my shoulder bag. I had not planned for confrontation.

Travis honked the horn. After all, we weren't ICE—*Immigration and Customs Enforcement*—and we weren't here to make an arrest. If the growers ran and hid, it would be okay with me. I wasn't surprised that no one came to greet us except the dogs. Travis rolled down the window and the first pit, over sixty pounds of liver-colored red-eyed white-fanged rage lunged forward, sticking face through the open window and catching a blast of mace into his open jaws. Yelping and snarling, he fell back and, since no one else was available, ran around trying to bite himself. Travis kicked the door open, knocking the dog in the head and stepping out, quickly spraying him again. The two remaining dogs turned tail and chased after Bruiser who now led the way, foaming and yelping into the woods.

We weren't exactly off to the best start, but since no one was there to control their dogs, it worked.

No one was in sight, but I sensed the presence of camo-clad gang-bangers behind every tree. Travis took the safety off his gun and told me to stay alert as we approached the shabby looking cabin.

So much for pretending to be a social worker. I knocked on the rickety wooden door; the hollow echo conjured images of a lid being nailed on a coffin.

"Maria? *Ma-ri-a!*" I called. I thought I heard something. Just as I reached for the door, a white pit bull returned, running full tilt around the corner as it barreled down on Travis.

Bam! A single shot and the dog dropped in its tracks. I stared in horror, paralyzed with fright as blood and gore splashed across the walkway. More frightening still—was the silent chill of cold metal pressing into the back of my head and the choke-hold that took me from behind. Travis swung back around, responding to the threat that he could not have seen, but must have sensed.

"*Hola amigos.* Drop it!" Travis dropped his gun. "And you." He tightened his chokehold and I dropped my bag.

"What the fuck you want?" the menacing voice wheezed into my ear.

The arm around my neck was huge and bare with a tattooed sleeve. The breath on the side of my face heavier than a six-pack of beer and his body odor rivaled Neil Road landfill. The gun felt like death jammed against my head.

My entire life didn't exactly flash before me, but thoughts of Chance did. Unexpected thoughts; like remembering how proud I'd felt the night he received an award for saving the life of a little girl. She had been buried alive for three days under a building that collapsed during an earthquake in Haiti. Mercy had pointed the way and Chance had risked his life going beneath the rubble to save her. With an overwhelming pang, I wished Chance were here to rescue me.

"I'm a social worker, here to give Maria and Paloma a ride to the woman's shelter," I lied. "Are you Ramiro?"

He laughed with a deep guttural cough and tightened his chokehold. "You bring a cop with you to get the bitch and her kid?"

"He's with CPS—Child Protective Services. They wouldn't let me drive out here alone."

The man gestured with his gun pointed at Travis. "Now the other one, Señior CPS," the man spoke with a thick accent. The world was fading into shades of gray as I gasped, sucking in my last breath. My knees buckled and I dropped as low as the chokehold would allow.

Travis stood with one hand in the air, using only his fingertips, he carefully pulled a second gun from his waistband at the small of his back and tossed it toward the first gun already on the ground. The instant the guns clanked together, I summoned every drop of caffeine in my body and jumped back on both of Señior Bad Man's feet and straightened my legs, jack-knifing us backward onto his butt. The heat of the gun blast scorched my ear with a deafening shockwave, reverberating through my head and burning the fold of my ear as the shot went wild. I rolled away, grabbing for the mace from my bag as Travis raced for the guns.

A giant paw reached out and grabbed my free wrist. I groped for the mace with the other. Ramiro rolled, pulling me on top of him, once again using me as a shield. With Ramiro's focus on Travis's gun and my bag just out of reach, I resorted to tried-and-true Plan C: jerking my knee into Ramiro's crotch with a force that turned his brown face blue, then white. His groan bugled through the hills like a castrated bull, only releasing his grip when Travis pointed a gun at his head.

Travis continued to subdue him. *That is to say;* Travis watched with a pained expression as my assailant writhed and rolled in the dirt, cursing in Spanish and moaning in agony as he clutched his now-wet man-parts. I crawled toward the second gun, got it and rose, stumbled to the house and slipped inside.

Muffled sounds led me to Maria who had apparently wriggled her way off of a dirty, ragged sofa and onto the living room floor. Her wrists were bound with duct tape and a second strip of tape was wrapped around her head and over her bruised and battered mouth.

Hurrying to her side, I froze, terrified, heart crashing wildly when the door slammed.

It was Travis. He took in the scene and moved to our side, whipped out a knife and neatly sliced the duct tape from Maria's wrists.

The thought blazed through my head: *I will never criticize men and their pocket knives again.*

Freed, Maria ripped the duct tape from her head, pulling out hair that stuck to the tape and waved about like corn silk on a husk.

"Paloma! *Mi niña! Por favor.* Please! Maria motioned to the screen door at the back of the cabin. *"En el hoyo!"*

Okay—I got the "Paloma" part, and I got the idea.

Travis pulled the shaking Maria to her knees. "Is there anyone else here? *¿Cuántos?* How many?"

"Si. Seis o siete."

I knew those words meant six or seven. Evidentially Travis knew some Spanish too.

He crouched, looking past me as he surveyed the room. Softly, urgently, he asked, "Sunny, are you hurt?"

"I'm o..." before I could finish, Maria shot up from the floor and raced toward the kitchen. "She's going after Paloma!"

Travis held me by the arm. "Hold on. Wait here while I call for backup."

"That'll take too long!" I argued.

"I'll call, and then we'll go together. Sunny... use it if you need to," Travis said, pointing to the gun I'd left on the couch while helping Maria.

I nodded to Travis, who winked and nodded back. He slipped out of the room, opening the front door and stepping over the gunman's now-inert body that lay on the doorstep with his ankle cuffed to a post that supported the porch. I watched him through the window as he passed by the dead pit, making his way cautiously back to the car, and then, I couldn't wait any longer.

Feeling more secure with a gun in my shaking hand, I ignored Travis's orders and quickly followed Maria. Slipping out the back door, I headed toward the only outbuilding I could see and caught up with her as she crouched behind an old well house. Kneeling in the dirt next to her, I looked into eyes that were equal parts terror and exhaustion. Fueled by desperation, Maria clutched my arm and raised her backside, preparing for another sprint.

"Alto! Stop! Who's the guy on the porch?" I whispered to Maria. "*Quién es el hombre?*" I practically flunked high school Spanish, but like most Californians, I learned in kindergarten how to count to twenty, and later, Mexican food. Then, I learned how to handle crisis calls.

"Ramiro," Maria said, pointing to the house. "*Ramiro, mi novio.*" Then she pointed at the woods, sniffling and wiping her face with her sleeve. "Paloma, my da-ter... *enterrar... cementerio.*"

"Cemetery? *He buried your daughter?* Oh. My. God." I gasped. Oh yeah, this *was* really happening. This wasn't at all like I imagined my day would go. I only hoped that Travis had been able to radio for help out here in no-man's-land.

"Lord," I looked heavenward, "please send some heavily armed SWAT angels to Paloma until we can get there."

Maria crossed herself in response. "*Gracias,*" she said. I guess the universal language of prayer is understood with the heart.

The door at the back of the house rattled from behind. I swung around, gun extended, finger taut against the trigger just as a demonic growl told me another pit was moving up from behind. I turned back again to face a new threat, every muscle in my hand aching to squeeze the trigger and release the tension. The screen door slammed, and I spun... to see Travis stepping out of the screen door; our guns aimed at each other—just as I heard a cry from Maria as the dog scrabbled for a leap.

Pivoting low, I fired—*Bam! Bam! Bam!* Three times without blinking. The air rent with the sound of gunfire and a single scream from the dog who fell, twitched, and sighed before he died. Dead silence. Blood seeped from beneath the dog. I had no doubt that the gunshots sent a warning to the men in the woods. I could only hope it had Cc'd the message to the last dog. I knew these men meant business. They would probably kill us and use us for fertilizer and then name the new strains Kop Kush or Blue Splat.

Sickened at the sight of the poor beast lying in a growing pool of blood, I willed myself not to faint, throw up, or burst into tears for the dog that had died while doing his duty. Travis moved past what was left of the dog, squatted next to us and whispered, "God, Sunny, remind me never to piss you off."

Ignoring the jibe, I swallowed. "Did you get backup?"

"911 babe. On their way."

We followed Maria who was heading for the hydraulic pits, left by miners in the 1800's who had hosed down the hills in search of gold, leaving the area pocked with holes and settling ponds. Catching up with her again, we had to hold Maria back. There were no guarantees that the other bad guys were gone, so we pulled her down with us as we squatted behind a rock pile. Travis shushed us with a finger to his lips. Minutes felt like hours.

Finally, the beat of helicopters turned the quiet forest into a military zone. The first helicopter flew toward us, then hovered overhead and radioed Travis who responded with a hand-held device he pulled from his coat pocket. A few more agonizing minutes ticked away before it landed, sending billowing clouds of dust fanning out and making us cough as it touched down on an old landing site.

A second helicopter completed aerial surveillance, and we got the "All Clear" to move safely toward the hydraulic pits.

"Paloma! Paloma!" Maria dashed to the closest pit, practically tumbling into the yawning hole before discovering it was empty.

We spread out in different directions to search the other pits. Cresting a hill comprised of tailings, I froze with a sense of foreboding, stomach clenched and heart racing as I spotted a child's pink tennis shoe half buried by debris. Something else, beyond the shoe and off the trail caught my eye. It looked like a child's backpack tossed, or dropped, lying tangled in a shrub. The pack had a big purple and pink star covered with glitter that flashed in the sun like a sign pointing the way.

Fighting an urge to run the other way, I approached the rim of an adjacent pit. I didn't want to look. I didn't want to have images of a child's dead body trapped in my mind forever.

I am an advocate.

It was my duty to shield Maria from whatever lay ahead. I moved to the pit and peered over the edge.

ⅎ 🕊 ⅏

Paloma lay motionless at the bottom of the pit; face down, tangled hair splayed across the dirt, wearing a short-sleeved t-shirt, dirty underwear, and one sad pink shoe. It was over 100° and getting hotter by the minute. Dread filled the air, filled my lungs, and weighed heavily on my heart. The squeeze in my chest made it hard to breathe, harder still to call for help.

Oh baby, please be all right.

"Lord..." I croaked, but had no need to finish. God knew.

With a leap of faith, I catapulted, sailing feet first, like an Italian mobster in cement shoes, straight to the bottom. Feet, knees, and head bouncing off the rock-strewn ground, propelling me forward for a second time before crashing to a stop on the far side. It took a minute for the twinkling stars in my head to fade into sunlight. I crawled to Paloma's side and gently turned her over and cradled her unconscious body in my arms.

"Paloma?" I whispered, brushing her hair from her face. Her mouth quivered in silent response. *Water! She needs water!* Paloma didn't weigh much. I dragged her to the shady side of the pit and whispered, "It's okay, honey. *Tu Madre* is coming.

"Here! We're down here!" I called out in a gravelly voice. No reply.
I looked back at Paloma. "I'll come back. I promise.

I struggled to climb; fell back several times, tore my pants and gashed my injured knees on jagged pieces quartz. Sweat bathed my face, stung the gunshot burn on my ear, and blurred my vision. At last, I pulled myself over the lip—and into a rush of an oncoming rescue team—with Chance leading the way.

Chance stumbled, startled. Recovered, "Sunny? What... ?" Chance tossed his gear down.

"The pit," I gasped, gesturing behind me.

"You're hurt." He quickly assessed my injuries.

"Go! Go!" I gestured wildly toward the pit and he moved ahead.

Maria was running toward us, arms outstretched. I could barely hear her cries over the deafening *thump-thump* of the helicopter. I didn't understand her language, but I knew what she was saying.

It was a touching scene when Chance was hauled up from the pit carrying Paloma in his arms. Maria's eyes shined with unbridled gratitude as she reached up and kissed Chance on the cheek. He was all strength, thoughtful and sensitive. The scene before me tugged at my heart, and I struggled to rein it in.

I refused medical treatment so there would be room for Maria on the helicopter. That, and I wanted to show Chance that I could take care of myself. They were all life-flighted down to Enloe Hospital in Chico, and I watched them fade into the horizon with a sigh.

CHAPTER 28

ॐ ༄ ☙

When the air had cleared and dust settled, Travis and I began our long drive out of the hills. We traveled in silence for the most part until I gave in to exhaustion and the post-adrenalin crash. Somehow I slept through the bumps and jolts of the dirt roads only to awaken much later when we pulled up to an ornate, black, wrought-iron gate. Travis reached out and pressed the key code for the electronic gate that swung open. I rubbed my gritty eyes and squinted. Chico has some very prestigious homes and I had never been to this particular gated community.

"Welcome to California Park," said, Travis.

A family of white geese drifted across the glassy surface of a large pond just as the last rays of sunset wrapped the water in a fiery hug and kissed it goodnight.

We pulled into a beautifully manicured stone and brick home. Curious, I looked to Travis, my expression asking the question that my lips were too tired to form.

"My place," he said. "Come on."

Travis walked around the 4x4 and opened the door. I dragged myself behind him and up the winding walkway like a tired puppy. The porch light came on and I paused to admire the beautiful full-length, etched windows on either side of the carved oak door. He unlocked the door, ushered me in and flipped a switch. I stopped and stared, amazed.

The entry pointed the way to a facing free-standing wall—only the wall was a solid upright single-cut slab of polished green and gold onyx about six feet wide—that showcased an intricate Chinese table and carved Buddha who appeared to be meditating between a pair of ornate sconces. The entire scene was backlit with a soft, golden light that illuminated through the translucent slender-cut slab and I gasped as the tranquil sound of water slid down the face of the rock, whispering its water-song through perfumed air. I felt as though I had entered a Buddhist monastery.

Travis led me around the shrine and stepped down into a white-carpeted living room and a plush white leather sofa with green and gold tapestry pillows that stood in an orderly arrangement along the back. I sat, and he disappeared.

More than curious, my eyes swept the room in a kind of fascination, pausing to admire the beautiful rockwork that framed a large, rugged fireplace with contrasting delicate Japanese maple and juniper bonsai trees gracing its mantel. The opposite wall featured a stunning mural of great blue herons in flight, rising from tall reeds on a lakeshore and soaring toward the high ceiling. The only other furniture was an ornate writing desk.

This place is Travis, I thought; precision cut, serene, elegant, yet substantial and enduring all at once. It was immaculate, masculine, and very Feng Shui. The practical me that had grown up hauling ashes from the wood stove to the garden was busy contemplating the sensibility of a fireplace and white carpet when Travis returned carrying two glasses of dark red wine.

"How do you keep the ashes from wrecking your carpet?" Even as the words left my mouth, I was embarrassed at my lack of sophistication. The fireplace was undoubtedly gas, not wood, and I blushed, feeling awkward and out of place.

A warm smile stretched across Travis's face as he held a glass out in offering. "Here, you look like you could use this."

He was right. I took a sip and melted into the soft cushions. Like everything else, the wine was perfect.

"Travis," I turned to look at him. "Why did you bring me here?"

"To get you out of your pants," he said with a boyish grin that made blood rush to my face. Embarrassed that I had blushed twice within minutes, I looked away, hating that he has that affect on me.

Travis gave a soft laugh and disappeared again, returning with peroxide, ointment, adhesive tape, and some large gauze pads. I zoomed from embarrassed to stupid in the space of a heartbeat.

"Drop 'em," he said.

What's a girl to do? Besides, I was too tired to argue, so I unzipped and dropped my pants, left standing before Travis with my thong, torn knees, and most likely my face in coordinated shades of fire engine red. Flushing was the only protest I could muster.

"*Nice,*" he said in a husky voice, trailing the word as his eyes slid up and down my legs. "You can sit." His smile made my pulses quicken, his words were calm and reassuring. "I won't hurt you."

He lied. A groan started at my knees and worked its way up into a yelp as Travis the removed the grit embedded my wounds. The cuts were pretty deep and threatened to pull open with every bend of the knee as I climbed back into torn jeans.

"Thanks, Doc," I mumbled as he dabbed burn ointment on my ear.

Travis gathered the first aid remnants, and I returned to surveillance.

The house was magazine perfect and the decor serene, but it wasn't natural. Things were missing; like an entertainment center, clock, phone, junk mail, animal dander, photographs and mementos from captured moments in time, dust. The Buddha was the showcase and central theme of his home, and I pondered this phenomenon as I took in the tranquil environment.

Do all roads lead to heaven? Is living for *here and now* really so bad? After all, *now* is all we really have in any faith, or even in the absence of faith.

Travis returned. "Hungry?" he asked.

I'm sure I saw a glimmer in his eye. "Starving."

"Tuna okay?"

I followed Travis, limping behind him into the kitchen with my wineglass in hand. He had set a small table for two with sandwiches and a platter of fruit and then dimmed the overhead lights.

"No candlelight?" I teased. His eyes darkened at my question. "Just kidding."

He reached for his food as I bowed my head in silent prayer. I thanked God that Maria and Paloma were safe and I was alive and hadn't gotten anyone killed. When I was done giving thanks, I asked God to bless the food and looked up to see Travis fully absorbed in watching me.

"How long have you been a Christian?" he asked in a respectful tone.

I gave him more details, how my parents had practically abandoned me, the years spent in Joyce's company, and how she had ministered to me. Travis continued to gaze in fascination. Then I breezed over the events in Sturgis again. Maybe I owed my talkativeness to the wine, the exhaustion, or even a part of what God had meant by "cleaning out my closet." It felt like a cleansing tonic until I got deeper into the story and saw Travis's face darken. I noticed a small muscle straining and pulsing along his jaw and felt a build up of tension that was out of harmony with the environment.

He interrupted to ask detailed questions about the motorcycle gangs, particularly the Bandido Nation and the Mongols.

"I thought we were talking about faith. Can we just have a conversation for once instead of an interrogation?"

"I'm sorry. Old habit. Please, continue." He looked contrite.

I huffed and concluded with the story of Tim, the motorcycle preacher who had brought me back to California, and how I had come to know Christ during that journey.

"So, how long have you been a Buddhist?"

"I grew up a Catholic," Travis said as he continued to study me, gauging my reaction. "I was an altar boy for a time. My mother took me to Mass every Sunday and I went to confession like clockwork, but nothing in my life changed. No matter how many Hail Mary's and Our Fathers I said, I still felt bad and stayed bad. Then one day it occurred to me that maybe I wasn't really such a bad person after all. Maybe it was just the church that made me feel that way."

"What way?"

"Unforgiven," he clarified. "I don't have your kind of faith. I need more than words in a book. I need proof." He looked into his cup of wine as if he were doing communion. "I need... I need to be an active participant in my own salvation."

"Do you believe in God?" I asked.

Travis grew thoughtful. "Buddha says it is fear that drives men to the sacred mountains, trees, and shrines. When I was in combat, I heard men crying out to God when they were wounded. Those that survived went back to being jerks," he chuckled, "a lot like I would do after going to confession."

Reaching for some fruit, I contemplated his words. "I don't worship mountains, trees, or shrines," I said finally. "I worship the Creator, not the created."

He was quiet again and his silence felt like an invitation to continue. "So," I asked, "do you believe in heaven or hell?"

"I've seen both, and it sounds like you have too," he offered, placing a warm hand over mine on the table between us.

"But... you believe in an afterlife that is all-inclusive? Right?" I didn't know much about Buddhism.

"Yes. Absolutely," Travis said with conviction. "There are many levels of existence before reaching a state called 'enlightenment.' Unlike Christianity, a person isn't stuck in one level for eternity."

I could have wept. "If that's true, then I guess Logan will be there—in your afterlife—raping me and stalking me for eternity. I mean, if he doesn't want to change here on earth, why would he want to change later?"

৪০ ৵ ৫৪

We finished our meal in silence. Travis slid his chair back and walked around and took me by the hand, guiding me back to the sofa in his sanctuary.

"What would make you think that Logan could abuse you in your afterlife?"

"Because... if there is no black and white, no heaven and hell, then we are left with too many shades of gray. What would keep me from being raped in heaven, if heaven is just a place where *everyone* goes they die—the angel police?" My voice tightened. "If heaven isn't perfect, then it's just like earth, and it isn't really heaven at all. And where do you draw the line, Travis? Is heaven filled with people who just tell 'little white lies?' Where they 'borrow-not steal' your stuff for eternity? Is it a place where it is okay to slap, but not punch? If there is no God and no boundaries, who the hell draws the line?"

"We do. For ourselves." Travis handed me a tissue as my tears fell in rhythm with the water skimming down the face of the fountain.

"Oh yeah, that's right. *Reincarnation.*" I exclaimed. The force of my convictions rose up and spilled over. "You probably believe in reincarnation. This time Logan is a killer. Next time he'll just be a child molester because he'll have evolved to a higher life form." I drew back, feeling a need to keep my distance.

"You know Travis, for a man who dedicates his life to the pursuit of justice, your faith has none. Unless you are telling me I deserve what Logan did to me."

Silence.

Exasperated, huffing again, I reached for my shoulder bag and rose from the sofa. Travis rose with me.

"If I am not a child of God—then I am a bastard of the universe," I declared. "I have no past, no future, and no inheritance. Only death! Or worse; evolution. I don't think so! I was created for more than that."

I knew he didn't have an answer, or else he was doing the Kung-Fu-Master silence-implies-wisdom thing.

"I don't want to argue. Please, come back and sit with me. We're talking, right? Isn't that what you wanted?" Travis's soft voice was at odds with the tension in his movements. I didn't want to leave on a negative note. Not after all we had been through and the kindness Travis had shown. This was his home and he was entitled to his beliefs.

Time to change the subject. Easing back onto the sofa, I sat. "You don't have any family pictures on your walls."

"No. I don't." He said bluntly.

Okay. I asked the obvious. "I take it that means you're not married?"

Travis leaned forward, taking me captive with his gaze in a way that shockingly reminded me of Ramiro, who had held a gun to my head just hours ago. We locked eyes.

"*No.* I am *technically* married," Travis said in a steely voice. "She had several *affairs* when I was deployed." His face darkened. Apparently, I had found his trigger. "Second tour in Iraq... and *'No'*... our divorce is not final. Did I miss anything? 'Is that the dirt you were looking for? Need more graphic details'?" Travis iterated, emphasizing and repeating the same hurtful words I had hurled at him in the restaurant. My words had returned, bringing tears to my eyes and stinging like a slap to the heart.

"That was wrong," Travis hastened to apologize. "That was a cheap shot." His eyes flickered as the last trace of resentment drained from his face.

The truth set aside the insult, illuminated by simplicity: We were both married—but not to each other. It was time to go. I got up and looked around, careful not to leave anything behind.

"Wait. Don't go. Don't walk out." Travis pleaded as he reached out. "I want you to stay with me tonight."

Just tonight?

"Sex won't fix your fractured marriage or my broken heart." I turned away, picked up the keys to the county SUV from the end table and hobbled across the room.

"That's not my intention." Travis quickly intercepted me, the look on his face was real, honest and raw.

"Then what is your intention?"

The strain between us was taut, stretched to the breaking point. I found myself sympathizing with the pain that cut across his handsome face, a pain I knew all too well, the result of betrayal by someone you love and trusted.

"Do you and your wife still talk?" I asked.

"Sometimes." He sounded defensive.

"Do you still see her?"

"Sometimes." His gaze dropped.

"Do you still love her?"

His voice and his face softened. "Sometimes."

Travis reached out and took hold of me, drawing me close enough to feel his breath on my cheek. His warm scent made me dizzy and feeling intoxicated. He cupped my face. "You are the most amazing woman I have ever known."

"What about...?"

Travis touched a single finger to my trembling lips as our bodies and minds pressed in, closer... deeper.

"Umm..."

"Shh. I love you, Sunny McLane." His lips grazed my ear, sending a shiver of want racing down my spine.

I pulled back, breathing hard. "Oh, Travis... that's the second time you've said that. What does that mean? for you? for us? What do you want from me? I need to know."

I've been used... so many times before.

Strong hands drew me back into a consuming embrace. "I want you."

I repeated "What does that mean?" in words so faint they seemed to evaporate in the heat of the moment.

His mouth enveloped mine, kissing with conviction, kindling an unexpected surge of need that coursed through every cell in my body. He worked his way down—hungry lips that ravished my mouth, explored my throat, and lingered as he sampled the sweetness of breasts...

"Travis!" I moaned, and he seemed to drink in the sound.

Talk is cheap. Men will say anything to get me into bed.

"What do you want from me?" I breathed a question that begged for details: get laid, get married, one night or a lifetime? All fizzled, sputtered, and died in the ensuing flood of desire.

Buttons flew open, liberating pent up inhibitions. Zippers swung back the doors to passion.

"You know what I want." Travis's voice was husky as his mouth pressed into my tortured flesh; kissing-kissing-nuzzling-nipping-tasting.

There comes a time when men won't talk. Cold reason turns to ashes in the flame of desire. And there comes the point when you can't say *No.*

Can't turn back and risk their anger, violence, or humiliation.

Or perhaps, I was using my past to justify recklessness. Real or imagined, I crossed the line and fully surrendered to soft skin over hard muscle as it found its hungry way into the deepest part of me.

Like the incense in the hall, the essence of testosterone and estrogen mingled in the air, fueling the force that drove each of us to scorching heights of passion. From the thick white carpet where we burned in front of the flameless heater, to the California king-sized bed, sleek with black satin sheets, to the floor in a tangle of soft fleece blankets and the erotic warmth of the six water jets that renewed us in the shower—the night wore away as we set fire to every room in his house.

Had there ever been such a night? Collapsing at last on his bed with my last ounce of strength, I sighed, "I think I love you too, Travis."

Morning came and went. We woke intertwined—arms, legs, bedding—still dizzy with exhilaration and exhaustion when reality dawned. Travis was holding me close to his heart when I sat up and looked back to find him smiling serenely into my face.

Oh, my God! What have I done?

CHAPTER 29

ಹ 🕊 ಠಿ

Travis was deliciously sweet—at first. He tried to understand as he stood before me, but the gap in our beliefs became a chasm in the days following our affair. A difference was so vast that I wondered if it could be bridged over the course of a lifetime. And I didn't know if I—*if we*—were ready to risk the investment of time and sacrifice necessary to find out.

"What is your problem?" A frustrated Travis closed my office door and stood close enough for me to take in his frustratingly sensual essence. "Didn't you have a good time?" It was an honest question, and his eyes probed as he asked it. He had joked and flirted over the past couple of days, like an actor before an empty house. I could not engage. It had been a lot easier to play the game before we had sex.

I blushed in spite of the fact that I had nothing left to hide. "You don't understand, Travis. Of course, it was good," I admitted. *It was amazing.* "But I feel guilty."

He sniffed. "Christianity will do that to you," he said. "Now you know why I'm a Buddhist." He was in no mood to deal with Christian fanaticism. "You take life too seriously." He looked hurt.

When I told him I needed to talk with my pastor, he shrugged, shook his head, and stared hard at the tips of his polished shoes. Then he agreed that talking with my pastor was a "good idea" and abruptly left on business with a still-unhappy Paige.

ಹ 🕊 ಠಿ

"Are you and Travis having problems you'd like to talk about?" I asked Paige.

It was late in the day and Paige, back from her field work with Travis, had brought me her briefs for review. She froze for a moment, blinking rapidly.

She looked almost decent today and I couldn't help but realize again what a beautiful woman she was. Some people are just born lucky, I thought with a twist of jealousy.

"No. We're good," she frowned. "Nothing that will affect my job. Is that all?" she added with finality.

"No." She paused, poised for flight. "I'd like to thank you for all the extra help you've given me lately. I appreciate it."

Paige looked as if I had spoken to her in a foreign language. Then her eyes narrowed and flickered with the familiar suspicion and repressed anger that had come to define our relationship. But I noticed something more. Something different. More than anger, she seemed to harbor an underlying hurt.

"Sure. Whatever," Paige snapped before hurrying away, closing the door behind her.

Not my problem, I told myself. Who knows how I slighted Her Majesty this time. *She probably missed a nail appointment.* Heaving a sigh, I returned to my stack of briefs. I had done my good deed for the day and I still didn't like her. Anyhow, I lacked both the time and interest to deal with Paige's mysterious problems. I had enough of my own.

℘ 𝒴 ℭ

This was one week I didn't want to avoid Mac. No amount of Travis, ice cream, or otherworldly distractions would keep me away from my counseling session. To his amusement, I called ahead and we agreed to meet at the church at 6:00 p.m. I had just enough time for a quick shower.

A war was raging from within; I was too Christian to be happy in Travis's world and too much a product of the world to be satisfied in a faith that dictates so many rules. Some churches regulate dress, some music, some holidays... not to mention once-saved-always-saved, saved-by-works, saved-by-grace, saved-by-baptism, saved-after-death. And then, there is the Tribulation: pre-trib, mid-trib, post trib, no-trib saints. How could one be sure of anything?

"Lord! Do *you* really care about anything besides our hearts"? I asked aloud. I didn't get an audible answer, but I recalled that "Out of our hearts comes every thought, word, and deed."

I stood in the shower and did my monthly breast exam, which led me to do a heart-check also. My breasts didn't have any lumps, but my heart listened to the murmurs of the evil siblings, Anger and Pride and their toxic therapy—Revenge and Guilt. So oppressed was I with fear, regret, and self-condemnation that I could hardly look at Travis, who had summarized our romantic encounter in one simple word: "Fun."

Which of us was right? While I am not sure of everything, I am certain of this: my faith isn't something I can throw away like the stuff in my closet that has become uncomfortable or unfashionable. Somewhere along life's ride, my faith had become much more than the fabric of my life, full of holes and stains. It wasn't something I put on to cover myself, but something that had taken root, like my baby once had, and grown in my spirit. I could not, would not, abort it. Sighing, I shook myself like a wet dog and let my worry's fly.

Mac unlocked the door, turned on the lights and led me through the empty church building with a protective hand on my shoulder and a warm smile on his face. "Sit over there, Sunny."

"Oh, Pastor." The waterworks came. I hadn't slept in days, but had lain awake with visions of a divine boiler rocking crazily under pressure and my sin-ometer gauge spiking well past the DANGER zone. I had committed an unpardonable sin. I was afraid... and my heart was breaking.

Just because Travis believes there are no consequences for recreational sex didn't make me exempt from the truckload of guilt that had parked on my chest. Joyce, in Feather Falls, had always preached that while God loves me, there is hellfire and damnation in store for sinners. And Lord knows, I am a sinner. In my heart, I understood that I was no different from Starla, Logan, or even Paige for that matter.

I confessed to Pastor Mac that I was "seeing someone," and Mac easily and graciously read between the lines.

"You're not going to want to hear this," Mac picked up where we had left off. "I understand and *believe me*," he said emphatically, "you have my sympathies. That being said, don't ask me for my blessings. The Bible is clear that you are to 'leave and cleave' and become one with your husband." He leaned over the desk and removed his glasses, so nothing stood between us. "You are still one couple, even though you guys live in different houses."

"But I won't go to hell if I divorce him. Right?" I asked. I needed to double-check this. "The Bible says that I can divorce Chance because he has been sexually unfaithful."

Macs' features softened, and I swear the man could see right through my hypocrisy.

"That is true. There is nothing, *absolutely nothing*," Mac asserted, "that will send you to hell. God does not go back on his promises, but there will always be consequences for our choices. Stopping smoking doesn't mean you won't die of lung cancer, and leaving Chance doesn't guarantee you'll find happiness elsewhere. I will not advise you on the matter of divorce. That is strictly between you and God, but I do urge you to pray long and hard before deciding. The deeper the wound, the longer it takes to heal. Perhaps, you should give it time."

His gaze was steady and kind. No accusations, no judgment. Just compassion.

"You see," Mac continued, "most people have the wrong idea about Christian forgiveness. They confuse *meekness* with *weakness* and think *forgiveness* is *forgetness*. Forgiveness is really a way of declaring your faith in divine justice. You can step back and let God fight the battle for you. A lot of angry people lose sleep while their offender snores on without a care in the world. Forgiveness will never change the other person. It can only change you.

Are looking for happiness or satisfaction? I want you to be happy, and my dear, you will never find it in revenge. Only regret. Living in a state of anger and bitterness is a lot like swallowing poison and hoping it kills the other person.

Talk with your husband, Sunny. Denying that you have suffered a serious hurt won't heal your wounds. They will only get infected and kill off whatever hopes you might still have for a future together. Chance stays away from you because you told him to and because he is afraid. Only you can offer reconciliation."

This felt like another religious burden. Everything was on me. It was always on me. Nothing ever offered me justice when it came to Chance. I should have left the meeting with Pastor Mac feeling justified about having had sex with Travis. Logan had taught me a lot about biker justice, and payback and my job had taught me about accountability and punishment.

Having sex with Travis was fair. It was payback. It was just. But the meeting with Mac hadn't felt like either. I had gone to my pastor in search of peace and returned home tied in emotional knots. I knew I was missing something important, but for the life of me, I couldn't figure out what the hell it was.

ℴxℴ

While reunification with Chance didn't seem likely, especially in light of my ambivalence and temporary insanity with Travis, I knew I wasn't ready to dig out and file the divorce papers that lay buried under a mountain of junk mail. Mac is a wise man and I trust and love him, so I decided to follow his advice and made the choice to keep the doors of communication open with Chance. Pouring a glass of wine for courage, I picked up the phone.

"Hey, what are you doing?"

"Mercy and I are sharing a plate of mango tofu tacos."

"Tofu tacos? Have you been talking to Ashley?"

"Sort of. I told Shane I needed a change and Ashley called to tell me that I need to give up meat."

"How's that working for you?"

"Mercy, no! Bad dog! Mercy! Argh... no!"

"What's she doing?"

"Taco is gushing out the sides of her mouth. *Outside!* Oh man, there's slobber everywhere... not the remote... She slimed it, brown with orange chunks. It looks like... Ugh! Never mind."

Mercy is a big dog and never does anything in a small way. I smiled at Chance's sounds of disgust as he cleaned up the Mercy mess.

When I asked if he still felt like going for a ride, Chance stopped grumbling.

"You bet! I'll pick you up around ten tomorrow," and later, "Have a good night. Sweet dreams."

I did not have a good night. It was plagued by disturbing dreams that

I was glad I couldn't remember later. It was almost 10:00 a.m. and Kissme was head-butting me to get up and let her out. The sun was heating up and I had just enough time to brush my hair and suck down a quick cup of coffee. I was ready to ride.

~ 🕊 ~

People typically think you're a wimp if you ride on the back of a motorcycle—unless you're wearing a patch that makes them think again. What they don't know is that it takes a lot more courage to ride hands-free, trusting the driver with your life, than it does being the one with both hands on the wheel, so to speak.

Riding has always been a kind of therapy for me. You have to love bikes to understand—or horses or airplanes, hiking or swimming, skydiving or trying a new recipe—anything that requires focus and risk. Chance pulled in the driveway, his bike refracting daylight like a piece of polished onyx burning in the sun. I hurried so he wouldn't turn off the engine. I didn't want to talk. I was tired from treading the mental hamster wheel round and round and getting nowhere. I needed to ride—in spite of a surge of post-traumatic stress from having gone over a cliff the last time I rode. I pulled on my helmet and gloves and prayed as I swung my leg over the VTX, "Lord, please don't let him kill me."

Like red-hot coals fanned by 1800 CCs, we blazed up the canyon like a firestorm, higher and higher. Truth seekers are always looking for God. For myself, I didn't see how they could miss Him. His presence was both evident and tangible. God was manifest everywhere I looked. At times we road level with the river; some places were calm and the river would sparkle like a string of polished diamonds, and there were times we rode past churning whitewater that foamed and splashed like pearls scattered before the wind. Then there were places where the river would grow so small and distant that the water looked like liquid poured from a crucible into a silver chain that graced the throat of the Feather River Canyon.

Hours later, Chance eased off the road just above the accident site where my old Harley slept beneath the pounding rapids. I pondered the joy and sadness that it had brought into my life, even as I now considered the new bike that Chance and I were riding together, wondering where it might take us.

Chance paused for a moment, seemingly lost in thought before killing the engine and motioning for me to dismount. We pulled off helmets and gloves, and the fringe on my leather coat swung in time as I walked toward the edge of the canyon. The leaves on the trees were turning color, and the roar of the water echoed off the steep walls.

"Why are we stopping—here, of all places?" My stomach knotted like a like a washcloth wrung too tight.

"This," said Chance, striding up and standing close to me, "is where it all began." Reaching over he took my chin, lifting it until we stood face to face. "And this," he continued, "is where I need to ask your forgiveness."

Chance is a big man. A strong man. Solid. Inside and out. Not perfect by any means, but big enough to admit his failures and shortcomings. I am trained, not to look *at* people, but look *into* people. And what I saw, as I searched the steady blue gaze of my husband's eyes, was bigness of heart and strength of character. What I saw, was a *real man.*

"I'm not asking you to take me back or anything you don't want to do," he hurried to assure me.

Chance placed his hands on my shoulders, and we continued to gaze eye-to-eye and heart to heart.

"I love you, Sunny, and I don't want to give up on our marriage. I understand that you're probably not ready to hear *that,* but I do hope you'll hear *this:* I have hurt you terribly, and I know *sorry* isn't enough. I know I have to make a new history and it's going to take time. I know that trust is something that has to be earned."

"I can *never* trust you again. It's more than what you did with Paige. It's that you lied to me! I can never be sure of you... of us... again."

"That may be so. We can only live one day at a time. I brought you here today to beg for your forgiveness." He radiated honesty from within, as warm and steady as the heat rising from the heart of the motorcycle.

I was surprised that he used the same one-day-at-a-time logic I had so recently used to justify having sex with Travis. He was talking forgiveness, while I had been plotting revenge.

Cars rushed past with bicycles and kayaks strapped to the top of their vehicles. Big rigs shifted through their gears as they slowed into the turns. All they could see was a motorcycle and two people. They couldn't see the damage or the disillusionment we carried. They could not fathom the risk we had taken by riding up the canyon together. They couldn't see a future hanging in the balance of indecision.

"That's good you understand because I'm not ready to take you back." Long pause. "But I am willing to ride with you."

A smile played across his lips, and his heart shined in his clear blue eyes. "I'm going to be the man you always wanted me to be, but not to try to get you back," he modified, shaking his head in determination. "I have to do it to get me back to being the man I want to be. I've been in counseling for months. I've been a regular part of a Christian men's group over in Paradise. It's a great group that offers help for any and every issue, from one man's food addiction to another brother recovering from porn addiction. They've asked me to lead the group, and I think I will. Between that and leading our church's Bible study, I've never felt so"—he paused to search for the right word— "so complete."

I gave him a quick smile, but I wasn't really listening. I was too busy rehearsing my response. This was the moment I had been waiting for; ever since the day I learned of his deception. The scene was set, the script memorized, and the time was now or never.

"I forgive you, Chance."

I had rehearsed this Christian epithet a dozen times in preparation for the grand moment I would bestow my holier-than-thou grace on him.

An image of Jesus in a Santa suit keeping a list of who's naughty and nice popped into my head. I had just lied. Lip service and nothing more. I had not forgiven Chance and now cringed as I visualized the hand of God striking a large check mark under Sunny ~*Naughty*.

"But I need to be honest with you," I continued. *About time.* "I don't know if we will ever get back together."

"Fair enough," said Chance. "That's more than I deserve." He reached over, surprising me as he pulled me into his arms and held me close for a joyful heartbeat, then turned with a smile, cinched down his helmet, mounted and fired up the bike without another word.

I felt like a flat tire as I rode along without touching him. The miles slid past and it occurred to me that I had won the battle and lost the war. I felt a stab of envy knowing in my heart that Chance had let go of an enormous burden. I guess that is what Mac had meant about anger and bitterness being like lead weights.

Chance shifted gears and we flew up the canyon; my heart feeling like a tombstone, and his, like a spirit set free from the grave.

ℂℂℂ

I stopped by Chance's house the next day to pick up some vegetables. He didn't answer the door, so I walked out toward the garden, pausing under a shady oak to observe him as he bent beneath a blazing summer sun, moving methodically between the rows of vegetables. I am jealous of his garden. The rows are perfectly aligned, lush, opulent, abundant as always, while the two potted plants on my front porch are weather-beaten victims of neglect.

Chance hummed a tune as the sun beat down, deepening the tan on his bare back and bleaching his hair an even lighter shade of blond.

He frequently leaves bags of produce on my steps and hauls baskets of surplus to the church and the Rescue Mission.

A pang of envy struck an arrow in my chest. My husband is a mystery. An enigma. How does he remain so darned happy knowing how I feel? Lord knows I remind him at every opportunity. And he knows I have feelings for Travis. Not to mention that Logan's buddies could be skulking in the woods—even now, lining us up in the crosshairs. Yet, there is Chance, singing along with KLOVE Christian radio and laboring in the garden instead of fishing or watching TV.

The door to the house was open and I slipped inside to raid the refrigerator and returned with two tall glasses brimming with ice cold lemonade. Chance locked the garden gate, petted Mercy, and brought up a basket filled with various red, green, and orange vegetables. It looks like salad is on the menu.

"Oh, hey, I didn't hear you come up."

"Great watch dog you got there. *"Kisses for Mercy,"* I cooed, reaching down to rub her finely chiseled head as she wagged her tail.

"What brings you here?" he asked, happy to see me again so soon after our ride.

"A question. Why are you are always so darned happy?" I was only half joking. "There's enough vegetables here to open a produce stand. You must like self- abuse."

He laughed and wiped his brow. "I like sitting with you and drinking lemonade and looking at the harvest. How can you look at my tomatoes and not smile?" he chided as he placed a basket in front of me. They were beautiful—full, practically sensuous, and ruby red.

"Seriously. In all of the years we've been together, you've always been more happy than not. How do you do it?"

Chance took chair on the porch and drank deeply, puckering his lips at the tangy taste of sweet and citrus, and then sucked some frosty drips off his mustache with his lower lip. "Aren't you happy?" He finally asked.

I rolled my eyes. "What's there to be happy about?"

Chance gave a sad smile and reached down to stroke Mercy who took up her place in the shade near his feet. "Before I was a Christian, I was like everyone else, going through one boring, repetitious day at a time. Some good, some not. I was *existing* more than living." His brows furrowed in thought. "But when I really got that Christ died to save me from another boring day, to give me the fullness of life, I figured the best to thank God is to be happy and appreciate my time here in spite of my circumstances.

A wistful sigh escaped. "I wish I had your faith."

"Good Lord, No!" Chance laughed. "Never! Why would you want my faith instead of finding your own? Think of all the fun you'd miss out on."

"You've got a strange concept of fun," I countered, feeling sad and a little frustrated. "It's just, how do you *really* know? You and Ashley, Mac and Shane. You are all so sure of yourselves while I am back and forth and up and down, almost moment to moment in my faith."

Chance smiled, his eyes holding more sparkle than the frost on our glasses. His full happiness had returned, while mine lay like the shadows beneath our feet. I envied Chance.

"Well," he said, "that's where you're mistaken. Actually, I have no confidence in myself." He gave a little chuckle. "But I do have faith in Jesus and his promises."

"Yeah, but how can you be so sure?" I felt like I was standing on the brink of discovery. So close...

"When you go to court, what does it take for the law to convict someone?"

"Evidence."

"What's the best evidence?"

I thought. "Um... eyewitnesses and physical evidence."

"Is that enough proof to get a conviction?"

"Always."

Chance nodded. "There you go. It's that simple. Or else it was mass insanity by the thousands of people who 'eye-witnessed' countless miracles; dead neighbors rising from their graves, people born blind seeing, people dying of leprosy healed. I don't have all that much faith. Like most people, I needed proof. And I got it. It's documented. You've got your eye-witness, and you have your evidence."

Can it be that simple?

"It's just history, no faith required." Chance wrapped it up sounding like Mac. "Belief is a choice," he said, "but the choice will never alter the facts."

Mercy got up and whined expectantly. It was about that time. "Hungry?" Chance asked. "How about a salad?"

෨ 🕊 ෬

Sometimes I think Chance missed his calling and should have been a preacher. He is always preaching to friends, co-workers, and me. While I love it, I sometimes think it was a huge part of my struggle to forgive him. I found the hypocrisy intolerable.

If Chance had of been a man who bought behind-the-counter girly-magazines, watched seedy X-rated movies, or if I'd caught him sneaking online pornography when no one was looking, I might have seen his adultery coming. But he had always been the complete opposite. He had always held himself out as moral and upright.

Well, I thought, *it just goes to show. You can't trust anyone.*

CHAPTER 30

జ 🕊 ౭

Blood from her broken nose was everywhere: sprayed across the kitchen wall, pooled on the cupboard, a splotch on the table, and partial handprint on the back door that slid from the window to the knob. Blood had even soaked Mickey Mouse on her t-shirt that proclaimed Disneyland to be the *Happiest Place on Earth,* but not for *Tinker Bell* who fluttered above him. Tink looked like Mickey had fired a round into her head.

The police had cuffed Rocky-the-perp, and his parole officer had been notified. Rocky wouldn't be bothering Lannah again for a few years. She would use the time looking for her *Next Man.* "Like they do on the TV show" she declared. "Kick 'em to the curb and find someone new."

The police had forced entry into the home when they heard Lannah's screams and the sound of dishes shattering in the kitchen, sounding like a skeet shoot in a china shop. Upon entry, the first thing the police saw was eight-year-old Manny sitting in front of the TV completely oblivious to all the commotion, laughing and cheering the characters in his bloody drug war video game. He worked the controls as if his life depended on it.

"Yeah! Get him! Kill him! Kill him!" Little Manny, dressed in Sponge Bob PJs and munching from a bag of Doritos was hyper-absorbed in his game, shutting out his dad's bellowing and his mother's frantic screams. Although his parents' fighting hadn't bothered Manny, it had been loud enough to alert the neighbors who had called the police. Amazing but true—Manny didn't even look up when the police cracked the frame on the front door and stormed in.

After Rocky had been cuffed and loaded in the cruiser, Lannah stood in the front yard telling her story to the police. She told them not to call an ambulance; a girlfriend would drive her to the ER.

Back inside, a second officer asked Manny three times, "Is there anyone else in the house?" before assuming the boy was deaf and turned off the TV to get his attention. The officer was rewarded with a hateful glare and "My sister, Becca. Her room's down there," he said, pointing down the hall before grabbing the remote and turning the TV back on.

Becca was not in her room, so a systematic search began for the missing three-year-old girl. Under beds, behind doors and in the closets. They finally found little Becca tunneled under an enormous pile of dirty clothes in Manny's bedroom, as if somehow her big brother's suits of armor could protect her.

I read the report with a kind of morbid fascination before setting an appointment with Lannah. She had blatantly told the police, "It don't bother them. They hardly ever hear it," she'd said, referring to her children. I wondered if I was like Manny, blotting out the horror and accepting violence as a normal part of life. Or maybe was I more like Becca, hiding under a pile of dirty work, sheltering from childhood memories.

ℬ 𝒴 ℂ

"Momeeeee," I sobbed, as Starla screamed. My world was very small when I was five. I rarely traveled beyond the cabin except to accompany my mother to the grocery store and emergency room.

I adored my dad who was always loving, tender, and patient with me. That my wonderful father should be hitting my beautiful mother, dragging her by the hair, kicking and screaming across the yard, was beyond horrible. Then he would go away, but not to prison. Starla never called the police on Lefty, and I suppose he must have known that she wouldn't.

Instead of going to jail, Lefty would be heading for Oakland, running from his past and the powerlessness he had felt as a POW in Vietnam. He had been a three-year guest of the Vietcong in the Hanoi Hilton, a prison that was infamous for inflicting severe systematic torture—not designed to gain information—but to break the collective and individual spirits of the men housed there. Lefty had left Vietnam, but Vietnam had not left him.

For some users, emotional pain feels as if life has filled a backpack full of stones they must carry until they are finally crushed and buried alive. Each stone bears a name: *mom-dad-husband-stranger-friend...poverty-accident-war-fate...* Fueled by outrage, the victim pulls those stones out one-by-one and hurls them, not caring who they hit: their children, friends, spouse, a perceived enemy... just to get the damned load off their back, no matter who gets hurt.

But the empty pack is a lie, for it soon fills up with new stones they put on themselves; *guilt, shame, remorse.*

Other perpetrators inflict abuse void of any emotion. They hurl accusations, telling their child to "Man-up!" as they beat them down. With detached observation, they measure their victim's reactions against their own history of abuse. *"Did I handle my beating better? was I stronger? am I a winner or a loser?"*

There are adult victims who say, *"I hate you,"* to their child because they see the child as weak. They despise the little mirror in front of them that reflects their own history of powerlessness.

Little Becca reminded me of myself because I mostly hid; although like Manny and many other children, I would sometimes disassociate and completely withdraw into other dimensions through games, books, and fantasy.

Puberty typically transitions abused children into adults that are hooked on painkillers, alcohol, sex, and drugs. Their addictions result in unwanted pregnancies for girls in need of male love, and juvenile hall for boys in need of attention and direction.

Like other child survivors of domestic violence, I had grown up knowing that I was different from other kids. I also endured the heartbreaking confusion regarding loyalty. Boys feel guilty that they were unable to protect their mothers, while girls believe abuse is an inescapable part of being female.

I brought Starla cold washcloths and hot coffee in the morning. Sometimes I would put a wildflower on her pillow. She did not thank me, hug me, or hold me. But I liked to imagine that she loved me all the more for my offerings.

As for me, I learned to feel guilty early on. I really missed Lefty. I adored my father. When he was gone, I missed the man who would call out "Hey, Baby Girl, how's my best sweetheart?" and shower me with kisses and hugs.

No wonder my mother left me, I thought with another load of guilt. *Daddy loved me more than he loved her. I was the beneficiary of all the dreams Starla had envisioned with the man she loved.*

෨ 🕊 ෬

The aroma of French roast wafted into the lobby like a beacon of light drawing the crowd. There was enough caffeine to power a small army, and that is just what it was intended to do. The huge basket next to the coffee pot was pregnant with a cholesterol lover's selection of poppy seed, blueberry, banana nut, and orange muffins. The silver tray next to the pot flaunted tempting slices of cantaloupe arrayed in a sunny orb that hugged bunches of voluptuous grapes and delectable lipstick-red strawberries. Napkins and small colorful paper plates, designed to make even a modest eater look piggy, sat at the head of the table. Bottles of water rested at the far end. The table to the right showcased name tags, sign-in sheets, handouts and blank notebooks laid out in grid-like precision. All this, designed to attract and mollify the employees attending today's seminar.

Continuing education is a necessary and often welcome, relaxing break for most professionals. Simultaneously, it can also be a time of stress and anxiety for the presenter. The PowerPoint slideshow was up and I did a quick head count, pleased to see so many agencies represented. I waved to Gina from Children's Services and nodded to Traci from the court. I ignored Marne from the SAFE Program but welcomed her excellent, dedicated co-workers. There were counselors from various countywide programs, representing both private and social services. I guessed about fifty to sixty people were there for the training and I was grateful to have the opportunity to teach on the "Impact of Domestic Violence on Children."

If it weren't for my faith, the traumatic events of my childhood would have been meaningless, *just plain bad luck*, and I might have grown up bitter and depressed. I do not believe that God created, designed, or intended for me to have the experiences of my youth, but that it is his joyful promise to make something good come out of the misery.

I silently prayed, "Dear Lord, let this training touch at least one heart and save one child. And God, please don't let me burp, fart, or have food stuck in my teeth."

Cups full, plates down, the room grew quiet. All eyes turned my way as I gave my educational pedigree for an introduction. After all, being a victim does not make one an expert. But then, neither does just reading about domestic violence in books.

"They were sleeping in the other room..."
"They were playing, watching TV..."
"They're used to it..."
"They see violence on TV all the time..."
"Kids are resilient; they'll get over it..."
"They'll forget..."
"...just a baby..."
"I've never heard them talk about it..."

I had heard every possible variation of the same theme and I was sure that most of my audience had heard them too. We started out on common ground, and from there, I let the facts speak for themselves.

"Preschoolers can become excessively clingy, fussy, fearful, and have digestive problems. By elementary school, they can become hyperactive or aggressive, or overly eager to please." Next slide.

I see myself as validation of my information. I was always trying to please my teachers with good grades. I clung to my neighbors, Joyce and Kenny, as surrogate parents. I felt guilty for loving my dad, yet submitted to Logan even as Starla had submitted to Lefty's abuse.

"Many of the boys from violent homes end up in juvenile hall, and the girls begin to self-medicate to escape traumatic memories. Children grow up to become violent men and battered women. Boys explode, girls implode. Men go to jail, women seek mental health services. Both are more likely to abuse their own children." My crowd stirred, glancing at their watches. Their minds were turning away from me and back to work. It was time to wrap it up.

"Because these children can have radically different reactions, some professionals deny or minimize the impact of domestic violence." Pause. "I want to thank you for your time and open the floor for discussion. Are there any questions?"

I hadn't tripped and fallen on my face or left the zipper on my skirt open. My nylons didn't run and the computer didn't crash. My presentation had been articulate and my answers clear and concise. *Whew…and thank you.* But would my message make any difference?

I mulled this over on the long drive home. As Chance would say, I hold more triggers than a gun safe.

ဆၣ 𓆰 ၶ

"I heard the presentation went well." Travis popped a stick of gum in his mouth and chewed it with a slow deliberation that caused yet another rush of warmth. He seems to find my embarrassment amusing. I had my clothes on, but he still makes me feel naked.

Travis hadn't asked me about my visit with Pastor Mac, and I was pretty sure he wasn't going to. He was back to being playful in his obnoxious, endearing way.

"Who did you hear that from?" I asked with a grin, hoping it was Jack or Amanda.

"Paige," he said with a nod and a smile.

"You lie," I said, tossing my head with a laugh. "Even I can see through that one. You're pulling my chain."

"Nope," he crossed his heart, "Boy Scout's honor." He considered me for a moment before adding, "You don't know her."

"Yes, I do. You could say that Paige and I have a history with each other."

Travis tipped his head to one side. "Just because you've shared experiences doesn't mean you know somebody," he said.

I suppose he had a point. I really didn't know much about Paige, except for the list of reasons I despised her.

"Her dad was a lot like yours," Travis went on, as we lingered in the atrium.

"I find that hard to believe. My Dad was a *good* man," I declared with a dismissive wave as if Paige couldn't possibly have been the product of a good man.

Travis stopped in mid-chew to evaluate me. "Her dad is ATF. Tactical Commander. Not too shabby."

I scowled. "And you know this, how?"

"I asked and she answered," he said with his chin up and a tight smile.

Increasingly peeved, with mounting resentment and possibly a little jealousy, I rushed to my father's defense. "My dad was a war hero. He was kind and good and I loved him."

"Sunny. Do you ever listen to yourself?" Travis reached out and took my hand. A leaf from the towering tree beside us, released it's hold and fell, swirling and tumbling from a height that almost kissed ceiling, to land on the walkway at our feet. "I hate to be the one to burst your bubble, but from what you've told me, your dad was just another wife-beater."

I jerked my hand from his in righteous fury. "Get away from me."

"Calm down and get real. You told me your dad beat your mom. Didn't you?"

"I have work to do!" I turned away, almost knocking over an elderly couple who had come to pay their land taxes. "I'm sorry. I wasn't looking where I was going," I said to the old folks.

"...or where you've been," Travis added.

"Screw you!" I said, to the horror of the white-haired seniors. "No, not you!" I hastened to apologize again.

Travis let out a sharp laugh. "You have issues," he said as he strode away. "*Serious* issues."

It's hard to say which of us was more upset. But at this point, I had lost everything I had ever loved: Frito, my dad, my husband, and yeah, my mother too. All I had left were a few fragile memories, and I wasn't going to let anyone—and I mean *anyone*—take them from me.

CHAPTER 31

ಙ 🕊 ಇ

"Whatever you do, *never* use the word *advocate!*" Traci leaned forward, tapping her finger sharply on her desktop to reinforce her point. The court-appointed mediator for child custody was such a... witch.

I had spent the night in the recliner and wasn't in the mood.

"Why? What's wrong with 'advocate'? I've only been one for three years."

Traci sighed, thoroughly bored at having to explain the obvious. "Public agencies *hate* advocates. The minute they open their mouths, our ears are shut."

"That's ridiculous. What's the point?" I was outraged and offended.

"Because the word *advocate* means that you have a single point of view. My job as a mediator, and in fact, the entire court system, is to get the *whole* picture before making a decision."

Holier than thou, Saint Traci.

"Stick with 'counselor,'" she advised. "After all, you *do* counsel. Besides, you'll get further."

"Jesus is an advocate," I declared in my defense.

Traci leaned back and rolled her eyes. "Holy crap, Sunny! Don't *ever* say that again. God has no business here." Her eyes snapped, and voice oozed with disdain. She sat tall in her chair and fidgeted with the papers on her desk. "Keep your religion to yourself, or you will be out on your butt."

I was speechless, but she couldn't shut up.

"You want people here to hate you? You want them to think you're an extremist? Keep tossing the J-word around like that and you'll find yourself on the God-Squad list."

Everyone knows about the God-squad list; rumored to be the brainchild of liberal administrators who want God out of the public system. It's simple: Make the list—Lose your job.

So now I am an undercover advocate. I couldn't help but wonder if anyone had bothered to tell Victim Witness or the other allied agencies that their advocates are hated. I was politically ignorant about so many things... or perhaps *innocent* is a better word. I had written the grant that funded the first Special Victims Unit in California and was proud that Butte County was leading the state. But apparently, our system had remained in the dark ages. Or at least, I was.

I attempted to set Traci straight. "Has it ever occurred to you that a woman who has just had her nose broken and two black eyes.... just *might* have a *tiny* problem speaking up for herself while sitting next to the guy who beat the crap out of her? *I am her voice,* so give me a break. Better still, give *her* one!" I turned to leave and then couldn't resist asking her the real question that had brought me to her office that day. I turned again and squared off with a hand on my hip.

"What now?" she asked.

"Why? Why do *always* side with the abuser? Why do you give good kids back to their mother-beating fathers?"

"Unlike advocates, it's my job to be fair and impartial." She sniffed with an air of superiority. "It's my job to listen to *both* sides before making a recommendation to the court."

Judges love mediators and will almost always utilize their suggestions. It saves them money they would otherwise spend on anxiety meds and adult beverages after listening to backstabbing, cutthroat couples duke it out through the justice system—eight hours a day, three-hundred days a year.

"Very noble," I said derisively, "but you didn't answer the question."

I had known Traci for years and believed she was susceptible to the charm that typifies wife-beaters. She raised her eyebrows and considered me for a moment. "Off the record," she said deliberately, "I think most women play the system to get the kids." She dropped her gaze and her voice, adding, "And a lot of them ask for it."

Clearly, I wasn't the only service worker with "issues." After working closely with hundreds of women, I had yet to meet a single one who had ever "asked for it."

ഌ 🕊 രു

"You don't understand! I don't want to press charges. I don't want to go to court. I just want her to get help."

There they were again. Same words, new face. This time the words belonged to a very masculine and extremely handsome Ethan Michaels. Ethan leaned forward on the sofa visibly upset, assuming an assertive, nonaggressive posture.

"I hear what you are saying Ethan," I said, looking at the bulky bandages that made one of his arms look twice the size of the other. "I know this can't be easy, but we both know it's the right thing to do."

At least I hope he knows it is the right thing to do.

It wasn't only his arm and shoulder that had suffered injuries. He had also suffered a major blow to his male ego. He had been stabbed in the back both literally and figuratively.

Violence against men is probably the most under-reported of all crimes. Men—nice men—who would never hit a woman, have a hard time telling a jury *"My wife beat me with a frying pan,"* resulting in head trauma. Or, *"My wife stabbed me with a steak knife,"* as with Ethan. Kitchen utensils are the most common weapons used by women who assault men.

The number of male victims cases have increased since hospitals became mandated reporters of domestic violence injuries. Hospitals and all medical practitioners, including dentists, optometrists, podiatrists, and chiropractors are all legally required to file a report with law enforcement whenever they treat a suspected domestic violence injury.

"Triggers" are words or actions that provoke another person to act, or in my line of work, react. Some triggers are amazingly consistent. Most women can be called every obscene name ever created by man and still refrain from physical violence. But call her the "C-word" once, and she will react with violence almost every time. The same is true if a man calls her "fat" while she is working with lethal weapons in the kitchen, or he throws the food she has just cooked as she sits at a table armed with a fork and knife. He increases his chance of getting sliced and diced faster than a stalk of celery at a Benihana restaurant.

Ethan had over thirty stitches on the arm he had used to block her thrusts and a dozen or more on his shoulder blade from when he had turned away. Still, God wired men to be protectors and Ethan was ashamed of his inability to protect himself. Had a man stabbed him, he might have gone to court to seeking justice, which is a legal way of way of striking back. But men consider it unmanly to be assaulted by a woman.

Like women, men suffer lasting emotional wounds from domestic violence. But most men won't discuss their wife's violence, not even with their closest friend. They learn to *suck it up* and *carry on*. Much like a rock in a gas tank, such attacks are damaging and sometimes result in a complete breakdown.

Violent women battering men is on the increase. There was a political slogan that promoted the concept of *change* as if *change* is is always good. Yet a healthy person can get sick, a family torn apart, or a job abruptly end, all resulting in some kind of change. "Change" of itself, is not categorically good. I advocate for the right of women to protect themselves, and yet it saddens me when some devolve into acting out the very behavior they condemn.

Cases like Ethan's helped to break the old myth that only alcoholics beat women. Previously, the state ordered abusive and violent men to attend Alcoholics Anonymous. Men would sober up and attend the meetings, then go home and beat their wives. Finally, after someone noted that there are non-abusive alcoholics, the state changed from court-ordered AA meetings to Anger Management, and later to a more comprehensive Batterer's Treatment Program. Good change.

When two women meet for the first time—say they are traveling on a bus across town—they will frequently learn everything about each other before arriving at their destination. *"Are you married? Do you have kids? Do you work?"* They may even draw conclusions as to whether the other woman is happy, and possibly exchange advice.

It is different when men first meet. The interchange is limited to a nod, a word, or a mere grunt of acknowledgment. In the first weeks of batterer's treatment, men mostly sit and observe. They are much slower to engage in interpersonal conversation.

California's decision to sentence men to fifty-two weeks of batterer's intervention had excellent results. As time progressed, so did the men. Males naturally gravitate toward behavior that gains respect, and unofficial leaders consistently evolved within the groups.

I suppose the same dynamics hold true for other groups of men. My father was a leader of men. He had been a hero in Vietnam. His friends said he never cracked under pressure, not even when the torture at Hanoi Hilton resulted in the amputation of his left hand. Men under his command had gravitated toward him and his inner strength because he had resolved to endure, adapt, and survive, no matter how painful.

Starla said when Lefty came home from the war he threw his service citations and ribbons in the trash. I know that is true because I asked my dad once if he ever got any medals in the war. Lefty just laughed, shook his hook at me and said, "This is your daddy's 'metal' of honor sweetheart, and don't you forget it."

I guess the army is a club or a gang of sorts, and I suppose, later on, it was natural for a man like Lefty to join and rise through the ranks of the most notorious motorcycle gang in the world. I don't know, but I imagine, his biker brothers had followed him for the same reasons the POW's had.

₭ ℯ ℛ

Sitting across from me at a candle-lit table for two, Kissme licked her chops in anticipation. Okay, maybe this was a little weird, but I was moody and depressed. Things had gone well at the morning presentation. I was feeling really good before Travis had wrecked my day.

"Travis is a jerk," I said to Kissme. She sat quietly and tipped her head in concern.

"Paige is a snake." Her low growl matched my own.

"I saw Chance today, walking through the courthouse. He didn't see me." Kissme whined. Maybe it's her way of saying she misses Chance too, or maybe she's afraid I'm taking the last bite of food without saving some for her. I gave a little laugh and dangled a spaghetti noodle and watched her suck up doggie style, then tossed her a meatball for making me smile.

Moving to the recliner, I tucked us under a throw and dimmed the lights, appreciating my dog but longing for human companionship as I chased my thoughts down a lonely trail. My mind wandered, traveling from childhood to children of domestic violence, and on to Braden. I remembered the case so clearly. Braden hadn't been a child, but he had been so young...

જી ૐ ભ

Not all victims keep their appointments with me. Some come to court with advocates from the SAFE center or Rape Crisis. Some come with support from Victim Witness Advocates and others with family or friends. Many will arrive alone, rejected by their exhausted families, or sometimes, they just refuse assistance.

"Sunny," Chance would say back in the days when our marriage was still fresh and new, "the good Lord has placed you right where he needs you. There are no accidents. The people you touch are divine appointments." I still believe that, even when they disregard my advice and increase the likelihood of harm. I respect their choices. Still, many of the cases that break my heart include people I have never met.

Braden Steffey was a handsome, virile young man who had graduated with honors from high school and enrolled for his freshman year at Chico State. Always funny, known for his practical jokes, he and his buddies had saved and planned their outing for months.

They packed a cooler with beer that one of the older guys had bought, grabbed some swim gear, lots of junk food, and rented a party barge, launching into a day that would change Braden's life forever.

The day started out hotter than a blonde in a thong bikini on the back seat of a Ninja motorcycle. Braden's prescription-strength antihistamines fueled a burning thirst. He hit the beer and hit it hard. His friends were getting angry that he was sucking down all of their beer when he suddenly puked it back up and passed out. Not only did his friends lose out on the beer they bought, but now they were furious at having to clean his vomit so they could get back their deposit.

As they worked, they devised a plan to get even with Braden. First, they bought more beer with the deposit money. Then they pulled off his shorts, leaving him naked and passed out in the bushes behind the marina parking lot. Good joke. Bad ending.

Braden woke up scared and angry. It was dark, the marina closed, and the parking lot empty. Braden, thinking he might find clothes or at least a beach towel, was walking along the dock under the lights when a car with three young women pulled up. Catcalls and whistles from the girls, Braden quickly forgot his anger. He thought he'd died and gone to heaven when they invited him to get in the car and "party" with them. Braden was laughing—all the way home to their lair.

Teased into the bedroom, they tied him to the bedpost where he was stroked, then tortured for hours. He was repeatedly raped and anally raped with several objects. He thought he was going to die. He cried and begged them to let him go. The women laughed. Braden was ashamed that his body responded to their touch, even though a knife was held to his throat. Then it was over.

They took him for a ride and let him out near his apartment complex. Next, Braden did what rape survivors should never do; he took a long hot shower, watching his blood, his innocence, and all of the admissible evidence swirl down the drain before calling the police.

Braden never recovered, physically or emotionally. His friends laughed at him and told him he was "gay" for not enjoying his "good luck." Terrified of people, unable to sleep or focus on his studies, he soon dropped out of college and walked away from his friends and his dreams. He didn't like men and couldn't trust women. He refused to press charges because he couldn't bear the publicity. Depressed and isolated, unable to live with the past or face the future, Braden finally found peace with a handgun to his temple.

∞ ☚ ℞

Life with Chance back in the time of Braden's case had been more than happy. It had been deeply satisfying. Like brandy and cigars, or a Harley ride on a California Sunday morning; all sunshine and smooth sailing. Chance possessed wisdom and spiritual insight beyond his years back then. He was also my best friend. The kind of friend you could always count on when having a bad day.

Inconsolable, possessed with the spirit of *What-if* and its twin Spirit, *If-only*, I had wept for Braden. *So young, so young. His whole life ahead of him... I could have, should have, might have...*

"Sunny... shh. Stop. Babe, listen to me for just for a minute." Chance had wiped tears from my face with his fingertips, tenderly kissing my cheeks. "Honey, this isn't about you. Don't personalize everything as if Braden had no choice in the matter. As if he had no destiny. Braden's death isn't about you, and in a sad way it isn't even about Braden."

He drew me close and we sat on the lawn gazing at a doe and two fawns nibbling brush as they worked their way up the facing slope.

"The real loss," said Chance, "is to all of the people whose lives he might have touched."

Looking into his crystal blue eyes, I saw him drawing his thoughts from the Holy Spirit within.

"Everything we do has an eternal effect. The world calls it 'cause and effect.' And it's true. But what they don't understand is that the effect ripples beyond time and space. Braden's grandson's- grandson's grandchild might have influenced someone to run for president. Or ten generations from now, a Braden offshoot might have comforted an advocate who cried for the loss of one young man." He sighed in calm acceptance.

"We have an eternal purpose, Sunny. The beauty is that we all get to make choices. The sadness is, that some of those choices turn out wrong. You are blessed to understand that more than most people. When Braden killed himself, he didn't even see that he had a choice. All he could see was the present going on forever. No faith. No trust that God can work all things for good."

"How could God or anyone make anything good come from what he went through?" I asked, drying my eyes.

"Braden could have used his tragedy to be a blessing to men in the same way that you are a blessing to women. But instead of helping others, he ended up hurting others by choosing to take his life. He couldn't see that his life still had a purpose." Brushing the hair from my face, he cupped my chin in his strong hands and softly repeated, "This isn't about you, Sunny. Be sad for him, but not for yourself."

The deer had worked their way to the top of the hill. The sun dipped low, casting a soft golden mist across the sky, silhouetting their forms and turning the trees to deepening shades of red. The doe turned to gaze at us for a long time, until at last her babies nudged her to move on.

CHAPTER 32

৯৩ 🕊 ৫৪

We had passed each other in the halls and in the restroom almost daily for three years, and in all that time, I had yet to see to see Ivy King smile. Her face seemed to have frozen like a dour Beijing Opera Mask, as though someone had run their fingers through the fresh paint and stretched her countenance into a permanent state of melancholy. She was the Queen of Grim, but then, she every right. She was the county's most respected child abuse investigator, and I told myself, *the day I look like that, is the day I quit.*

But I hadn't quit. Not even when I saw my reflection in a window that mirrored Ivy's after working a case where a child had watched her father stab her mother sixteen times. I kept my job but gave in to a burning desire to see my mom. A couple of months had passed since the call from her PO.

৯৩ 🕊 ৫৪

Rain clouds slid in like stealthy dark spirits that stopped to hover over the Port of Oakland. An early fall storm had crept down the coast from Alaska and would probably never reach the central valley. Rain began to fall, and a cold wind blew in off the ocean, chilling my heart.

I wanted—I *needed* to find my mother, and the Port of Oakland wasn't the safest place to hang out after dark. Day workers were already sitting behind locked doors eating their dinner and channel surfing through dreams and fantasies. It was time for the night shift. Time for night-people to take to the streets: the pimps and whores, stealers and dealers.

Still, I'd followed Mac's advice. Thinking a bodyguard might be a good idea, I'd told Chance I was going to look for my mother and asked if he wanted to join me. I was determined to be alone with her once we got to Oakland and rudely insisted that Chance wait in the truck when we finally arrived.

Chance sitting behind the wheel of the Dodge Ram made a much stronger impression than my little Volkswagen would have, but any empty vehicle, even a Heavy Duty Ram truck, made a likely target a for smash and grab. Then too, I needed to do this alone.

I found Starla's building by using the number that Tom Aural had provided and entered through a dingy glass door into a run-down tenement building. Cautiously, I stepped inside to find myself directly under a staircase adjacent to a long hallway. The sharp, pungent smell of urine, both fresh and old, tore at my lungs and stung my eyes. *Couldn't they hold it two more minutes?* I hustled down the hall checking room numbers as I went.

Gangster rap blasted from an open door about halfway down the corridor. Doing the math, I figured Starla probably wasn't on the ground floor. She must be up another level, so I retreated back to the stairwell.

Laughter floated down the stairs as a pair of women, one black and one white, clung to each other as they made their way down. Stumbling drunk, drugged, or both; it was evident by their excessive makeup, tawdry outfits, and spiked four-inch do-me-heels that they were on their way to the streets to conduct business.

"Excuse me. Excuse me. My name is Sunny. I'm looking for a woman named Starla. Do you know which unit is hers?"

They exploded with laughter and repeated, *"Do you know which unit is hers?"* in mocking tones. Somehow it didn't sound quite the same.

"She's my mother." I offered.

"You Starla's baby? Well, why didn't you say so?" The black woman asked. "You look just like your mama." Not sure that was a compliment. "Upstairs, end of the hall."

"If she's not there, she's probably already on the street," the white woman added as they went on their way.

I didn't think anyone would be on the street in the pouring rain. Must be a figure of speech, I thought, guessing the prostitutes would probably work the local establishments on a night like this: bars, hotel lobbies, and the like.

Squaring my shoulders, I made my way to the next floor. A trail of graffiti marked the way, and I paused to read the words of the local prophets. "God is Dead" and "Welcome to Hell," along with numerous other epithets and sexual references. I moved down the hall. Numbers were missing on both sides. TV was blasting on the left, so I knocked hopefully on the door on the right. No answer. No luck.

Taking a deep breath, I knocked on the left. A young black man, shirtless and shoeless, opened the door, checked me out and grinned. It was not a nice, "Hello. How are ya?" kind of smile. It was more like a cat gloating over a bird hooked its claws.

"Hello. I'm looking for Starla." I said, totally intimidated by his predatory gaze.

He slammed the door in my face. Sighing, I turned to go just as the door popped back open.

"Mom?" I was so happy to see her.

"Sunny? Wow! How the hell are you? Come in, come in. Don't let Darnell scare you. He don't bite. Not hard, anyhow." She laughed and led the way into the dark room and turned down the TV.

If possible, my mother had lost even more weight than when I had last seen her at the bus depot. She stared at me with glassy eyes and a contrived smile plastered on her face, absently scratching at her arms. I got the feeling she wasn't exactly thrilled about my visit.

"Sit down. Sit down."

I looked around at the living room—two mattresses on the floor with space in-between full of trash, dirty clothes, and dirty dishes.

"Hey!" Darnell barged in between us. "I want what I paid for, Starla. Hear me? Now," his voice low and threatening as he unzipped his pants and thrust his hips.

I was stunned, and Darnell loved the shock that registered on my face.

"Hello! This is my mother!" I got in his face with my shoulders squared, trying to act braver than I felt and regretted leaving Chance in the truck.

Darnel ramped up the intimidation. Belligerent, he shoved his face in my face. "You put out? I'll do you too! Probl'y got less chance of catching a fucking disease wichchoo anyhow. I can do you both; mama, baby." He rocked his head side-to-side. "Come on, girl, les play." He rubbed his nose on mine.

I jumped back, repulsed as his slimy eyes raked my body. I shouldn't have come. Starla barely knew me from the doorknob, but... she was still my mother.

Starla snapped out of her drug-induced stupor for a moment. "Baby, you go wait in the other room." She looked at Darnel with disdain saying, "We'll be done here in just a minute," and then to me, "then you and I can go have a drink or somthin'."

Did she really mean to "do" this guy right here, right now? With me in the other room?

I was in her world. Turning away, I walked numbly into what passed for a kitchen. My nose wrinkled with disgust as I studied an open can of beans with mold bubbling up from under the lid and some fast food bags sitting on a filthy counter with bits of wadded wrapping sticking out of them.

The Taco Bell bag next to me began to shake. *Earthquake?* I looked for a safe place because this is California, and that is what we do. The bag rattled around a bit more, then a furry little gray head with inquisitive beady eyes poked out. The mouse looked at me, twitching his whiskers, unimpressed. Apparently, humans weren't much of a threat, and I didn't bother to chase him away. Instead, I focused on his antics to blot out the sounds of my mother's orgasmic screams from the front room.

My mother was right about it only taking a "minute," but the minute was enough to pound yet another filthy and indelible memory into my brain. It made me long for a hot shower under a steady stream of antibacterial soap.

ఈ 🕊 ల

Darnel left with a smirk as Starla tapped a cigarette from the pack she pulled from beneath her dirty mattress. She looked at me defiantly. "What? You got a problem?"

"No. I..." I looked at the floor to avoid her stony stare and sat down next to her. "Did he hurt you, Mom?"

"Not as bad as I hurt him. Don't you worry, baby girl." She laughed heartily as she flicked her Bic. The hardened lines of her face deepened in the flickering glow of the disposable lighter. She sucked in smoke with deep satisfaction, then jet-streamed it out with a sadistic smile. "I just gave that little turd AIDS."

My old friend, disassociation, came to my rescue. I must have misunderstood. As fast as I heard her words, I dismissed them—for a time.

"I gotta go, Mom. It's a long drive home."

"Wait, honey. Gimme a minute. You just got here. Don't go yet. Just sit back down," she urged, rising and pushing me back onto the mattress. "I'll be right back." Starla slid around the corner, and I heard her mumbling on the phone. Probably lining up more clients, I thought bitterly.

She came back with two cans of generic beer. "Hey now, you can't leave without having a drink with me."

"I hardly ever drink, Mom. And I have to drive home." I didn't mention Chance.

"Here!" She thrust the open can at me. "Stop acting so damned prissy. What's wrong with you, Sunny? Lighten up, for God's sake. One beer isn't going to kill you."

Logan had once said the exact same thing. My lips fluttered as I exhaled frustration. I had made a big mistake. But I took the beer obediently and listened to Starla ramble on about different people we both knew from the old days.

Thinking about Chance waiting for me in the cold truck, I slammed back the beer as quickly as possible and rose to leave over her protests. Between inhaling a tall can on an empty stomach and the slow acceptance that my mother had HIV, my head spun.

I have no memory of saying goodbye, good luck or get well soon. I was numb. Not even tears could break through my invisible wall of self-protection as I backtracked down the dimly-lit smelly hall on autopilot, scarcely noticing the man who was moving purposefully toward me. Avoiding eye contact, I dropped my gaze as he drew near, hoping to walk past him without incident. Then I froze as his vest came into focus. Bandido Nation.

I never saw the punch coming. Hollywood teaches us that a strange man will grab the woman from behind or tackle her and wrestle her to the ground, but guys just don't sucker punch a strange woman into a wall. Except in my case. My world shrank to the size of a blurred stain on the carpet as I doubled over fighting for breath, stunned that the impossible had happened. Then reality grabbed my hair and yanked me upright, slamming me back against the wall.

A brown face with a scraggly beard hovered inches from mine. Sneered, "Hey, Chica. Been lookin' for you for a long time." His words slurred, diffused through a fog of alcohol. I might have been tipsy, but he was hammered. Cold, wet hands clutched my throat as he leaned into me. "Where're the fuckin' guns? Huh? Your boyfriend thinks he can double-cross me? He left you the money with you, maybe, huh?"

I struggled, pulling wildly at his muscled forearms to free myself.

"Maybe your boyfriend wants ta trade, huh? You for my guns!"

I gagged, and he relaxed his grip enough for me to answer. This allowed three things to happen; his face came into focus enough for me to see his rotten teeth, watery brown eyes, and pocked skin. I saw that he wasn't much bigger than me. I could breathe again and sucked in enough air to clear my head and charge my senses. Tried and true; I recalled Ramiro on the ground and that a knee to the crotch always worked in the movies. Turns out the move also works in the slums of Oakland.

The tables turned. Now the biker was the one bent over with bulging eyes, fighting for breath, thinking the impossible had just happened. I shoved his fat butt with both hands and heard his head bounce off the wall, then took off down the hall like my pants were on fire. I cleared the stairs two at a time and grabbed an anchor post, swung around and down into the lobby— right into the arms of a second biker.

Another round of grappling ensued. I kicked and fought the new guy as he strong-armed me backward, under the dark recess beneath the stairs. One arm clamped across my chest, another over my mouth, he growled, "Shut up!" And again. "I said, 'Shut up!'"

I redoubled my efforts. When sweaty hand over my mouth failed to muffle my screams, he reached up with his other arm and pinched my nose. I kicked and thrashed, madly fighting for air. And then, night fell in the already dark hall, as if a soft black blanket were thrown over my head. Everything w fading into darkness when I thought I saw Chance. *Maybe I'm dead*, I thought. Then—blackness.

80 🦋 CR

I opened my eyes with thoughts that transcended time and space. Was I dead? Chance was speaking to me through a white haze. Had I drowned in the Feather River?

"Sunny. Oh, baby. Oh, God. What happened?"

"Where am I?" I squinted and tried to sit up without throwing up as the world around me spun and teetered.

"Thank God." Chance was crying, tears streaming over the angles of his rugged face as he pulled me onto his lap and rocked me in his arms. His heart pounded out a love song through his shirt. The world slowly came back into focus. I was looking up from the underside of a stairwell into the faces of several tenants who looked back, their expressions ranging from mildly curious to totally bored. Starla was not among them.

"Chance?" Sitting up, I rubbed my head as everything came back. "Oh... Chance!" Trembling, terrified, threw my arms around his neck and held on.

"It's okay, baby. I got you. It's okay."

The biker lay in an unconscious heap in a pool of blood. One of the male onlookers rolled him over, exposing a pulpy face, saying, "Looks alive to me. Missing a few teeth, though." Some soft laughter and joking followed the people as they left to resume their business. Violence was not a big deal in this neighborhood. Chance stood, scooping me as he did, and quickly carried me out to the truck. The cold rain on my face felt good.

"Am I okay? Are we safe?" I asked as he set me on my feet to open the truck door. A kiss to the side of my face assured me that I was still alive.

"Not for long. He'll be calling other gang members as soon as he's conscious. Let's get out of here. I'll tell you on the way home."

Chance took off his flannel jacket, wrapped it tenderly around me, and boosted me into the truck. He stood on the running board and reached over to buckle me in, paused to press his head tightly against my chest for a few beats, then jerked back. Pulling himself together, he closed my door and locked it before walking around to get in. He wasn't taking any chances.

"I nearly killed him." Chance swore as we pulled onto the freeway and sped away from the inner city.

"Am I really okay? Are we going to a hospital? Did he... was I ..."

"No, honey." He reassured me with a gentle touch. "You're going to be all right. I came looking for you. I heard your screams when I when I opened the door and saw him..." Chance struggled with his emotions as he gripped the steering wheel. "I could have killed him!" Chance sniffed and then laughed a short, tough-guy laugh. He looked grim and vengeful.

I gazed at him in fear and gratitude. This was a different Chance. One I rarely glimpsed. The same tender man who majored in rescue and comfort was also powerful and dangerous. I loved him—this man who fought for me and shed tears for me—unashamed.

Chance called 9-1-1 and reported that a man was in need of an ambulance at the tenement building. He didn't offer any more information. His reasons for getting me out of town were the same reasons that I had been dodging Logan for years.

"Hon, did you know those men?" Chance glanced anxiously.

I paused to consider my options. Lying would definitely take too much effort, and I was tired. My resolve was crumbling.

Maybe I should just blog about my life or post it on Facebook, I thought hopelessly. *What's the use?*

"I never saw the man upstairs before."

"There was another man *upstairs?*" Chance tensed, putting on his cop face. "Did he have a gun?"

"I don't know if he had a gun or not. I didn't know him, but he wore Bandido colors. I've seen the guy downstairs, though. At the cabin."

Chance paused to call 9-1-1 again; this time to advise the responding officer that there was a second, possibly armed man upstairs.

"You know his name?" Chance asked after he hung up.

"No. He was just some guy Logan brought to the cabin a couple of times. The first time was right after he got back from Laughlin when my dad died. I thought it was weird he would bring two riders with him from other clubs. One was a Bandido, and one was a Mongol, just like tonight."

Chance's brows pinched in thought. "You know, it was no coincidence those guys just happened to show up while you were there."

Startled, I replayed the sequence of events carefully back through my mind, telling Chance everything that had happened while at my mom's, from beginning to end. The thought flashed through my mind as lightning branched across the night sky and thunder rumbled over the throaty sounds of the turbo engine.

"Oh, Chance. Do you think it was my mother? You think Starla sold me out?"

"You tell me. How could she have known you were coming?"

I thought of Sheena but immediately dismissed the idea. I hadn't told Sheena when I was coming. Then I thought of something else. "When I wanted to leave, my mom went into another room to make a phone call. Then she guilted me into staying and drinking a beer with her." Silence filled the cab, drowning out everything else.

"Why, Chance? Why would my mother do that to me?"

I stretched out across the seat, pillowing my head on Chance's warm lap and wept softly. I felt his chest heave as a tear fell and mingled with mine.

"I am sorry you have to go through this. You've been through so much." Chance's voice was thick with emotion as he tenderly stroked my hair from my face. "I expect Starla needed drugs or money. But why do the gangs want *you*? What is it you know?"

Everything. And nothing, I answered to myself.

"Not much," I said. "That man you beat up did business with Logan, and the man upstairs thought I still had a relationship with him."

"What kind of business?" asked Chance.

"Guns. Drugs. Money. I don't know. I didn't want to know. I mostly stayed in my room when Logan did business. I think it was some kind of gun deal. I don't know anything else."

Chance recalled that a Mongol rider had started the fire below my house. But neither of us could figure out what was going on.

I lay in silence for a long time, listening to the rain drum on the windshield and the wipers beat a gentle rhythm that lulled me toward sleep. The last thing I felt was Chance's comforting arm wrapping around my shoulder, protecting me from the terrors of the night.

Chance took me home and tucked me into bed next to Kissme while making his own bed on the couch. He was gone when I woke up, but he had left a fresh pot of coffee and note that read, "Call me if you need me. You are in my thoughts and in my prayers. Love, Chance."

ཐ ༝ ཚ

I waited all weekend for the Laundry Fairy to arrive. In spite of the pain of being punched in the stomach and the terror of my brush with death. In spite of my mother dying of HIV and the frightening possibility that even more bikers might be trying to locate me. In spite of the confusion and passion that welled up from a deep desire to love and be loved, I still needed clean underwear. Life goes on.

CHAPTER 33

෯ 🕊 ඃ

Moonlight slipped through the moon-roof on the car, peeking in and out of cotton ball clouds, bathing the hills with a pale yellow light. The air was warm, rich with the smell of parched summer grasses as I wound my way through the valley and up into the foothills. My brain flipped between the ethereal beauty and processing the night's CODA message.

CODA expects me to accept responsibility for my behavior. The program focuses on how we have hurt others as opposed to how others had hurt us. Much like religion, CODA was proving more of an anchor than a life jacket.

Tonight I had a very real ache for Chance to be back in my life. I still loved him but couldn't deny my feelings for Travis. Wild, crazy feelings reminiscent of the exhilaration of skinny-dipping in a cold river. The thrill of Travis was different from what I felt for Chance. I sighed, as hungry for security and friendship as I was for intimacy and passion. I drove along, concluding that having feelings for two men did not make me a slut. I hoped.

I parked and gathered my things. Daydreaming—*is it still considered day-dreaming if it's already night?*—I beeped the car shut and headed for the door. Fumbling, I dropped the keys.

෯ 🕊 ඃ

The doorpost exploded into fragments as I bent to retrieve the keys. My heart leaped and body arced into a massive spasm as if hit by a defibrillator before dropping to the ground. Stunned, I hugged the porch, panting as panic surged through every cell.

The Glock was in the gun safe. *Crap!* Teeth-grinding, I waited for the kill-shot. Ten heartbeats later, rolled off the porch, dropping down some two feet into the flowerbed where I would make less of a target. Didn't even feel the rose bush whose thorns peppered my body, except for the one that hooked through my eyelid. Silence reigned except for the ringing in my ears and Kissme's frantic cries from the house. Time was ticking and every second of delay worked against me as I fought ropes of terror that held me captive. A salty tear trickled, igniting a flame that freed me from the trance. Moaning softly, I pinched my eyelid and pulled it up, twisting the thick, thorny stem. The shrub and I both shuddered, and the sound of whimpering cut through the night.

No one needed to tell me the shooter was Logan. I didn't need to look for a Bandido or a Mongol or a crazed former inmate. I could sense him— the presence of evil—and the hair stood up on the back of my sweating neck. I groped for options, knowing that my life would depend on my next choice.

Tick-tick-tick.

If I tried for the door, I would be a clear target. I could crawl to the side of the house, but Logan might have moved around and lined himself up for the next shot. I was pretty close to option number three, doing the sobbing-girl-thing when the roar of a motorcycle shattered the stillness. He was leaving!

"Oh, thank God. Thank you!" I let go and took a deep breath. It was too good to be true.

Literally.

The sound of the bike grew... louder... closer, instead of fading away.

Chance! It was Chance! Oh, my God. My head spun. *No!*

Would Logan kill Chance?

೫ 🕊 ೞ

Tick-tick-tick.

From a far corner of distant memory, I heard Lefty calling out to the guys with his signature rally cry: "Let's do this!"

"Thanks, Dad," I whispered, not sure if I was talking to Lefty or God.

My dad had taught me that courage isn't an absence of fear, but a determination to act in spite of it. Either Chance would be Logan's next target or I would have to risk a bullet to warn him. I had a choice to make and doing nothing was not an option.

Like a racer off the line, I jumped up, legs driving, arms pumping, heart hammering as I sprinted into the woods, away from Logan and toward the bend in the driveway. Another shot whined past my head, blasting a nearby tree and spraying shards of bark that burned into my neck and arm.

Hungry branches reached out, clawing my clothes and ripping strands of hair as I raced on. Blood trickled into my eye and sent me crunching and crashing into a mound of debris; dry, crackling leaves and branches that popped like bullets as I fled through shadow and moonlight. I was an easy target.

"Lord!" I gasped. And the Lord heard my prayer. A cloud sailed in front of the heavenly beacon, and suddenly it was dark. God had turned off the lights.

Scrambling up the incline, torn, bleeding, hair matted with dead leaves, Chance rounded the corner as I tumbled onto the road and into his headlight shrieking and sobbing like a ghoul from Stephen King's worst nightmare.

"Stop! Stop!"

Chance grabbed the brakes, swerving and skidding on the dusty road, laying the bike over as a third bullet cracked through the night air. Together, we pulled the bike upright, and I leaped on the on the back screaming "Go! Go! Go!"

Chance didn't pause for an explanation. He just cracked the throttle, churning up a smokescreen of dust between Logan and us as we fish-tailed our way back up the road to the safety of Chance's house.

80 ❦ ℭ

Few people would have understood why I sat, weeping for my dog. Filled with visions and memories of little Frito, I imagined Kissme being flayed or dismembered, or worse.

I wanted a gun and I wanted my dog, but Chance would not allow either. He told me to call 911 as he grabbed his 9mm handgun and his AR-15 for distance. Calm and in complete control, he took me by the arm on the way to the door. Blue-hot eyes burned into mine.

"He'd better hope the cops catch him before I do." Spinning on his heels, Chance called Mercy. Jumping in the truck, they sped off down the road.

I called 911. Then I called Travis.

80 ❦ ℭ

Four days later:

It was more than an invigorating smell of coffee and far beyond the intoxicating scent of his body wash. Perhaps I had simply reached a sexual level of awareness in his presence. I knew he was there before I looked up.

Travis stood in the doorway of my office, chewing gum and twirling a bullet between his thumb and forefingers in one hand, and holding a file folder in the other. One eyebrow rose in question, and his head tipped slightly forward, expecting a response.

"The lab tests are back? Ballistics?" I asked, not waiting for an answer. "You must have great connections." Nothing important ever happens fast in Butte County.

Seeing the shell casing scared me as I recalled how close it had come to taking my life. That bullet had my name on it, but the hand of God had deflected it. This time. *Guess he still has more for me to do,* I thought.

Travis straightened. "The bullet is M-16, military issue," he said. "Nevada?"

I eyed him suspiciously. "Is that a question or a location?" Beyond asking if I was okay on the night of the incident, I hadn't seen Travis since. When I had asked where he was, Amanda looked perturbed and said he was "probably working." I didn't need another morality lecture, so I let it go.

Chance had written the official report down at the sheriff's office. I tried being honest this time, but my memories were sketchy. I neve did get involved in Logan's business. Women were never a part of gang dealings, so staying aloof wasn't weird. It was expected.

Travis entered the room, shutting the door behind him. "Both," he answered to the "Nevada" question, and then asked permission before sitting down to engage me at eye-level. *Have we really become this formal?*

"I know you're still upset over what happened and you have every right to be. We need to talk."

I wondered which "happening" he was referring to. I swallowed, feeling my throat bob, and he almost responded with the old familiar, teasing smile that now barely touched the corners of his mouth.

"We'll start with the outdoor incident," he said, as if reading my mind. Then, he reached over and tenderly brushed the side of my face with his fingertips," thus tabling our intimate indoor incident for another time. "That okay?" Again, asking permission.

I nodded.

"Do you know if Logan had business ties to Nevada Chapters or the Bandido Nation?"

The question was a two-pronged fork jabbing into painful places I didn't want to revisit.

"It's in Chance's report. I don't want to go through this again." I said, drawing back.

Travis settled on the corner of my desk, one leg cocked lazily over the edge, just inches from my face. I watched, fascinated by the taut muscles that played against the fabric of his trousers, then snapped out of it when he tossed a copy of the report in front of me. "I read it. These are my questions, not his."

Green eyes drew me like a moth to a flame. I shrugged in resignation. "Shoot," I said, not caring if he took the word figuratively or literally.

"Do you know if Logan had business ties to Nevada Chapters," he repeated.

Vivid memories reached back to Lefty's funeral and flashed before me. The motorcade had stretched from one end of the Bay Bridge to the other, Harleys riding two abreast. It seemed that every chapter from California, Nevada, Arizona and others had been present.

Travis doesn't understand Hells Angels very well, I thought. Business ties are Brotherhood ties. And Brotherhood ties are stronger than blood ties.

I pursed my lips, glancing down at the corner of a postcard that poked out from under a file and drew a breath.

"He had ties with all the chapters. Including Nevada." I said, recalling that some of the men that returned from Laughlin with Logan had worn Nevada patches.

"Can you pick out their faces?"

Yes. "I don't know. Maybe."

"And the Bandido and Mongol that came to your home?"

I glanced at the protruding postcard again. It had arrived in the morning mail at the district attorney's office, addressed to me. I was relieved that Travis couldn't see it from where he sat.

Travis pulled a picture out of the folder and slid it toward me, covering the postcard and everything else, forcing me to look at it.

I pulled back with a gasp, unintentionally answering his question. It was a crime-scene photo. One of several. It showed the half-charred body of a man lying inside of a burned-out building. Some of the victim's limbs and part of his face was missing—but I still recognized him.

The memory was crystal clear. I had passed out beers and cooked meals for the men that returned with Logan from Laughlin. The man whose body I was now looking at had been particularly scary, the way he had followed me from room to room. He rode with the Mongols, a gang with a reputation for violence and viciousness.

"What happened?" I whispered.

"The picture was taken after the bombing of the Mongol clubhouse a few years ago. How did you know him?

"Sunny?" Travis repeated with a touch.

I didn't hear him walk around the desk, but all at once Travis kneeling was next to me, stroking my hair. It was soothing, but he never let up is line of questions. "How did you know him?" he coaxed.

"He came to the cabin a couple of times," I said in a voice so soft I wasn't sure he heard me. "The first time was right after my dad died, and then he came back later, once or twice... with a rider from Bandido Nation. Logan was showing everyone his new tattoo: The Filthy Few."

Travis nodded and emitted a deep "Humph." It was Logan's written declaration that he had committed murder. Travis pulled out another picture. "The other rider; was it this guy?" he pointed to a tough looking Hispanic man, the man who had choked me until I passed out.

"Yes," I whispered. "He's the one who tried to kill me in Oakland when I went to see my mom. Who is he?"

There was a brief knock and Paige slunk through the door. She looked smug and sleek in her skin-tight pants, wearing a top with more plunge than a fleet of septic trucks—and just as nasty. It is a little-known fact that she is the reason our office does not have a dress code. The men enjoy the view.

I shuffled the pictures on my desk into a pile to indicate that our meeting was over. Travis reached over and took the pictures, placing them back into the folder. "We'll talk more about the other incident later." He said as he rose to leave.

Other incident? Would that be you and Chance, or us? It was awkward.

"Sunny, your 3:00 o'clock appointment is here," said Paige. She had one eyebrow arched like a cat ready to strike, with a matching half-curl on the opposite side of her mouth. "Travis, got a minute?" she asked in a velvety tone. They left the room together.

I called Gayle at the front desk and asked her to hold my appointment for a few minutes.

Then I slid the postcard out and studied it again.

CHAPTER 34

ಋ ᵛ ಛ

"Go away. Just go away." Carissa looked like a fashion statement. Nineteen years young, she was a slim woman with dark blue eyes and radically textured brown hair shot through with hot pink highlights.

The men at the office, however, failed to notice her hair when she showed up wearing a midriff top cut above her short-shorts. Her pants were unzipped and laid wide open in a V, revealing what appeared to be an absence of underwear in front, and a pair of thong straps riding high above a pair of sweet cheeks in the rear. A fake diamond accentuated her bellybutton, and a tramp stamp marijuana leaf was inked across her low back in shades of red, purple and green.

Everything about her walk, talk, and pheromones exuded a message that even a dead man could read. Except for today. Today her finely modeled face had been hand-hammered by her former high school boyfriend, a construction worker that left her with lips that rivaled Mick Jagger's.

The University police was working with Chico P.D., and together, they made seven arrests for the gang rape of this young woman. Her abuse had been posted on a very popular, highly questionable website, and now the hunt was on for her missing boyfriend.

Carissa was just another freshman university student wanting to be accepted by the most popular young people on campus. She had been excited at the prospect of attending her first frat house party—and Carissa loved to party. Lots of booze and hooking up with cute boys afterward was her "normal." But what happened to her that night, was anything but "normal."

Date-rape drugs are frequently manufactured in bathtubs. They have no odor or color and I knew firsthand how they affect the body and mind. Some of them are like a giant memory eraser. You literally never know what hit you. Or in this case, *who* hit you. You might wake up without a trace of remembrance, but you would know with certainty that you had been grossly violated.

Carissa had become a target the moment she entered the party looking eager and sexy in her come-and-get-me outfit. Before the night was over she would be on a mattress in the basement with seven men and a webcam; streaming live rape. Thanks to modern technology, if you missed the first part of the crime you could replay it, watching it over and over as the young men took turns with an incoherent Carissa. It was the most frequented video ever to hit campus.

Unfortunately for Carissa, her former boyfriend, Jach, a coarse drug dealing, drug using muscle-bound roofer, who had *not* been invited to the college party, also saw the video. It didn't matter to Jach that she had been the drugged victim of gang rape. It only mattered that other men were doing his girl for the entire world to see. Jach found her the next day and brutally beat her for being a "ho." When a girlfriend took Carissa to the hospital and details of the rape and subsequent beating came out, the hospital called the police.

"I am not going to go away, and neither is this. You've already been the victim, now it's time to hold the perpetrators accountable," I said, restlessly tapping my pen against her very thick file. "They need to go to prison for what they've done."

Carissa began to cry, and I handed her a box of tissues.

"I don't want everyone to see it," Carissa said, referring to the jury who would see the video entered into evidence.

I bit my pen, holding back the thought that this was coming from a girl who seemed to want *everybody* to see *everything*. Moreover, I wasn't going to remind her of what she already knew—that the video had already been seen by hundreds, if not thousands of people on the internet.

"I'll be there with you," I assured her. "You won't have to go through this alone."

Carissa looked up. "I talked to a woman at Rape Crisis who said I don't have to do this at all."

Sounded like Marne to me. I have found that disagreeing with people puts them on the defensive and it is aways wiser to begin by agreeing.

"You *don't* have to be here, Carissa," I told her in all honesty. Then I added; "I just want to help you get justice." Then I qualified my statement. "We both care about you. It's just that Rape Crisis and I see your situation in different ways." Now... drive it home: "The other advocate... Marne?" Carissa nodded. "Marne believes that you can walk away from your problems and put them behind you. She sincerely believes that memories will fade with time."

Carissa looked at me. "You don't think they will?"

"I think Marne was once a victim who now uses pain and anger like two strips of Velcro. That is holding on, not letting go. I don't believe a person can truly heal without justice."

Carissa looked me in the eye. "Can you promise me justice?"

⅚ 🕊 ⅛

I was thankful that Logan had left the scene before Chance and Mercy arrived at the house. I didn't want anything bad happening to them because of me.

Travis arrived a short time later with several squad cars and a helicopter that swept the forest canopy with powerful searchlights.

Logan always gets away, I thought with a taste that rivaled cold, leftover sauerkraut. He slithers through dark places like slime in a horror movie, and then, Poof! He's gone. For a while.

Carissa's words were but an echo of many women before her, and it had been my question for Chance just days ago.

"Can you promise me justice?" I had insisted Chance answer when he interviewed me at the station after the shooting.

The question upset him. His brows knit together as he tried to read me. "Why are you asking me that?" He was terse, knowing that I understood.

"Can you?" I demanded angrily, frustrated because I really did know.

Chance's gaze never faltered. "Not this side of heaven," he'd replied.

ജ 🕊 ൌ

I'd held Carissa's gaze. "No," I told her truthfully. "I can't promise you justice. But I can promise you your day in court. I can give you an opportunity to hold your head high before a jury, look them in the eye and tell the whole world what those beasts did to you. That is your strength, Carissa. Not what the defendants say and not what the jury decides, but what *you* say and what *you* decide. That is your healing."

"What if they don't believe me? What if the judge just lets them go?" she asked.

She looked so vulnerable, so... innocent.

How many times had I stood outside of the courthouse after a 'Not Guilty' verdict and held weeping women in my arms? I can't count the numbers, but I always reassured them, dramatically looking at my watch to make my point.

"I'm off the clock now, so I would like to say something on a personal note." They would look at me expectantly. "As long as we have juries made up of humans, there will always be human error. For myself, I believe in God, and I think there will come a day when your abuser will be held accountable and perfect justice will be served."

The impact of that statement has always amazed me. The gratitude that survivors would show because I shared this spiritual truth still warms my heart. It's a God-Thing.

Carissa didn't look like she cared a whole lot about spiritual truths. But, you never know. The Bible says that the Holy Spirit is like the wind; we never know where it will go or whom it will touch. Timing is everything.

"Some people get away with crimes," I answered honestly. "But it's not very likely in your case."

"Yeah, but what if they do? What if I go through all this for nothing?"

It was a fair question. I gave it my best shot. "I believe in divine justice. As long as juries are made up of imperfect people, they can always render a flawed verdict."

She frowned, her etched brows visibly bitch-slapping each other over my reply. "What's that supposed to mean?" She fumed.

"It means that I can't promise you a guilty verdict, but I can promise you this: If you do nothing, they will go free."

₮ 🥺 ℞

It was Labor Day which is the complete opposite of everything Chance and I had in mind. For us, it has always meant Recreation Day. We would pack up the truck, boat, dogs and camping gear, then head to Eagle Lake for the last days of fishing before fall.

When Chance came to my office and tentatively asked if I would like to go, I tried to look as if I needed to check my calendar. In truth, I couldn't say "yes" fast enough. I had to put aside my quest for justice for the weekend. There simply wasn't any room left in the camper for unnecessary baggage. *If I wanted burdens, I could stay at work,* I told myself. I was going on vacation!

Okay, maybe I am not all that noble. Looking forward to a weekend with Chance was mostly true, but it was also true that I was afraid of Logan coming back to finish me off. Ashley and Shane were going on a motorcycle run, and I had turned down an invitation to have dinner with Travis only hours ago. *More dangerous than Logan,* I had joked to myself, so I told him I already had plans for the weekend. Travis had stiffened, his tone velvet but edged with steel. "Sooner or later we need to talk."

That was true. It's just that *talking* was not high on the list of all we would do.

The high-country always provides the three R's; not the usual relax, refresh, and renew. For Chance and I, it meant rods, reels, and romance.

We launched our old aluminum fishing boat instead of the Chris-Craft showboat. Maybe we were looking to recapture our early years, where we had camped and the way we felt. Out on the cold, crystalline waters of Eagle Lake, basking in the late summer sun, we found ourselves talking about justice. Which led to divine justice. Which resulted in...

"Really, Chance. Don't you believe most religions are all pretty much the same?" That's what I thought. Or hoped. Especially for non-believers.

Chance knows a lot about religions and is a committed Christian in spite of himself. Anyone who believes in reincarnation and knows Chance would have concluded that Chance was a Christian in his past life, too. That is how deep his faith goes and is one of the things I cherish about him. Chance loves the Lord. He never tires or acts ashamed, awkward, bored, or embarrassed when talking about Him.

"Sorry to disappoint you," said Chance as we trolled along the edge of the lake, the little motor purring with all the satisfaction of a cat with well-trained owners. We settled into a private cove feeling as if we had the whole lake to ourselves.

"It's like the story of the three pigs. They all built houses from different materials. One straw, one wood and...?" He looked pointedly to me.

"We built ours on the Rock," I finished. "So what are you saying? That houses of worship serve the same purpose, but are built on different foundations?"

"You got it," said Chance as he reached over and cut the engine. "Ready for a story? There's an allegory that makes it easy to understand."

I love a good story, so I hurried to do the icky part of baiting my hook with half of a night crawler and watched in disgust as it break-danced on the point. They say it doesn't hurt the worm to halve them, but either that is not true, or it's a girl worm excited over her 50% weight loss. I hoped she would keep on dancing when I cast her out and then settled back to listen.

Chance also cast his bait into the water, not far from mine. Then began his tale.

"A man was on a journey when he fell into quicksand. He was waist-deep and screaming for help.

"Confucius came along and looked at the man's condition. Thoughtfully stroking his beard, he advised, "Confucius say, you should avoid such situations," and walked on.

"The man struggled and cried out for help again.

"Buddha heard him and arrived soon after Confucius left. Seeing the desperate man, he offered his sage wisdom. "Let this be an illustration for us," he said, before he too, walked away."

Chance slowly reeled in both the bait and me.

"By this time, the man was freaking out. He knew the end was near and kept thrashing and screaming. Sure enough, Mohammed came to see what was going on. He solemnly observed the sinking man and determined, "It is the will of Allah," and went on about his business."

I waited in anticipation as Chance finished reeling in his line, then watched as he cast farther out, in deeper water.

"Hurry up," I said, knowing he would take his time, whetting my appetite for more.

He smiled, dimpling, his eyes reflecting both the intense summer blue of the sky and the subaqueous purple of the water. He finally continued the story.

"By this time the man was chest deep in the quicksand. The more he struggled, the faster he sank. Just then, Krishna happened along. Krishna put down his flute and sadly shook his head over the man's situation. Then he brightened and offered words of encouragement.

"Better luck next time," he said, and left the man to his destiny."

I leaned forward expectantly, and Chance returned my smile. My pulses quickened as I took in the color of his tanned skin that mirrored the color of the earth, tousled hair as flaxen as the leaves on the slopes as they prepared for fall, and eyes that sparkled liked the diamonds the sun had cast over the alkaline water. I knew I was still in love.

"And?" I demanded. "Come on."

"Well... by now"—Chance clearly enjoyed the telling of the story as much as I was enjoying listening—"the poor man was up to his eyeballs without any hope at all. He was gagging as mud filled his mouth, but somehow he managed to croak out one word: *'Jesus,'*" Chance choked the word with his hand at this throat. "Jesus heard his name and was instantly at the pit, *waiting*. The man has just enough breath for one... last... word: *'Help,'*" Chance whispered. "Immediately Jesus reached out, grabbed the man and pulled him from the filth that was sucking him under.

"Then Jesus said, 'Come. Live.' Jesus took the shirt off his back and wrapped it around the man, but he didn't stop there," said Chance. "He went on to give him food, water, and rest before they continued their journey—*together forever.*"

A rainbow trout leaped from the water, splashing and spraying us with water. Chance whooped, reeling in a trophy-size fish while I sat in silent wonder.

Chance was all aglow. "Isn't it beautiful?" He demanded.

"Yes," I replied softly, watching his every move.

"Have you ever seen anything like it?" His boyish joy was contagious.

"No," I said, as I continued to stare at him. "And the fish isn't bad either."

Chance packed the fish into the livewell and turned to take me in his arms. Removing my hat and sweeping my hair back, he held my face in one hand while softly tracing the lines of my mouth with the other. I could feel his breath, warm on my skin. His lips brushed mine leaving me dizzy. "I love you, Sunny," he whispered, holding me close as he kissed the world away. No boat, no Logan, no Travis or Paige. Just us.

The weekend was perfect, starting and ending with a kiss and nothing more sexual in-between. We walked to the edge of the lake at sunset and stayed there until the stars came out. The wind breathed the promise of autumn, crisp and cold as it swept down from Mt. Lassen's snow-capped volcanic rim and the other soaring peaks that look down on Eagle Lake. Chance grabbed a blanket and wrapped it around the two of us. We huddled until the stars glittered with cold and the lure of a warm campfire called us back.

That night, we crawled into the camper that Chance had mounted on the truck. I slept in the cab-over, and he slept where the table converted into a bed. Kissme, bundled in doggie pajamas, burrowed under my covers, and Mercy lay on a huge dog pillow on the floor next to Chance.

We made it back by Monday afternoon, and I helped Chance unpack. Then he drove me home. I got out and thanked him, said "good-bye." He got out and came around and pulled me into his arms. His face radiated love and his eyes brimmed with peace and happiness. "That was the best weekend ever," he said, and kissed me again. Softly, this time. Less sure of himself.

ഇ ୬ ഌ

It was Tuesday morning, and I sat at work, more upset than frightened by the audacity Logan had shown by sending me a postcard in care of the district attorney's office. The card was large and glossy with a sweet little Chihuahua wearing a colorful sombrero beneath the caption, "Greetings from Cancun." The little dog's left eye had a burn mark that resembled a cigarette-burn. On the back, written in a familiar hand, was written, Hotter than Hell, wish you were here. The card didn't need a signature for me to know who had sent it or what it meant. The words on the card were a veiled threat. Not a crime, but typical of his blatant contempt for authority. Throwing the postcard in the trash, I sat rooted to my desk, trying to sort my thoughts from my feelings.

Someone is going to die. I acknowledged this with a start as I considered that all of the men in my life were experienced killers. Chance and Travis were both fully trained to handle outlaws like Logan. But then, Logan didn't fight according to the U.S. Military's Rules of Engagement. He was a killer too. I paused to correct myself. Logan was not a *killer.* He was a *murderer.*

I didn't want either Chance or Travis dying in the line of duty, taking a bullet that was meant for me. I loved both men, each in his way, and if anything happened while I sat by and did nothing, it would be my fault. *Justice is not limited to a courtroom,* I told myself. Sometimes, you have to take matters into your own hands.

I fished the postcard back out of the trash for a third time, studying it again with a fresh charge of anger and frustration.

I can kill Logan, I thought, weighing my options. This quickly turned into an invitation-to-a-migraine-moment. Something about, "Thou shalt not murder," thundered through my brain.

There's always Plan B. *I can kill myself.* I paused thoughtfully. Maybe not. I wasn't quite there yet. There were still victims to save, coffees to drink, roads to ride, men to... love.

"Snap out of it," I scolded myself, trying to shake off my fears. "Time to pony up." I decided to go to Feather Falls. The timing was perfect. I would check things out while Logan was busy *wasting away in Margaritaville.*

I left a voice mail for Paige to attend court with Amanda. She would be at Jach's arraignment after he had spent the holiday weekend in jail. I told her to be sure to notify Carissa whether or not he made bail. Then I gathered my things and checked out of the office.

I told Gayle I would be in Feather Falls assisting Keira Gilman in writing a victim impact statement for her father's sentencing hearing on the incest conviction.

And I did help Keira.

Then headed for the cabin.

CHAPTER 35

৪০ ᘐ ൦੧

I'd stayed up late watching a movie called *Apocalypto*. My favorite part was when the victim, Jaguar Paw, realizes he is being hunted in the very place he grew up and boldly declares, "This is my jungle!" The knowledge enabled him to turn the tables and defeat his pursuers

I thought about Jaguar Paw's wisdom as I turned onto the dirt road that led to the cabin and eased the car behind an old slash pile on a logging landing above the property. I left my things in the car and locked up. I wanted to see if the place was empty. My hope was to find evidence that would put Logan away for a long time. He was in Mexico, and this was my window of opportunity. I imagined him being attacked by a shark, and then spit out.

The old deer trail cut down through the brush and into a dry wash that ran behind the cabin just below the ancient Maidu grinding stones. Following the thicket of manzanita that bordered the wash, I came within sight of the back of the house, not far below the bomb shelter. There was little likelihood of being seen. These were my mountains, and I knew every inch of them.

The cabin had a new back door and some shutters over the windows. No dogs, no bikes, and no cars. I remained on high alert. The spare key was still under the loose rock that borders the flowerbed. I let myself in and scanned the living room and dining room.

No one was in the living room. Just a couple of generic beer cans sitting on the living room floor. The air was rank from the stale beer and the soggy cigarette butts floating in them. Nothing more threatening in the dining room than a couple of dirty dishes scattered around a rickety table.

The mess told a story. No mold on the plates and coffee still floated in the bottom of one cup. The cabin hadn't been empty for long.

Glancing upstairs, I shuddered at the memory of the brutal rapes. It's true; I didn't call it "rape" back then. I thought that Logan could do whatever he wanted because I belonged to him. That false belief wasn't just the result of social ignorance and isolation. Outlaw bikers dominate their women and sometimes beat them.

Looking around one more time, I locked the door and replaced the key. Glanced up the driveway and headed back toward the forest. The underground shelter was about twelve feet wide and twenty feet long, completely buried and naturally camouflaged beneath layers of fallen oak and pine duff. I searched for the key to the padlock, hoping to find it as easily as the house key; under a little cleft at the base of the structure. It was gone.

I broke into a cold sweat. Panic was building. Whoever was staying here might have ridden into town, or possibly gone on a short run to the Gold Flake for a six-pack.

I searched, checking around the edges of the hidden steel doors and moved some rocks and logs. I shivered when I finally found the key, stuffed deep inside the knothole of a gnarly oak branch that stretched over the shelter and could have passed for a rotting finger pointing toward a grave.

The steps lay at a steep angle, securely concealed deep under the natural debris of the forest floor. The lock was corroded but industrial strength and required a short battle before surrendering with a click. The massive double doors groaned and screeched in protest as rust broke loose and the metal hinges released their grip.

Glancing nervously around once more, I stepped down into darkness.

ജ ✵ ദ

Inside, I groped along the cold metal wall, searching fervently for the Maglite where Logan used to keep it. To my great surprise and deep relief, it was still there. Switching it on I breathed a "Thank you" that it still worked.

Sweeping the light back and forth, I looked for clues. It was hard to believe that I had spent many carefree days of my youth in this place. But there wasn't time for memories. I continued down the steps, casting shadows that tip-toed before me. The chill scent of earth, metal, and rust assaulted my nostrils. The air seemed to pool at the bottom of the steps, thick with the smell of death and decay.

The shelter hadn't changed much, except the shelves that once held cases of MREs and vacuum sealed buckets of rice and beans had been pried from the framework, leaving sharp, twisted pieces of metal waiting to gore the inattentive. In their place, stacked six-deep on the floor were oblong wooden crates that looked like coffins. Swallowing my fear and focusing the Maglite's beam, I studied them up close, tracing faded words with my fingers, barely able to read them. Stamped on the sides of the oily looking crates were the words: Silver State Armory, NSM 7th Battalion. M-something-something, followed by some serial numbers.

Shocked, I stepped back and swept the light again, pointing it toward the back wall. There, in the far corners, was a stack of smaller square, olive drab crates with rope handles stacked to the ceiling. Moving closer I held my breath, then slowly released it, initiating the four-square breathing technique that Chance had taught me—to prevent heart failure—and I was pretty sure I was in serious danger of heart failure.

Breathe in 1-2-3-4, Hold, 1-2-3-4. Breathe out 1-2-3-4, Hold, 1-2-3-4. Repeat.

No time. I had to keep moving.

Setting the flashlight off to one side, I reached up and tugged at one of the relatively smaller boxes. It didn't budge. I set my will against it. Although they were bulky and cumbersome, I grabbed a rope handle, yanking and pulling until one broke free, falling off the stack and narrowly missing my head.

Panting and sweating as much from fear as the intense heat. Mascara melted into my eyes, burning and producing watery pools with zombie smudges beneath. Swiping at my eyes with the back of my hand, I bent to the new task, wrestling with the metal latch on the box. No luck. It held tight. Tired and frustrated, I grabbed the flashlight and did a quick search within the radius of its pale beam. I noticed metal brace that had once been used to hold a storage shelf, hanging limply from a wall. With great effort, I worked it loose and returned to the mysterious green box.

Sticking the brace under the latch, I jerked it back and forth and side to side. Finally, the lock cracked and splintered, breaking free. Gasping from exertion, trembling with fear, I stared at the box that gaped like an open wound on a battlefield, exposing its entrails.

"Oh. My. God.—Oh. My. Lord!"

The crate held thirty grenades, all nestled neatly inside.

Then—*Boom!*

ഇ 🦋 ര

The sound of grinding, tortured metal banged again. *Clang!* The percussion jolted every nerve in my body as I spun toward the sound and light. One door was now closed and latched. Looking out, I saw a familiar black silhouette framed against the forest canopy. Logan! Standing, dressed in trademark black; pants, boots, and a sleeveless wife-beater shirt, holding a gun to a man's head. The man's hands were tied behind his back.

"Well, well. Looky here," Logan panted. "*Hola*, little wife! Greetings from Cancun. And you even opened the door for me! Still my best sweetheart."

He shoved the man hard with his boot, pitching him forward down the steps, sending him thudding off each one and landing on the floor of the shelter. Logan laughed. "Looks like I get to kill me two birds with one stone," he said.

I dropped everything, rushing to aid the man who lay groaning before me, then just as fast, drew back in fear and confusion. I knew this man! He was the Bandido biker who had tried to kill me in Oakland. The same man Chance had beaten. He should be in jail. Or a hospital.

"Logan," I cried out, looking up in bewilderment at the dark frame that filled the doorway, his face masked in shadows. "What is this? Who is he? What's going on?"

"Get real, Sunshine. I find you hard to believe. Even you can't be that stupid," he drawled in his old familiar style. "But—no problemo! You two are gonna have lots of time to get acquainted." He spun away and pulled the second half of the heavy steel doors shut with a groan that unleashed another resounding *boom*, followed by the scrape of a metal bar as it slid into its cradle. Before I could blink, came the final *snick* of the padlock.

Head spinning, heart pounding, I jumped to my feet. Leaping over the fallen man, I sprinted up the steps and hurled myself against the door. Too late! The force of the impact sent waves of pain like aftershocks, rippling through every muscle in my body. We were trapped inside the belly of Jonah's whale. It swallowed both light and air, smothering my very screams.

&ℭ ℐ ℭ&

I couldn't breathe. The overwhelming stink of unwashed bodies and liquor filled my nostrils, the reek of pot and tobacco-stained hands clamped over my mouth, one after another. There was light. A searing, blinding red light, a pain-filled agony that stabbed into my mind and belly again, and again, and again, until dark rushed in, overshadowing the red and releasing me from the horror. The memory of Sturgis had returned liked demons to a party: a wild, vivid, orgy of cruelty and flesh.

"The memories. Will they ever go away?" I had asked through swollen lips and tear-stained bruises.

"No dear, they won't," Katie, the CMA Chaplain's wife, had said. "But with time and the peace of God, they can lose their power. You will gain control over them instead of them controlling you." It wasn't the answer I wanted to hear.

I remembered it all as I clung to the unforgiving door, vividly reliving the horror of my rape. All of the terror and pain returned, yet somewhere in the back of my mind, I could hear Katie's words encouraging me. Then I heard another voice, a deep voice that snarled; "For God's sake lady, shut the fuck up!"

I stopped screaming.

Breathe in 1-2-3-4, Hold, 1-2-3-4. Breathe out 1-2-3-4, Hold, 1-2-3-4.

The sweat of my labors had left me icy cold. I shivered and hugged myself as I battled fear. I called on the name of the Lord, but all I heard was the cursing man that moaned in the dark and Logan humming a tune as he raked, burying the door to the shelter under oak leaves and pine needles—burying us alive.

$$\text{ℬ 🕊 ℭ}$$

All sense of time was lost in the absence of light and sound. The total blackness was like a living death. Maybe a coma. I don't know. But as I sat, trembling in utter darkness, my frantic mind latched on to something Lefty had said long ago.

I only asked my dad once about his experience as a prisoner of war after the two of us had watched a war movie called *Apocalypse Now.* Our little TV had been powered by a set of jumper cables that stretched through a hole he'd cut in the window screen and clamped onto the battery under the hood of Starla's van.

I'd taken my dad by the hand and asked, "Daddy. What was it like... being a prisoner?"

He had paused, his eyes searching mine, perhaps assessing what kind of answer he thought I could comprehend. "It's like being asleep, baby, but with your eyes open."

I had been disappointed and thought he was evading my adult question—until now. Right now, for the first time, I completely understood my dad.

"Sorry." The man was breathing heavily. "Hey, I know you're scared man, but I need you to help me." His pained voice called out in the dark, "Help me untie my hands."

"You tried to kill me," I said in my bravest voice, still hugging the door. "You're a lying piece of crap."

"If I wanted to kill you, Sunny McLane, you would have never woke up. I just needed you to shut up. Now your husband—I'd like to kick his ass." He groaned, moaning some more.

"You shut up!" I yelled. I needed to think.

It was so difficult to think. It was harder to breathe. I wondered how much air was in this place. I felt trapped in a steel drum, and in a sense, I was. *Think, Sunny!* I chided myself. *Get a grip!*

This is a bomb shelter. There must be a way to filter the air. They wouldn't make a bomb shelter air-tight. I wracked my brain. Things like air, light, and water hadn't top priorities for a little girl at play. The shelter had been my cave, my corral, my palace. Now it felt like my tomb.

Okay, I remembered. Somewhere, there is a handle that cranks something. And now that I thought about it, I recalled Matt the Rat asking Daddy, "What do you do if a tree falls on the door?" Lefty had laughed and called him a dumb SOB. Why?

"I'm a cop," the voice came again with a jolt, shattering my contemplation. "I work undercover with ATF," he croaked. "Come on, Sunny. Untie my hands. I'm telling you the truth." I could hear him grunting in pain as he struggled to move about.

"Yeah, right, and I'm David Copperfield working on a trick to get us out of here. I think you're just another stupid one-percenter, so shut up so I can think. Okay?"

First, I needed the flashlight I had dropped. It was probably dead, back somewhere by the grenades. Tentatively stretching out an arm, I decided to follow the perimeter and avoid the man at the bottom of the steps. That made more sense than screaming and crying, although I was still on the verge.

Easing off the side of the steps, I dropped down about three feet to floor of the shelter and slowly groped my way along the wall. Hands out, forward motion. A razor of jagged metal sliced across my face and I cried out, falling backward. Touching my cheek, my hands grew warm and sticky. The metallic taste of blood reached my lips.

"Oh, God, where are you? I can't breathe. Help me, Lord. I am so thirsty. I need the flashlight," I unconsciously rambled in prayer.

"Hey, it's okay." The voice seemed to reach through my wall of fear, and he continued in a reassuring tone. "Listen, I'm scared too."

I could hear him grunt in frustration as I inched forward, terrified that the next piece of metal might skewer me in the eye.

"Look, you have no reason to believe me, but I really am a federal agent. That's why I'm here. Your, whatever-he-is, Logan, he found out. Someone on the inside blew my cover."

"What are you talking about?" I demanded.

"The guns. They're down here. Aren't they?"

The sound of metal-on-metal startled me. Hope surged and set me screaming for "Help!" then gave up as I keyed into a new sound. *What the...?* The screeching stopped.

Maybe this guy can help me with the doors, I thought. "Hey, pal. I don't know if you really are a cop or not," I panted, "and to tell you the truth, I don't give a care. Can you help me push on the doors?"

"Untie my hands. Hurry." He didn't sound good.

It was a risk I would have to take. I made my way toward the voice, nearly stumbling over him. He lay where he had fallen. With shaking fingers, I ran my hand along his muscled arm to the rope that bound his wrists and worked frantically to free him. I knew I would never get out of the bomb shelter alone. I struggled to loosen the rope.

We stood up and tentatively groped our way up the steps to the doors.

We pushed, shoved, and pounded to no avail. They didn't budge.

Then came the banging. Loud. Like a hammer. Then twisting and turning. Suddenly, a small shaft of diffused light spilled in, just for a moment, from a point in the ceiling. It was followed by darkness and more cranking.

"Oh shit!" My brain screamed *be careful what you wish for* as I heard... water? "He's filling the shelter with water!" I cried out in desperation as a wave of terror swept over me.

"Hush. Don't move." I could feel the man's hand on my arm, and I didn't pull away. I didn't "hush" either. I screamed.

"Logan! *Logan!* Let me out of here! Let me out!" I didn't want to drown. I didn't want to die.

"Wait! Listen, will you? Hush!" The man's voice was deep and urgent. He led me back down the steps toward the sound and waited.

There it was again: a soft hissing noise. Not water. No, Logan wouldn't willingly damage his arsenal. Arsenal? Nerve gas? Was he going to gas us? I didn't scream. In fact, I held my breath for as long as I could.

Breathe 1-2-3-4.

"I don't want to die." Logan was possessed by demons and capable of anything.

Again, the brief light. Again, the soft hiss of gas passing through a hose. Gasping for air, I wet my pants. A sign of poisoning by nerve gas? I was shaking so hard with terror that I couldn't be sure. *Please Lord, let it be quick.* More cranking, then darkness.

I waited for the white light of death to show me the way home. Then I heard it.

There is a peace that comes with knowledge. Imagination, the unknown, is almost always worse than truth.

Reeek! Crank-crank! Shhhh-hissss! There it was again; the sound of metal followed by a flash of light, then darkness, and the sound of metal again.

The spirit of peace descended upon me when I realized I wasn't going to drown. I wasn't going to bleed from my eyes or blister inside and out from nerve gas. I knew that sound! I knew it well. We were not alone. Logan was dropping rattlesnakes through the airshaft—one at a time.

CHAPTER 36

ഇ 🕊 ൙

I can't explain the supernatural mantle of peace that enfolded me. I stopped screaming and crying. I could breathe again. My racing heart subsided to a strong, steady rhythm.

We stood there, side by side in the black void. It was the man's turn to panic. "What is it? What do think he's doing?" he asked in a harsh whisper. His voice cracked, and I heard him swallow hard. I might have even heard him break into a sweat. Fear radiated off him like a wood stove on a cold winter night.

"What's your name?" I asked the man.

"William. William Barros. They call me Wild Bill."

"Well, Bill, I suggest you sit down and don't move."

"Why? What is it?" he asked.

"Snakes. Lots of snakes." I replied.

I heard him running back to the door, tripping on the stairs and cursing in pain as he fell. He was the one yelling and beating on the door this time. For myself, I sat very still for what seemed like hours. At last, Bill was silent too. I imagine he was exhausted from his assault on the steel doors and the beating Logan had delivered. I began to sing, softly. I sang every worship song I could think of from "Amazing Grace" to "Silent Night." I sang, but I did not move. Not even when I heard a rattle low and to the right. I didn't flinch. *These are my mountains,* I thought to myself. I just sang, and out of my songs birthed words of hope, and grace, and mercy.

I knew I stank. And while the scent of urine may attract bears and bobcats, Lefty always said it repelled snakes. I could only hope he was right. I know rattlesnakes prefer eating mice over people and that their rattle is comparable to a growling dog. The rattle stopped, but I sang on until some time later when the Lord gave his angels charge over me, and the sweetness of sleep washed my fears away.

ഇ 🕊 ൙

I have no idea how long I slept. I only recall waking up with a painful longing for my mother. It was a familiar emotion, one I frequently experienced growing up here, at the cabin. There were long, lonely days, months, and years of yearning for my mother's love. But never more than at this moment did I ache for her arms to wrap around me. I could almost hear her whispering, "Don't you worry. Mama's here. Everything's gonna be okay," and in my spirit, I saw her sweep the hair back from my forehead with a soft, gentle touch.

Then the spirit of my dad came to visit. "Get up, baby girl. Daddy's here. Find a shovel and kill the damn snake," he commanded in the vision.

Kill the snakes? I didn't have a shovel and I had lost the flashlight. I couldn't even see my fingers in front of my face.

Next in the apparition-parade came Travis. I saw him clearly in my mind.

"Use the Force, Sunny. Close your eyes and feel the Force." I could practically hear *Star Wars* music playing in the background as he faded away. It was all so surreal that I thought perhaps I had been bitten in my sleep and was dying. But the visions overpowered my fears, and they continued.

Next came my husband, the rescuer. His fierce countenance pierced the darkness, ordering me to "Hold on. Never give up. Never give in. Help is on the way."

And sadly, as usual, He who came last, should have been first. My Jesus came into my spirit saying, "I am the light. I am the way. I put before you both life and death. Choose life."

Okay, Lord Life is good, but I could use a little of that light here.

What to do with all of this information in the great darkness?

Darkness? Wait a minute. Where was the flashlight? What happened to the light? Sitting up, I prepared to do a mental rerun when I heard a sharp hiss. Something was moving across my leg.

It was time to transcend from victim to survivor. The minute I trusted the Lord who gave me life, I had my epiphany. The divine revelation of my vision was revealed. Instantly, I believed: *everything was gonna be all right,* I would *hold on, let "The Force" be with me* and *kill the damned snake.*

Snakes move fast, but I moved faster. This one was not coiled but stretched out over my leg. I had the advantage. Using the "Force," or maybe it was the Spirit, I grabbed toward the hissing end of the weight on my legs with both hands, clamping down on a powerful timber rattler, desperately clutching its head and feeling the sting of its tail as it frantically lashed at my face and body. In a frenzy of adrenalin-driven strength I screamed out "Daddy!" and smashed its head repeatedly on the metal floor between my legs until at last, the colossal snake lay limp across my lap.

My heart was crashing in my ears. "Come on snakes! This is what I do," I roared, "I catch snakes... so come and get me!"

Flinging the carcass hard, I heard it slap against the opposite wall. I heard the Lord say, *"Fear Not. I will give you the power to trample on serpents!"*

Then I heard

say, "God, Lady! I don't know who's crazier; you or Logan." Bill was still alive and still huddled somewhere over by the door.

"Hey, Bill," I said breathlessly, "there's a flashlight somewhere in here. We should try to find it."

"Yeah, right. I'm right behind you." Even in the dark, I could sense the sarcasm on his face.

"Listen. If you're really a cop, shouldn't you have cop-people who will come looking for you?" I asked.

"No... Maybe." he paused. "I lost cell reception when I followed you up here."

I laughed, somewhat hysterically. Nerves jagged. "Yeah," I said, still breathing hard, "That is a problem up here." I wet my lips. So thirsty! Then I asked, "How did you know I was coming up here?"

He seemed to be considering whether or not to tell me, and then reluctantly said, "Our informant sent me a text."

"Informant? What informant?" I demanded, squeezing my eyes shut in a vain attempt to block his answer even as I asked, anticipating yet another stab to the heart. "Tell me."

I heard him sigh. "Pretty, young, blonde," he doled out the clues like columns and rows of hints on a crossword puzzle.

"Paige?"

If it weren't for the likelihood of multiple snake bites, I would have run over there and bitten him myself.

"What about you?" he demanded. "Are you saying Travis doesn't know you're here?"

I was stunned. "How do you know Travis?"

"Jeez, my head is killing me," he groaned. "We work for ATF."

My head reeled as I absorbed the possibility. I ran various scenarios through my imagination, alternately accepting and dismissing what he was saying.

"I saw you with Logan. You're no agent. You're just another Bandido dealer."

The man gave a short laugh of contempt. "I almost have to agree with you, Chica. After a few years of undercover, you start to question your own identity," he said, more to himself than to me. "Your Logan is a pretty smart guy for a dirt-bag. He managed to put a lot buffers between himself and his crimes. He solicited traitors inside other gangs and paid them with Hells Angel money. Risky as hell, but brilliant. He paid a Mongol in guns to take out your dad."

My head spun, and sparkly flecks of light danced before my eyes in the absolute blackness of the shelter. "I don't believe you. You're a liar." My voice trembled in rage, anger, and denial. "Are you saying that Hells Angels sanctioned my father's murder?"

"Course not. You're not that stupid, and neither am I. Logan and his buddies are traitors to their clubs, you know?"

"Even if you are an agent, you're in with the Bandidos, not the Angels or Mongols. How could you know these things?"

Bill made some more noises as he moved around. "Logan agreed to pay a couple of our... let's call them, 'independent contractors' in guns to blow up the Mongol clubhouse."

"Why?" I whispered. "Why?"

I could hear him exhale. "To kill Lefty's killer. Make it look like a gang war."

The pictures Travis had shown me of the charred remains of the burned-out clubhouse pixilated before me in shades of gray, like a thick cloud of smoke before my eyes. And like smoke, it sucked the oxygen from my lungs.

Logan was the man who had my father killed! Had Travis known that?

Bill continued, "They blew the place to hell, but Logan never made good on delivering the guns. That's where you come in, and that's why we're stuck in this God-forsaken snake hole."

"You tried to kill me!"

"You nearly blew my cover!" I heard him stumble against something. "Holy shit! Ohh...! Jesus Christ! I've been bitten. God! It bit me! God damn it... Ahh—"

"Bill don't! Get a hold of yourself!" I tried to maintain as I listened to him alternately crying and cursing. "Take off your belt. Put a tourniquet above the bite," I ordered. He was breathing erratically.

"Bill?"

I stood up slowly, hoping to reduce my body-target size, and inched my way in Bill's direction and toward where I hoped the flashlight had fallen when the doors were slammed shut. Moving carefully, with extreme caution, I tentatively felt along the floor with my foot until I bumped into something solid. A crate of guns. Good!

Lifting the lid and reaching in, I dug around until I felt one. It wasn't loaded, and it wasn't as if I was going to shoot my way out, but it would make a much safer probe in the darkness than my foot. No sooner had I pulled the rifle from the crate and turned around, then I heard a warning rattle from another snake.

The difference between victim and survivor often depends on a person's immediate response to the threat. The natural action-and-reaction to a snake's rattle is to jump backward. Instead, I pushed with all of my might— tipping several crates of M-16's, sending them sliding and crashing toward the sound.

Wiping my face with my arm, I moved forward again, past a silent snake and toward a silent Bill.

I wondered how many more snakes were entombed with us. I wondered if the one I had just dumped the crates on was dead or just wounded. I knew from my childhood that snakes can still deliver a deadly bite long after they are dead. Lefty always cut their heads off with a shovel and then buried them for safety's sake.

Tap-tap-tap! I inched my way toward Bill, making lots of noise and vibration with the rifle butt in hopes the sound would frighten the snakes.

"Fear not, Fear not," I repeated in time to the taps. This was my mantra.

My toe bumped something that suddenly moved away from me. Or rather, *rolled* away from me. Squatting down, I reached out tentatively in the darkness, fingers wrapping around a cold, hard cylinder. The flashlight!

Trembling with hope, I pushed the button. Darkness. Banging the Maglite against my leg, it flickered on just long enough for me to see a giant timber rattler, fangs protruding, silently sailing through the blackness... sinking them deep into my leg. Startled, I cried out in pain.

The flashlight fell and rolled, blinking off and on. I seized the rifle, gripping it with both hands, and leaped after the snake as it hurried to escape. A lethal cocktail of rage and adrenaline surged through my veins as I repeatedly hammered the snake with the gun butt into a writhing, bloody pulp before collapsing on the steps next to Bill and the flashlight with its spasms of faltering hope.

Tears falling, hugging the flashlight, I offered up a "Thank you, Lord." At least I wouldn't have to die alone in the dark.

Ⅎ

People from the mountains and country know all about rattlesnakes. It is no surprise to us that between seven and eight thousand people in the country are bitten every year. And every year we get updates on what *not* to do: No tourniquets, no sucking out the venom, no ice or elevation of the body or affected limb. We are told there is a progression of shock, followed by fainting, or *blacking out.* So, it was with some surprise that I found myself falling from darkness into light instead of the other way around.

I looked around for my dear friend, Jesus, to welcome me home. Joy unspeakable, there He stood in a cloud of light, just as I had imagined; all aglow, hair flowing, eyes unearthly. The clouds rolled back, revealing all of my hopes... I blinked rapidly. Make that—all of my nightmares!

It was the devil himself, Logan, and he hovered just inches from my face. The light I'd seen from above was filtering in through the open doors of the bomb shelter as Logan disentombed Bill and me.

Laughing. Stinking. Spitting out, "Hey, baby. Got you a little love bite?" More laughter as he slid his arm under my neck, lifting me onto his lap and squeezing my face as rolled my head from side to side.

"Sunny side up. Wake up! Are you alive, sweet thing? How about a kiss for old times' sake?"

My leg was numb; the rest of me tingled. Overwhelmed with nausea, I gagged. I must focus or die. I felt a mass of slime and gore under my fingertips. The dead snake I had pulverized, and something else. Something hard.

"Time for a quickie, baby? A little send off for the hubby?" Logan pulled my shirt open and lifted my bra. Fresh air on bare breasts. My head spun, making bile rise as he worked to unbutton my pants.

Not this time!

Now or never! I gagged violently, cheeks ballooned, and vomit erupted from behind pinched lips. Logan pulled back to avoid the stream of spew. I leaned over, my hand madly groping through entrails to grasp what was left of the snake's still-solid head. Pulling myself upright, swung hard on Logan's neck—driving the open mouth of the dead snake straight into it.

Screaming, jerking erratically, Logan clawed his way backward from under me, frantically clutching the viper head that was latched firmly to his throat. He crawled over Bill's inert body and up toward the light.

ఐ 🕊 ෬

"Freeze! Police! Get Down! Get Down! Get Down! You're under arrest." Bam! Bam! Warning shots? Travis had arrived with the cavalry.

"Poor Bill," I mumbled, fearing the worst as the world swam around me. I remember thinking that Logan had probably ignored the advisement and quietly hoped that Travis had shot him.

"Sunny, I'm here. I'm going to save you." Chance appeared through shadows and light, kneeling over me as he checked my vitals. The last thing I remember was Chance's strong arms carrying me, and him desperately shouting orders for someone to bring him Crotaline—whatever that was.

Part Three

"FORGIVE US OUR TRESPASSES..."

CHAPTER 37

ॐ ✣ ॐ

There was that light again, temporarily blinding me as I squinted, blinking my way back to reality. Sounds filtered through brain-fog that slowly dispersed. Noise was replaced with a misty vision that faded into the worried face of my husband.

"Doctor, she's waking up!" Emotion glistened in Chance's eyes, threatening to spill over, like a heady foam bubbling up and spilling over from the mug of a tired and thirsty man. His red-rimmed eyes were underscored with dark circles. Chance looked like a soldier who had stayed his post through a long night of battle. He brushed his fingertips across my cheek, and his simple gesture answered my questions before asked them.

"You're 'kay." He wet his lips. "You're go...ing to be alright." Worry lines etched his brows, and concern broke his words like waves upon rocks. His heart was not on his sleeve, but in his face. "I swear... I don't know... whether to kiss you, or divorce you," he exclaimed. "I am so angry. And so relieved."

"And I am *so* sick."

I perceived many things: (1) I was not in heaven, (2) I had survived the snake bite with both legs intact, (3) I had a bandage over my cheekbone, and (4) Chance was pretty upset, albeit relieved about (1) and (2).

Dr. Lance entered the room and intervened before things could escalate. Moving to my bedside, he beamed down in his characteristically assuring way. I knew Dr. Lance. He was a gifted, generous man who had donated his skills to provide cosmetic surgery for disfigured victims of domestic violence. I felt privileged to know him and was relieved that he was my doctor.

Dr. Lance winked and said, "It's true. You are a very lucky young lady." He pointed to my bandaged leg. "Just a small amount of venom in your leg, but your pants died a terrible death," he joked with hands across his chest.

"Not my Gloria Vanderbilt's." I tried to joke back, but my voice was thick with emotion.

"Don't get too excited," scolded the doctor, his expression turned warm with confident assurance. "The leg is swollen and there will be some scarring, but I have you on an antibiotic drip and we're monitoring your blood pressure. You're stable for now but I am keeping you here for a couple of days until the swelling goes down." He tapped me with the chart, "And we want to make sure there are no complications." He gestured with a tilt of his head toward Chance and continued in a more serious tone.

"You know, Sunny, your husband's quick thinking with that shot of Crotaline probably saved your life, or at least saved you from possible amputation." He turned to Chance and bumped knuckles. "Good job!" Then, turned his attention back to me. "I did my best work on the cut on your face. You'll barely notice it when it heals. Questions?"

I couldn't think of any.

"I'll be back to check on you later. Meantime, get some rest. Doctor's orders," he said, tapping my chart with his pen. He left the room.

So much had passed between Chance and me—so much love and so much hurt. We each spent a few moments in quiet contemplation of one another. People who are close can comfortably do that. One thought, however, took center stage in my mind.

"That's twice you've saved me," I told Chance. "Um, make that three times. I almost forgot being used for target practice at the house." A scripture rose in my mind: *There is no greater love than to lay down your life for another.*

His peaceful mood shifted. "Yeah, we have to stop meeting like this. Let's move to Alaska and start over."

I laughed until I noticed that he wasn't laughing with me. He looked serious.

"Brrr! Get real. You know I can't stand being cold. My feet don't thaw until the Fourth of July."

That got a chuckle. Chance knows all about my icy feet on his warm legs. "Okay. Hawaii, then. It's always warm in Hawaii. We'll move there." He still had that determined look in his eyes. "I can get work with their police department, and you can walk the dogs on the beach every day. Great sunsets, moonlit nights, pineapple grilled mahi-mahi..." His lips turned up at the corners, but the intensity of his gaze never wavered.

I studied him for a time. "What aren't you telling me, Chance?"

His features tightened as he paused to gauge my reaction. "Logan survived."

☙ 🕊 ❧

Abuse victim, Sarah, arrived right on time. Only she didn't see herself as a victim. Like half of the population I work with, she was there to "drop the charges," so he could "get the help he needs."

If abusers had half of their victim's compassion, I'd be out of a job.

Settling on the sofa and accepting a cup of tea, she began.

"My faith means everything to me," Sarah murmured, dabbing at her tears with a tissue. "I used to be a nun, you know."

"No," I said, genuinely surprised. "I didn't know that. How long ago was that?"

"Oh..." Sarah ran her fingers thoughtfully through graying hair, pulling wisps back into her attractive, upswept hairdo as she pondered. "I think about twenty-five years ago. Maybe closer to thirty. Time flies."

Sarah was lovely. She had aged gracefully. Or maybe she had simply aged in a state of grace.

"I always knew when it was coming," she said thoughtfully, referring to her husband, Preacher Pollard's violence. "Parker would turn up the TV and pull down the blinds. He'd be rambling about religion and then get into this... state. Like he was there, but he wasn't there." She twisted her Kleenex, knotting and unknotting it nervously as she considered her words. "Oh, ma'am, I don't know what religion you are and whether you believe in such things, but it's like... he gets possessed. He just isn't himself."

"And then?"

She studied the tissue in her hand. "Then he would take me into the garage and bend me over the workbench." Her face registered pain and shame.

"And?"

"Parker would quote scripture, then take his rod of chastisement and whip me. He says it's for my own good... that it makes me a better wife."

"A rod?"

"The top of an old fishing pole. He says it's his responsibility as head of our home to smite me and that it's right for me to submit to his authority." Sarah's delicate shoulders trembled with controlled grief. "I thought he loved me. And, well, he wasn't always like that. He is a pastor, you know."

"I read that."

"Yes. Well, Parker's first wife and their young child died in a car accident. They were arguing while he was driving home from the city. His little girl died right away, but his wife was... horribly disfigured. She died a couple of years later. He was so angry. So lost." Her sweet face glowed. "I tried to help him. I thought my faith was strong enough for both of us."

80 🕊 ⋈

Life isn't so bad, I thought, as I lay next to Logan, moonlight flooding through the sliding doors of the upstairs bedroom, bathing our bed in watery light. I studied Logan's features, so sharp and stern when he was angry, yet soft and boyish when asleep. His hair, dark as a raven's wing, lay feathered across his pillow and I thought how desirable he was. I smiled, remembering the day he had undressed me in the lake, taking off my swimsuit and making love under a fiery sun in a warm bed of water.

I thought I loved him.

When I was still young, I thought he was "misunderstood." *Poor Logan*, I would tell myself. *He's had such a hard life...*

God knows I tried for years to understand Logan. I knew he had survived a rough childhood and grown up in a violent and abusive home. His real dad was a biker, a one-percent outlaw who had abandoned both him and his mom early on. His stepfather rode with a gang, too. The stepfather loved motorcycles and crack cocaine. His mother loved the stepfather's lifestyle, and the expensive gifts he would buy her during the Honeymoon Phase of their "Cycle of Violence."

The cycle starts with "tension," where the batterer internalizes a pressure cooker of mounting anger and frustration. Next, comes the "release-of-tension;" an episode of explosive, violent abuse. And finally, "reconciliation," also called the "Honeymoon Phase," complete with contrition, romance, and gifts. Woman's dreams come true during the honeymoon phase. The man is sweet, the gifts extravagant, and the sex is hot. Round and round the cycle spins, except—with the passing of time— the violence increases in frequency and severity, and eventually, the honeymoon phase, "phases" out. Instead of "Honey, I am so sorry," he says, "The bitch asked for it."

Logan's first trip to the juvenile hall was the price he paid for smashing his stepfather's motorcycle with a baseball bat. His first trip to prison was when he killed the same stepfather using the same bat three months after his release. Logan had fallen into the thirteen percent of boys between the ages of thirteen and eighteen who are in prison for killing their mother's abuser. Logan was tried in court as a juvenile and under California law, released at age twenty-three.

Yes, I thought I loved Logan; the easy-going man with a southern drawl, careless air, and flattering tongue. He was strong, like my dad, tough and fearless. I thought if I could just love him enough, if I could take away his pain and the stigma of his past, he would heal.

Like so many other victims, I always excused him. I blamed his past, his stepfather, his friends, his meds, and most all, myself. There was always an excuse. The years came and went, and the honeymoon ended.

He stopped being apologetic for his abuse and started saying things like, "Don't make me do this, Sunny." "You're not going anywhere!" and "If I can't have you, no one can."

I stopped excusing him the day I looked in the mirror and saw a woman with a black eye—who looked shockingly like my mother—staring back at me. It was about that time I started thinking that Logan was crazy. I shifted the responsibility for his behavior where it should be; square on his shoulders. I blamed no one but him. And he scared the hell out of me.

80 ॐ ଓ

Some people would look at Sarah with contempt; both for her faith in an apparently faithless God, and lack of faith in herself. But I admired her spirit and sympathized with her disillusion. It is so easy to feel disappointed when God fails to carry out *our* plans for *our* lives; those times when you find yourself saying, "It wasn't supposed to happen like this."

Sarah had submitted to her husband out of love, not fear. She had faith, duty, and a sense of obedience beyond anything this world could see or accept. Unless, like me, you admire the spirit of the wild salmon whose sad bodies, even now were drifting back to the vast ocean.

I love this woman, I thought. I understood her and wished I could help her lay aside the suffering-Christ she was trying to model, and know the joy of the living God. If only Sarah could free herself from the shackles of her religion.

"I don't blame God for what Parker did. He is a very troubled man. I made a promise, *for better or for worse,*" she said, "and I won't leave him."

We talked as I walked her outdoors to her car. "No. I didn't expect you would leave him," I acknowledged.

She got into the car, closed the door, and rolled down the window. "Do you think I'm crazy?"

"I think God loves you, Sarah. Very much. Real love is about *freedom,* not *bondage.* Christ came to set the captives free. You might love Parker, but what he did to you... that isn't love... and it isn't worth dying for."

Sarah stared at me thoughtfully as she started the engine.

"The restraining order is court-ordered. It will stay in effect while Parker gets the help he needs," I advised, touching her lovingly on the shoulder. "I suggest you use your time to do the same."

℘ ❦ ℘

"It's not possible. How can Logan still be alive? I saw it. The snake. It had him by the throat."

Chance continued to hold my hand softly, a marked contrast from the tension that gripped the rest of him. "It had him by the skin of his throat," he said. "He's still in intensive care. I think they are doing skin grafts, probably off his butt. I guess he'll be an official butt-head after that." Chance tried to make light of the matter, but I was too sick to smile, and he dropped his head as if exhausted from the effort. "I'm sorry to say it, but it looks like he's going to live."

"Chance? What did you mean when said earlier that you didn't know whether to kiss me or divorce me?"

Chance pressed his lips together, wearing the strained expression that was all too familiar. "I can't believe you went up there alone, without telling anyone. That was..."

"Stupid? Are you calling me stupid?"

"Irresponsible. Unprofessional. Unnecessary."

"Stupid?"

"Stupid!"

The tension increased and Chance responded by getting up. "I have to go. I need to feed Mercy and I'll have Ashley pick up Kissme. You need to rest."

"Yeah, you look pretty tired yourself. Go home; get some sleep."

Exhausted, he nodded, acquiescing and promising to return in the morning.

I lay in bed, stunned that Logan was still alive. I started to wonder if he really was immortal. I know he always thought he was. My old fears rose as I slipped deeper into a drug-induced sleep. I dreamt that I could hear him shuffling down the hall. He was searching for me, high and low, calling my name. *"Sunneeee..."*

CHAPTER 38

਒ 🕊 ੭

I was ever so grateful to be alive after surviving the snakebite, but I wanted to die when Travis entered my room. It was early, before staff woke patients with the rumble of breakfast carts.

Flowers and card in hand, Travis looked painfully attractive in casual denim pants and an earthy green T-shirt and matching sports coat that perfectly highlighted his sylvan green eyes and sandy brown hair.

"I brought you flowers," he announced. "Sunny yellow ones," he added with a grin as he attempted to arrange a riot of dazzling yellow blossoms in the crystal vase he placed on the table next to me. They were as alluring as the man himself. Leaning over the bed, he tenderly kissed me on my forehead saying, "How's the leg, partner?"

਒ 🕊 ੭

"I'm not your partner. I'm not your anything!"

My voice was low and menacing. Rage boiled from within; betrayal and deception making a toxic brew. Hot tears sprung to the tips of my lashes, but I wouldn't let them fall. Not for anything.

"You said you loved me, Travis. But you're just like every other man, using women to get what they want."

Travis froze, but I could hear the whirr of his brain racing full throttle. "Exactly what drugs do they have you on?" he asked, taking a futile stab at bad humor on a rotten day. "You're not serious."

"You!" I spat it like a dirty word. "I was just another merit badge for your ATF career and another trophy for your bedroom wall. You used me in every way a man can use a woman. And now you stand here with flowers, making jokes like I am some kind of idiot."

"Sunny, wait," he pleaded. "Please. You need to let me explain."

Why do men always "need to explain" when things are perfectly clear?

"You knew!" My voice was high and tight as I jabbed an accusing finger at him. "You knew that Logan had my father killed! You knew that dead Mongol was the one who pulled the trigger! —How dare you keep that from me?!"

Travis didn't back down. Dropping all pretense of a relationship, he went to full-on cop-mode. He steeled himself. His features hardened as his eyes chambered high-velocity rounds.

"My feelings for you have nothing to do with this," he countered. "I don't owe you any apologies for doing my job. I do it, and I am damn good at it! ATF has worked on this bust for years and now we have the perpetrator—Logan—in custody. Are you angry about that?"

"You deceived me. You made me think you cared about me. You're just like Chance. You and Paige, all of you. Laughing behind my back!"

"This isn't about you!" he interjected. "You want to hear about it, or you want me to leave?" His didn't flinch.

I clenched my teeth and fixed a stony stare, crossing my arms over my chest, fuming. Nothing Travis could say would ease my rage, but I needed to hear the story behind the events that I had just survived.

Travis studiously turned away, staring out the hospital window as he began his story. "It started back in back in 2002. I was working undercover for ATF. It was a joint operation called Operation Black Biscuit. It was a big one, involving over 500 agents from three different states."

I had to struggle not to disassociate from the emotional battering that punched me with every word.

"I worked for over a year as a prospect for Hells Angels. I got close to Sonny, and I knew Lefty." Travis paused, a soft laugh escaped as he finally turned to look at me. "Your dad told me he had a daughter. He said that naming you Sunny was the only thing he and your mom ever agreed on and if you had been a boy he would have named you Sonny, after Sonny Barger." He dropped his gaze, looking down at the floor, lost for a moment in memory.

"It was a good bust. We got hundreds of guns, grenades—even some napalm. We knew we didn't recover all of it. And we knew the theft didn't involve the entire club, just some renegade members working with Logan."

Travis lifted his eyes, but he wasn't looking at me. He was elsewhere, back in time.

"Logan wasn't a major suspect until after Lefty's murder in Laughlin. That was no spontaneous casino brawl. It was a diversion. Lefty's body was found in the desert, a few miles out of town. Alone. It was a professional hit. We now know, thanks to Agent Barros, that Logan took a contract out on your father.

He shifted uncomfortably.

"CSI matched the bullet pulled from your front doorpost to Operation Black Biscuit and the break-in at the Silver State Armory." Travis tightened his gaze. He focused on me now. "Lefty didn't want his club involved in the armory heist, but it seems Logan had other plans.

"I'm sorry about your father. He didn't deserve that."

A mantle of sadness overshadowed us as we made eye-to-heart contact. The background hospital noise—voices, telephones, and equipment rolling down the hall—drifted in from under the door, but the silence that lingered between us was deafening.

"What about Paige?" I finally asked. "How does she fit into all of this?"

Travis dropped his gaze and took a deep breath, like the pause of an engine down-shifting, steady and smooth.

"Paige was my wife."

I tried not to go into anaphylactic shock as I struggled to understand. "Your...?" I trailed, wordlessly.

"Sunny," his urgency felt like a slap on the face, jolting me back to reality. "We need you to testify."

This was more than I could bear. The tears of anguish I'd fought so hard to restrain unleashed, spilling down my cheeks. Travis had my tears—but I kept my pride. Gathering the remains of shredded dignity, I lifted my quivering chin and met his gaze with fierce determination. "Why? Why do you need me? You have everything you need. All of your loose ends are nicely tied up now."

"No. Not everything," he countered. "You can ID the man who killed your dad. You can also ID the Bandido that Logan hired to blow up the Mongol clubhouse."

"Tell it to your good buddy, Wild Bill. That's his job, not mine. Now get the hell out of here."

Travis worked his jaw, his eyes as hard as polished jade; then looked away to control his emotions. "Bill's dead," he said. "He died at the cabin."

I felt small and mean. Clearly, Bill had been more than just a colleague to Travis.

"I was undercover with the Angels during Operation Black Biscuit. Bill joined the Bandito Nation later as a part of Operation Black Rain. I had to get out. Bill found out the guns were headed to Mexico, to Mexican drug cartels.

This case is bigger than you, Sunny. Bigger than me." The hollowness between us gaped like an open wound. "I was safer in the Army, so I did a second tour in Iraq."

The only sound was possibly that of my heart, shattering like fine china splintering across cold tiles, sending shards of glass like shrapnel into my soul.

Travis was first to break the ensuing silence. "It's not a card," he said with finality.

"What card? What are you talking about?" I scowled and wiped my eyes.

Travis picked up the get-well card and handed it to me. "It's a subpoena."

Reaching over, I grabbed the vase and hurled it across the room, cursing as it exploded into flying chunks and clumps. Dr. Lance ducked, throwing his arms over his head as he entered the room.

"Whoa! I didn't do it!" the doctor exclaimed. "What's going on in here?"

"Oh my gosh! Oh my gosh! I am so sorry!" I sobbed as Travis stalked out of the room.

Much like the vase, my heart had shattered, the blossoms of hope dashed to pieces as the doctor hurried to inject something into my IV.

"Easy does it. Take a deep breath," said Dr. Lance. "You're going to feel better... fast."

Alternately sobbing and cursing, my breathing rapidly slowed. My eyes grew heavy. Someone wiped my face, and then I surrendered to the doctor's promise of peace.

It was night when I woke. There was no clock in sight and the curtains were drawn, but there was stillness, a pervasive hush that told me the time. I moaned softly, remembering everything. I replayed it all through my mind until I was exhausted. As I drifted off, the face of Madison Crowley floated into memory.

80 ❦ 03

The jury leaned forward in a single motion as if joined at the hip, their faces visibly registering uniform frustration.

"Ms. Crowley." Amanda Cross, sporting a leopard spotted kaftan and matching turban, raised her voice. Jury members weren't the only frustrated people in the courtroom. Amanda was not happy. "I repeat. Please speak up! The jury cannot hear you."

I wondered what the problem was as I squirmed in my seat, wishing I could shake some sense into Madison.

She was a tall, middle-aged woman, dressed in clean, green cargo pants and a light sport-cut sweater. She had a lean athletic look with her carefree messy-styled haircut and expensive cross-training shoes. She had spoken loudly just a few days ago when standing in my office asking for the charges to be dropped on Al-Pal. But today, even the judge was straining as she squeaked out her timid replies.

"I ask you again. How is your husband employed, Ms. Crowley?"

"He's a contractor," she replied audibly.

"And specifically, what type of work does that include?"

Maybe she won't need a cattle prod after all, I thought hopefully, although a few volts wouldn't hurt.

Amanda's bulk, brass, and aggressive style are usually formidable enough to subdue people into compliance.

"Drywall and painting." The defendant's voice returned to a whisper.

"Excuse me? Did you say drywall and painting?"

"Yes, ma'am."

"And these pictures, taken at Enloe Hospital following the incident and arrest," said Amanda, holding them in front of the victim, "are these pictures of you?"

The victim nodded, making another inaudible reply.

"We can't hear you. Please state your answer for the jury."

"Yes."

Amanda shot me a fiery look as she passed the photographs of Madison to the bailiff, who in turn, would hand them to the jury. The pictures were now Amanda's only hope for a conviction. Madison was turning out to be an impossibly uncooperative victim, and it fell squarely on me.

The pictures produced sharp intakes of breath from the female jurors and an equal but opposite exhalation of disgust from the men. Half a dozen glossies showed Madison standing in her shorts looking pathetic; dripping with paint from the top of her tangled hair to the soles of her Nike shoes.

According to her husband, Alan Crowley, she had "nagged him night and day for weeks," complaining; *"How come you can paint for everyone but me? My mother is coming and you can't even... you said... you promised... what is your problem?"* until he "cracked" under pressure. He duck-taped her mouth and painted her with a roller brush—which was criminal, and then began caulking her ears and nose—which could have been fatal.

"Lucky it wasn't a homicide," I mused as Travis leaned close, brushing against me.

"She's lucky the jury doesn't kill her," he whispered back, as Madison continued to mumble.

I sighed. "It's fear," I whispered behind my hand, avoiding stern looks from the bailiff for talking in the courtroom. Travis nodded in silent agreement.

Having assessed her during previous interviews, I initially thought her quiet responses were a form of stage fright, coupled with a double dose of embarrassment and humiliation. Her husband had no history of abuse or violence. The jury would take that into consideration. The defense kept playing up the poor, exhausted man being nagged beyond his limits, whose actions did not result in physical injury.

The trial dragged on... and on... and on. You could see the outcome before the jury ever retired to deliberate the case. They were no longer frustrated or sympathetic. They were angry.

None of the myths typically attributed to DV cases were present. There were no drugs or alcohol to blame, neither was the defendant or victim impoverished, uneducated, or of minority status.

Ultimately, the seniors in the jury had missed their afternoon naps and soap operas. They were cranky and frustrated over their inability to hear testimony in spite of having their hearing aids cranked to the max. The younger jurors had been agitated, repeatedly glancing at their watches, upset over wasting a day in court when they had better things to do. Once again the jury reasoned: If she doesn't care, why should I? In the end, Al-Pal got a free pass.

৪০ ❧ ೞ

My cases continued to reach and teach the vicissitudes of life in the strangest places, at the oddest of times. Turning over in the hospital bed, the soft, steady beep of a monitor seemed to resonate, helping me to understand Madison on a much deeper level. I related to the depth of her fear. *Oh, God! How I knew the depths of fear!* But that night in the hospital, I learned that survival mechanisms are rooted in the core of our being, and our response to threat is as unique as our individuality. Just because we cannot relate, doesn't mean we shouldn't respect.

I examined and reaffirmed my own fears; the depth of which no one else could plumb. Perhaps Logan had been right when he declared to his friends that he was "bullet-proof," invincible and immortal. *He will kill me if I testify*, I acknowledged to myself. And if he can't do it personally, he will most certainly take out a contract out on me—just as he had done on my father.

CHAPTER 39

~ ✣ ~

I am a crisis worker, an advocate. The one with all the answers, a fount of wisdom, a bedrock of stability. And yet, I was crumbling.

I had cried so much over the past two days that my tears had become like pets, so familiar that I called them by name. Left eye outside corner, *Rage*; the inside straight, *Hurt*; right eye center, *Self-Pity*. Whoops, there goes *Remorse* off the chin and on to the back of my hand.

It would have been better if Chance had let me die any one of the three times he had saved me. I would have been okay with *dead*. It would be so much easier now if he hadn't cried each time he faced the possibility of losing me. If *only* our passion through the years had not been so consuming or our love so deep. *If only...*

It was my third day in the hospital. Chance had arrived long after Travis had left and after I woke from Dr. Lance's sleep-inducing cocktail.

"I'm worried about you. You need to stop crying. This isn't like you." Frustrated, Chance got up and paced the room, his cowboy boots drumming a restless rhythm that disrupted the quiet hum of the hospital.

"Don't tell me what I need." Another day. Another confrontation.

I looked at him, wishing he had a giant ketchup stain on his shirt, a pus-filled pimple on his nose or something... anything besides the broken look on his face. Neither of us was making it easy.

"You worked with them, didn't you?"

"Who?"

"Travis and Paige. You knew they were spying on me all along."

Chance turned away, his expression rigid and fixed, pushing his hands deep into his pockets.

"How does that go?" I asked him. "'Hurt me once, shame on you. Hurt me twice, shame on me.' Guess it's my fault this time."

His shoulders drooped along with his gaze. He stood there, slumped in defeat.

"Well?"

"You've already got your mind made up. What is the point of my saying anything? You wouldn't hear a word."

"I almost trusted you again. I almost..." The end of the sentence hung there in the air, unspoken, but not unheard.

"Everything I've done, I have done for you," said Chance.

"Like when you did Paige?"

Chance chewed on his lip. "You know... you have never let me be your husband. That was my job, but you hid your past and refuse to let me protect you in the present. Paige is *your* problem now. You and I can never move ahead because *you* will never let go of the past. You will keep her alive and between us forever."

"Your working in some grand undercover scheme with Travis and Paige *is my present*, Chance. And since when is telling me to *'Go be with Travis because I deserve a good man,'* while you're screwing his ex, a part of the sheriff's protocol?"

If it were possible to slam hospital doors, Chance would have rocked the building. Instead, all I heard was an excruciatingly slow sigh, like the final wheeze of a dying man, as the door closed behind him.

My friends returned in full force: *Regret* cascading down one cheek, *Resolve* marking the other. My leg didn't hurt at all compared to the emotions wreaking havoc in my soul.

ဆ ಲ ೞ

"I hate men," I said to no one. I really hated men right then. All men. *They all lie, they all deceive. They are all the same; Lefty, Logan, Travis, Chance. Not a trustworthy one in the bunch.*

Only God was left, and I am pretty sure, contrary to popular belief, that "He" is both male and female. After all, I reasoned, Adam was created in God's image, and God pulled the female half out—*my point*—dividing him into two people instead of one, leaving poor Adam only partially reflecting God's full image and the woman reflecting the other parts. Both sexes forever divided and forever in search of their counterpart.

I am going to enter a convent and surround myself with nuns, I thought with a sense of relief. *And if I ever see another man, I will strangle him with my rosary!* Nice fantasy, but of course what I really hated at the moment, was my life.

Emotionally spent and desperate for the respite of sweet sleep, I sank deeper into my bed, feeling as if I were being sucked into a black hole.

Not really, I admitted as I let go. I didn't exactly hate *all* of my life. What I really wanted was for none of this to have happened. What I really longed for, was a sense of "normal." I have always hated being different.

"God, I wish I was normal," I whispered in despair.

I am just the freak offspring of a Hells Angel that fornicated with Earth Mother.

Somewhere from the vast galaxy of inner space, I heard the Holy Spirit speak. *"You might have been a surprise to your parents, Sunny, but you were no surprise to Me."*

"Lord, you are the only thing in my life that has any worth," I declared.

"If you are angry with me, I am sorry. Whatever I have done, I am sorry. Please take my pain away."

Exhausted, I let go, falling into warm dark arms of sleep.

છ ✥ ભ

"Sunny. Sunny? Wake up, Sunny."

I woke with a start to the dim light above my bed creating a halo around the kindly face of Dr. Lance.

"Ready to go home?" he asked.

I was more than ready. I had never felt so alone. There had been one short visit from Shane and Ashley, and Ashley had promised to return to take me home. Two more long days had followed without hearing from Chance or Travis. I desperately missed my dog, my house, and my bed.

"I was going to stage a breakout if you didn't let me go."

"Well then," he chuckled, "you will be pleased to hear that your ride has arrived."

An hour later I was discharged from the hospital and sitting in the car next to Ashley.

I told her everything on the drive home: the good, the bad, and the ugly. I couldn't help myself. I needed to get everything out. Men and women were created to be perfect opposites. Men keep their own counsel, "suck it up" and swallow their pride. But I am a woman and women look for answers; in magazines, groups, self-help books, TV talk shows, and girlfriends. Females understand the need to reach out.

So I told all to Ashley as she drove, quietly absorbing the information. This is never a good sign. When Ashley is supportive, she engages. When Ashley is silent, it means she saving up to download on me later, and I probably won't like it.

She helped me into the house, propped me up with pillows on the sofa and put the teakettle on to heat. Kissme, nearly hysterical with joy at our reunion, was barking and spinning in circles. She can't really help herself; she is a Pomeranian. And a blonde.

Then came the judgment seat as Ashley dragged over the high wingback chair and positioned herself in front of me. I knew this was coming. This was *so Ashley*.

"Chance was right, Sunny. You never should have gone up there alone. That was really foolish."

Her words stung. The truth always hurts.

"And you never should have gotten involved with Travis, much less told him that you love him," she said, reaching to hand me a cup of tea. "Even if it is true. You're a married woman, and you were acting like a high-schooler."

"Yeah. What was I thinking?" I asked, rolling my eyes. "I actually thought I had a shot at marrying a man who might be faithful. I thought maybe, just *maybe*, God would give me a break. Well, you can stop worrying about Travis, Ash. I know better now. Men are all the same. They are all cheats and liars."

It was Ashley's turn to wince. "Shane doesn't cheat or lie," she hastened to defend her husband. "And anyhow, God hasn't betrayed you. You just need more faith and patience. God will work this out for good. He is faithful."

Shooting her an incredulous look, I fired back, "Not all of us were lucky enough to grow up in a perfect little churchy home. You had perfect parents, the perfect childhood, and now you have the perfect little marriage. God knows you are the perfect little Christian, and I am not.

"God let me down, Ash." Disappointment swelled the lump in my throat. "He dangled hope in front of me and then pulled it away, right when I was beginning to believe that I could lead a normal, happy life. Where's the faithfulness in that?"

Yeah, I loved God, but I had to blame someone. If I didn't blame God for my miserable life, it would just be bad luck. And when you trust to luck, God never gets the credit for the good.

"Oh, Sunny." Ashley was by my side. She wrapped her arms around me, holding me tight to keep me from falling apart. Then she turned my sad face to hers. "You need to listen to me. You just need faith and patience. God hasn't left you, and neither will I."

80 🕊 CB

My first day back to work and there was a voicemail waiting from my boss, Jack Savage, directing me to meet him in his office at 10:00 am.

Jack's office, much like the investigators' intentionally uncomfortable interrogation chairs, is similarly designed for psychological impact. Something about the towering bookcases, the flags standing at attention at his right and left shoulders and the President of the United States frowning down from the portrait hanging directly behind his head as if confirming his every word.

During the meeting, Jack made it abundantly clear that I was legally obligated to respond to the subpoena Travis had served me. Simply put—I would lose my job if I failed to show up for court.

Part of Jack's cooperative agreement with ATF had included putting Travis undercover in the district attorney's office. Savage slipped him in as an investigator with the Special Victims Unit, and the arrangement proved beneficial for both agencies. This was Jack's spotlight, his center-stage moment. And Jack-the-DA thrives in the spotlight. The successful seizure of the stolen weapons stockpile would probably get him reelected several times over.

Both Travis and Paige had been placed in SVU for the purpose of getting close to me and finding out what I knew, who I knew, and the degree of my involvement with both the gun deals and the bombing of the Mongol clubhouse.

I would rather be waterboarded than sit across from Jack another minute, I thought, as he delivered his intimidating speech. I squirmed at the idea that he knew I had sex with Travis.

It was degrading to imagine Travis and Paige watching my every move. How many times had they watched me scratch myself, pick my teeth, palm a tampon and run for the bathroom, plus a zillion other unmentionable acts?

"Are Travis and Paige really married?" I asked Jack.

He paused for a second. "They were practically divorced when they came here."

"Isn't that a little weird?" I asked.

Jack shrugged. "Her dad thought Paige might benefit from working in victim services, and I agreed."

"Her 'Dad?'" That sounded pretty informal like maybe Jack knew him personally.

"Yes." Jack cleared his throat. "He's with ATF."

"You look a little uncomfortable," I said. "Are you uneasy talking about your political relationships?"

Jack scowled as politicians will do when caught in the fudge zone: responding with an air of righteous arrogance. "This discussion isn't about me. I know the facts behind this investigation and assume it may be problematic for you, but I need an answer. Given the circumstances, are you able to continue your work here?"

I stared. "How much did Chance know? Was the sheriff's office part of this operation?"

Jack fidgeted again. "We had operational agreements with both ATF and the SO."

"How convenient. One big happy family."

"I'll ask you one more time," he warned. "Can you continue in your professional capacity as an advocate, or not?"

ॐ 𝔶 ଓ

I didn't want the next meeting, but I needed to hold one of my own. Like Jack, I decided it was best to have it on my turf. I needed my own answers and spent the day steeling myself to receive them. I had invited both Chance and Travis to my office and had Paige make the arrangements. I doubted they would miss my not-so-subtle implication.

Dressed in a conservative suit with my hair swept up, chunky jewelry and pointy heels, I was all business. Eyeballing the clock as the countdown-to-meeting ticked away the minutes... only a couple more to go.

The phone rang and I answered in my best professional power-voice.

"Special Victims Unit, this is the advocate, Sunny McLane."

There was a long, hard silence. Then, "You're mine, *bitch!*" The line went dead.

I dropped my jaw and dropped the phone. It was dangling off the edge of the desk, still spinning in erratic jerks of insanity at the end of its cord beeping a signal to hang up the receiver just as the guys walked in.

Travis did what he always does. Surveying the situation, he took immediate action and began tracing the call without a single word to me. Chance walked in behind him and did what he does best. He asked for an explanation, assessed my condition, and headed back to the sheriff's office.

The call was traced to the jail. It was Logan's first day out of the hospital. Transported and booked into the facility, he was given the standard "one phone call." He used it to call me.

Later, he would tell his attorney that he had said I was a "fine bitch" instead of "You're mine, bitch!" He said he had called me because I was still his wife and he was still in love with me. If Logan had not been spawned a dirtbag biker, he would have made an excellent dirtbag attorney.

Was there a contract out on me? What was I supposed to think? Say? Do?

Travis suggested the Witness Protection Program.

Chance voted for the Husband Protection Program.

Dr. Lance renewed my prescription for Xanax.

Jack Savage insisted that I take another extended leave of absence. After all, it wouldn't look good to have his star witness end up DOA in an election year.

And me? I skipped the meeting idea and went home, locked my door, poured a glass of wine and loaded my gun.

So now my boss and I have a love-hate relationship. He hates paying me to stay home, but is thrilled that I am his election miracle. Talk about job security!

Ashley came over and stayed with me for three days and three nights before Shane showed up with some lumber, tools, wood fillers, and a can of paint. After checking in to say a quick "Hello, how are ya?" he went straight to work, banging and sawing, as he repaired the damage done to the front porch by Logan's shot and CSI gouging the bullet out of the doorpost.

Shane's thoughtfulness made me cry. More tears came when he announced, "Sunny, I spent the last four hours fixing your house because I love you. I am taking Ashley home with me because I love her. Chance has an extra room at his place. It would be a good idea for you to use it for a while."

He saw my tears.

"I talked to him, and everyone knows it's for the best. He loves you, Sunny." Shane is a man of contrasts. He is as rough as a grizzly bear with the heart of a teddy bear. He knows how to stand his ground and bend his knee. He can be sharp as a sword and blunt and a baseball bat. I love Shane. His eyebrows and the corners of his mouth all turned up in sincerity. "Chance is an ass, but he never meant to hurt you. You don't have to make up with him, just don't be stupid and stay here alone. You don't need to be dead to be right." Then he kissed me on the forehead, gathered both his tools and Ashley and they headed home together.

I wondered why it is that everyone thinks they know what is best for me, yet it always comes out sounding like what is best for them.

80 🕊 ⊗

Ashley is my forever friend, but there are times when she is like sand in your shorts, a rock in your shoe, poison oak on your...

Still, annoyances are temporary, and love is forever. Her heart is gold, her laughter music, and her love genuine.

It was Sunday afternoon a week later, and I was still alive. Logan was in custody, and I finally felt safe enough to venture outdoors. Maybe part of the plan for killing me included making me stir-crazy enough to lure me outdoors, because I had to either go outdoors or shoot myself.

Ashley and I talked as we power-walked the dogs down Nelson Bar Road, past the flocks of sheep and traditional ranch houses that grace the oak-studded foothills. More accurately, Ashley was power-walking her dogs, and I was power-limping as I carried mine.

"No, no! Don't tell me. Let me guess!" I said, stopping to gasp for air. It is hard to think with oxygen deprivation. "You sold a piece of toast with a picture of the Virgin Mary on it?"

"Nope," said Ashley, beaming and laughing. "That's already been done, except it was a picture of Jesus on the toast." She frowned thoughtfully adding, "But I'll keep a lookout for Mary."

I hoped she was joking. We both laughed and kept walking until we were out of breath. Okay, until *I* was out of breath. It didn't take long. Ashley is always eating healthy foods and working out. I am into easy foods that are mostly healthy and enough exercise to keep me not-fat.

"Seriously, I got a bottle of pins and screws," she said, wearing her I-did-it-again smile. "I could retire on this one."

"You could retire any time you want, sale or no sale."

"I figure," Ashley said, rolling her eyes towards her think-tank, "I'll start the bidding at $1,000.

My eyebrows narrowed. "What *aren't* you telling me? I already know whatever it is, is weird, just by the look on your face."

Her smile got bigger. "Evel Knievel! I got the screws from the aluminum plate in his right arm after he bent the plate and broke some pins in his elbow. I have to do my homework before I can auction them," she said, tapping her head. "I'm not sure if they're from the time he landed in the box of rattlesnakes, jumped the aquarium full of sharks, or rode through the mountain lions. It was one of his animal things."

Good thing Evel Knievel was born again.

"Anyhow, they had to rebuild his arm with all new plates and pins. I got them from a guy who came into the shop and told Shane that he won them in a game of five-card stud with Evel Knievel back in the day," she said with a wave of her hand.

"Let me guess. His bike was a broken Harley?"

"Well, *yeah*. We own a Harley shop! Besides, Harley endorsed Evel Knievel." Ashley hated to admit that they might be prosperous because Harleys are notorious for breaking down and expensive to repair.

Kissme was wriggling in my arms, so I put her down, and we started to walk again, slower this time so Ashley could finish her story.

"And you got this stuff from him, how?"

"He traded them to Shane for mounting his new tires."

"And you got them from Shane, how?"

Ashley blushed and smiled. "I have my ways."

When we headed back up the hill toward the truck, she asked about Chance, and the conversation turned somber. Chance and Shane had ridden their bikes down to San Jose for a Promise Keepers convention, returning yesterday, elated. There is something powerful about three thousand men gathering for three days of worship, supporting one another and rededicating their lives to God's plan for marriage. I was happy that Chance and Shane had maintained their friendship through our break up, but I kept thinking about the hypocrisy of Chance going to a *Promise Keeper's* meeting; pretending to be something he was not.

"Ashley, I need to tell you something."

There was a pregnant pause before I continued.

I talked with Pastor Mac about my marriage, and he said that Biblically speaking, I have grounds for divorcing Chance. I've had divorce papers filled out and sitting on my desk all summer. I think it's time to file them."

Ashley raised one eyebrow to heaven and flat lined the other in a look of exasperation.

I instantly regretted my decision to confide in her.

Here comes da judge.

"What do want me to say? Are you looking for validation to get out of your marriage?" She pinched her lips and frowned. "You're not a baby Christian anymore. You know right from wrong, and you knew what I would say before you ever told me."

Ashley must have sensed my disappointment. She slowed her pace and stopped to rest in the shade of an oak tree. "I'm sorry. Life doesn't always turn out the way we want. They say the way to make God laugh, is to tell Him our plans. Seriously, I will say this:

You have to choose to either live by your *convictions* or live by your *feelings* like the rest of the world. I can't tell you what to do."

That was a first.

CHAPTER 40

సం ✌ ఐ

Early in my career, I learned that one-sided stories are just that: One-sided.

"Those stupid cops didn't even arrest him. Did you see what he did to the house? That hole in the wall could have been my face! He threatened to shoot me, and the cops didn't even care," Gala ranted, furiously waving her arms to emphasize the severity of her situation. She was outraged, and rightfully so. No one had taken her seriously.

Considering that domestic violence makes up one-third of all violent crimes in our county, little four-foot-something-in-platforms Gala had my full support. The bottom line in my work is the certainty that violence, *without intervention*, will always get worse. I intended to show the responding officer that he might be able to intimidate Gala, but he wasn't going to intimidate her advocate. It was past time for a change! It was time local law enforcement learned to be *proactive* instead of *reactive*. They needed to do their job and *protect and serve*, not just wait around for someone to get hurt, or worse. I was personally going to put an end to the redneck, good ol' boys network.

Flushed with righteous indignation, I stormed down to the sheriff's office. After all, Gala's husband had been drunk, punched a hole in the wall and made verbal threats. Okay, he had never been charged with a violent crime, and there was no history of calls or complaints from the victim. But this is how the cycle starts.

Going to the criminal window in the lobby of the sheriff's department, I demanded to see the officer who had responded to the call. The buck stops here! *Whatever that means.*

Minutes later, I had been taken back for my first ever meeting with Officer Robert—AKA Crazy Bob—Martel.

Declining the offer of a chair, I squared off in front of his desk, keeping the introductions to a minimum to emphasize that this was anything but a social call.

"My name is Sunny McLane, and I am the victim advocate from the district attorney's office. I represent Gala Burton who called you last night asking for protection. Her boyfriend, Michael Hyatt, was threatening to shoot her."

Bob leaned back with a thoughtful nod. "Umm-hmm," he responded.

I carried on with my sanctimonious tirade about ethics and his inept performance in failing to protect Gala. "The report indicates that you only charged the suspect with being drunk in public. That is unacceptable!"

Bob nodded again, still saying nothing but continued to carefully evaluate and analyze me as he sat there. I know this because I do the same thing for a living.

"Gala said that Michael will be released this morning and he will probably be home in less than an hour. Is there a reason you failed to charge him with making threats? Or at the very least, since it happened on the weekend, issue an emergency restraining order? My victim is in extreme fear for her safety because you minimized her danger. Michael has threatened to shoot her!"

It's true, Gala had told me that Michael didn't own a gun, but he could always borrow one.

Bob sighed and looked at his watch. How rude! Was he brushing me off? He stood up.

"Come on. Follow me," was all Bob said as he walked off down the hall and through a maze of offices with me in tow.

Disoriented at first, it took me a minute to realize that we had stopped in a room directly above the visitor's reception at the jail. Bob walked to the large window that overlooked the parking lot and motioned for me to join him.

Suspicious, but curious, I stood next to him searching and seeing nothing. "Nice parking lot," I said with a full measure of sarcasm.

He smiled and said, "Wait here a minute." He turned away and walked off to pour himself a fresh cup of coffee from an urn sitting on the counter.

I waited, scowling and drumming my fingers impatiently, seeing nothing more than a blue jay pause in a tree to make a deposit on a car. The silence was broken as the doors beneath us were thrown open, and several inmates, visitors, and one harried-looking attorney exited the building. My eyes narrowed.

There was Gala, looking like she was joking around with Michael as they walked amicably, hand-in-hand to a small, beat up, used-to-be-red car. She got into the driver's seat, and he slid into the passenger seat. A minute later, they drove away.

Bob was back, peering over my shoulder. "Humph," was all he said before leading the way back to his office and his chair. Once seated, he leaned back again and asked, "Anything else?"

I was dumbfounded. Totally embarrassed. I might as well have had the word *rookie* tattooed on my forehead. "No," I said, in complete humiliation. I started to leave and then stopped and turned back. "Yes," I stated as an afterthought. "Why only the 'drunk in public' charge?"

Bob shrugged. "He hadn't done anything I could arrest him for. He was drunk, in his home, on private property. I got him to follow me out to my car and and then arrested him for Drunk in Public. It was the only legal way I could get him away from her."

Shaking my head at Bob's brilliance and my stupidity, I threw him a charming grin. I had learned a valuable lesson about one-sided stories. "You *are* good," I said with a wink, and headed back up to my office.

The next day I sent him a dozen donuts and a gift card for Starbucks. It was the beginning of a long and close friendship.

℘ ✝ ℭ

Rocket is a flaming-red two-pound terrorist that lives in my neighborhood. Every time Kissme and I walk to the mailbox, we have to cross Rocket territory.

Rocket's owners aren't very sympathetic. In fact, they stand on their lawn and laugh as I reach down to rescue Kissme who trembles every time the teacup Chihuahua runs bristling and snarling onto the road. He might have been funny except for the nasty row of little spikes in his mouth and my bare legs in sandals.

Rocket's Mama is pretty, although it is almost impossible to look her in the face without fixating on the two large hoops that pierce her lower lip, the matching mini-hoops lining the rim of each ear, and the large silver tongue stud that has a reptilian way of darting in and out when she speaks. She is a young, freckle–faced redhead who reminds me a lot of Rocket. No amount of smiles at the Dome Store or "Hellos" at the post office ever resulted in more than a snarl.

There are always kids in their yard, ranging from diapers to about five and they are usually running amuck like a litter of frolicking puppies. I used to think Rocket's mama ran a day-care, and in a way, I guess she does. So, I was completely surprised when she showed up on my doorstep.

"Hello. *Kissme, hush!* Sorry. Uh, how can I help you?"

"Hi, I'm your neighbor. The last house on the road?" she said, pointing down the graveled road. "My name is Jolene, and I'm a friend of Ashley's. She said it was okay for me to come here."

A friend of Ashley's?

Folks often wonder how people in my profession keep their sanity while working every day in the world of violence and victims. One way is by setting firm boundaries that include *never* bringing your work home with you. Instantly upset with Ashley for violating the sanctity of my home, I stepped outside to speak with Jolene on the front porch.

"How can I help you?" I asked again.

Jolene looked nervous as she glanced back down the driveway. When her head was turned, I considered the tattoos on her arms. I know jail tats when I see them. But I also know the look of a frightened woman when I see that, too.

Suddenly I felt guilty for not inviting her indoors, but I didn't want to risk her casing my house and possibly breaking into it later when she needed a fix or blazing a trail to my door for her possible addict boyfriend to follow.

Being a Christian isn't always comfortable or safe, so I led her around to the back porch for safety's sake and asked her if she would like something to drink. I was thinking of coffee or maybe a soda and I wasn't too happy when she said, "How about a beer?" I am not really a beer drinker myself, but I like to support Chico and usually keep some Sierra Nevada brews on hand for special occasions.

"I hear you're a Christian," said Jolene, tipping the bottle and taking a long swig of Chico's finest.

Thanks, Ashley! I thought with a mental grimace before putting on my plastic Christian happy-face. "Yes, I am."

"I'm... hiding from Tanner, my boyfriend. I was wondering... can I stay here? With my baby? He'd never look for me here."

If I were a Catholic, I would have had to go to confession for the unchristian thoughts stampeding through my brain. Then I recalled something Pastor Mac had said after church one Sunday: "That's what the 'meat of the word' is; Action. When the Bible talks about baby Christians getting the 'milk,' that means they are learning the word. But 'meat' is putting the word into practice."

"Let's talk," I said. I needed the details to determine the seriousness of Tanner's threat.

I knew the battered women's shelter was probably full over the weekend, and of course, it was Sunday so no one would be available from Catholic Ladies Relief to get a voucher for a hotel room. *Maybe,* I thought, *I should send her up to Good-Samaritan Ashley's for the night.*

"He threatened to kill my baby," said Jolene, opening a second bottle of beer.

Why did I bring out the whole six-pack?

Okay. Now I took Jolene seriously. "Exactly what did Tanner say?"

"He said he's going to take the baby for a ride and throw him out of the car and tell everyone it was an accident." Jolene began to cry, so I brought out the standard issue of tissues from the house.

"Not my baby. Dear Lord, not my baby." Jolene wept, bent over in grief.

I did a quick threat analysis. Tanner had a plan and the means to carry it out. I asked her where the baby was now.

"He's got him. He'll do it. I've never seen him this mad. He's always been so *good* with the kids."

I patiently got the names and ages of the children. They were all with their dad, and their dad had been drinking all day.

"No, he doesn't beat the kids. Much. Once in awhile."

Not good.

It took a long time to convince Jolene to let me call the police. Maybe she was starting to accept that both she and the children were in need of protection. Maybe it was the third and fourth beer. The reason didn't matter, but I had to do something because she kept spinning those rings through her lip with her tongue and it was making me sick. Nervous habit maybe, but when my stomach started to loop in time with her hoops, I left to call the sheriff's office. The dispatcher, Kelina Morgado, immediately dispatched an officer to respond, along with Gina from Children's Services.

Another beer and Tanner's life history had been detailed with expletives that mostly included four-letter words, none of them nice, until the sheriff's car rolled into the driveway with my friends and associates, Crazy Bob and Gina.

I summarized the situation to Bob, providing him with Tanner's history with the kids, the threat level, and Jolene's statement that he had done jail time for drugs. Nodding his head, Bob left us to pay a call on Tanner. Jolene was in tears again, and Gina was her incredible supportive self as we tried to reassure her that everything would be okay. Both Gina and I knew that we weren't completely honest. Sometimes things are never okay again.

After what felt like an eternity, Crazy rolled up the drive again. To our utter amazement, he opened the door and stepped out with a snarling Rocket in hand.

"Baby! *My baby.*"

Rocket bolted from Bob's arms and fairly leaped into Mama Jolene's embrace. Jolene slobbered and fussed and carried on over the dog before setting him on the ground and crying out with joy as Rocket ran, yapping and snarling, at each of us. Jolene kept repeating, *"My baby!"* over and over again.

I felt the "stupid" light blinking over my head, thinking, *Ashley is so dead!*

"We'll be right back," said Bob, smothering a smile as he herded Jolene and *baby* Rocket into the cruiser to take them home. Gina and I looked at each other in stunned silence until they were out of sight before exploding with laughter. Within minutes, Crazy Bob was back, doubled over the hood of his car, laughing so hard that his eyes ran harder than twin taps at the Sierra Nevada Brewery on St. Patrick's Day.

"Baby! *My baby!*" he mocked, holding his sides and gasping for air. Gina and I tried our best to help him get a grip. At last, Gina rolled her eyes, and we pushed Bob into the car. I could still hear them laughing as they drove off. I knew the story would become legend and I would *never* hear the end of it.

୫୦ 🐾 ଓ

My personal trainer, Kissme, sat on the couch next to me, intent on the steaming slice of pizza in front of my face. She was clearly thinking, "I'm here doing my job, Mom. Just rip that baby in half, and I will personally save you fifty percent of the calories." As my personal trainer, Kissme is always willing to help me diet. The moment was broken by a knock on the door that triggered Kissme to bark and spin. I wasn't sure if she was doing her watchdog thing or a "Wait! Don't forget the pizza" thing.

I sighed, wondering why it is people always call or come over when I am eating my dinner, watching the last five minutes of a movie, or just want to be alone.

I knew Logan was in jail, but just in case, I looked through the peephole before opening the door. There was Travis, decked out in a black suit, purple shirt, and dark sunglasses, looking more edible than the already-forgotten pizza. I resented the fact that that he looked so gorgeous. My body responded, but my heart... that was a different matter.

Not happy to see him, I frowned and opened the door. "Travis. What are you doing here?" It was easy to see that something was wrong—terribly wrong. He just stood there silently, too choked up to speak. "What's wrong?" This was a different side to the man of steel. The man who is in control of every situation

"Looks like you'd better come in."

I led the way into the kitchen. "Let me get you something to drink." It was my auto-responder speaking. One of those awkward moments when you don't know what else to say.

Travis removed his sunglasses to reveal the emotional struggle going on within. He reached over and took me gently by the hand, drawing me close as he blinked and spoke in halted words.

"Sunny... Crazy... Bob is dead."

Hands to mouth, I muffled the wail that started low and rose, escaping with startling clarity. "Wha...?"

"He responded to a domestic call a couple of hours ago." He wiped his eyes. "Bob was shot by the victim."

Swaying, I felt myself go weak in the knees. Travis supported me with his hands on my shoulders.

"The victim?" *I must have misunderstood. I must be in shock.* I shook my head, trying to make sense. "How? Why?— Oh my God."

Travis clouded up. "God had nothing to do with this. The victim didn't want her boyfriend arrested. She was in violation of her parole by being with another parolee. He cut her up pretty bad. She was screaming. Bob tried to wrestle him into the squad car." Travis paused to steel himself. "She grabbed Bob's gun from his holster while he was bent in the car and shot him twice before back-up arrived and arrested her. He died at the scene."

The room spun. Travis helped me to the sofa, and I sat in a state of shock. *Not possible,* I thought. *Not possible.*

The truth is, most of Bob's fellow officers didn't like the man, but he was still considered family and they would grieve. I guess I was used to men like him. I understood them. He wasn't so different from Lefty, war-torn and burned out, trying to manage as best as he knew how. Simply put, Crazy had liked me because I had seen through him and accepted him. I had looked through his defenses straight into his heart and saw a gentle soul. And where was he now? I wondered.

I swallowed a growing lump of grief that threatened to strangle me, and probably continued to breathe, although maybe not.

God has everything to do with it, I thought, vaguely aware that I had never talked with Bob about the Lord. Now it was too late to know where his final home would be.

When I least expected it, Travis tipped my head back and kissed me, slowly, deeply. Completely off guard, his kiss was an unexpected micro-therapy session, a Band-Aid on a bullet wound, a fix for a junkie, a thirty-second Xanax for a mind on the verge of breaking. Or perhaps, it was sweet release from an inner anguish so deep that I couldn't reach it alone.

Then, from somewhere in the distance, I thought I heard Kissme. Had she run out of the house? Was she okay? Drawing back, I turned to call her. But she was already there, wriggling with joy in Chance's arms.

I don't know who would have won the fight. Chance is more powerful, but Travis is an expert in martial arts. But there wasn't any fight. It was more like mutual defeat as Chance just turned and walked away.

"I'm sorry. I had no right..." Travis began.

Having returned more or less to reality as I watched Chance fade into the distance, I turned to Travis, whose worried eyes searched mine.

"No," I agreed, "you didn't have any right. You never have and you never will again," I said. "You need to leave."

And he did. Without another word.

I am not sure how long I stood there staring at the closed door before the waterworks came, but the next thing I recall was the sound of Kissme hacking up pizza all over the couch.

ဆ ⅋ ભ

Officers and dignitaries arrived from all over the state for Bob's funeral. Chance and Travis were each assigned to service-related duties, so I was on my own. Thank God. News cameras rolled. A large color guard marched in perfect precision, carrying the state and U.S. flags. Dozens of fire engines silently lined both sides of the route from the church to the cemetery, light bars flashing as the procession of mourners passed through. At the cemetery, the red carpet was rolled out, and bagpipes pierced the air with "Amazing Grace" as five fighter planes screamed overhead, one breaking away as they flew over the gravesite. I couldn't stop the tears that coursed down my face.

Bob would rather have had no one present, except perhaps some deer or maybe a rabbit. People had caused him too much pain in his life. All he really wanted was to move away and be alone. Life can be frightening in that way. Sometimes we get what we wish for.

People talked endlessly about what a great guy Bob was and how funny and kind he had been. Shaking my head, I had to wonder if anyone here had really known him at all. They sounded like a bunch of pompous windbags to me, but then I wondered if anyone of us ever really knows another.

I mulled the thought over as the stories continued to "celebrate Bob's life," droned on.

I recalled a different kind of story: one about an old man who taught his four sons a lesson in life by sending each of them on a distant journey to observe a pear tree. One went in the winter, one in the spring, the third in the summer, and the last in fall. When all of the sons had returned, he called them together to share what they had seen. The first son reported that the tree was ugly, bent and twisted. The second said it was budding and full of promise. The third said it was lush, filled with fruit and ready for harvest. The last said it still had some color but looked like it was dying. The brothers argued over who was right until their father, after hearing all the reports, told them that they were all correct. He said it was important to remember that we only know a person for a season and easily forget there are other stages in their lives. He taught his sons that they must never judge what they have seen as the whole picture.

Maybe, I had just known Crazy Bob in the autumn of his days. Maybe all of those out-of-character eulogies had only reflected different seasons of his life.

I sat there, contemplating my own life and the inevitable changes that seasons bring. I had choices. I could see the present for what it really was or I could continue to live in the memory of all that Chance and I had once shared, in the springtime of our lives.

CHAPTER 41

੩ 🕊 ੨

"It was just a matter of time. I am not mad at you. I brought this on myself." Chance said from his sofa where he sat with head down and shoulders slumped, refusing to look me in the eye.

I had raced to his house after cleaning up from Kissme's pizza puke, and when he didn't answer the door, I had let myself in.

"You can lose the guilt trip," I said. "It wasn't what it looked like."

Or maybe it was.

"Really?" Chance looked up with a bitter smile. "Because it looked a whole lot like you kissing Travis. I must have missed the part where you were telling him to stop."

Yikes.

"I'm not in love with Travis," I said defensively, and at the moment, the words rang true, although I knew that he would always have a piece of my heart. I might have done some mud-slinging at this point and dredged up Paige, but Chance had been right. I was the one keeping Paige between us. The pain in his wide blue eyes told me that I didn't need to add to it.

Chance tipped his head to one side, brows squeezed tight as he asked the million-dollar question. "Do you love me?"

Yikes, again. It was my turn to hang my head. I wanted to qualify my answer, but I wasn't fast enough.

Chance nodded in silent acceptance of my unspoken reply.

"Yes," I hastened to assure him. "Of course I still love you. It's... it's just not the same. Maybe... after we separated... I was looking at Travis and hoping to find what I once shared with you."

He brushed a thoughtful finger across his mustache. "You deserve happiness, and I am sure you'll find it with someone else. I was wrong to hope. I know that things that are broken and repaired are never the same. But..." Chance got up, picking up a small white box from the coffee table. "Here." He offered the box without a hint of emotion.

It was the kind of box that a woman instinctively knows holds jewelry. "I made this for you." He shrugged. "For us, really. I was going to give it to you. Surprise you, when... when I was at your house."

I took it, speechless. Mesmerized. The little box had a big hold on me, flooding me with shame. I didn't deserve anything. In my mind, I saw the divine scales of justice tip, and another heavenly checkmark dashed against my name. I know I am responsible for my own behavior, and Chance's bad judgment will never justify mine.

"Go ahead. Open it. I guess there's no point to it now, but you can open it if you want to."

I tugged gently at the slender satin ribbon that broke loose too easily, slipped through my fingers and landed in a shimmering coil at my feet. The lid came off just as effortlessly to reveal a small wooden cross nestled in the bottom of the box.

Brows raised, I tried to muster a smile but doubt if it reached my eyes. Chance couldn't have missed my surprise—or disappointment.

It was not at all what one would expect of a wooden ornament.

The cross was not crafted from ancient polished olivewood or aromatic cedar of Lebanon or any other exotic Middle-Eastern wood. More likely it was cut from a Home Depot scrap pile and topped with clear resin. On closer inspection, I could see that what the cross lacked in beauty was compensated by an elegantly designed, feathered mount and hung from a delicate gold chain.

"Particleboard," said Chance, his eyes fixed on the tangle of forgotten ribbon. "Particleboard is made from a million pieces of shattered wood and held together with a bonding agent. The end product is stronger than the original slab. I had hoped our marriage could turn out like that; better, stronger."

Chance shook his head and retreated deeper into his man-armor. "To tell you the truth Sunny—while I really do love you—I am tired. No. I am *sick and tired* of always apologizing. I get more respect and appreciation from the men in my recovery group than I do from my wife."

"That's because you haven't cheated on them... yet. And which are you tired of apologizing for? The affair, or the lies and deceit that continued afterward?"

"When is enough, enough? How many times will I have to say I'm sorry? A hundred times? Two hundred? A thousand? A lifetime? Will being sorry *ever* be enough for you?" He shook his head. "I don't think so." Chance looked as if his thoughts were marooned on a deserted island.

"Believe it or not, I've been trying to protect you from Logan and his friends the only way I know how... the only way you'd let me."

"Excuse me?" I bristled.

Chance got up and walked to the kitchen, returning with a bottle of wine and two glasses. "Would you like some?" He asked, wearing a tired but otherwise unreadable face.

I realized that my entire body was clenched. *Maybe a glass of wine wouldn't hurt.* "Okay," I said, trying to let go of some tension before I snapped. Chance poured the wine and sat back down.

"Jack was approached by ATF last April with a collaborative proposal.

Being Jack, he was totally stoked. So they made a unified pitch to the sheriff's office for a joint venture. I'm just a sergeant, not the Sheriff, and you know what happens when you get two elected officials in one room. I didn't make the rules."

"But you followed them. You put your work ahead of our marriage."

"You put your *past* ahead of our marriage. Besides, I didn't see it that way, and I doubt if you'd understand. You think everything is about you."

I tensed up again as Chance took a slow, thoughtful drink, running his hand through his hair. "I was ashamed. Ashamed and embarrassed when I learned more about my wife in one afternoon, sitting in a room full of strangers, than I had in three years of marriage.

"I talked with Pastor Mac, and in the end I decided that joining the operation was the only way I could protect you. No matter the cost."

"You talked to Mac? Mac knows about Logan?"

"No. Well, yes. Some. Not all. I talked to Mac about me."

I gripped my glass, feeling like the fool that I am. "And Paige?"

He slighted his head with a shrug of indifference. "I think she got the job through some political back-scratching."

"That's what Jack said. Something about her father."

"Meaning Paige's daddy is a ranking somebody at ATF who wanted Butte County to babysit his baby. Now *we* cut her paycheck, not the feds. Still, Paige was supposed to work with you, tracking your phone calls and reporting any suspicious activity."

"Suspicious activity? What does that mean? I used the office phone to call the dog groomer on company time?"

"No." He traced the rim of his glass thoughtfully. "More like using the county car on county time to go to the cabin. I guess you could say that Paige's surveillance saved your life. That's how we knew that you and Bill and Logan were all up at the cabin."

I wrinkled my nose in disdain.

"And the meetings at the casino?"

He sighed. "We met several times. It started as business, and then..." Chance grimaced and leaned back in surrender.

"Did you know she was married to Travis?"

"I knew they were going through a divorce. Paige had an affair with her POST training officer, and that was the last straw for Travis. And of course, everyone knew she was hooking up with Mark." He considered his next words carefully. "She made it easy. She kept hinting that you and Travis had something going on and, well..."

Where is a defibrillator when you need one? I must have paled. I could barely spit out the words. "You believed her? Without asking me?"

"She convinced me that you had never been a child victim. She said you were this wild biker girl; *Property of Hells Angels.* And I knew what that meant." Chance sighed, drained his cup and sniffed. The glazed look in his eyes was not from the wine. He worked his jaw to ease his tension. "Of course, all that happened before we spent the day on the lake and you finally told me everything. But by then, it was too late."

A couple of tears escaped. One found its way into my cup and I deliberately took a drink, swallowing it. I needed to toughen up.

"And since then?"

"I haven't talked to her anywhere except at the office. Strictly business. I told you, I need to be accountable to God and to me. It's not always about you."

Mercy got up from her bed in the corner of the room and padded over to Chance. Sitting in front of him, she placed a paw on his leg and whined softly as she licked his face.

He was still hugging her when I got up and left without saying good-bye.

Back home, I skipped dinner. I wasn't hungry. The only food I was interested in was food for thought. And my mind drifted like a breeze sighing in the night, stirring memories until they finally came to rest on Aissa Williams.

℘ 🕊 ℭ

"I do." I dutifully swore to tell the truth and nothing but the truth, so help me God.

My curriculum vitae had been reviewed by the court and my qualifications established me as an expert witness in felony domestic violence cases. Until now, I had always been an advocate for the victim. In this instance, the victim was dead and his wife, Aissa, was charged with first-degree murder.

Taye Williams was dead. Aissa had stabbed him in his sleep and then set the house on fire. The coroner had already testified that Taye was still alive at the time of the fire. There were legal issues regarding the time lapse between the years of separation and the murder.

Aissa's face was set in stone. No remorse, no shame, no denial. An aura of defiance radiated from an otherwise impassive countenance. I had met Aissa and didn't like her. But that was not a consideration. My job is to educate juries.

Amanda Cross advanced to the witness stand like a hungry tigress. Garishly dressed and thoroughly intimidating in her Bengal striped tunic and carved ebony earrings, she paused, and pounced.

"Ms. McLane. As an employee of the district attorney's office who reviews criminal reports, would you agree that we live in a culture where it has become a social norm for perpetrators to cry "victim" as a justification for behavior; blaming their childhoods, blaming their addictions, blaming..."

"Objection! That calls for conjecture," the defense attorney leaped to his feet. John Kingman was an elderly married man that never tried to hide the fact that he kept a twenty-something girlfriend on the side. He was a deplorable, rotten husband, but one heck of an attorney.

"Sustained." The judge scowled at Amanda, who raised her eyebrows in mock innocence. "Strike that."

"Humph." She turned to me again. "Ms. McLane, in your line of work as an expert on the dynamics of domestic violence, would you share with us any contributing factors that might influence a victim to contemplate, and perhaps retaliate with murder?"

I launched into a narrative about *battering and its effects*—a newly litigated phrase for the previous *battered women's syndrome*—both of which refer to a victim's mental state from constant and severe physical abuse. The dynamic didn't change with the new terminology, just the application. The condition remains controversial but is legally applicable when considering the defendant's behavior in the matters of self-defense, provocation, insanity or diminished capacity.

I used to dramatize this dynamic for the jury by repeatedly stretching a rubber band to demonstrate that, "Everyone and everything has a breaking point if enough pressure is applied."

Unfortunately, during this particular demonstration, the rubber band snapped, firing out of control and smacking Defense Attorney Kingman on the forehead... which was promptly followed by dead silence... then "It was an accident, Your Honor!" and "Order in the Court!" as the jury exploded into hysterics. The resulting red welt did not rise to the level of an assault charge, but I had proved my point in a memorable way.

Jack Savage formally reprimanded me—and then promptly gave me a raise. My model was disallowed in future cases, but the defense attorneys came to regard me with new respect.

The bottom line question and answer in this case, and for my own circumstances as well, is this: *At what point does past trauma, cease to excuse present conduct?*

&) ℘ ($

I had seen Travis at Bob's funeral, but he had been working, and we'd distanced ourselves from each other. Monday morning was just another day in the life of the world. Business as usual in spite of the gaping hole left in the fabric of the universe by the death of Officer Robert Martel. Officials would later rename a bridge that spanned the Feather River in his memory.

It was past lunch and I was tired, hungry, and thirsty. Court had dragged on until the rumbling of the judge's stomach could be heard from where the attorneys sat.

Although I teach on the subject of interpersonal violence, it never ceases to amaze me when I consider the devastating consequences that one person's choices can have on future generations. At work, this phenomenon is termed "learned behavior." At church, it is called a "generational curse." We know that boys who watch their dads beat their moms will most likely grow up to be abusers. But this guy, Aden Beltzier, had witnessed far more than domestic violence.

As a young boy, Aden had frequently sat in the back seat of the family car with his little sister, watching their drunken mother have sex with various men in the front seat. On the flip side, there were times he had watched Dad doing the babysitter on the sofa and an occasional barmaid being "served" on top of the bar. So it was no great shock when, as an adult, Aden swaggered home bragging to his wife, Pauline, that he had spent over one-thousand dollars of their retirement money on a one-night-fling at the infamous Mustang Ranch outside of Reno, Nevada, where prostitution is just another business.

What amazed Paula was that Aden actually thought his escapade would leave her dazzled and impressed by his masculine prowess. Instead, the whole incident backfired, leaving Paula feeling violated and furious, spewing a steady stream of fairly accurate profanities at Aden all the way to divorce court, where he took a swing at her in front of the judge.

Out on bail, Aden was facing either a fifty-two-week batterer's program or up to fifty-two weeks in jail if the jury found him guilty. Why this case had even gone to trial instead of being pled-out was a mystery, except that every citizen has a right to a jury trial, and Aden was big on rights. But the hour was late, and the jury was half-past overdue for a lunch break.

We were crossing the parking lot to the sharp tap-tap of Paige's stilettos clacking behind Travis, when the tap-tapping was buried beneath the scream of a hungry engine. Heads snapped around at the sound and I turned to see a monstrous black truck with custom flames wreathed around its grill wildly careening as it accelerated toward us at the speed of fear.

"Paige!" I cried. Jerking Paige by the arm, I yanked her from its path and slammed her to the ground like a WWF superstar as the force of the truck blew past. The air was rent with a resounding ear-splitting shriek as Aden's Ford F150 tore its way through his wife's little blue hatchback.

Paige came up spitting fire; palms bleeding, with a broken heel on her new shoe and her skimpy skirt jerked up to expose her thonged bare bottom to a stunned crowd standing outside of the courthouse. Clueless as usual, Paige failed to realize that she had just brushed death and that the drama was still unfolding as she struggled to rise on the broken shoe.

Crouching low behind a nearby car, I heard gunshots as Aden unloaded his .45 into the wreckage. Without thinking, I reached out and yanked Paige's one good shoe from under her, sending her back on her bare bottom as a bullet exploded through the car windshield, right where her empty head had been only a moment before.

Travis, who never missed a beat, drew his weapon and executed a smooth takedown on Aden.

"Put it down, put it down! Now! Drop it, now!" Travis drilled Aden in the arm, sending his gun flying across the lot and promptly pounced on him, doing a nifty "cuff him and stuff him" to a cheering crowd.

Or maybe they were cheering Paige's indecent exposure. Hard to say which, in Butte County. Not that it mattered. Paige would never forgive me for saving her life in such an inglorious manner.

What mattered was standing up to see Paige rushing to Travis, sobbing. What mattered was that I couldn't hear what he whispered into her ear or forget the tender way he had brushed away her tears.

80 🕊 CB

I have never seen Travis caught off guard. He *always* sees stuff coming: trucks, pit bulls, bullets, knives, plots, and threats. So I couldn't believe my eyes when his head ricocheted from the force of Paige's slap across his face. The man who is always in control looked paralyzed as he stood before a now-shrieking, anorexic blonde bimbo armed only with her tantrum and a pair of broken red stilettos.

"You crazy bastard! You rotten son of a bitch! I hate you! I hate you!" she screamed through her tears.

Even the arresting officers stopped loading Aden into the back of the cruiser to watch with interest as Paige drew her arm back to slap him again. Travis snapped out of his shock and caught her by the arm. Her hair was snarled and her dress still hiked half way to heaven. The local men were entranced by the spectacle. The women were shocked. I was disgusted.

"Paige! Stop it. It's over." I shouted her down and the screaming stopped, but not the tirade.

"You let that guy run me down and shoot at me," she shrieked at Travis. "She... she... *of all people...*" Paige sputtered, pointing at me. *"You trusted her with my life?!"*

Travis spun around and stalked back toward the arresting officers. I knew he would consult with them and carry on as if nothing had happened. *Mr. Tough Guy.*

I was shaken and furious. "Psycho bitch! You're fucking insane. I just saved your worthless life." I growled, and she snarled back.

"I hate you! Almost more than I hate him." Her voice shook with emotion as she tugged at her skirt, trying to cover what little remained of her dignity.

"I should have let you die," I barked. "I wish I'd pushed you in front of it... you ungrateful, lying skank!" People were still listening.

"Sunny! Paige! Ladies!" Amanda ran interference as she hurried us away from the courthouse. "Are you girls all right?" Amanda puffed from her short sprint.

"Fuck all of you! I'm out of here!" Paige swore with indignation, tears streaking twin tracks of mascara like so much war paint.

"Good! And don't come back!" My sin-ometer tank blew to pieces as I reached out to grab her hair.

"Stop it this instant!" Amanda caught my hand as Paige stormed off. "Let her go!" she commanded with complete authority. "Upstairs!" she ordered. And to Travis, who was returning to join us, "You too, I want you upstairs as soon as possible. My office!"

Angry and shamefaced, I followed Amanda back to her office where she promptly shut the door, passed me a box of tissues and took her seat.

"I am surprised and disappointed in you. Paige is still practically a kid. I expected more from you."

Stung that Amanda would defend her, I spat, "I hate her! She has wrecked my life and I dispise her. I should have let her die."

Amanda pulled herself upright and leaned forward. "Sunny, you are one of the most compassionate people I have ever met, and furthermore, you call yourself a Christian. I fail to understand that you have no sympathy for that wreck of a girl."

"You don't know..." I started. *Or maybe she does. Everybody knows.* "She was put in my office to spy on me. And she had an affair with my husband."

"I know, and I am truly sorry about your marriage. But let me remind you that this is a law enforcement agency and not a high school clique. What I do know is that ATF has given this office legitimate cause to investigate you. But it's not all about you. Paige is a part of this picture with a story of her own." Amanda's brown eyes softened. "Girl, she was put in this office with hopes that this job, and you, might help her."

"I don't..."

"No, apparently you don't." Amanda leaned back without backing down. "That child has been through hell."

"She's made my life hell!"

"Sunny McLane, you can listen to me, or you can talk to Jack. Which is it going to be?"

"Go ahead," I mumbled. I didn't really have a choice.

"Paige's father is the assistant director of ATF's Intelligence Division. He was in Mexico vacationing with his wife when his thirteen-year-old-daughter, Paige, was kidnapped by a drug cartel right off the beach. Kidnapping is a regular industry down there. When her father failed to meet their demands, Paige was sold into sex-trafficking."

The shock was a sharp slap in the face, and I drew back in disbelief, stunned by the impact of this information. I could only stare.

The moment was interrupted by a knock at the door, and Amanda glanced through her window into the atrium walkway. "Come in Travis," she said. "I was just filling Sunny in on Paige's history."

Travis pulled up a chair and sat down as Amanda apprised him of our discussion. "I can't believe that Paige—or *you,*" she looked pointedly at Travis, "have never told Sunny what happened to her. I thought that was supposed to be a part of her coming to work for us; to get counseling and therapy."

"Why didn't *she* tell me about her past?" I demanded.

"Have you told Paige about *your* past?" Travis rose to the challenge.

"Travis." Amanda interrupted, clearly irritated. "Are you done with Aden Beltzier, because I would like to finish up here?" Travis nodded in quiet assent.

"Good," said Amanda as she repositioned herself, "because I need to speak with Jack about the Beltzier incident and I would rather omit the details regarding the conduct of my SVU team in the parking lot." We sat as quiet as schoolchildren in front of Mother Superior. "As I was saying, there was a lot of political pressure on the Mexican government to intervene when Paige was kidnapped. Still," she said, turning her piercing gaze on me, "it took months before Paige was finally located and they negotiated her return. ATF is still trying to bring down that cartel."

𝕰 𝕸 𝕮

"Travis. I don't know what I am supposed to say," I said as we exited through the front of the county buildings. The back area was still busy with law enforcement taping off Aden's crime scene. "Why didn't you tell me about Paige?"

"What good would that have done?" Travis huffed. "Would you have forgiven her for what she did with Chance?" He slowed his pace so we could talk as we walked toward a bench near the upper lot.

I still thought Travis should have told me. "So tell me everything now. Please. And don't give me half of the story. I still have questions about Paige and about us. I deserve answers."

Travis shrugged. "Go ahead. Ask." He sat next to me but kept his gaze on the buildings.

"Okay. Let's start at the beginning. Who is Christy?"

"Christy?" Travis turned to look at me, genuinely bewildered. "Who's Christy?"

"There is a picture in your desk of a woman with two kids. It says, 'Love, Christy and the kids' on the back."

Travis gave me an incredulous look. "You went through my desk?" he demanded.

"Screw you and the ATF horse you rode in on! After you invaded my privacy?"

Travis shook his head and then pulled a piece of gum from his pocket. He unwrapped the gum with slow deliberation and started to chew before answering. "Christy is the wife of an old friend of mine. He died when we were in Afghanistan, the day before Christmas. I keep in touch with them. I visit them every Christmas and take toys to his kids."

A long, uncomfortable silence followed as I took this in. If guilt were measured by the ounce, I'd be buried alive at the bottom of a mine shaft. But I didn't stop.

"And Paige. How did you two meet?"

Travis sighed, his expression open but impenetrable, like a coat of chain-link armor. "Her Dad got her a computer job at ATF. We started dating when I went undercover with Hells Angels. She thought I was exciting—what with my Aryan Brotherhood look and black Harley. She told me about her past, and I really wanted to help her. Be the hero. So I married her."

"And?"

"Unfortunately, I married her victim issues along with her. So when we had the opportunity to work in SVU, we—especially her dad—agreed it could be a good thing."

"She came to us from Chico State." It was more of a statement than a question, and Travis just looked at me as if to say, "Haven't you been listening?"

I frowned, trying to get the whole picture. "So, Paige's dad has a vested interest in guns that are going to the Mexican cartel?"

Travis nodded, and silence rushed in to fill vacuum between us.

"But you were divorcing Paige when you came here. Why?"

"Because she was self-medicating having extramarital sex with everyone in pants."

Work was over and employees were gravitating toward their rides home. "That must have hurt," I said, "and yet you stayed near her and worked next to her. Why?"

"Because I love her."

"And me?"

He half-smiled through his pain-filled eyes. "I love you too, Sunny."

Chapter 42

ಖ 🕊 ಞ

"Christians are nothing but a bunch of brainwashed idiots," Starla raved. She'd lit the fuse with gusto and watched expectantly for me to blow.

I peered at her ravaged form through the safety rails of her bed, located on the fourth floor of San Francisco Medical Center, her expression pleased with her rebuke. She had been in the hospital for almost two weeks, and it was a good thing that it had overlapped with my leave of absence.

The time off didn't exactly feel like a blessing, but in a way, I suppose it was. The extra time allowed me to make the long, tedious drive to and from the Bay Area. I had been thinking about relocating Starla to a long-term care facility closer to home. Like the rubber band illustration I had used in court, I was stretched to the breaking point. I was tired of pouring out my heart and wasting time and energy trying to be the good daughter.

When I had told her about Logan, the cache of weapons, being trapped with deadly rattlers and my subsequent stay in the hospital, she just looked bored. "You look okay to me. I need a cigarette. Sunny, you got a cigarette? Oh, that's right, you're too good."

Today my fuse was short and the explosion that followed did irreparable damage.

"Everybody's brainwashed, Mama!" I shouted back. "What's washed your brain? Drugs? Alcohol? Disease?" My voice rose and temper burst from her constant vulgar and blasphemous attacks.

"At least my love comes from the God of the Bible, not self worship—like you. And don't try to tell me that your Hare Krishna and Yogi crap hasn't brainwashed you," I fired back with a stupid *I'm-so-stoned* face and jabbing the air with the two-finger *peace* sign.

"Yeah," she drawled sarcastically. "I can see your love, baby girl."

Starla would have none of Christianity. She said no more but gestured angrily toward the TV with the remote. That was sign language for *"Shut your face, I'm watching the Wheel of Fortune."*

Stomping to the end of her bed, I turned the TV off and spun around to confront her again. Before I could open my mouth, Starla used the remote to flip the TV back on, ratcheting the volume high enough to rattle windows. Stung by her snub, I reached behind the television and jerked the plug from the wall.

"Look where it's gotten you." I was spitting mad and on a roll. "What do you hope for, Mama? In your next life the wheel of fortune will evolve you from whore to pimp? You're dying!" My voice caught as I choked back a sob. "You have no hope of heaven and you are at the front of the line on the highway to hell!" The dam had burst; anger and bitterness flooded the room. Starla cursed, I cried, and nurses came running in to see what the commotion was all about. When they determined that another crazy Christian was at the root of the problem, I was promptly banned from the building.

ↄ ℞ Ↄ

In spite of everything, I followed through with my plan to move Starla closer to home. I borrowed the money from Chance but refused his offer to go with me to pick her up. He suggested I ask Pastor Mac who had a small RV, to accompany me. The hospital could have, and probably should have sent my mother by ambulance. But Starla didn't want an ambulance, so I was relieved and grateful when Mac said he would be "happy to help."

"We don't know what the future holds..." said Mac led as we drove I-80 into San Francisco.

"...but we know Who holds the future." I finished. "I know, I know. Thanks, Mac."

It was a long drive, and I used the time to talk to my pastor friend about my childhood and how my mother had repeatedly abandoned me.

"Do you have any good memories of her?" Mac asked kindly.

I listed off memories of how beautiful she used to be.

He modified the previous question. "Do you have any good memories of things you did together?"

I thought for a time before recalling, "She saved me from getting Property *of Hells Angels* tattooed across my back. She talked my ex into putting it on my vest instead."

Mac smiled at that. "Maybe we should make you a new vest with *Property of Jesus Christ* to wear on your next visit."

We laughed easily together. I was glad to be talking with Mac. He had been an outlaw biker, and he understood.

Then, somewhere around Berkeley, I told him the story of my last visit with Starla; my failed attempt at sharing my faith, and how the argument had escalated until I was kicked out of the hospital.

"Are you nervous?" He asked as we crossed the Bay Bridge and entered downtown San Francisco.

"Nervous? No. More scared than nervous, I guess."

Mac laughed at that. "It's got to be a lot like your work as an advocate," he said thoughtfully. "You never know when the one you are trying to help will turn on you. Don't give up," he encouraged. "Don't *ever* give up."

"How do I not give up?"

Mac took his eyes off the road for a moment. "Starting your day with a negative outlook is like eating breakfast off a dirty plate."

"Is that in the Bible?" I snickered. "So whose job is it to clean the plate?" He cocked an eyebrow at me in reply. I thought for a moment. "Is that how you feel when you preach every Sunday? Like it's the first time?"

"If I didn't, next Sunday's sermon would probably be my last. It's all about the attitude of the heart. You can always ask God into your heart. Maybe you should try to forgive your mom. She is a shattered pot, and you'll want to handle her gently with care and respect."

I sniffed, feeling short on both.

"Timing is everything," he continued. "Try again when it feels right. And then try again, and then again."

If it weren't for Mac's encouraging words, I'd never have considered the possibility.

The final transfer arrangements for Starla's placement in a long-term care facility in Paradise were made. She was dressed and ready to go by the time we arrived. I signed papers downstairs while Mac and the attendants made her comfortable on the queen size bed in the back of the RV.

Once we were out of the city, Mac gave me his *go-get-'em* nod. Releasing my physical and spiritual safety belt, I headed to the back, sliding through the RV to the edge of Starla's bed with a soft, tentative, "Hi Mom."

Starla looked pale and thin; blue veins under tissue paper white skin. Sad, watery gray eyes looked everywhere, seeing nothing. Moved with sadness, I leaned over and kissed her forehead. She smiled at me, and I knew I had her attention for the moment. Sometimes a moment is all we get.

Offering up a mental, "God help me," I took a giant leap of faith. "Can I pray for you, Mom?"

She nodded yes and I kept it short, humbly asking God to restore "both my mother's health and our relationship. Amen."

Still smiling and peaceful, Starla patted my hand and whispered, "You keep that... and I'll keep you."

Stunned at the impossibility of ever reaching her, I leaned into her, looking deep into her eyes. Embracing her hand with the last vistage of remaining love, I spoke. The words came low and hushed. "It doesn't work like that. I won't be here forever. Only the Lord is forever, Mama. I can't save you."

ജ ✤ ൙

"Mommy? *Mommeeeee*. Where are you?" I begged, sniffling and wiping my runny nose on my sleeve as I wandered through the cabin, crying and calling for my mother. "I'm hungry. Please! I'm scared."

Starla made her way down the steep, narrow staircase, *bump-bump-bump*, dragging a beat-up leather suitcase she had found at the local dump. She was wearing a short halter-style dress that she had made from a purple India-print bedspread and a pair of black military boots. Her face scrunched with frustration as she blew at a long blonde hair that had stuck to the sweat on her forehead.

"Shut up, Sunny, and grow up! You're always whining. Can't you see I'm busy?"

"But Mommy, where are you going? Can I go? I wanna go too!" Hysteria wrung from a rising tide of desperation.

Red-faced, out of breath and out of patience from her battle with the suitcase, Starla dropped it and turned to face her grubby child that looked so much like her father. "You're not going, and that's final!"

"I'll be good. I'm sorry. I'm sorry. Please don't go..."

"Having you was *his* idea. Fine! He can have you. I'm outta here!" She kicked at Frito who yipped and ran behind the couch as Starla continued tugging and swearing at the suitcase. The bag wedged against the frame of the front door and she yanked on the suitcase until a new gash ripped through the leather, setting both it and her free. Then she was gone, kicking the door shut behind her.

It wasn't the first time she had left. And it wouldn't be the last.

ℝ 𓃭 ℞

Starla was in the new long-term care facility for two short weeks before being transferred again. This time to Paradise Hospital. My mother was dying. I received an update from the hospital when I went to visit. Her time was now marked in days, not weeks, as her organs were slowly shutting down.

I poked my head in the room. "Hey, Mom. It's me, your Sunny."

The corners of her mouth twitched up into a smile. She looked emaciated, but alert.

I couldn't make out her words, but her eyes spoke volumes. I read fear, maybe *terror*.

My heart ached for her, probably more from sympathy than love. I don't know if my mother had ever loved me. I'm not sure if Starla even knew what the word meant. She had dedicated her entire life to self-realization, self-actualization, and self-gratification. The Bible confirmed what I already knew. That real love, *Christ love*, is the opposite of selfish love. True love is other-realization, other-service and the resulting gratification is because it really is "more blessed to give than receive."

Compassion is walking a mile in another person's shoes. *Love* is giving your shoes to someone who needs them more than you. Maybe Starla felt wistful, but I doubt that she ever lost sleep over the decisions she made. Sacrifice was not a part of her DNA. I mulled over her situation. She knew she was dying. The time to make a final decision, one that would determine her eternal destiny, was rapidly running out.

I wanted to talk with her about heaven and the hope I have in Christ. Because he died and came back to life, Starla could inherit the promise of life after death. Every time I started to testify, we were interrupted. A nurse came in to check her vitals, a janitor took out the trash, and a pastor peeked in but was warded off by my mother's hostile looks. And then, there was the TV repairman. You have to be kidding. *TV... At a time like this?* I asked him to leave, but Starla managed to croak out, "No. Stay!" It was like she thought her life would end if the stupid TV were turned off. And maybe for her, it really would. As long as the TV kept her attention, she didn't have to think about the future or the past.

I returned to her side and held her hand in hopeless silence as she watched some shows. After a time she whispered, "Roof."

"What did you say?"

"Roof."

There is a lovely patio with a beautiful view on top of the hospital. There are tables with striped umbrellas where both staff and patients can buy food, relax, and take in the sunshine and fresh air. I had taken Starla up there several times over the past week following her lab work.

"You want to go up on the roof?"

Starla nodded yes.

"Hmm... I need to check with the nurse and see if it's okay." I doubted it would be, what with the IV in her arm and the oxygen tube in her nose, but if that is what she wanted, it wouldn't hurt to ask. At least we would finally get some privacy.

To my complete amazement, the staff hurried to accommodate Starla's wishes. I guess dying has become a bit like the Birth Day Place, where they try to make you comfortable and honor your wishes as much as possible, both coming and going. Nice touch.

And it was nice. More than nice. The nurses unhooked the IV tube leading to a shunt inserted in and anchored to her wrist, then helped her into a wheelchair with a portable oxygen tank attached to the back. They carefully wheeled her into the elevator and up to the sky lobby. Then they left us, after telling me to press the "panic button" near the patio door if she showed any signs of distress.

It was early in the day and we had the place to ourselves. Starla pointed to a private corner that she liked, so I wheeled her over to a table with a view that stretched into forever; cascading across ranks of mountaintops, dappled with sunshine that filtered down through wisps of clouds. Standing at the rail, drinking in the majestic scenery, my heart fairly leaped with thankfulness. I knew the Lord had orchestrated this divine appointment.

"Mom, I love you."

She nodded in agreement and smiled at me.

"Me too," she said in a hushed voice.

"Mom? Can you forgive me?"

Starla squinted, puzzled. "What for?"

"I think I have been angry with you for most of my life," I said. "There were times... well... I just blamed you for everything." I had her attention. "I'm sorry for the times I judged you. I'm sure you did the best that you could." She stared at me in silence. Kneeling down, I took her hand and looked into her eyes, asked, "Can you forgive me?"

She turned away, staring out over the flowers and emerald lawn below, and then at the clouds brushing across the rain-washed sky. Everything smelled so fresh and intoxicating. Turning back, her eyes heavy with sadness, she nodded "yes, " and I kissed her withered cheek.

"Thank you, Mom." I took another deep breath. It was now or never. "Mom? I want you to know that Jesus forgives us in the same way you just forgave me. And he loves you more than I could ever love you." Her eyes were unreadable: a closed book.

"You don't have to die. You can have eternal life in heaven, a place where no one will ever hit you or hurt you again. A beautiful place moved by love instead of lust, joy instead emptiness, laughter instead of tears."

I poured out my heart and hope from the deepest part of my soul. "It's all *good*, Mom. It's about letting go of the sorrows of this world and taking hold of Him."

Tears came quietly, tracking down the deep lines that creased my mother's tired face.

It was a Holy-Ghost moment. "I could baptize you right here, right now," I hurried to add.

Starla struggled for words. "Water," she croaked in assent.

Thank you, Lord! My feet fairly flew as I rushed across the patio to the sky lobby and ordered a bottle of water and a paper cup from the girl at the food service window. I felt blissfully alive as I poured the water into the cup. "It's a miracle," I whispered. I turned around. I looked. Transfixed. But Starla was nowhere in sight.

The wheelchair was there, the oxygen cord dangling over one arm, but Starla had disappeared.

"Mama..." I strained, terrified, eyes darting around the deserted terrace. Nothing. No one.

I never felt the water splashing down my legs, never heard the glass shattering as I plowed my way back across the terrace; coffee cups, glass table tops, and chairs pushed over as I raced across the patio frantically searching and screaming, *"Mama!"*

No Starla.

Ghostly hands of terror stretched their fingers to pluck away my failing hope. My mind cast wildly about sifting through possibilities. *Maybe this, maybe that, maybe...* I reached the wheelchair and the short wall bordering the terrace. Then scorching fear gave way to cold reason.

There is only one place left to look.

Peering over the edge, a strangled cry erupted; *"Nooooo,"* and the word was caught up by the breeze and carried across the land.

Far below lay my mother, arms spread wide as if to embrace her destiny, eyes wide open stared heavenward with an expression of shock. Her body lay splayed amidst a tangled thicket of morning glories.

The blossoms crushed beneath her seemed to cradle the once-beautiful flower child, while a stray tendril of delicate blue blossoms draped across her brow like a forlorn crown, sadly mourning her passage.

CHAPTER 43

ॐ ಃ ಜ

Things had not been going well for Kia Xiong for quite some time. Growing up in a home and culture that tolerates domestic violence and considers it a private and sometimes justifiable matter, she had often watched her father slap her mother and drag her into their bedroom. She remembered how her grandmother would scold her for listening at the door as her father shouted all manner of accusations and her mother screamed and wept on the other side. But that was all in her past.

Kia was a mature woman of almost twenty-two now and living in an apartment of her own. If she could slap Teng, she would. She knew he was cheating on her and she knew the consequences of marrying someone unfaithful. Her mother had often been sick, barely able to cook or clean for days following a beating. Kia shivered at the memory.

Kia had never met Teng, but he had been a part of her life for a very long time. Arranged marriages are still acceptable in her culture and in her circle. In an age where text messages fly back and forth at the high school, and sexting explicit nude pictures of your privates to boys is considered fun by some American girls, Kia had resisted the temptation to join in such activities. She wanted to be a good daughter and someday, a good wife. She had kept all of Teng's love letters in a box. Including the last one that said he had met another girl at college.

She stared at the letters now, her tears staining the handwritten pages. Lovingly, she piled them in a heap on the little three-burner stove in the corner of the kitchen. Pressing her fingers tenderly to her lips and then to the letters, she placed a kiss on top of the stack, then turned on the burners and went out to her car.

The local news later detailed Kia's suicide drive off the Berry Creek Bridge into the lake. She left behind her parents, two sisters, three brothers, a grandmother—and the charred remains of a neighbor— a single mother with two children who had died trapped inside the burning apartment.

Suicide is the ultimate act of selfishness. A moment in time when a person is unable to see beyond themselves. They lack the capacity to externalize, consider, or care about the wreckage of lives left in the wake of their tragedy. Some people take offense, thinking I am cruel to apply the word "selfish" to such a helpless, hopeless, broken state of mind. Nevertheless, I would also cite an unborn child as the epitome of *selfishness*; unable to see beyond its own needs. They too lack the ability to externalize, respond and reciprocate. I guess my definition of the word "selfish" does not refer to a state of mind, but rather, a state of being.

Right or wrong, unborn or dying, they are no less precious in the eyes of God.

გა ❦ ൬

I pulled the blankets up and kicked them off again as I tossed and turned in restless anxiety. I groped for the clock, hoping it was morning, but its luminous hands told me it was much too early to get up. I wondered if I had slept at all. I was desperate for sleep but feared the onset of another nightmare. They had become a nightly occurrence since Starla's suicide six days and five horrific nightmares ago. I lay in torment for hours, drifting on clouds of sad memories until one seemed so soft, so inviting, so compelling, that I succumbed to its temptation.

"Momma, don't go." Hands... young, but no longer tiny, reached out again to clutch her floor-length paisley skirt in an all-too-familiar rerun as Starla headed downstairs. This time she was dragging luggage of a different sort—her child—as she yanked and pulled at her skirt, trying to free it from desperate young hands. Tears and snot coursed down my face as I begged the usual refrain, "Momma, I need you!"

Three steps up from the dining room floor, Starla snapped, pushing me down the stairs with one arm. I landed in a heap at the bottom, terrified and wailing at the sight of her other arm; dangling, broken, and covered with a rash of festering cigarette burns. Patches of hair had been ripped from her scalp, leaving angry pink patches of bloody bumps. Her puffy face ranged from plum purple to army green. Blood teared from one eye that had swollen shut. Just above her split lip, her nose bent at a horrific angle. I gaped in horror as she stooped over my body and screamed in my face, "Well, I don't need you! And I don't need this!" She eyes cast daggers of resentment. "I can't be who you need me to be." Then the door slammed shut, again.

I bolted upright in bed. Kissme growled as she scrambled to the other side. Gasping for air, heart pumping madly, I knew upon awakening that Starla's nightmare injuries had embodied every woman I had ever worked with.

I am sure a psychiatrist would have a field day analyzing my dream, but I saw it as a spiritual attack. I rolled off the bed and onto my knees and prayed, "God, please hear me. I know I don't deserve your help. I have no right to ask, but I am begging you. Please, *please* take this burden from me."

In less than a heartbeat, I heard it; *Fear not, child. I am with you. I will never leave you or forsake you.* "Thank you," I whispered in the night as I crawled back in bed. Kissme moved next to me, giving me an encouraging nudge as she wriggled under my arm. Wrapping my arms around her I held her close, and my nightmares fled from the presence of God.

৯০ ৶ ৫৪

I flipped through the pages of the county crime statistics that Victim Witness tracks and sends every month that enumerate cases categorically; summarized by felony and misdemeanor, case type, and the percentage of violent and nonviolent crimes. The compilation looked thorough at first glance. However, this report came about six months after the death of Kia and the same day Chance called me from the sheriff's office with information on Bobbi Lancaster and Dalton Freeman. That call had left me thinking about the domestic violence cases that nobody tracks.

"He begged me to kill him, I swear! That crazy SOB kept a loaded shotgun in the bedroom. Every time we'd fight, he'd march in there and get it, sit in his stupid chair and stick the barrel in his mouth going, 'Pull the trigger... Just pull the trigger!' Shit, I wish I had of. But I didn't. He even tried to get the kids to shoot him!"

Heroine addict, Bobbi Lancaster took a hard pull on her cheap cigarette, rolled her eyes and cursed some more. "Hell, I used to tell him to do it! Quit talkin' about it and just go for it! I mean, I didn't push too hard because I didn't want him to turn the gun on me. Crap!" She tapped the ash to the ground. "I never really thought he'd do it."

But Dalton Freeman had finally done it. Men are the most likely ones to seal the deal and end their lives. I wondered about the demons that had haunted him. What internal pain or hollowness would lead a person to take their life? A deep sorrow sweep over me. There had been no warnings, no domestic disturbance reports. Suicides weren't even a statistic; at least not on my desk. No one tracked domestic suicide, but Dalton was dead all the same.

Not everyone thought Dalton's story was a sad one. Like Bobbi and the officers who had responded. They didn't lose a lot of sleep over another dead junkie. Moreover, when Kia had killed herself, there had been a lot of anger from the community over the loss of innocent lives at her hand, and only her family grieved for her. As for me, I felt a great sadness. Each suicide was an abortion of God's plan for their life. Both Kia and Dalton were much too young to die. *How is it, that someone in their twenties, has no vision of being thirty or forty or sixty?*

Everyone dies. I know that. Shuffling papers on my desk, I paused to wonder if statistics were kept somewhere on deaths that result from heartbreak.

Maybe in heaven, I thought, *but not on earth.*

ဆ ℣ ଔ

"Hello, Sunny." Travis leaned against my door with a no-longer-familiar latte in hand. It had been a long time. I had forgotten how much this simple gesture had meant. "I was sorry to hear about your mom. I can't imagine how difficult that must have been." He seemed sincere, coming from deep within, but it failed to plumb any depth in me.

"Truce?" He offered me the coffee.

"Where's your wife?" I asked in a tight voice. Page had been out for a week.

He set the coffee on my desk and shut the door.

So much had happened since I had seen Travis at the hospital. When he left, I'd built a fortress around my heart, one stone at a time, determined that he would never hurt me again. Then later, when delivering the news of Bob's death, he'd kissed me, and his kiss had been like the trumpet that brought down Jericho with a single blow.

"Actually," Travis said, "Paige is sort of an ex-wife."

"And just what is *sort of an ex*?" I challenged.

His gaze narrowed. "An X," he continued," is where two lines or two lives intersect, and then move on in opposite directions. Paige and I haven't lived together for years."

"An X is also a signature that establishes a contract or covenant."

Travis's mouth tightened into a hard line. "You should have been a lawyer."

"No, I should have been a prosecutor. They seek the truth. Lawyers deceive. *You* should have been a lawyer."

"I am very sorry for the pain I've caused you, Sunny. But I'm not at all sorry *or* ashamed of how I feel about you." He paused for a couple of heartbeats as his words sank in. Travis's features softened, "Now... when and where is the funeral?"

I sat in silence for a moment, tears gathering in the corners of my eyes. "Saturday. Foothill Mortuary. Noon. It's not a funeral. It's just a memorial."

I returned to the present and my eyes, which seemed to hold an inexhaustive supply, filled with tears again. Travis pulled a tissue from the box on my desk, leaned close and dabbed at the corner of my eyes, then placed his hand on my shoulder with a gentle squeeze.

"You okay?" His eyes thoughtfully searched mine.

"No. But I will be. Starla wasn't a nice person, but she was still my mom."

"Yeah, I know. But you are. A nice person that is."

ဆ ℣ ଔ

I had met with Pastor Mac at noon to begin the memorial service, such as it was. I opted to use a flower arrangement that beautifully framed the large canvas portrait of Starla I had made from an old picture. I chose a single image over the more traditional collages and mosaics that cover the course of a lifetime. I didn't think Starla's life would paint a very pretty public picture. If anything, I thought, a photo-documentation of Starla's life would make a great deterrent for the "Scared Straight" program; where juvenile offenders tour the "Big-House" as a foreshadow of their destiny if they don't change their ways.

The portrait was a truly amazing picture of my mother. She looked like a radiant princess right out of a fairytale, draped in a flowing white gauzy dress with billowing sleeves and a wreath of tiny white flowers adorning her long, golden tresses. The picture appeared to have been taken somewhere on the coast, with sunlight filtering through towering majestic redwoods in the background. I thought it was her wedding picture and it came as no surprise that my dad was not in it. I suspect he was straddling his Harley somewhere behind the camera.

Some friends and work associates attended the memorial; Serena from Rape Crisis, the director of the SAFE Program, Mark from Search and Rescue, Gail, Amanda, and Jack, from work. Paige, to my great surprise, was there. Alone. She was dressed appropriately but didn't look well. She avoided eye contact as she mumbled her sympathies on the way out of the service. No one came for Starla, but of course, I didn't announce to the biker world where it would be or that I would be there.

I thought it ironic that the precious women from our little church in Concow were the ones who brought food and provided music for my Christ-hating mother's memorial. But that is the kind of women they are— genuinely kind and thoughtful.

Starla's life had been reduced to less than four pounds of natural elements, poured into an eight-by-six inch plain wooden box. I packed it up after the memorial and seat-belted her securely next to me, anchoring her like a priceless treasure for the drive home. I couldn't bring myself to put her in the trunk. That wouldn't be right.

More tears came when I told her we were "almost home." This was something I had wanted over the past months, or perhaps years. It had been a long time since we lived together under the same roof in a place called home. It felt right. I wanted to look after her and talk with her for a while before releasing her ashes.

The phone rang almost daily. My always-caring Ashley provided me with a daily dose of scripture with the same fervor and conviction that Jewish mothers dish out chicken noodle soup to a sick child. *Dear Ashley.* At least she refrained from stating the obvious: that Mom is in hell.

Chance had given me a supportive hug at the service and continued to send fresh flowers to the house every week, and every week I would place them in a vase next to Mom's box on the end table.

Pastor Mac reminded me that my mom had vehemently rejected my repeated efforts to lead her to Christ. "Not everyone will be saved, Sunny," he reminded me with conviction and sensitivity.

Travis assured me that my mother was "at peace." I have no idea what in the world would lead him to believe such a thing, other than the hope that he too, will find peace when his time comes.

Joyce and Kenny from Feather Falls called with their sympathies and came to the memorial. Joyce said that Kenny had burned sage and beat his drums, singing ancient songs to help Starla find her way home.

Taking off my shoes, I poured a glass of wine and pulled Kissme onto my lap as I pondered the differences in all of our beliefs. There is *fate*, and there is *faith*. If *fate* is true, then I am already a victim of an inevitable future. But if I have *faith*, then I have *hope*. Without faith, I have no hope. And my personal hope is that I don't end up in outer darkness with Starla. For the Bible says that the light came into the world, but people—like my mother— preferred darkness, seeking to hide their shameful deeds.

Kissme licked my face and wagged her tail, knocking over the Serenity Prayer plaque that rested against Starla's box. I think it was a special delivery message from God as I picked it up and read, "God grant me the serenity to accept the things I cannot change, the courage to change the things I can, and the wisdom to know the difference."

"My heart is broken, Lord," I whispered. "I don't want to be alone tonight, and I don't think I can survive another nightmare. If you are willing, I could really use a double-portion of the wisdom-thing."

I must assume it was my answer to *God's* prompting—or maybe it was God's answer to *my* prompting—that led me to my next decision.

ဆာ ༀ ལ

I don't know what it is about sex and funerals. Studies have shown an extraordinary increase in sexual activity among mourners. Maybe it has something to do with sex being life affirming. Probably right up there with the heightened sexual activity that precedes an invading army. Perhaps it is instinctive; a God-driven desire to create and sustain life in defiance of the certainty of death. I can't guess. I suppose it is just as likely to be the result of the first three letters of the word "funeral" being f-u-n... and the fact that funerals are frequently followed by ingesting vast quantities of food and alcohol.

Then again, maybe the answer does not require an analyst. Perhaps it is as simple as a waterfall taking the plunge, a chick cracking out of an egg, or an infant reaching for a warm breast full of milk. Some things just happen. They are part of a greater plan that cannot be denied. All I know is that night; I longed to be a wife to my husband. I had a desperate need to be held and loved. To be swept away into the blissful land of sweet forgetfulness.

Wearing only a soft print beach wrap and my hair hanging loosely across my shoulders, I kissed my little dog good-night, assuring her I would see her in the morning and stepped out into the fading light.

Chance opened his front door, and there I stood, silently drinking him in with a hungry look that any man could read. His blond hair tousled, his blue eyes flashing like tinder and flint, they ignited a promise of warmth and fire to follow. His lips parted in response to my own stirrings, and I could see he was reading me with guarded caution.

"Sunny..." he began. I dropped my wrap with a single tug on the cotton tie, standing naked before him in the setting sun whose fiery colors kissed my skin and turned my creamy tan to polished bronze.

"Sunny..." he repeated in a low, husky voice. "Are you sure about this?"

A smile touched my lips. Wordlessly reaching for his hand, I led him across the porch. He stopped me at the steps, spun me around and easily caught me, lifting me into his arms and carrying me down the steps to the inviting stretch of lawn beneath the jacaranda tree. The last rays of sun turned his eyes to violet as he sat me down.

Kneeling next to me, he brushed my cheek lightly with his lips, nuzzling my eyelashes, then kissing my eyes, his breath as sweet and warm as the summer night. Whispering my name in my ear, he trailed kisses, deeper, more heated, down my neck—kissing, tasting, teasing, pausing. Drawing back, he stared, taking all of me in with his bold, confident gaze. Reaching out, he plucked a flower from the bed that wraps around the base of the Jacaranda. Slowly, tenderly, he brushed its pink petals across my lips, tracing the contours my face, its velvet softness sliding down my throat and across my breasts, where he lingered until I sure I would cry out if he stopped. He didn't.

He moved lower and lower still, bending over my body as his mustache continued to tickle and tease every inch of my frantic skin until I shivered, flesh quivering with ecstasy. I cried out, gasping, trembling and eager—my love soaring, fresh and alive, as if carried on the wings of a bird's first flight.

"Open your eyes," he whispered. "I want to see all of you." He tugged his t-shirt over his head and spread it on the grass next to him, moving me onto the fabric still warm from his body. The musky scent aroused me, unashamed. I could see his muscled features against a darkening sky as he stepped out of his pants.

Again he slowed, restraining his need as he whispered in my ear; words of need, words of love, words that set my pulse racing and heart soaring as I returned touch for touch and kiss for kiss.

We embraced; locked into each other's arms and each other's gaze, all the while touching, touching. Running his fingertips over the soft curves of my body... stroking and pausing here and there... until I lay back in surrender, closing my eyes with a soft moan and little cries of urgency.

We kissed. Kisses that burned, kisses that devoured, kisses that were soft as butterfly wings, wave upon wave of ecstasy until we came to a place where sand and surf meet in an explosion of ecstatic joy, becoming one for a moment in time. All through the night we rode the waves, from all-consuming tsunamis to gentle fingers of probing inlets that joined in a single sigh of fulfillment.

The stars in the heavens seemed to whirl softly, colliding and cascading. Like the delicate sound of wind chimes, I could hear them singing praises to their Creator.

I woke up in Chance's bed, rolling over, drowsily plucking at the sheets and snuggling into his pillow. If not for his scent, I might have thought it all an exquisite dream.

I stretched and sat up. Pulled on one of his T-shirts and padded to the kitchen.

Chance left me a note propped up against the coffee maker, a sure-fire place where he knew I would see it. "Good morning Sunshine. Do you have any idea how beautiful you are when you are asleep? I'll stop by your place and let Kissme out and feed her. Mercy and I are heading down to Fresno for the field trials. Won't be back until Sunday evening. Wish us luck. Better still, pray for us!

~ Chance

At first, I was relieved that he hadn't signed it *Love, Chance*—or burdened me with anything that smacked of obligation or renewed commitment.

Then again...

CHAPTER 44

෨ ⸙ ଔ

Victims don't visit perps in jail. It just isn't done, at least not by anyone thinking straight. The attorneys involved would have a collective fit, to say the least, and at most, Jack might have me fired for unprofessional conduct if my visit affected the outcome of the trial.

Ashley would have admonished, "Did you pray about it?"

In a way, I guess I did, if "God help me" counts as prayer.

My mind was made up. I refused to be bullied and live in fear for the rest of my life. When I left word that I was going down to the jail, no one thought anything about it.

I sat across from the smudged Plexiglas window that separates inmates from visitors. It wasn't as if I thought Logan could reach through the glass and strangle me. I felt safe enough with the two guards that took up their positions at the door behind him after depositing him in a chair across from me. He was wearing the striped jumpsuit that branded him as a violent inmate.

Inmates in Butte County Jail are classified by the color of their jumpsuits: orange for minimum security, red for high-security risk, yellow for anti-socials, and green for persons charged with sex crimes. Then there are the Logans; inmates who wear black and white stripes and are not allowed out of their cells without being handcuffed and accompanied by two guards.

His tangled hair was tucked behind his ears leaving his neck exposed. His sleeves were rolled up to show off his SS lightning bolts and Filthy Few tattoos. His countenance was arrogant and pretentious.

"Umm, baby." He licked his lips and visually stripped me before I could speak or think.

Disarmed, but not dismayed, I managed to keep a poker face intended to reflect fearless determination.

"I want you to call off your dogs," I said in as commanding voice as I could muster.

"I've missed you, baby!" He grinned. "So much so, that I lie in my cell and picture you naked every time I think about your love bite," he said, twisting his neck to expose a hideous scar; a thick scarlet-red rim that ringed a hollow cadaverous-gray crater.

"It looks good on you," I said. "Fitting!"

Raw hatred flicked across his features before he resumed his act. "I know you're here because you miss me and you want me. You're *mine*, Sunny. You'll have always be *mine*," He whispered as his eyes melted into black pools.

"You never were very smart, Logan. I'm here to warn you to call off your pals. You're not the only one with friends—and my *friends* are a lot higher up on the food chain than yours."

And God, it better be you, I thought, realizing my mistake. I should not have come. Too stupid. Too late. But at this point, I had no choice but to play it out.

"Uh-huh." Logan smirked. "Just remember, Sunburst, I got *friends* too, in low places. *Really, really* low places."

"Of course you do," I said, tossing my head in agreement, "but which of our friends run these facilities?"

Logan snarled as he leaped for the glass, pounding and yelling, "You can go to hell, Sunny!"

"After you, Logan! After You!" I fired back, pushing my face next to the glass and smirking as he pounded away.

"I'm not done with you, bitch! Not by a..." he continued his rant as the guards intercepted him, his threats trailing down the hall as they dragged him back to his cell.

"Lord, help me," I gasped as I staggered outside. That was possibly the stupidest thing I have ever done.

80 🕊 ଓ

"That was the stupidest thing you have ever done!" Chance was here, and his presence left me stunned. Chance never comes to my private office. The decision had to do with space, boundaries, respect, and probably Paige and Travis as well. But, here he is. My butt barely warming my chair after the incident at the jail.

"I can't believe you went to the jail. What in God's name were you thinking?"

It wasn't a question. Chance was furious. And his remark was as close to taking the Lord's name in vain as Chance ever got.

"I don't need your permission to go to the jail," I said, angry that he was angry. Okay, I was angry because he was right. The best defense is a good offense, they say, and I thought anger masked my fear fairly well. But whoever thought up that pithy saying has probably never confronted Chance or Logan.

"If Jack finds out..." Chance let the threat hang in midair for me to fill in the blank. "You might have prejudiced the case."

"All right already!" Jaws, fists, buns—everything that could clench, did. "Jack doesn't own me! Logan doesn't own me! Travis doesn't own me!

And you—"

"I know! I know, Sunny. Please. You're making this *really* hard for me. Again."

"*I* make it hard, for *you*?" I said with rising indignation.

Chance's brows collided as he struggled to control his temper and response. "You have never let me confront Logan in my own way. And I admit, there were times it was for the best." He nodded in agreement with his own head talk. "I could have killed the filth. And part of me is sorry I didn't. I've killed people who were less deserving of death than Logan," he said, referring to his military days. "I risked our marriage to work with agencies to put Logan away for good, and now you might have jeopardized the case."

"You think I can't take care of myself? Think about it Chance—I probably changed my own diapers."

My mind flashed through all the times I had survived trauma. I saw my dad, who had survived war to be murdered by my husband. I recalled the searing agony of gang rape. Burying Frito, my best friend. Watching my mother get zipped into a body bag. And I can still hear the hiss of rattlesnakes and Logan's cruel laughter. Hadn't I survived all that... and so much more on my own?

I am a survivor, not a victim!

"Of course you can take care of yourself. You never fail to remind me."

Chance leaned in, his muscles tight and jaw set. He lowered his voice. "I am your husband! It is my duty, my *privilege*, to fight, and even die for you if necessary."

That was my husband speaking. No cliché. No melodrama. No Oscar performance. I knew Chance meant every word.

"And you wanted me to stay out of it. Don't be a man. Don't be a husband. Go mind my own business, as if I were a child!" His words swung like a sword between us—sharp and dividing. "God knows I was wrong for what I did with Paige. But everything I have done to protect you was done because I love you."

৯০ ♋ ൦ଓ

A single tear escaped, and it was one too many. I was tired of the tears. Chance had left, still angry. I robotically maneuvered through the remainder of the day with zombielike enthusiasm. Disassociation has been a tried and true friend for most of my life, but even that failed to rescue me today. So I fixated on work and it was only the sound of the custodian, methodically banging trash cans into his cart that broke the spell, reminding me of the late hour.

A knock on my door startled me. "Paige?" I hastened to pull myself together. "Why are you still here? It's after hours."

I had done well avoiding her since her appearance at the memorial. She hadn't looked well then. She looked worse now.

"I need to speak with you, Sunny." Her voice cracked with strain.

I looked at my watch. "Sure. I have a couple of minutes."

She moved slowly, tentatively toward the sofa, avoiding eye contact. I was curious, but couldn't imagine anything short of an *I-give-a-care* feeling from me today. I was already running on empty.

"I know it's late. I was hoping you were still here when I saw your light on."

I put on my best, bored, professional face. "How can I help you?"

"I'm going to have a baby."

My first thoughts were neither kind nor Christian. I gave a shrug. "And you're telling me this, because?" I searched her face, and she returned a blank stare. "I don't know what I am supposed to say, Paige. Congratulations? I am so sorry? What?"

She stiffened, throwing her hands in the air with a curse and shaking her head.

"What do you want from me? A baby shower? An abortion fundraiser?"

She jumped up and dashed for the door. I didn't care. In fact, I felt vindicated; thinking she finally got what she deserved. *She probably doesn't even know who the father is.*

I flicked the overhead light off, simultaneously flicking on my Stupid Light. Maybe the baby was Mark's. Maybe it was Travis's. Maybe... OMG!

ℴ ✧ ↚

The motor in the little red Beemer was running and I would not have blamed Paige if she "pulled an Aden" and ran me down in the parking lot.

"Come back! Stop! Wait," I gasped, rapping on her window.

The window slid down to reveal fresh tears on a helpless, hopeless, looking Paige. She paused, cast her eyes down and turned off the engine.

"I am so sorry, Paige. Really! I am. That was mean of me. Please don't go."

She stared at her hands that seemed limp, barely able to hold onto the steering wheel. "I just needed someone to talk to. I don't have many friends—women friends, that is. None who would care about this," she said, touching her belly. "I know you hate me. It's okay. I have it coming." Her voice trailed off.

I had to know. The suspense was so taut that I could barely squeak, "Whose baby is it?"

"Mine. Just mine." Her lower lip trembled and jutted out as she turned a sad but determined pair of hazel eyes on me.

"You don't know who the father is?"

"I don't care who the father is! I thought I could talk to you—you being the big Christian and all. I was wrong. But promise me you'll keep this just between us... if you can handle that."

"But..."

Paige gripped the steering wheel in fierce determination. "Promise me!" Her voice rose, shrill and demanding.

"Okay. Okay. I promise."

"Good!" She started the engine, and I stepped back as she put the car in reverse. The last thing I saw was her *All About Me* bumper sticker fading into the night.

₨ x ₒ

"You should move back in together. It's the best way to solve your problems. You'll never solve anything living apart." Ashley grew thoughtful as we sipped the steaming mochas she had made for us in her kitchen. "If I had moved out on Shane the time he..."

"But you didn't." I cut in.

Ashley raised her brows in surprise. "But if I had—"

"Stop it, Ashley! I interrupted." I need this to stop."

Sometimes Ashley is like the blind leading the blind. For all of her good intentions, she cannot take me where she has not been. I knew I was risking it all. I seemed to be doing a lot of that lately. Ashley is my best friend, but the truth is, I had been preparing, possibly even rehearsing this moment for a long time. I didn't want to offend her. I couldn't bear to lose her too. But everything has a tipping point, and our friendship was balanced on that point right now.

"This is really hard for me to say, Ash. You're my best friend and I love you. But I need you to stop telling me what to do."

Complete silence.

Ashley always tries to edify me, which is Christian lingo for *teach, instruct, enlighten,* and *improve*. Those aren't bad things if delivered with sensitivity.

"*Really?*" Ashley's eyes grew big and round, then rapidly narrowed. She bristled, "And this, coming from *The Advocate?* You can dish it out, but you can't take it? Is that it?" She stood with arms crossed.

Mental *ouch* followed by another awkward pause. "I love you, Ash. But you're wrong. My work isn't about telling people what they should and shouldn't do."

"Really?" She sounded skeptical, defensive... and deeply offended.

"Really! I give people options based on my training. I say things like, 'Have you thought about... Do you think... What would happen if...' kind of stuff. Then I offer options; like services and resources. I would never tell someone what to do. They need to find their own strength and figure things out for themselves. I just show them different paths they can take and where those paths might take them. They have to decide for themselves which path to travel. That's how they grow."

Ashley continued to monitor me as she analyzed the information.

"Okay," I teased, "I'd like to tell a few of them '*where to go.*'" I said, laughing and rolling my eyes to break the tension between us.

"Seriously," I said, reaching out to touch her sleeve, "I appreciate it when you share ideas and options. It's just really upsetting when you try to correct and direct," I said, hastening to add, "even though I know you have the best of intentions."

Pause.

"I know you've been a Christian longer than me, but I am getting there. I will discover things as God reveals them to me. It's a process. And maybe, once in a while, I'll even have something to offer you, to build you up. Usually, I never feel I have anything to offer you."

Ashley's eyes shifted rapidly right and left, up and down, and finally came to rest on mine. "Are you calling me self-righteous?"

I laughed. "Yeah, I guess I am."

Quiet.

Then the air filled with the music of our laughter. After all, Ashley really is a mature Christian. She got up, walked around the table and hugged me, whispering in my ear, "I'm sorry. Forgive me?"

This conversation was part of the changes I sought as I struggled to reposition myself in my relationships.

ಐ ೫ ಲ

A jagged splinter of early morning sunlight pierced the slit between the blackout curtains, poking me in the eye and waking me at last. I don't know how I knew, but without a doubt, I knew the time had arrived. Today was the day.

After the morning coffee ritual, I poured a second cup into a travel mug and filled a water bottle for Kissme. Bundling up in a fleece-lined sweatshirt, jeans and a pair of thick, furry socks and hiking boots, I stuffed Kissme into her "I HEART MOM" sweater.

The sun was shining, but the wind sliced through the layers of clothing and made me shiver. Tucking my mother under one arm, I nodded to Kissme, who flew out the door and beat me to the truck. I took inventory as I surveyed the pile on the seat. "Let's see. Mom, coffee, flowers." Thanks to Chance, their fragrance filled the cab. "Miss Kissme and the Bible."

I tucked an old black and white photo—one I had a local glass company seal between two pieces of glass and then frame for me—under my Bible. It was a picture of Lefty, Starla, and baby Sunshine, taken just one hour after I was born. Lefty was beaming from ear to ear, my little face that peeked out from a receiving blanket was pink and wrinkled with a tiny rosebud mouth, and Starla was gazing at the bundle in her arms with a mixture tenderness and radiant joy. It was irrefutable proof that I was once loved.

We drove up a narrow, twisted and gutted dirt road high up above the old railroad town of Pulga. Winding ever upward, I would occasionally pause to admire a majestic tree and listen to the melody of the brook that splashed and danced its way parallel to the road. The wind would catch the watersong and whisk it away, scattering it across the mountains.

I talked with Starla, Kissme, and God, then popped in a favorite worship CD and sang along, filled with the Spirit. Still, we drove until at last we arrived at a small white bridge that crossed the water beneath a crystalline waterfall.

Getting out, I set about fastening the picture to the little bridge and then lovingly placed the flowers, bundled as if they were a baby wrapped in a blanket of white tissue, beneath. Drinking in the sound of the rushing water, the melody washed away the last of the rag-tag remnant memories that tried to intrude on the serenity of the moment.

A yellow swallowtail butterfly sailed along, first pausing to drink on a wet boulder, then sipped from a tiny red flower that bloomed inside the sheltered cove where the water gathered before leaping down the mountain to the Feather River far below.

Telling Kissme to stay in the truck, I hugged Starla to my breast as I carefully climbed over the rail and onto some rocks. Climbing down the rocks, I stepped easily onto a short deer trail that led to a pool at the bottom of the falls. It was calm and peaceful, out of the wind; but the rush of the water created its own mist and spray that swirled up softly, seeming to drench my face with kisses. Sliding open the lid, I saw my mother. Not the ashes or the dust, for ashes and dust they were, but I saw the flower child that once danced in the garden and did yoga to the rising sun. I saw her broomstick skirts, blonde hair that shimmered down her back, and laugh lines around azure eyes. She had been so young, so alive, and so very beautiful.

"Good night, Mama. May the angels of God escort you to your destiny," I whispered, releasing her into the rushing waters to begin her journey to the sea. The powder seemed to float and swirl, pausing in farewell. The yellow butterfly returned to hover for a time, before each of us went our different ways.

CHAPTER 45

ഇ ✣ ൠ

Change was in the air. No doubt about it. Things were coming to an end, or maybe a new beginning, depending on your point of view.

The wind chimes rang out in reckless abandon as the sizzling grip of an Indian summer continued to give way to cooler mornings and chilly nights. Lofty clouds scudded overhead casting magnificent displays of wind-swept blue and black shadows parading across jutting foothills. Jake brakes are popping, thuda-thuda-thuda-thuda, from the cattle trucks as they slow passing the observation point, hauling livestock down the canyon from summer pasture in the high country to winter pasture the valley. Farmers look at the sky, students check their new class schedules, and I? I am looking at a fat gray squirrel, larger than a house cat, stockpiling acorns in the black oak not far from the deck.

Amazing how fast the world can change. One day you are a little girl, walking home to your mother. An hour later, she will vanish from your life for the next three years. One day your heart is full, and you are happily married to the man of your dreams, and the next day a text message shatters the promise with the force of a deer flying through your windshield. One day you are a cop who dreams of finding sanctuary from a turbulent life in the wilds of Montana, and the next day, the dream is laid to rest with the man.

Dead leaves swirled, piling up against the railing on the deck. They look so sad. Like mortal remains of dreams gone by, leaving behind only the memory of their beauty and their bounty.

People at work are watching their inboxes for the dreaded pink slips as the county faces another round of budget cuts. Everyone is perched like vultures, preparing to either take flight or feast on the remains of the newly unemployed. This has become an annual event as we wait for the county administrators to decide our fate.

But today is Sunday, and I am sitting here wondering if church will come to me.

ɡ 🕊 ʒ

"Good afternoon, Sunny!"

Kissme flipped out as little dogs will do, thoroughly embarrassed at being caught cat-napping and giving me heart palpitations as I snapped from my contemplations back to reality and the friendly face of Pastor Mac.

"Didn't mean to startle you like that. Guess you didn't hear me pull up or knock on the door." My pastor climbed the steps up to the deck and crossed the distance to give me a warm, heartfelt hug that quieted my heart and silenced the dog.

"When you asked me to stop by after church, I had this crazy idea you were actually going to be at church. So what's up, sister? You looked like you were a million miles away."

"Sorry. Would you like a cup of coffee?" I asked, knowing he loves coffee almost as much as I do.

"Love one! But don't get up."

"I wasn't going to." I teased. "Through the door to your left, there's coffee on the counter and half & half in the refrigerator. Oh,"—I held out my empty cup—"would you mind filling mine while you're at it?"

I could hear Mac laughing as he made himself at home. I always like that, when people come to visit. No entertainment required. We are all just family and friends.

"Here you go," he said, stepping back outside and handing me a cup, and settling into a chair across from me.

One of the many changes I was going through was the realization that I had nothing left to hide—and nothing left to lose. So I hugged my cup, dropped my eyes and took a cleansing breath.

"A lot of bad things have been happening to me, Mac. I guess I want— I need—absolution."

Astonished, Mac tucked in his chin, lifted his brows, and drew his cup tight against his chest.

"My job is in jeopardy, and my leg still hurts from the snakebite because I went to the cabin when I shouldn't have. My mom died because I left her unattended while I rushed to save her soul. I was getting close to Chance, and now we aren't even talking. The other night a woman came to me for advice because I was a Christian, then ran out in tears when I said a lot of mean, hurtful things. I feel terrible. I am ashamed and I feel guilty. Mac, I know God is punishing me for being such a fool. And I know I deserve every—"

Mac interrupted. "Stop! No more." His expression tightened with concern.

I have become nothing more than an artesian well for an endless supply of tears that push their way to the surface. "I'm sorry," I whimpered as tears spilled from my eyes.

"It's okay, Sunny. Take a deep breath. I need you to listen. We'll take it slow." We both took deep breaths. Mac gathered his thoughts like the squirrel harvesting acorns. "I need to ask you something."

"How is it possible that you have sat in my church... for, what? about three years now? and you never heard me read the Bible verses that clearly state; God has *already* forgiven you."

I sat there, sifting through memories. "Because that's what I learned from my neighbor in Feather Falls and *her church*. Besides, Mac, I have to confess; I sin all of the time. I try. Really, I do. I can't seem to get through a day without sinning. Sometimes I lie awake at night thinking—"

"Say no more." Mac reached out and put a comforting hand on my arm. "Tell me... and I am serious," Mac said earnestly, "how do you visualize God? What does He actually *look* like to you?"

I had to think about that one. "I don't know." I paused, hesitant. "I guess the usual way. Kind of like Gandalf in Lord of the Rings. You know, an old man with a long white beard. Or maybe wearing a gold crown and sitting on a big throne." I swallowed my pride. "Lightning in one hand, rod in the other."

"What else?" he probed.

I exhaled, releasing pressure so I could dig deeper. "Well—*don't laugh*—sometimes I imagine God is like an uptight Santa Claus, keeping a list of who's naughty and nice. *Nice* gets your wishes granted and you go to heaven. *Naughty* gets you a lump of coal and you get hellfire." Mac didn't laugh or interrupt, so I wiped my eye with my sleeve, sniffled, and continued. "Sometimes I imagine this meter. I call it a sin-ometer." I winced, embarrassed by my admission. "It's like this giant pressure tank in heaven, with a gauge and a black needle, and a red *danger zone* on it." I blushed. "Do you think I'm weird? Do you think God will punish me more for thinking the way I do?"

Mac's face lit with joy. "Sunny. I think God loves you, and you must make him very happy! I'll bet you are one of the more interesting and honest people he's met, but let me help you." And it was my turn to be surprised.

"Try to think of yourself as God's *friend*, not his *subject.* There is no list. There is no *sin-ometer*." He chuckled." There's just love. He's already forgiven you for every thought, word, and deed on the very day you asked him into your heart and into your life. Everybody sins, every day. We are just human, and that is the whole point of Grace— that God knew about our sins when he died for us. He knew that through his sacrifice we would be forgiven, not just for our past sins, but for the present, and all of our future sins too. You are already forgiven, Sunny. Clean slate! He loves you just the way you are. Right here, right now."

"But I was taught..."

"No buts," he admonished. Mac was the image of patience, and there was wisdom in his eyes. "Sunny, my very dear sister. Let me tell you about my dog."

"Your dog?"

"Yes," he said. "It's a true story. I guess you could even say it's a love story. All my life I have loved dogs," he began. "I've had them all, big and small, but my heart has always had a soft spot for Dobermans; they are a special breed for me. And my heart broke when my female died, and my male Dobie disappeared. So I had been praying and asking God to bring a new dog into my life."

"Did He?"

Mac nodded. "He did indeed. But God has some pretty unexpected ways of answering prayer. We have it planned one way, and God has it another. I was working outside on my property one day when a call came from a little old lady who lived just down the road from me. She was terrified and asked me to bring a gun to her house. She said she was trapped indoors by a vicious stray dog she suspected was rabid. So I got my gun, and then, almost as an afterthought, I grabbed my old Doberman's pinch collar; one of those heavy kind that are used control unmanageable dogs."

"Did the dog have rabies?"

"No," said Mac, "but it was very sick. And it was a Doberman." He smiled, warmed by the memory. "It was starving and had several large scars on his body. It was lying in a patch of star thistle outside of her house, dying and snarling at me. He wanted no part of me and wouldn't let me get near him."

"Did you have to shoot it?"

"I'm not sure what made me do it, but I put the gun away and kneeled down in front of that dog and held out the pinch collar. To my amazement, he got up, walked over to me and put his head right in that collar.

You see, the chain was *familiar*. And that's how it is with a lot of Christians, Sunny. They readily trade in one burden for another. They trade the freedom that Christ offers us for the weight of a set of laws and rituals. That dog knew he was dying, yet he readily submitted to a familiar chain.

So, I got him in the truck, and I drove him home. When we entered the gate to my property, I took the collar off and we had a heart-to-heart discussion right there."

"Really?"

"I said to him, 'Look around you, buddy. You know where you've been, and this is what I am giving you. These nine acres and everything inside this fence is yours to rule over and protect.'"

"So it worked out," I said, thinking it was a beautiful rescue story.

Mac chuckled. "Well, over a thousand dollars and a daily dose of medicine later, he was a new dog. Almost. For all the years I had him, I could pet that dog any place on his body *except* for his head. And I still have scars to prove it," he added, showing me a scar on the back of his hand where the dog had bitten him.

"Then the day came when I woke up to find him lying in a pool of blood from his sickness, and I knew once again that he was dying." Mac paused, tears forming in his eyes and mine.

"I lifted him up and carried him to the car to take him to the vet. And you know what? That dog crawled over and curled up on my lap like a puppy. He finally let me pet his head and comfort him as he died in my arms.

You see, Sunny, that's how it is with our relationship with God. First, we are dying in sin. Then God comes along and we are given a second chance—a new life—when we live within the boundaries that he sets for us. But most people hold something back. They say, 'Yes Lord, I give you my life, except for this one little part I am holding back, when we could have had an intimate relationship all along. This is what it comes down to. You can have a business relationship with God with rules and regulations and duties, or you can have an intimate relationship with forgiveness and mercy and love."

I choked up. I had never thought of God like that.

"There is no scorecard," Mac reiterated. "There is no sin-ometer. No list of naughty and nice. *Forgiven* means just that. The Bible says your sins are forgotten. Erased. Our past, present, and future sins too. God cares about your heart. He loves you, my sister, right where you are. Don't ever doubt that. Not ever."

℠ 🕊 ℞

"Not my problem. Not my problem. Not my problem," I chanted over and over, idly twirling the three-month commemorative token CODA had presented me. *Who am I kidding? This is definitely my problem*, I thought as I sat at my desk on Monday morning.

"Step one," I paraphrased aloud from the Codependents Twelve-Steps as I waited for my computer to boot up and I could begin my workday. "I can only control myself." *And this time,* I thought, *I won't be asking my co-workers, my husband, girlfriend or former lover for advice.* I didn't need to ask *everyone* until I found *someone* who would tell me what I wanted to hear.

I had spent most of the night thinking about Paige, both her present condition and her past. I knew what it was like to be gang raped, yet allowed anger to smother my empathy for her. It wasn't hard to imagine the horror of being ripped from your family and forced into the sex trade. One minute, she had been an innocent child, and the next, a victim of violence. I understood the kind of damage such trauma leaves behind; like a sudden flood that strips you from your foundation and washes away all sense of security and stability, or an accidental fire lays waste the land, and leaves permanent scars where there once was life. Paige had been a child when her kidnapping happened, and I had to agree with Amanda, it wasn't all that long ago. She is still very young.

I passed the night talking with God about what he would have me do. The voice that spoke to my spirit was not subject to my feelings.

The fact remains that Paige is pregnant and only God knows whose child it is. At this point, only God knows whether she will keep it or abort it.

When looking back at recent events, I like to think I have matured over the summer. Pastor Mac says "We are like tea bags, never knowing how strong we are until we are plunged into hot water." I know now that we are not defined by our problems, but how we respond to them.

With that thought in mind, I picked up the phone and dialed Paige's extension. She arrived at my door with a pink slip in her hand and a look of aggrieved indignation on her face.

"They're letting me go. They're cutting my job. You did this, didn't you?"

"I'm sorry, Paige."

"I'll just bet you are!" she retorted she crossed her arms and hugged herself.

I looked at her for the first time, seeing her as a child trying to be brave, instead of the woman I had grown to hate.

"I called you here to ask you how I might help. Is there is anything I can do?"

"A job would help. I'm going to need money for this kid."

I was genuinely surprised. "Does that mean that you're not going to... that you're going to keep it?"

"I told you. This is *my* baby."

Bewildered, I lowered my voice, and asked softly, "But Paige, don't you *want* to know who the father is?"

"No. I don't. I don't care."

"But," I stuttered, "but don't you think the father has a *right* to know?"

"No! No one is taking my baby from me. It's mine! And you promised you wouldn't tell anyone."

"I know, and I won't go back on my word. You've been through enough."

ℬ 🕊 ℭ

My heart clenched. Caught off guard, I was unprepared for the emotions that rose as I looked over the police report and photographs of the latest victim's injuries. I knew this woman, Alawa Rose. Gayle called to inform me that Alawa was in the lobby to "drop the charges" against her live-in boyfriend, Johnny Meeks.

I grabbed the keys to the county car on my way to meet her. Alawa greeted me with a thoughtful, silent look of recognition. She was a beautiful, mature Maidu Indian woman with copper skin, silver hair, and chestnut

brown eyes. She was both a neighbor and a close friend to Joyce and
Kenny in Feather Falls. Savagely beaten about the face, her swollen
eyes were ringed with redish purple circles. I had seen the attached
photos where Meeks's steel-toed logging boots had pounded her back,
arms, and legs, leaving lumpy blue-black masses of inflamed tissue that
were now hidden beneath a long, brown, soft cotton skirt.

"Ms. Rose? Please, follow me." Veering away from the office, I
headed for the stairs and the parking lot. "What do you think, Alawa?"
I asked. "Let's get out of here and take a drive. Are you okay with that?"

Relief softened the deep lines that etched her aging face. "Thank
you, Sunny," she whispered as we took the stairs. I nodded, and in true
Indian tradition, we maintained a stoic silence until we were on the
road driving toward the solitary quiet of the Forebay. I respectfully
asked permission to talk with her once we got to the bay, and she
replied with a slight nod.

I have found that people are generally more inclined to be open
and honest when they are away from the county complex. This seemed
particularly true of Native Americans and rural mountain dwellers
who have little trust or love of government.

The Forebay is an off-stream reservoir west of Oroville with
about ten miles of shoreline. In season, the park is alive with children,
picnickers, barbecues, and birthday parties. This morning it is quiet
except for a few geese skimming the water and an old man with his hat
pulled low against the cool breeze trying to rein in his dog, lunging
and barking at the indignant geese. Alawa and I walked to a bench,
brushed away the colorful autumn leaves and sat next to each other,
gazing at the hills across the bay.

"Alawa, it hurts me to see you in pain."

Alawa nodded and turned her gaze to the geese. "I fell," she said.
"We were drinking with friends at the Gold Flake. On the way back up
the mountain, I asked Johnny to pull over so I could pee. I was really
drunk. I got out and tripped on a rock... fell off the edge." She paused.
"I hit a lot of rocks."

"Johnny has a long history of beating his women," I said, my heart
brimming with love and concern. "Please don't let him get away with
it again."

Alawa gazed at me and then back at the wild geese and the old
man, contemplating. "Should I fly north?" she asked.

"You should tell the truth."

"If the dog gets loose, it will kill the geese."

I considered this. "But it doesn't have to kill the geese. Right now,
it's just barking. Loudly, but it can be controlled."

She shrugged with a sad, tired look. "A dog is a dog."

I thought about Logan. She could be right.

"But you are not an animal, Alawa. You are a person. You are the
only one like you in the world, and that makes you both rare and

precious."

This is a lot easier to preach than it is to receive, I told myself.

The dog broke loose, ignoring its master, yapping and splashing in joyful abandon along the edge of the water as the geese took flight.

"Do you know where they will go?" Alawa asked, not waiting for a reply. "Look!" she pointed. "They cross to other side of the lake because this is their home. They have nowhere else to go." With grave dignity, she looked at me sympathetically. "You are young, Sunny. My mother is buried here, and her mother, and her mother's mother, back to the first woman made by the Creator, right there," she said, pointing this time to Table Mountain, the place where the Maidu believe God created the first man and woman. "I have nowhere to go but the other side of the lake," she said. "Drop the charges."

℘ 🕊 ℂ

Work has taught me that there are many different kinds of bondage. Mia, Kia, and Alawa are bound to their cultures, others are tied to drugs, poverty and the false confidence that they can change others, but no confidence that they can change themselves. Some are held by physical restraint, some by constraints of religion, and those who are bound with emotional ties. Then too, there are people like Paige and me, who are slaves to our past.

I went to Jack in the afternoon with an amended Needs Assessment, stating that our unit needed Paige in the program, and that she was an invaluable contribution to SVU. Okay, so I stretched the truth a bit. Or maybe I stretched it a *lot*. Paige and I have had a disastrous past, but now I was trying to focus on her potential instead of her flaws. With patience and some sensitivity, she might become a decent advocate one day.

Paige already had the primary requirement as far as I was concerned. She had been a victim. Having endured great physical and emotional trauma, she can become a survivor. It is a God-thing, making good come out of bad. Making gossamer butterflies from ugly worm-like creatures. With time and help, Paige could learn to use her pain to reach out and help others. It is hard to say what she will do. The sad truth is, not everyone survives. Even if they survive physically, many victims stop "living" and remain trapped by emotional injuries that never heal.

Jack has promised to submit the amendment to the county administrators. Whatever Jack wants, Jack usually gets. He has a way of being persuasive. Perhaps that is why he is such an excellent prosecutor. I am pretty sure that Paige will be keeping her job.

℘ 🕊 ℂ

Dressing in a soft skirt and sexy, low-cut clingy sweater, I took Kissme with me to Chance's house. Needless to say, my relationship with Chance has been strained since my trip down to the jail. But he invited me for dinner, and I am newly committed to doing the "right thing." Not out of guilt this time, but out of love. I am free! Just knowing that God has forgiven me, I am ready to extend genuine forgiveness to others, and I really wanted to reconcile with my husband.

With a strong sense of anticipation, I knocked on his door. "One day at a time," I told myself. The feeling was positively liberating.

Chance answered the door wearing Wranglers and a light blue denim work shirt that perfectly matched the sky blue color of his eyes when he looked at me. "You're just in time. Dinner's about done." He said, ushering me in.

The smell of beef stew and warm bread filled the house and whet the appetite. A rustic vase, overflowing with autumn flowers, sat on the table next to a sleek bottle of champagne, designed to stir appetites of a different sort.

It felt a little awkward. So much has happened between us. Passions had soared during our last two encounters—both making love and fighting. I had been surprised when Chance called and asked me to join him for dinner.

New beginnings? I hoped so.

The food was great, the talk was light, and somewhere around mid-bottle, Chance announced, "Sunny, I've decided to take a leave of absence. I have given a three-week notice."

I rolled my eyes. *There he goes again, thinking I can't take care of myself.*

"That's really sweet of you," I said, dabbing my mouth with a napkin. "But Logan's already been indicted, and I'm sure his attorney will be filing continuances to extend his right to a speedy trial."

"What did Travis say about that?"

"I haven't talked to him. He's back with ATF in Oakland." I didn't add that I sometimes miss him, now that he is gone. "You don't need to worry or take time off because of me," I hurried to assure him.

Chance tipped his head, looking at me curiously. "It's not about you, I'm doing this for me. This is something I want and need to do. I am moving to San Diego, at least until June." His steady gaze was calm and determined. "I have come to accept that you are more than able to take care of yourself. You don't need me for that."

Be careful what you wish for, danced through my mind.

"But some people do need me," Chance continued.

"What are you talking about?" Anxiety rose, burning the back of my throat.

"I've been accepted into Bethel University. I'll be studying for the ministry."

Did I have that freshly stun-gunned look on my face? This might be a good time for Chance to practice his CPR because I am pretty sure I stopped breathing.

"School starts on the first of the month."

I think he kept talking. Something about "mercy and calling," or "calling Mercy." Whatever. I couldn't reconcile the words with the person, the time, or the place.

How could I have been so wrong? I wondered. *Wasn't this dinner supposed to be his attempt to win me back? Wasn't it part of his master plan for us to move back in together?*

I had felt secure as long as I was the one controlling our relationship. That Chance might move on without me, never entered the vanity of my heart.

"Sunny? Are you listening? Sunny?" His mouth framed the word "listening," but all I heard was "leaving."

"I want you to come with me. I know this sudden and unexpected, but I've been thinking a lot about it these past months. I know"—he touched my arm reassuringly—"it would mean giving up your job... might be good... you'd be safe... get a fresh start..."

CHAPTER 46

ಚಿ ⸾ ೞ

Travis escorted me from the courtroom and across the busy parking lot of the federal courthouse in downtown Oakland.

As we walked, I noticed a long line of Harleys that bikers had ridden in spite of the threatening rain. Perhaps their hot tempers and blistering stares had kept them warm. So far, I had managed to avoid harassment, threats, and physical assault from Logan's outlaw MC brothers. But Logan is a patient man. Whether he gets years on death row or life without parole, he will have a long time to dwell on revenge.

The trial lasted for weeks but felt like months. Kept secreted in a safe room down the hall from the courtroom on the days I testified, I only appeared when called to the stand. Logan sat there looking like a choirboy in a tailored suit that covered his tattoos, wearing a GQ haircut and a timid, hopeful smile that charmed everyone but me.

His high-priced low-life attorney was probably paid by influential people in drug cartels; those who had a vested financial interest in seeing Logan walk. According to Travis, there are still large caches of money and guns stashed away somewhere.

Logan's attorney reminds me of Satan dishing out dessert, and the ever-liberal Bay Area jury was lapping it up.

Kidnapper or Lover? That is the question they ponder since Logan swears that I went up to the cabin for the purpose of seeing him, and later visited him in jail because I was still in love with him.

The guns are another matter, and the bombing may never be proved since ATF Agent Wild Bill is not alive to corroborate my testimony, and Logan's testimony has left "reasonable doubt" as to my relationship with him and the events. But the Mongols, the Bandidos, and probably members of Hells Angels who loved Lefty, have their own agendas with Logan. Whatever actions they might take, remains to be seen.

"What now?" I asked Travis, having made peace with him in my heart. He was right. He is a damned good investigator. I sometimes wonder how things might have turned out between us under different circumstances.

"Now might be a good time for you to reconsider moving to higher ground," he said as we reached his car.

"Higher ground, huh? Mountains aren't high enough?" I laughed and then shuddered as I turned to him. "Travis? There's no way Logan can walk on this, is there?"

Travis sighed, his brows pinched with concern. "Not likely, but he might walk on some of the charges. And he can still enter into a plea agreement—guilty to some of the charges if they drop others."

"How can that be?"

"You know the game, Sunny. He's saying you came up to the cabin for love, Agent Barros was investigating an open shelter, and the snakes were just a tragic but natural consequence of living in the woods. There's no proof that you were ever locked in the bomb shelter. The door was open when we arrived. And they are saying the weapons belonged to Lefty. That's the position the defense is pitching.

For a moment, the ground moved underfoot, and it still wasn't an earthquake.

Travis took me by the elbow to steady me, saying, "One of Logan's buddies, Lester the kiddy molester, has produced a doctor's report showing that he, Lester, was bitten by a rattler in the shelter just a few months ago. His friends will testify that they knew the shelter was a rattlesnake den and wouldn't go near the place. That's why the guns hadn't been sold off.

"Listen, Sunny, besides his scum buddies, you've probably noticed that Logan has a lot of powerful and influential friends." Travis frowned. "You should seriously think about moving."

We got in the car and started to drive across town. I tried to think it through.

I choked up, thinking back on Alawa Rose. "You don't understand, Travis. There is nowhere to go. This is my home. I was born here. I don't have any family. Where would you send me?"

We stopped at a red light. Pulling his Oakley's down on his nose, Travis studied me, his green eyes flickering before responding. "Away."

Silence.

"Away?" I repeated, frowning in irritation. "Away where? This is who I am and what I do. I am the one who didn't want to testify. Remember? Now I'm not even safe in my own home."

We locked eyes and Travis had the faintest smile at the corners of his mouth as he offered, "You could move into mine."

I smiled back, reached over and kissed him softly on the cheek.

Lord, he is a temptation.

ഇ ⁂ ൝

"Have you been to a doctor?" I asked Paige. "You don't look well."

"I'm fine," she snapped. "I just wish I wasn't so fat."

I bit my lip. "That's not fat, Paige. It's a baby. A little person."

She shrugged in resignation. "I know. It's just... I don't know if I can do this."

I went over and sat next to her on the office sofa. "I am sorry you have to go through this. But you don't have to go through it alone. You can find out who the father is and tell him," I gently offered.

Paige looked at me with an air of desperation. "You don't understand," she said. "This baby is mine. I want someone who will love me without judging me."

"God loves you, Paige. He doesn't care about your past. He just wants the same thing you want."

"What do I want?"

"A relationship based on unconditional love."

She gazed at me for what seemed like an eternity. "If I can't handle it—the whole motherhood scene—will you take my baby and raise it?"

The irony didn't escape me. Paige, who hated me for being a Christian, wouldn't trust her child to anyone else.

"One day at a time, Paige. You don't need to make that decision yet," I said with an encouraging smile. "It's enough that you have decided to carry the baby to term."

ഇൗ ൚ ൚

"Look at that, Sunny," said Chance. "Out there," he said, pointing toward the distant hills still bathed in the shadows of a new morning. He was dressed in a red flannel shirt and denim pants and finally taking a break from the job of cutting and stacking firewood in preparation for his departure and the upcoming winter.

I had been sitting on Chance's porch stroking Mercy's head, reading random passages from the Bible that Chance left lying in his chair. It was a new day and my heart filled with peace. The coffee was hot, but the Word, I thought, was stronger than a triple latte, sweeter than mocha, and more enduring than a venti double espresso.

Laughing at my own silliness, my eyes strained as I squinted into the distance. As if responding to a divine cue, a large bird soared into view, silhouetted against the brilliant fingers of first light that fanned across the ridge tops.

"Is this a Pastor Chance message?" I teased. "You know you're going to have to change your name to Pastor Positive if you plan on building a church. *Pastor Chance* sounds a little risky."

Looking back, I wonder at my shock about Chance's dream of entering the ministry. I guess I had been so busy thinking about me, I had forgotten to listen to him as he shared his love of leading the men's group, doing Wednesday night Bible studies, and ministering to others. Saving people is where his heart has always been. I was learning to see, accept, and respect him in a whole new way.

Chance laughed with the good natured easy laugh that has always defined his character. "This is a test," he said. "And you know what they say. 'Behind every test lies a testimony.'"

"Okie-Dokie, Preacher Man. Give me a clue?"

Chance got that inspired, spirit-filled look he always gets at times like these as he pointed to the bird. "Eagle or buzzard?" He asked.

At first glance, it is almost impossible to tell them apart. They are both masters of the sky.

"Can't tell yet." I was waiting for the bird to get out of the sun's glare. You have to get close to see them for what they are. The face of one is hideous and terrible, and the face of the other is noble and majestic.

Chance's eyes glistened with excitement. "Stay with me on this. The eagle takes its live catch and soars up into heaven, ingests it, and the two become one. But the buzzard"—he paused and shook his head— "the buzzard feeds on dead flesh on the earth, ingests it, and the two become one."

I put down the coffee and Bible and continued my surveillance of the bird drifted, hunting for its breakfast. "We're not talking about birds, are we? Is this a parable?"

Chance laughed and kissed my hand, looking up at me with adoration.

"I'm just thinking that's how it must be with God and the devil. At first glance, we can't always tell them apart. You just get caught up in the hope and the idea."

Chance was quiet as he let me draw my own conclusions.

"I guess it was like that for my mom, huh? She never could tell them apart. Those popular far eastern religions must have looked beautiful against the backdrop of boring Christian rituals. She probably never looked too close."

My mom, like so many new age people I have met, refused to see or even consider the God of the Bible in any personal way. Starla had worshiped the water instead of the Living Water. She idolized the trees instead of the One who was nailed to a tree. Starla never knew or wanted to know the eternal God; the Way, the Truth, and the Life. Instead, she had created and customized a god into her own image. It broke my heart to think of all her drug-induced highs, but she never soared with angels. For all her consumption of liquid spirits and mystical spirits, she had been adamant in rejecting the Holy Spirit. In the end, she got just what she wanted: No God instead of Knowing God.

I sighed deeply. The thought weighed heavy on my heart. And then, I just had to ask.

"Chance?" I asked, "What do you think about salmon?

"Salmon?" He cocked an eyebrow, then tipped his head, questioning and curious.

"Yeah. Salmon. What do think about salmon?" I let the question simmer as we continued to gaze at the horizon and the bird until it melted into the endless sky.

He turned to study me.

"Is this a Sunny Sermon?" he returned the tease. "If you go into ministry, you'll have to change your name to 'Serious' and give Serious Sermons." We both laughed at the prospect of *Pastor Positive* and *Serious Sunny Sermons*, and as we did, our hearts entwined.

"How did we go from birds to fish?" he asked.

I threw him a playful look. "It's a test."

With that, he grew serious, sensing the earnestness in my voice. Deliberating for a time, he finally smiled and said, "I love the salmon, Sunny. They follow their destiny, whatever the cost."

80 🕊 CB

I am following my destiny. One day at a time. And that can be exciting on days like this.

The bikes glistened like a row of dragonflies perched on a wire fence under a bright summer sun. Everyone says to *shop around* and *never buy the first one* you see. But the truth is, when I am done dutifully comparison shopping, I always come back to the first eye-catcher and buy it.

The sunny yellow Fat Boy I straddled didn't make me feel like either. In fact, it felt perfect. Shane was happy to have negotiated a sale. He never could understand why Chance bought a VTX instead of a Harley. Ashley was stunned and took up her usual, "If I were you, I would..." before catching herself.

Dear Ashley!

That was yesterday. Today the sky is blue and the California sun holds the promise of a perfect ride in the face of winter. Chance will be dropping off Mercy at my house and leaving for San Diego in the morning. It's not exactly that he is going on without me, but that he is moving on with himself. I feel a little insecure, but I will be okay. Kind of like riding solo instead of two-up with Chance, it is time to take responsibility and control. Time to face my fears and live the dream. I will be here, if and when Chance returns.

The moment of truth arrived, as it does this time every year. I hold my breath, suck it in and zip my black leather chaps, relieved once again that no seams explode as I tug the zipper over my thighs. I kiss my Kissme-Dog on her furry little head, tuck her into my bathrobe lying on the sofa, and turn the TV to the Animal Planet before slipping outside.

Chance doesn't live far away, as the bird flies. In the distance, I can hear the faint roar of the VTX coming to life. Smiling, I finish gearing up, fire up my new bike and twist the throttle. It is going to be another beautiful day as I ride out to fully embrace it. I am not sure where we will go from here, uphill or down, but I am confident that we are headed in the same direction.

80 🕊 CB

Homicides remain my hardest cases. Murder is an inevitable, tragic part of the work of an advocate. I stand here in a cold courtroom, subpoena in hand, and am required to examine grotesque photos of the victim's remains. I am asked to identify a once vital woman who has become no more or less than a series of exhibits.

Is this how Jasmine's story ends? How coud it possibly have come full circle? Jasmine had been my very first case, on my first day working as Victim Advocate for the district attorney's office. I smiled, fondly recalling Crazy Bob Martel and the way I had immediately broken all of the rules of advocacy. I remember it clearly.

ℬ ⅄ ℭ

"Is he still in the house?" I had asked the woman on the phone. "No?" He had left for work. *Just another day in his mind*, I thought bitterly. "Are you safe?" I knew she was, but it was a standard question that I was compelled to ask.

The sheriff's office had called me instead of Marne. The politics behind the call had escaped me. I was new on the job and trying to be precision perfect. I ran through a quick list of things for her to pack. "Be sure to take your important documents: your Social Security cards and birth certificates, health insurance and food stamp cards, credit cards, driver's license and the pink slip to your vehicle."

"Okay," she said in a timid voice. "Anything else?"

"Don't forget money, keys, medications, and a change of clothes. And be sure to bring a favorite toy for each of the children," I added.

I could hear her crying on the other end of the line, completely overwhelmed. The sobs told me that my information was too much for her to handle in her state of crisis.

I knew the officer was probably impatient to be off doing cop-things, like arresting Jasmine's husband, so I asked her to put Deputy Sheriff Martel on the line and offered to pick up Jazz and the girls and drive them to the hospital and shelter.

After several hours in the SART room, I took Jasmine to my office, closed the blinds, locked the door, and photographed her external injuries.

Rule #1. Never get emotionally involved. And yet, who can control the heart? I loved this courageous young woman and her two daughters from the moment I laid eyes on them. There was no resisting those precious little girls dressed in Hello Kitty pajamas with riotous halos of golden curls crowning their angelic faces. They looked just like their mother. Except Mom was missing handfuls of curls where her hair had been ripped out during the struggle. Injuries courtesy of her husband, Bryan, the plumber.

Jazz and the girls had recently moved to Palermo from Mt. Shasta, which is also located in northern California, shortly after Bryan inherited a trailer and the Ready Response Plumbing business from his elderly, recently deceased, stepfather. Jazz was without the support of family or friends.

There would be no returning to the trailer park. I could have arranged for a civil standby, where an officer literally "stands by" making sure the victim is safe while she removes her personal belongings. Not an immediate issue, because Bryan was in jail. But then, Bryan had brothers, and Jasmine was too afraid to return to the trailer. Apparently, with good reason.

The shelter was full and the hour late by the time we reached Chico. I had thanked God for Catholic Social Services, that wonderful community resource that sometimes pays for an emergency motel room in this type of situation. Like many women, Jasmine's bank account and credit cards were in her husband's name.

Seeing them tired and hungry, I broke Rule #2 by pulling into the parking lot at Collin's and Denny's market and buying a bag of groceries with my own money. This was against the rules, but it was after hours, and it was my money. Anyhow, it felt like the right thing to do. I knew they would not walk through the strange city of Chico after dark, trying to find the Jesus Center for a hot meal.

Charged with sexual battery, Bryan had followed Jazz to Mt. Shasta where he had savagely beaten her. The morning news broadcast of that event had been the source of my distraction—on the day of my motorcycle accident—the day that Chance came into my life and pulled me from the river. Amazing, how many lives were changed by just one man.

The murder case has taken years in coming to trial. It turned out to be a complicated case, requiring extensive investigation and top-notch lab work. Now the hard labor and dedication of the investigators and prosecutors have finally come to fruition. They believe that Bryan strangled Jasmine and disposed of her body by hiding it in a septic tank. The body had been horribly decomposed by the time they found it.

Back at my desk, I shuddered at the snapshots of her ravaged remains. I reflected on her courage and her vitality with great sadness.

In the recess of my mind, I could clearly hear the question that people so frequently ask me: *"Sunny, how can you stand your job?"*

"I love my job," I still reply.

If I can save just one life. If I can inspire just one person and convince them of their infinite worth. If I can make a difference...

I am pulled out of my reverie and back into the world by the ringing of the phone. I take a deep, cleansing breath—*because the cycle never ends.*

"District attorney's office. This is the advocate, Sunny McLane."

—END—

If you have enjoyed this book, would you kindly take a moment to leave a review on Amazon and Goodreads? Please tell your friends about my books and consider giving them as gifts to survivors of abuse.

AFTERWORD
from
DAWN MATTOX

Lost my job to budget cuts, lost my health to breast cancer, and lost my heart to my husband, all in the same year. As bad as that sounds, it was also a time of great discovery. I learned that I am precious, I am loved, and so are YOU.

I returned to my lifelong passion for writing. One day at a time. One page at a time. Sometimes with a tear, but mostly with joy and hearty laugher. Like a giant transfusion, I poured my heart onto each page.

Special Victim's Unit was five long years in the making, written while working night shifts and weekends as a Psychiatric Emergency Crisis Worker. At first I thought SVU had been inspired by my decade of work as a Victim Advocate for Butte County District Attorney's Office. I have since come to realize that SVU, and the books that follow, come from the heart. The story was always there... waiting on me... waiting for you.

Be the Difference!